Jim saw two of the Pathet Lao soldiers trying to flank him on the right, shifted his firing position slightly, and waited until he had a clear shot. The first one folded like a cheap accordion when the burst of fire hit him. Jim shifted fire and was fairly certain he'd at least winged the second, who dropped out of sight.

He shifted again, low-crawling to a position he'd picked out earlier. To stay in one spot too long was to give them a target.

Three soldiers burst out of the brush in front of him, firing into the position he'd just left. He shot the first, moved to the second, and pulled the trigger, only to feel the unresponsiveness that told him of a bolt locked back on an empty weapon.

Goddamn amateurish shit!

He punched the magazine release, the empty falling away even as he was clawing at another from his pouch. Not enough time. Not nearly enough. The other two Pathet Lao were no longer shooting at the empty position, and were cranking off rounds that cracked by his head. They'd be on top of him in less than a second.

Praise for John F. Mullins and his Men of Valor novels

"Articulate and forceful, Mullins gives readers the facts . . . as only a veteran operations man can."

—Mark Berent, bestselling author
of *Phantom Leader*

"Mullins brin   close and personal. The combat is real. . . .

C. Pollack

Also by John F. Mullins

Napalm Dreams
Into the Treeline

Published by Pocket Books

Bayonet Skies

A "MEN OF VALOR" NOVEL

John F. Mullins
Major, U.S. Army
Special Forces (Retired)

POCKET STAR BOOKS

New York London Toronto Sydney

An *Original* Publication of POCKET BOOKS

 A Pocket Star Book published by
POCKET BOOKS, a division of Simon & Schuster, Inc.
1230 Avenue of the Americas, New York, NY 10020

This book is a work of fiction. Names, characters, places and
incidents are products of the author's imagination or are used
fictitiously. Any resemblance to actual events or locales or
persons living or dead is entirely coincidental.

ISBN-13: 978-0-7434-7769-7
ISBN-10: 0-7434-7769-3

This Pocket Star Books paperback edition September 2006

10 9 8 7 6 5 4 3 2 1

POCKET STAR BOOKS and colophon are registered
trademarks of Simon & Schuster, Inc.

Cover art and design by James Wang

Manufactured in the United States of America

For information regarding special discounts for bulk purchases,
please contact Simon & Schuster Special Sales at
1-800-456-6798 or business@simonandschuster.com.

To all the troops out there still fighting.
My most heartfelt thanks for your service and sacrifice.
I'm impressed and immensely grateful that we
can still produce people like you.

Bayonet
Skies

CHAPTER 1

Falling silently through night skies, at one with the wind and dark. Above only the stars and the faint contrail of the plane. Below the embracing dark, broken only by the winking of the marking light on the base jumper's back-pack. No feeling of falling. More like flight without wings. Move the hand just slightly forward, and the body turns in the opposite direction, the invisible cushion of air below reacting to the asymmetry. Tuck both arms back to the sides and the head points down, the body becoming an arrow, speed building up—flare back out now, or you'll shoot past the base man like a rocket! The sound of the aircraft, fading now, is barely heard over the rush of the wind. To anyone on the ground it is but another jetliner, following the specified air corridor. Unlikely any radar operator would have picked up the exit of the team on his scope. The blips would be so small as to be confused with the usual screen clutter, passed off as atmospheric anomalies by anyone not looking specifi-cally for twelve tiny shapes, falling at over 120 miles an hour toward the earth.

It seems a long time, these two minutes from thirty-six

thousand feet to opening altitude at two thousand. Long enough to get very cold, though it is still summer. The face, where it is not covered with goggles, helmet, and oxygen mask, feels frostbitten. Your fingers are stiff and inflexible even through the gloves. Gloves aren't very thick anyway—can't be. If they were you couldn't feel those critical things that you hope you'll never have to use: reserve parachute ripcord handle, knife tucked in the elastic on the top of the reserve to cut away shroud lines should you get tangled in them, quick releases for releasing the main chute if it doesn't open properly.

Dark shapes barely seen are on either side, other members of the team keeping respectful distance. All too easy to slam into one another here in the dark; speed is deceptive, doesn't look like you're moving at all relative to them. Hit one another and you'll likely be knocked unconscious, unable to pull the ripcord when the time comes. You hope the automatic opener will work but you know it probably won't because the most reliable automatic opener is made by the East Germans and of course you can't get them because after all we can't patronize the Commies. So you'll hit the ground at full speed and bounce. Nice descriptive word, that. Soldiers are famous for their inventive ways to describe dying. Buy the farm, get waxed, get blown away, bounce. And you do—bounce, that is. Ten, even fifteen feet back in the air, jagged bones sticking out at odd angles from the coveralls, back down and bouncing only a few inches this time before finally coming to rest, looking like you're much less thick, because of course you are. *Whoa, boys, need a spatula to pick this one up.* Lots of ways to die on a night HALO jump, buddyboy, just pick one. And if you survive it, well, not to worry, because once it's over there will be all kinds of people down there on the ground trying to kill you.

Glance down at the altimeter making its slow unwind, crossing through six thousand, now four, get ready. Pull the left hand back to the chest while crossing the other hand in front of your face. Maintain your symmetry. If you don't, you'll go into a flat spin and that's not too good when the chute is opening because it will get all twisted and probably malfunction. Then it's a useless piece of cloth hanging above you; you have to cut it away with the quick releases before opening the reserve. If you don't sure as hell the reserve will get twisted around it. And you'll have two useless pieces of cloth hanging over you, slowing descent only slightly. So you'll hit the ground at maybe a hundred instead of 120. But you'll still be just as dead. The others will hear you as you flutter by them, just as you heard it when Sergeant Barnes bounced last month. And they'll mouth, "streamer," in voices so low as to be just at the threshold of hearing, as if to say it louder would in some way attract it to them, too. And they won't sleep for many nights, imagining the horror of your last minutes, projecting it upon themselves.

Two thousand and pull. The ripcord comes away smoothly, no burrs to get hung up on the cones of the back-pack. A soft feeling, barely noticeable at first, as the spring-loaded pilot chute leaps away, grabbing the air. Then stronger as it pulls the sleeve-covered main chute out: a noticeable slowing of momentum. The main grabs air down at the skirt of the chute, pushing the sleeve up like rolling off a used condom, and with an audible WHOOF it fully inflates. The crotch straps bite. They always do, no matter how snugly you tighten them. Get them too loose and a testicle will inevitably get underneath and you'll be walking funny for a while. The sleeve alleviates most of the opening shock, allowing the main to inflate relatively slowly. Back in the old days they didn't have sleeves or deployment bags, and the old paratroopers were always joking about having their nuts jerked so high it looked like they were wearing hairy bowties.

The sound of other chutes opening all around, like the cracking of a sheet shaken out. Not much noise but still you cringe because it sounds so loud here in the night. If someone who knows what the sound means is waiting below you're in deep shit. No worry about seeing the parachutes. They're black, blending in with the dark. Only way you could see them is as a cloud coming between you and the stars and of course you'd have to be almost directly below to see that.

Follow the base man as he weaves back and forth, dumping air from the canopy as quickly as possible. The MC-1–1 is a good chute, the military version of the Para-Commander all the sport jumpers are using. It is a little larger to make up for the extra weight you have to carry: weapon, ammo, rucksack, radio, batteries, claymores, sleeping bag. It gets cold at night here in the mountains and you've learned by hard-earned experience that "travel light, freeze at night" isn't all that great an idea.

Ground coming up now, more sensed than seen. Pull the quick release holding the rucksack to the harness and let it fall free. It comes up short, held by the fifty-foot lowering line, jerking the harness sharply. It hangs there, increasing the oscillation. But you don't want to ride it in unreleased; it makes it almost impossible to do a proper parachute landing fall, and that's a good way to break a leg.

The tops of trees suddenly cut out lateral vision. Good, that means the base man found the clearing. No rides through the branches tonight. Tuck the feet together, toes pointing toward the ground, knees together and slightly bent. Release of tension as the rucksack hits the ground and then so do you. No matter how many times you've done it the contact is always a surprise, no semblance of the carefully learned parachute landing fall, just flop down and hope you don't break anything. The usual three points of contact tonight: feet, ass, head. Pinwheels of light behind the eyes as the head hits hard. More wind than was forecast, evidently. The chute is pulling along the ground; pull hard on one riser and flip up and over as they taught you so long ago in jump school. That doesn't work, dumbass—you're still dragging the rucksack behind you like a big anchor. Screw it, release one side with the quick releases and the air spills from the canopy like a punctured balloon.

Get out of the harness quickly, stuff it and the chute and the unused reserve into the kitbag. Can't leave anything on the drop zone. The enemy often patrols open areas like this and they'll find even the smallest trace and then you're in for some tracking. And they use dogs. Big fucking mean dogs.

Crouch down beside the kitbag and rucksack, weapon at the ready. Listen to the night. The only sound is the soft sighing of the wind and the tiny scratches and scuffles of the other team members. Of course this doesn't mean anything. If it were you, you'd be biding your time too, waiting until the team joined up so you could get all of them. But maybe tonight you're lucky. They didn't stake out this DZ. And there weren't any hunters, or lovers, or insomniacs out for a walk who are even now scurrying toward the nearest telephone to tell the police about the men who came from the sky.

Pull the compass from its pouch, take an azimuth, the luminous numbers glowing softly in the blackness. Head for the rallying point. The rucksack on the back and the kit-bag slung atop it makes it hard to walk. You're carrying well over a hundred pounds, and feel every ounce. Someone jumps you now, you're screwed. No way you can get rid of all this stuff in time to fight, much less get away. Feeling terribly vulnerable out here in the open. Better get to the trees as soon as possible. There at least you can hide.

A shape converging on your path, laden like you. Good, two of you. Not that it does much good, two of you can be taken as easily as one, but it gives a psychological boost anyway. We all hate to be alone. Spread out slightly, so at least they won't be able to get the both of you with one burst.

Into the sheltering trees. Easy moving here. The forest floor is kept clean by the *Forestmeisters*. Few sticks to trip you, just the soft rustle of damp leaves and the whip of evergreen branches let go too soon by the man in front of you. Even more black here; all you can see of him are the two luminescent strips on the back of his helmet. You wonder how he can see anything at all. Probably can't, the way he's stumbling.

"Halt!" comes the whispered command, seeming even more urgent because it is said so softly and because it is accompanied by the snicking of a rifle taken off safe. The man in front stops suddenly. You drop down slowly, get close to the ground. Point your own rifle in the general direction of the sound.

"Who goes there?" comes the whisper.

"Friend," the man in front of you says.

"Zulu," challenges the unseen sentry.

"Goundcloth," the man in front replies, giving the correct password to the challenge. You let out a breath, aware for the first time that you have been holding it. "Two," the man in front says, telling them that there are two of you coming in. If there's a third, they'll know he's a tagalong bad guy. He'll be allowed to get close enough to kiss with the knife.

"That you, Cap'n?" asks one of the shadowy figures inside the small perimeter.

"Yeah. We got everybody?"

"You and Chuck were the last two."

"Any injuries?"

"Jerry banged his elbow pretty hard on a rock, but it ain't broke. Nothing else."

There is the soft chink of an entrenching tool striking soil, the hiss as dirt is thrown out of a hole. The shadowy figure, who by his voice you recognize as the team sergeant, says, "Gimme your chute and we'll bury it with the others." Gratefully you shed the load.

You take the starlight scope out of a side pocket of your rucksack, flip the switch, hold it to your eye. The light of the distant stars, amplified forty thousand times, shows up sickly green, bathing the figures in the small perimeter. Two are still digging. Others are facing outward, weapons at the ready. One of those, you see, has another starlight on his weapon. That would have been the man who challenged you. He was able to see you clearly as you came in. Just one more security measure. You can't have too many of them.

You scan the area outside the perimeter carefully. No movement. Good. Switch off the scope, take the compass out again. Line up the north-seeking arrow with the preset luminous spot on the bezel. You'll move out on an azimuth of sixty degrees for a thousand meters, do a dogleg on twenty degrees for twelve hundred, and, you hope, somewhere in that neighborhood find the objective rallying point. From there it's supposed to be an easy walk downstream to the target, a massive hydroelectric complex. Too big a target for an A team. You'd tried to tell the brass that, but of course they wouldn't listen. As usual.

Most of the weight the team carries is explosives and rockets. If you can get in—and that's a helluva big if—you can do tremendous damage, but not enough to put the complex out of action. Seems a lot of risk for not much reward, but that's always the way of it.

"We're good to go, sir," whispers the team sergeant.

"Then let's move." Everyone falls into place like the well-drilled entity they are. Jerry Hauck, the light-weapons man, takes point. Hauck has that most rare of things, an almost preternatural ability to sense when things are not as they should be; a branch slightly out of place, a noise that doesn't go with the area, a smell that tells him that humans are about. More than once it had saved them from ambush, back in Vietnam.

You walk directly behind him, keeping him on azimuth. The others, no two men with the same specialty close together, walk with weapons alternated to one side or the other. There is little sound, only the slight shuffling of feet in the moist leaves of the forest floor. All equipment is taped to keep it from rattling, canteens are full so there is no gurgling of water, clothes are tied down where they bag so they won't catch on branches. All exposed skin is darkened with camouflage stick. No one has taken a bath in several days, so there is no odor of soap or cologne. You smell of the woods—of dirt, pine needles, and smoke.

You are a well-honed, superbly competent fighting team. Members of one of the most elite forces in history.

And completely out of your depth. The wartime mission of a Special Forces team is to enter the enemy rear areas, make contact with local partisans, then organize, train, equip, and lead them in guerrilla warfare against the occupying power. A twelve-man team is regarded as the appropriate size to lead a thousand to twelve hundred guerrillas in an area many hundreds of square kilometers in area. It can tie down thousands of enemy troops in rear area security, strike at will against the enemy infrastructure: trains, power stations, airfields, command and control elements.

But the Special Forces team is not designed for direct action missions, such as this one. There are no known partisans in the area; in fact most of the population can be expected to be hostile. The Army had spent years and millions of dollars training the team, and it was very likely that some, if not all, would be killed on a mission like this. A hell of a waste of assets, you think. And the target just isn't all that important. Certainly not of any tactical value, and little strategic. It will inconvenience the enemy for a while, that's all. Other portions of the power grid will make up for the loss while it is being repaired. It is a far more appropriate target for the Air Force; a couple of fast-movers with a load of two-thousand-pound smart bombs. Hell, you think, as big as the place is, even the zoomies can't miss it.

But the Army fought for every possible target. It was a policy that had less to do with tactical matters than with budgetary. There was a finite amount of money to be divided up; if you let the Air Force have most of the targets it wouldn't take some sharp congressional staffer too long to figure out that's where most of the money should go too.

As you walk you count silently. At each 110 steps you put another knot in the piece of string carried in a side pocket. One hundred meters, give or take one or two. That way if you lose count all you have to do is feel the knots.

When there are ten knots you halt Jerry, then give the whisper back down the line to take a break, and watch as everyone takes his place in a small perimeter. The forest is very quiet. Not like Vietnam where there were always small animals stirring, birds or monkeys rustling in the branches above, short sharp cries of pain as the implacable logic of the jungle took its place. Here if there are birds they make no sound, and the animals don't venture forth at night. It is also much easier to move than it was in the jungle. The branches of the coniferous trees start well above the head; there are no vines and thorn bushes to catch clothes; there are few rotting logs and felled trees. No bomb craters, no punjii pits, no land mines. Just the clean smell of pine. Almost pleasant.

You pull a poncho from the rucksack, get underneath, and flick on a penlight. Study the map. Hard to tell if you are exactly on track; there are no prominent terrain features close that you can guide on. But up ahead, four hundred meters away, there is a wide break in the trees where the pylons march away from the power station. Each pylon will be numbered, and by correlating that number with the distance from the station you can get a good fix. It is a hell of a danger area, over two hundred feet wide and no vegetation higher than your knees, but the team has to cross it anyway. Might as well make the best of it. You turn off the light, fold up the poncho. "Saddle up," you whisper to the team sergeant.

The break is exactly 440 paces away. You allow yourself a small feeling of satisfaction at your navigational skills. The team stops. Everyone knows what to do. Ten men fan out, taking covering positions. You and Jerry will cross first, get to the other side, and make a box recon inside the treeline. If you find no one, the remainder of the team will cross in one rush. If there are bad guys on the other side, perhaps the covering fire of the team will allow you to get back. It sounds good in theory, but you hold little hope that you will be able to cross two hundred feet of open ground without being shot to pieces by one side or the other. Still, it's better than sacrificing the whole team. In the planning for the movement the team sergeant had tactfully suggested to the captain that he might want to remain behind while two lower-ranking people went across. To which you had replied that the lower-ranking people were far more important than yourself, because it is they who will be setting up the demolitions on the target. Your only mission, once they get there, will be guard duty. And everyone could see the logic of that.

Besides, you've never asked anyone to do anything you wouldn't yourself do, and are not about to start now.

You and Jerry shed your rucksacks, leaving them with the team to carry across. Through the starlight scope you detect nothing on the other side, but that doesn't mean a lot. Anyone there, if they are any good, won't be moving. They will be lying quite still; uncomfortable, cold, and stiff. They won't stir, even to take a piss. And they'll stay that way all night. You've done it often enough yourself. After a while you look forward to the terror of battle, just because it seems infinitely preferable to this miserable wait.

You nod to Jerry, who walks forward in a crouch. You follow, slightly to the left and behind. You feel terribly exposed. Out of the forest the night is uncomfortably bright, the moon having finally come up. It is not full, and for that you give thanks, but it still sheds enough light to silhouette you clearly. Each step takes you farther and farther away from cover, from safety. The sour taste of bile rises in your throat. What the hell am I doing here? you ask yourself. This is remarkably stupid behavior.

Halfway across and nothing. Jerry holds up while you quickly check the pylon. Number 69. That should be about right. Forward again, the dark treeline looking ominous. The familiar pain in the pit of your stomach gets worse. Right about where the bullet should go in, you think. The old wounds ache. The new ones wait to happen.

Close now and as yet nothing. Just a few more feet.

The clearing is suddenly and blindingly flooded with light. *Jesus Christ!* you have time to think, spotlights. We're fucked. Jerry, quicker than you, lets off a burst at the nearest light. It had absolutely no effect. You turn to run, get less than twenty paces when you hear, then see, the armored car roaring toward you, machine guns blazing. You yank a smoke grenade from your belt, pop it, hear it hiss as it spews dark smoke. Not enough to screen you, but maybe it will help the guys on the other side.

Jerry stumbles, goes down in front of you. Reach down, jerk him to his feet. "Run!" you scream.

The armored car is almost atop you now, the 7.62mm machine gun in the turret still blazing. People are dropping off the sides, running toward you. Turn and fire a burst at them, the first time you have used your weapon. Another car comes from nowhere, gets around behind you. Surrounded. You and Jerry stand back-to-back, ready to fight.

From one of the figures, wearing the white band of an umpire around his hat and sleeve, comes the words, spoken in a heavy German accent, "For you, gentlemen, I think the exercise is over."

"Shit!" you swear, lowering your rifle. Jerry does the same. Two of the figures come forward, take your guns. Their uniforms are those of the *Bundesgrenschutz*, Border Guards. They pull your hands behind you, roughly tie them.

"Where is the rest of the team?" one of them demands.

"Captain James NMI Carmichael, 445–16–9379," you reply.

The man laughs. In German he says, "Pack these two up and take them to the compound," he says. "The rest of you, fan out! There are more of them out there."

During the debriefing back at the Special Forces Operational Base, SFOB, you again make yourself popular with the brass. "And what, in your opinion, went wrong with the operation, Captain?" asks the general from the Pentagon.

"Simple, sir. We were the wrong people on the wrong mission in the wrong place. If we had been in our wartime AO, it would have been a hell of a lot worse. There would have been more than just a couple of battalions of BGS looking for us. The team wouldn't have gotten anywhere close to the power station. The Army would have lost a strategic asset, for a mission that the Air Force could have done, and done more effectively."

The colonel from the SFOB, who is also your commander in Bad Tölz, reddens. Colonel Casey had been on the planning committee that had set the policy of using Special Forces teams for direct action missions. "And your recommendations?" he asks, clearly thinking that a mere captain obviously has no idea of the overall picture.

"Leave the teams with the mission they were trained for. As you know, our AO in case of war is the southern Ukraine. In the first place, whether we can get in there or not is problematic. If we wait until after the balloon goes up, there aren't going to be any civil flights we can hitchhike on. It's sure as hell too far to walk. That leaves air infiltration, from a military aircraft trying to evade the most sophisticated air defense system in the world. And once we're in, we're not going to get out. Not until the war's over. So you send the team in for one strike, and whether or not they make it, you've lost them. They're not coming back out.

"Whereas if we manage to get in, or better yet, if you allow us to infiltrate before hostilities start, we can set up a hell of a guerrilla army. Every report we get from assets in the area tells us that the ordinary people are fed up with the Soviet government. Just like they were before the start of World War II. Even as badly as the Germans treated them afterward, the hatred they felt toward Moscow was such that many of them fought on the side of the Nazis."

You see the deep frown on the face of the commander, the bland indifference on the countenance of the general from the Pentagon. You're really screwing yourself, Jim. Grimly you press on. "And that guerrilla army could strike all sorts of targets. Keep thousands of troops tied down where they won't be in breakthrough armies, heading through the Fulda Gap on their way to the channel."

You wait for the ass-chewing you know you'll get. Generals didn't like to be lectured on tactics by captains. But the man disappoints you.

"Very interesting," he says, looking at you speculatively. "I'll remember your points." He gets up and, followed by a whole retinue of aides and colonels, leaves the hangar.

The group commander doesn't disappoint you. Colonel Casey wants to make general, and having one of his captains speak up, telling the Army chief of staff for Intelligence that his plans are all wrong, is not the way to go about it. Especially when the colonel had a hand in formulating those plans.

CHAPTER 2

He would a thousand times rather have had the ass-chewing he got from the colonel than the one he knew he was in for from Alix. She started almost as soon as he closed the door to their quarters.

"I'm not going to put up with this much longer," she said. "I'm damned tired of you being gone all the time. When are you going to put in for the staff job? You promised me!"

"God, it's great to see you too," he said dryly. "I've missed you. You look great. Gained a little weight, though, I think."

That was when she threw the glass at him. Not for the first time he was glad for adequate reflexes. She was wickedly accurate. The glass smashed against the wall behind where his head had just been.

She collapsed on the couch, crying; ashamed, once again, at letting her temper get away. It was happening more and more often. In a way he could understand. She was not taking the pregnancy well. And he was away a lot. Unfortunately, he'd told her that Germany would be an easy tour. The peacetime army. Nothing much to do but occupy time. And, it was true, he'd said that he would try to get a staff job. But every time he thought about it he just couldn't force himself to make the move. God, to sit around in an office all day, pushing papers! It was bad enough, this playing at war while there was still one going on.

He moved to her, put his arm around her. She tried to shrug it off but he persisted. Her rigid body trembled. So much anger in such a small frame! He felt helpless against it. And he, who had faced death on so many occasions, who had been wounded more times than he cared to count and had still kept going, was afraid.

"I love you," she said in a whisper after he held her so long his arm had gone to sleep.

"Me too," he replied, glad that the storm had passed. It would be okay now, as long as he didn't say something stupid to set her off again. He kissed the top of her head, all he could reach. She had her face tucked into his chest.

"Don't you think you ought to take a shower?" she asked. She looked up at him and wrinkled her nose. "You smell like you want to be alone."

He kissed her, tentatively at first, then with growing fervor; was aware of aching need. It had always been thus, from the moment they had met in Monterey.

He'd been browsing the racks at the local bookstore during lunch break from the language school, aware as usual of the disapproving looks his uniform attracted from the locals. Not that he'd cared. Bunch of damn hippies anyway, he thought. If they didn't like it, they didn't have to look. Look and make whispered disapproving comments were about the only things they felt courageous enough to do. He'd only been spit on once since being in Monterey, and that by a foolish young man with long hair. Who had instantly, and almost permanently, regretted his actions.

But her look had been different. Frankly appraising, then, as he smiled at her, interested. And he had felt that vaguely uncomfortable heaviness at the pit of his stomach, just as he was feeling now.

"Guess I better," he said finally. "Didn't get the chance before we left the U.K. Damn near had to run to catch the plane. You want to join me?"

"No," she said, frowning. "I don't want you to see me fat like this. You won't love me."

She was inordinately sensitive about her body. Sometimes he caught her at the mirror, staring at the gently swelling belly as if she hated it. Yet, he knew, she wanted the baby. Had wanted it from the beginning. Even before he had.

"You, my love, are full of shit. I think you're even more beautiful. And I could never not love you. Come on."

He scrubbed himself quickly the first time while she was still getting undressed. It would take more than one time to get the field dirt off. The water ran brown down the drain, little leaves and pieces of bark swirling briefly in the whirlpool. By the time he had rinsed she got in, keeping her face turned away. He smiled, pushed her under the water, gently soaped her back. Scrubbed, using his nails just slightly. She arched like a cat. He ran his hands around to the front, the soap slick on her small breasts, her nipples hard under his palms. On down, over the swelling stomach, feeling its roundness. It was true what he had told her; the pregnancy only added to her attractiveness, made what had been a hard little body honed by dancing into something more womanly. Something softer. Something infinitely more desirable. He touched her breasts again.

She turned, pushed his hands away. "Not yet, you horny bastard," she said, a smile in her voice. "As usual, you come home with a rucksack full of dirty clothes and a hard-on."

"Guilty," he admitted.

"Let's get some of this grunge off you first." She soaped him, scrubbed hard at his chest. "Did you have to bring half the countryside with you?" She pulled a dead insect from his hair, flicked it toward the drain. Her face was comically serious, set in a little frown as she worked at getting him clean.

He gave himself over to the pleasure, letting her move him about as if he was an inanimate object. She scrubbed hard, pleasure almost pain, his skin red and glowing. He became aware of how tired he was, how bone-tired. Almost dozing there in the shower.

Until with a wicked little grin she started soaping lower and lower down his stomach, reaching the hair, grasping his suddenly responsive hardness. Being quite thorough there too, making sure everything was scrupulously clean.

"I think," he said, his mouth dry, "that's quite enough. Unless you want this to end right here."

"Not on your life, soldier," she said. "Let's get to bed."

"Don't go to sleep yet. Talk to me!" she said later.

"Mphh," he groaned, flinching from the sharp little fist in his side. He had been in that ecstatic state just between awake and sound asleep, thoroughly satiated, warm, feeling good. Now there wouldn't be any sleep for a while. "I'm awake," he lied.

"I'm ugly, aren't I?" she asked. "And a bitch, and a real pain in the ass."

"No, no, and sometimes, yes. But I love you anyway. You make the doctor's appointment last week?"

"Mmh hmmh. He says everything is fine. Just like it was the time before. That I'm not gaining too much weight. Did you tell him to say that?" she asked, suddenly suspicious.

"Nobody could tell Beau Huckaby anything," he said. "Only person he pays attention to is himself. And that's only in the mirror." The group surgeon, a former football hero from the University of Alabama, was widely considered to be almost as vain as the group commander, who kept ten-by-fourteen glossies of himself posted conspicuously throughout his office: Captain Casey with General Westmoreland, Major Casey receiving the Silver Star, Colonel Casey pensively looking out over the wall in Berlin.

"And when are you going to go see Colonel Casey?" she asked, switching subjects with the speed that always left him befuddled and slightly behind. "About the staff job," she continued. "Nora Benson told me her husband isn't going to extend his tour. You're senior enough. You could be the S-4."

He tried to show no outward sign of the inward shudder that ran through him. S-4. A fucking supply officer! Hell, being in the staff would be bad enough in the S-3 (Operations) shop. At least there he'd get to plan operations, update the Warplans, pretend at least that he was doing something worthwhile. Even the S-2 (Intelligence) job wouldn't be too bad. Maybe he'd get to use the Russian he had so painstakingly learned in the course of a year at the

Defense Language Institute at the Presidio of Monterey. But the S-4? No way.

"I'm not sure the colonel is going to want to see me any time soon," he said, and explained what had happened back in England. "I don't think he's real happy with me right now."

"Then he's stupid!" she said. "You only told them the truth."

It was one of the features he loved about her, the way she defended him against outsiders. She might be pissed off at him, think he was doing things in an incredibly stupid way, but God help anyone else who thought that.

"Yeah, well, that's been said before. But it doesn't really matter, because he's the colonel, and I'm not. Told you before, I'm convinced that as soon as you make major they trephine a hole in your head and suck out half the brains. After you make colonel they go after the other half."

"I think you'll be cute with half a brain," she said, playful again. Her moods shifted with bewildering swiftness. "What would that leave you, about two ounces?"

"No worry about that anytime soon," he said, ignoring the jibe. "Hell, I'm lucky I haven't been riffed, much less make major. Promotion lists are gonna stretch out forever. Probably won't even have a new selection board for a couple of years. Not too much use for a soldier, once the war is done."

"Poor little whatever-its-name," she said, patting her belly. "He or she'll never see its daddy, because he'll always be in the field. He'll be this stranger who walks through occasionally. Poor little thing will say, 'Mommy, who is that strange man?'"

He realized that she was joking, but it hurt just the same. Was he being selfish, allowing his own feelings to get in the way of familial responsibilities? He wasn't the heedless bachelor officer any more. The decisions he now made affected more than just himself.

"I'll go see the colonel," he promised, "after he's had some time to cool off. Now can we get some sleep? Else I'll be AWOL tomorrow, and it'll take him a hell of a lot longer to get over that."

She was still asleep when he left the next morning. She'd never been one to get up and fix coffee, stating early in the marriage that if he wanted to persist in keeping such a ridiculous job and getting up so early in the morning, there was no reason for her to suffer too. He didn't mind, liking the early morning solitude. He fixed his own coffee, drank it while staring out the window. The Braunick Mountain, where he had learned to ski, was hard to see in the autumn fog. He shivered. It would be an early, and cold, winter. Despite being here for over a year, he was still not used to the cold.

He walked to Flint Kaserne, just across the street, admiring, yet again, the old buildings. The Kaserne dated to before World War II. It had been an SS Officer Training School, turning out thousands of young lieutenants who went on to lose their lives in a series of battlefields across Europe, Asia, and Africa. Young idealists, for the most part, who believed as strongly in what they were doing as he did in the cause for which he had fought. They had been Waffen SS, of course, not the Totenkopf SS concentration camp guards, who had largely been drawn from prisons. The Waffen SS had been good soldiers for the most part, and brave. But that hadn't done them much good, had it?

His team sergeant and several others were already at the team room. The others wandered in shortly after. Some of them looked like their first stop last night had been the club. But their uniforms were clean, and they were shaven. No matter how much they partied and how late they stayed up they always looked like soldiers the next day. Some of them, he knew, would have had no sleep at all. Back in the old days he had often partied right up to the time he had to get cleaned up to go to work. He couldn't imagine doing it anymore. Perhaps he was getting old. After all, he'd just turned thirty.

After battalion formation they returned to the team room to clean up the gear. The parachutes, recovered from the cache point, had to be hung, shaken out, and dried at the rigger shed. They would repack them later. Weapons were thoroughly scrubbed. The blanks used on exercises caused them to foul badly. Medical and demolition kits were repacked and requisitions made to replace supplies used.

By early afternoon they had finished the physical tasks, and then came the part he liked least, the paperwork. After-action reports had to be written, long detailed narratives of what had gone right and wrong with the operation. Unhesitatingly, he wrote down what he had said at the briefings. Colonel Casey wouldn't like it, but what the hell. Unlikely he would get around to reading it anyway. His time was far too valuable for such mundane tasks. Someone up at EUCOM, European Command at Stuttgart, would, and perhaps it would strike a chord. In any case he had already done as much damage as he could to his career, this wouldn't hurt it more.

And finally the day was over. He wanted to go home and take a little nap, but it was impossible. It was Friday, and Fridays meant mandatory happy hour at the club. Every officer was expected to be there, and woe be unto you if you weren't. Those who missed it, for any reason other than being on exercise or deathly ill, would read about it in their next efficiency report. And one small negative remark on an OER, anything, in fact, less than perfect, would mean that you would get some very unwanted attention at Department of Army the next time they were reviewed. So many good officers had already been riffed that only those whose efficiency reports said they walked on water on a regular basis still hung on.

Perhaps happy hour was a good idea, he didn't know. At least you got the chance to let your hair down, communicate with the other officers on something other than a professional basis. On the negative side it had started him drinking again. He'd avoided it a long time, stayed away from parties, skipped going to bars. He'd decided that many of the bad decisions he'd made over the years had been due to having too much to drink.

But happy hour, with its cheap booze and the general attitude that if you didn't drink there must be something wrong with you, had been too much to resist. Many times he had dragged himself home early in the morning after far too much happy hour. But then at least he was able to sleep.

He was late, so the place was already crowded when he got there. The two bartenders were working as hard as they could, the jukebox was playing Vicki Leandros's latest song, the other officers were shouting to make themselves heard. He looked around, spotted Al Dougherty, threaded his way through the mass of green-clad men over to him.

"Jimmy, me boy!" Al shouted. "I hear you made yourself popular again. Ursula, give Jimmy a stiff scotch. He looks like he needs it."

Jim accepted the drink, and the smile Ursula gave him, in gratitude. He took a long draught.

"So when are you going to give Ursula a chance, Jimmy?" Al asked as she moved back down the bar. "She wants you so bad she can taste it. And from what I understand, she's not so bad tasting herself."

"You know better than that shit," Jim said, fingering his wedding ring. Not that a wedding ring made much difference around Bad Tölz. Adultery and drinking were the two major sports, easing out skiing by a wide margin. Perhaps it was a function of too many American women cooped up in too small a spot, with their husbands generally gone. A form of cabin fever.

"I know, Jimmy." Al laughed. "True love, and all that shit. Glad I'm not afflicted. This is a bachelor's paradise."

"So you know so much about what happened to me," he said to Al to change the subject, "what about you? Did the old famous Aloysius Dougherty luck hold?"

Al frowned. "Not exactly," he said. "We jumped into Kiel Bay, couple of klicks off the coast, scout swam to the shore. Landed in a little inlet 'bout halfway between Oldenburg and Schönburg. Territory is about the same there as it would be if we had to go a little bit farther east. They were on our ass from the beginning. Never did get anywhere close to the target. Spent damn near all the time running. Then my belly started acting up. Puking blood the last couple of days. Guess I wasn't as ready for this shit as I thought I was." Al had been shot in the stomach a few years before, in Vietnam. They'd removed several feet of his intestines.

Al's team's wartime area of operations (AO) was East Germany. As such, he had even less chance of survival than did the teams who were targeted at the Soviet Union. The East Germans were widely regarded as the best troops the East Bloc had to offer.

"Coin check!" someone yelled, followed by the slap of a piece of metal on the bar.

"Shit!" Jim swore, searching frantically for his. You were supposed to carry the silver-dollar sized coin, engraved with the Special Forces (Europe) logo and your name, at all times. Tradition was that if a coin check was called and you didn't have yours you had to buy everyone a drink. If, on the other hand, everyone had theirs, the one initiating the check had to buy.

Jim finally felt the familiar piece of metal in the pocket of his field jacket; slapped it on the bar. Colonel Casey, he saw, had initiated the check. And it appeared that the colonel was going to have to buy. Good. The colonel had all sorts of little tricks like that, like checking to make sure everyone had dogtags, or that their uniforms were perfect, or that they carried the requisite cards in their wallets. In his mind it maintained morale. Everyone else just thought it a pain in the ass.

The colonel paid, and the liquor flowed. One thing about him, Jim had to admit, he wasn't cheap. Didn't have the vaguest idea of what to do with his command, followed slavishly the orders of the generals in Washington who would just have soon disbanded the Special Forces, but he wasn't cheap. That was something, anyway.

"You see the news in the *Scars and Gripes* today?" Al asked.

"Yeah. Looks like the NVA has a clear path all the way to the South China Sea. Why?"

"They cut the country in two, it'll be all over."

"Only a matter of time now. Think we'll do anything about it?"

Al snorted at the thought. "With stumblebum in the White House? Not hardly. And you sure as hell know that even if Tricky Dicky had lasted we wouldn't have done anything either. Hell, it was him and the good doctor that gave it away in the first place." He took a long drink.

"Besides," Al said finally, "what could we do anyway? Army's gutted. Air Force and Navy aren't much better. Hell, we couldn't even mount a good rescue effort when the Cambodians took the *Mayaguez*. So how are we gonna stop the NVA? Nuke 'em? You know better than that."

"So we just let it happen."

"That's about the size of it. C'mon, have another drink. Don't mean nothin' nohow."

Christ, Jim thought, he's right. And I'm getting to the stage I just don't care anymore. Numb. So much bad news already, a little more doesn't matter.

"So tell me, what did you actually do to piss the good colonel off? I heard rumors, but you know how that goes."

Jim shrugged. "Just got on my high horse again about Special Forces missions. And the chief of staff for Intelligence was listening to the briefback."

Al whistled. "Not a good plan, mate. Hell, you and I both know there's not gonna be a war in Europe anyway, so why bother?"

"Yeah, but suppose we're wrong? You want to be attacking some East German power plant, instead of putting a guerrilla band together? Hell of a waste, don't you think?"

"Shit, my man, if the balloon ever goes up, we'll go nuclear before any of us get a chance to do anything, so what the hell? We can't stop them with conventional forces, so we'll throw a tactical nuke to slow them down. They'll throw a little bit larger one in our rear area. We'll nuke one of their cities. They'll get England. And so it goes, until all the big stuff is flyin', and there won't be anything left. You know that, no matter how crazy we think the politicians on either side are, none of them are going to risk that."

Al drained his glass, signaled Ursula for a refill. "So I'm gonna just sit back, ride it out, retire, and then do what I'm gonna do."

"Yeah, and what's that?"

"Get me a little piece of land down in Florida, collect my retirement check, and shoot at anything that comes around in Army green. Drink beer with my buddies. Do a little fishing. Purchase some honest affection now and then."

"And go right out of your fucking mind."

"Oh, I don't know. I'm not as hung up on this shit as you are. I think I might not do bad at all. And if I do, there's always a war somewhere. Suspect they might pay a hell of a lot better money than this. Look, here comes Ursula again. Sure you don't want a taste of that?"

The club got even louder and more raucous. Other officers drifted by and talked, mostly about work. From the ones who had not been on the exercise he found that there was yet another exercise coming up, this time in Crete. His team was scheduled to go. More problems with Alix, he thought. Perhaps he'd better inquire about the S-4 job.

Later, much later, some of the wives showed up; some to reclaim their drunken husbands and take them home, others to join the party. Alix was one of the latter. She refused to drink anything, thinking it bad for the baby, but she'd never needed to drink to have fun anyway.

He watched as the men's eyes followed her, and was proud and the same time jealous. Not that he blamed them. She was beautiful. And not that he was worried. She had never shown the slightest inclination toward other men.

She pecked him on the cheek, smiled at Al, whom she genuinely liked. "My husband being a bad influence on you again?" she asked.

"Hell, you know me, Alix. I never needed any help." Al offered her his barstool.

"Glad there's at least one gentleman here," she said, shooting a look at Jim, who had been getting ready to offer his own. Al laughed. Jim glared at him.

"Sonofabitch," he said, "you're always getting me in trouble."

Al looked offended. "Me, get you in trouble? That'll be the day. Alix, I'm very much afraid you've married an ungrateful wretch here. My advice is to divorce him immediately and marry me. I'll be a good husband and father to whatever-its-name. Trust me!"

"No offense, Al my love, but a woman would have to be out of her mind to marry a reprobate like you. Of course, there are some who would say that one would have to be out of their mind to marry Jim, too. Including me sometimes. Can you get your girlfriend to bring me a cola, darling?" she asked Jim. "Or do we poor ladies not rate around here?"

When he had asked her to marry him, he had wondered how well she would fit into the military society. Nothing in her background had prepared her for it. Daughter of a Russian immigrant who had used his medical skills to become one of the foremost surgeons on the West Coast and a San Francisco society lady, her life had been one of privilege. He made less money as a captain in the Army than she had received as an allowance while going through college. His friends were rough, profane, rakish. Hers, the ones he had met, were refined, educated, and to a person, devoutly antiwar.

He needn't have worried. She had an easy manner about her that made friends wherever she went. From the beginning she had engaged as an equal in the chaffing banter that always went on when he and his friends got together. As Al had said of her admiringly, shortly after they met, "That girl don't take no shit from nobody!" She had thoroughly charmed everyone, from the colonel on down. Was it any wonder, he thought, that he loved her so much? He didn't know what he had done to deserve this luck, but he hoped it would never run out.

They talked, laughed, danced a couple of times. Occasionally she would leave him, go and talk with other wives. And their husbands. He watched as she turned away, with laughter and grace, yet another pass from one of the bachelors. The more she turned them down, the more they liked her. Perhaps, he thought, because of the male tendency to want something they could not have, and scorn something they could. Many of the other wives were not so picky, and were treated accordingly.

Amused, he watched the usual Friday night flirtations. It wasn't difficult to surmise who was having an affair with whom. The little looks, the surreptitious touches, the dancing just a little bit too close; all were telltales. He doubted that the affected husbands or wives were blind to it. Perhaps they just didn't want to see.

Finally Alix made her way back to him, smiling that little secret smile that said, I know something you don't know. He wondered what delicious little piece of gossip she had picked up now. She loved the little intrigues, the palace politics, the jockeying for position that went on constantly. He, on the other hand, hated it, wanting only for them to let him alone so he could go on trying to be a soldier in this goddamned peacetime army. He often thought that she would have made a far better officer than he.

He wondered what she had found out. She'd tell him, sooner or later. After she'd had the chance to see how to manipulate it to his advantage. And sometimes after she'd already performed the manipulation.

"You about ready to get out of here?" he asked.

"You're not having fun?" She laughed at the face he made.

"Just afraid if we stay here much longer we'll get cornered by the battalion commander again." That individual could be seen telling one of the new lieutenants, for at least the twentieth time, about the Ia Drang Valley. The lieutenant's eyes had a distinct glazed look. Lieutenant Colonel Grimstead had been a company commander in the 1st Cavalry Division during that bloodying, and had been quite a hero. But he was one of the most boring men on earth.

He was also, Jim knew, having an affair with the lieutenant's wife. He hoped the colonel was better in bed than at conversation. Though he doubted that the wife, a notorious social climber, cared much one way or the other.

"Besides," he said, "I was in the field for a long time. And last night just whetted my appetite."

She laughed, loud and long. "And just what do you think you'll be able to do about that? With as much scotch as you have sloshing around in you? Still, you may have a point about Colonel Grimstead. Come on. I'll make some coffee and you may be of some use yet tonight."

CHAPTER 3

He got a call the next morning to come and recover Jerry Hauck from the MPs in Munich. Christ, just what I need, he thought as he got out of bed. He sat back down quickly, his head threatening to fall off and roll around the floor. Alix slept on, oblivious. He looked at her longingly, wanting nothing more than to crawl back in beside her. Sleep late, until the hangover went away, and then make love again. She had a little smile, as if she were dreaming of the same thing.

No! Duty called. God damn Jerry Hauck, anyway. What had he done now? The MPs hadn't said. Probably fighting again. This certainly wasn't the first occasion. Jerry was one of the finest field soldiers he had ever known, and one of the worst in garrison. When Jim had arrived at Tölz Jerry was on his way to being kicked out of the Army. All the other team leaders had despaired of him. Jim had asked for Jerry to be assigned to his team, remembering the debts he owed the man from Vietnam. He doubted that he would have survived a couple of missions if it hadn't been for Jerry. And in the field he hadn't been sorry. Mostly in the garrison it had been okay too. Jerry, after a long and painful counseling session behind the team room, had been straight for quite some time. Now, it seemed, he was back up to his old tricks.

Finally he got up, took a handful of aspirin, and by the time he got out of the shower was feeling almost human. He dressed, left a note for Alix, and went downstairs. The German kids from across the road were already in the playground, having a wonderful time with the American children. The group was chattering away in a half English–half German patois that none of the parents could understand. Too bad the adults didn't get along as well. The Americans thought the Germans arrogant, which they were, and the Germans thought the Americans uncultured. Which, for the most part, they were.

The drive to Munich was pleasant. The used BMW he had bought upon arrival in Germany purred away, the road was just tortuous enough to be interesting, and the scenery was, as always, perfect. Almost too perfect, as if it were a set by Disney. The fields were even and green, the cows fat and clean. The houses were painted white, with sharply pitched roofs and window boxes spilling over with pink and white flowers. The streets of the little towns looked scrubbed. He had to slow down only once, while a herd of cows ambled down the road from field to farm. It would have been a much more pleasant drive had it not been for the German drivers behind him who, infuriated because he presumed to drive at less than eighty to ninety miles an hour on the narrow winding road, constantly flashed their lights, honked, and, when there was even the slightest chance, zoomed by. The German driver thought it his or her god-given right to travel just as fast as the cars would go. On the autobahn it made for some truly spectacular accidents, thirty- to forty-car pileups not being uncommon.

He refused to let it bother him. Time enough to get pissed off, when he got to Munich.

"Germans want to get him for inciting to riot," the MP captain said. "Along with aggravated assault and battery, assault with a deadly weapon, resisting arrest, and about a dozen other charges. Lucky they let us have him. He'd be staring out between the bars of a Munich jail for a long time. Frankly, I think they're overreacting, but you know the Germans. They don't like us too much anyway."

"Christ, what did he do?"

"Not that much really. Punched out some fat burgher. Then when the security guards came he tried to take them on too. The ADW charge is for when he smacked one of them in the head with a beer stein after the guy tried to use a nightstick on him. Near as I can tell, when the police finally came he didn't really give them a lot of trouble, except for calling them Nazis. Thus the resisting arrest charge. They worked him over pretty good before we got him. You know I'm going to have to send this Delinquency Report up to USAREUR, don't you?"

"No way around that?" Jim knew that when CINCUSAREUR, Commander in Chief, U.S. Army Europe, got the report Jerry's career was effectively over.

"No way. They're super-sensitive about any American-German incident. Like the Krauts are doing us a favor, letting us stay here, instead of it being the opposite. Sorry."

"Okay." Jim sighed. "Where do I sign?"

Jerry had, indeed, been worked over. One eye was puffed shut, and he walked with a limp. Taking deep breaths caused obvious pain. Jim helped him into the car.

"Okay," he said as they pulled away from the city, "you want to tell me your side?"

"Nothing much to tell, *Dai Uy*. Guilty as charged. Fat fuck pissed me off, so I dropped him."

"And just what did the fat fuck do to piss you off?" Jim persisted. He knew there had to be a story behind this, and he was desperate to find something that would help exonerate his NCO.

Jerry snorted, then winced with the pain. He was silent for a moment, then, "You know what that son of a bitch tried to tell me, sir?"

"That you're ugly? Hell, you didn't have to come to Munich to hear that."

Jerry tried to laugh, winced again. Then grew serious again. "We were talking, laughing. He said he'd been in the German Army during the war. On the Russian front, of course. I sometimes think the Western Campaign must have been the easiest one in history, what with all the Germans being on the Eastern Front. What'd they have at Normandy? A platoon of Boy Scouts?

"Anyway, I told him I was a soldier too. At Bad Tölz. And the son of a bitch said, well then you understand."

"Understand what?" Jim asked.

"That's what I wondered. When I asked, he said the Special Forces had to understand what the Germans had to go through, because they had been accused of war crimes too. And that, of course, there were no real war crimes. I couldn't believe what I was hearing. So I asked him, what about Dachau and Auschwitz? And he said that nobody had actually died in those places, that the story of the Holocaust had been cooked up by the Allies in order to justify what they wanted to do to the Germans. Which was to keep them from their rightful place in the world. So I punched him."

Jim had heard the claim before. And each time it angered him more. There was a whole group of Germans out there who, it seemed, had learned nothing from the worst war in world history, people who still believed that Germany had a historic mission to rule the world.

Still, his anger could be as nothing to Jerry's. Jerry Hauck was half Jewish, half Sioux Indian. As he sometimes joked, lucky enough to be a member of both groups of people upon whom genocide had been attempted in the last hundred years. His father had grown up on a reservation, watching the last of his people and his culture succumb to alcohol and assimilation. His mother's parents and most of the rest of her family had perished in one of the concentration camps the German had claimed didn't exist.

They were silent for the remainder of the trip, Jim searching his mind for a way out of the problem, Jerry undoubtedly pondering the various injustices of the world. Jerry, Jim often thought, suffered too much. Not for himself, necessarily, but for anyone else who found himself oppressed anywhere in the world. In Vietnam he had regularly stolen food from military convoys to give to the Montagnard villagers he had adopted. When one of his indigenous troops was killed he made very sure that the family was well taken care of, many times taking money out of his own pocket when he thought the official death gratuity too skimpy. And, Jim thought, God only knew what was going through his mind now that those same people were being shot wholesale. If he was suffering, Jerry must have been being ripped apart.

Then a strategy to save Jerry came to him. It would be

risky, and probably wouldn't do a hell of a lot for his career, but that was okay. He didn't have much of a career anyway.

"Jerry," he said, as they neared the gates of the Kaserne, "I want you to go to your BEQ, and I want you to stay there. The only time I better hear of you coming out is to go to the messhall. Else I'll make what those Kraut cops did to you look like a love pat. Understand?"

Jerry, who had been on the receiving end of the captain's "counseling sessions" before, signaled his agreement. All he wanted to do right now was go to bed and try to heal up anyway. And wonder what he was going to do when they threw him out of the Army.

"You wanted to see me, Captain Carmichael?" the battalion commander asked, shortly after Monday morning formation.

"Yes, sir." He told the colonel about Jerry Hauck's transgression, leaving nothing out. Including the reasons, as he saw it, it had happened. Then he said, "I'd like you to give SFC Hauck an Article 15."

"Are you out of your goddamned mind!" The colonel clearly thought he was. An Article 15 was the highest form of nonjudicial punishment in the military. As such, any commander could administer it. Since, technically, team leaders were just that, leaders, and not officially in command, Lieutenant Colonel Grimstead was the appropriate official to administer it.

However, the colonel's attitude clearly showed that he knew what Jim was trying to do. If he gave Sergeant Hauck an Article 15, the NCO would already be punished. And thus they couldn't court martial him and throw him out of the Army. Which would leave Colonel Grimstead in a very ticklish position with CINCUSAREUR. Not to mention with Colonel Casey, who had just that morning told him of his intention to finally get rid of the troublemaker.

"No sir. At least I don't think so. SFC Hauck deserves an Article 15. Nothing more. You've heard the story. The German deserved it, and probably a lot more. Sergeant Hauck is a hell of a fine soldier. He's got four more years to retirement. Let him have it." Jim was almost pleading by now.

The battalion commander started on what Jim knew would be a long, boring, and totally irrelevant speech about the responsibilities of the United States Army and its men to the host country of West Germany, and how NCOs had to live up to the highest standards, and so forth. Jim cut him off.

"Do those standards include not fucking your subordinate's wife?" he asked.

Grimstead was suddenly and uncharacteristically quiet. "And what do you mean by that?" he asked finally. The blowhard tone had left his voice. It was down to business.

Jim pushed on. "Remember a small gasthaus just outside Lenggries? An afternoon in March last year? You coming downstairs with Joanne Whaley? Someone turning away so you couldn't see his face? That was me, sir. So don't give me any shit about standards. Now, are you going to give that Article 15, or am I going to have to go to the USAREUR IG and see if they want to give me a talk about standards?"

"You son of a bitch," Grimstead said, getting up and starting around the desk. "I'll whip your goddamned ass!"

"Oh, that'll solve a hell of a lot. We duke it out here in

the office, you whip my ass or I whip yours, and we've still got the problem. Admit it. You're fucked. But you can at least plead ignorance if you do what I want. I'll tell whoever asks that I didn't give you all the facts in the matter, led you to think it was less serious than it was. You go on screwing Joanne, and I'll keep my NCO, and sooner or later everyone will forget all about it."

Grimstead subsided in his seat. After a moment a small smile played about his lips. "You're a devious son of a bitch, Carmichael," he said.

"I've been told that, sir."

"Siddown. I'll give him the Article 15. You're probably right. Hauck does deserve it. Lots of us deserve a lot more than we get. You think I'm a clown, don't you?" he asked suddenly.

"I know you do," he said when Jim didn't answer immediately. "Most of the other officers do too. Sometimes I wonder about it myself. Why I always feel so fucking useless. Could be I'm in a useless job, with nothing to do and nobody who gives a shit. Could be I'm a boring old fart anyway, and this just makes it worse. Could be I felt the need to be a young man just once again, even if it was between the thighs of a little slut. You ever feel useless, Jim?"

"Fucking nearly every day, sir," he replied.

"Hell, you don't need to call me sir," said Grimstead. "I feel like we're coconspirators now. That ought to call for first names." He grinned. "Why do you feel useless? You've got a beautiful wife, soon have a kid; your career sucks, but so does everybody else's here in this wonderful fucking peacetime Army. So why do you feel useless?"

"You hit on the point. This wonderful fucking peacetime Army. Couple of years ago we were doing something. It might have been wrong, we might not have done it right; hell, for all I know maybe we shouldn't have done it at all. But we were doing something. Now we're practicing for something that will never come. Sort of like dry-humping."

Grimstead laughed. "That's a good analogy," he said. "I'll remember it. Well, get Hauck in here and we'll go through this charade. And if he fucks up again, neither you, nor I, nor God himself can help him. Your responsibility, Jim. I hope you're ready for it."

Lieutenant Colonel Grimstead gave SFC Hauck the maximum allowable punishment under the provisions of Article 15 of the Uniform Code of Military Justice. He was restricted to quarters for three months, banned from the NCO Club, and the colonel assured him that the paperwork would become a permanent part of his records. It was not enough to keep him from being promoted sometime in the future, but made it highly unlikely. Still, he would be allowed to stay in the Army.

"Thanks, Captain," Jerry said later in the team room.

"Don't thank me," Jim said coldly. "There are a lot of good people who've put their asses on the line for you for a long time now, and frankly I'm beginning to wonder if you're worth it."

A look of pain, frightening in its intensity, crossed Jerry's face. He said nothing.

"Here's what's going to happen now," Jim continued. "First of all, you're going to get some help with your drinking problem. You're to set up an appointment with the counselor immediately, and you'll do everything she says. You're not to drink, at all. You're restricted from the club officially, and that means the Rod and Gun Club too. If I get any reports you've been seen in a gasthaus off the Kaserne, I'll increase the restrictions so that the only time you'll be able to leave is when you're on official duty. Is all that clear?"

"Yes, sir," Hauck said, his face now set in grim lines. "Will that be all, sir?"

"And don't pull that bullshit on me!" Jim exploded. "We've been together too long for you to go into that officer/NCO mode. You need help with the alcohol. Like probably 50 percent of the people on this Kaserne. Difference between them and you is that it inevitably gets you in trouble. So you're going to straighten that problem out. Christ, Jerry, don't fight me on this."

After he had gone Jim sat thinking, what right do I have to come off as so holy? What I said about at least 50 percent of the people here needing help was true. Including me. The combination of cheap alcohol, boredom, and frustration was deadly. Maybe I should be the one seeing the counselor. But that was almost a sure kiss of death for an officer. Soon the word would get around, and you would be regarded as just a little bit off-center, not able to handle your own problems, the attempt to get help being regarded a sign of weakness. In a perverse way the system was far better disposed toward those who had an alcohol problem than those who were trying to get rid of it.

The next couple of weeks were spent in normal garrison duty. Up at five, a quick cup of coffee, and to the battalion area for physical training. It usually consisted of twelve repetitions of the "daily dozen," the standard Army calisthenics, and then a four-mile run. To spice up the standard fare, different events were often scheduled, like running up and back down the Brauneck Mountain. Only two miles up, but running steadily uphill was a killer. Few made it all the way to the top. Or there would be organized athletics: combat volleyball, pushball, grass drills. Injuries were common. The Special Forces soldier is by nature aggressive; has to be. Games were played with the intensity and commitment of combat. It was not uncommon to send five or six people to the dispensary after a particularly good game of pushball.

Other days they would swim, endless laps in the Olympic-sized pool in the field house. Or go on rucksack marches, up and down the mountains so close outside the Kaserne. Those soldiers coming from Fort Bragg, which since the end of the involvement of the Special Forces in Vietnam had slacked off considerably on training and readiness, were in for a shock once they got to Bad Tölz. They could be seen behind the formation on the runs, puking and reeling from fatigue, falling farther and farther behind. But soon the fat around their middle would melt away, and they would be there ready to harass the next group of new guys. Nobody doubted that there was a need to be in shape. It was just so easy to fall out of the habit when not forced to do it. In this they were, as in other things, reflective of the society from which they came. Jim was often amused to see in the media the depiction of the Special Forces soldier as some sort of fanatic jock, a loner who spent all his time pumping iron and biting the heads off snakes. Such a person existed, he knew, but did not last long in the SF, where teamwork was all.

After PT a quick shower, some breakfast, then on to the normal daily tasks. A lot of time was spent in maintaining proficiency in one's own military specialty, and a lot more in cross-training. All detachments had to be skilled in cross-country and high-mountain skiing, since most people agreed that the only real way to get to the wartime operations areas would be on the ground. Everyone went to the ski schools; first to those given by the detachments, then to the more specialized courses conducted in the Winter Warfare Schools of France, Italy, Spain, and West Germany.

It kept them busy. Jim thanked whatever powers might be for that. Otherwise his personnel problems would have been much worse.

No one was content. Like him, they knew that they were preparing for a war that would never come. And they saw what was happening in the United States, a progressive gutting of the Army that most felt would end only when another war did come. One that they would not be ready for.

Twice a week, after duty hours, he went to college courses given by the University of Maryland. All officers were supposed to have a college degree. It looked bad on your records if you didn't. He had never figured out how having a degree made you a better combat leader, but that didn't matter. Much to his surprise, once he started he found that he enjoyed it. He had always been a good student, able to grasp complex material, and now excelled at the classwork. In particular, the history classes fascinated him. Human existence, he saw, had been a regular progression of wars. There was always someone, somewhere, who wanted what the other person had. And was willing to kill him for it. And the ones who got killed were the ones who were not prepared to fight back. It made him sad for his country.

He would probably have achieved higher grades were it not for his propensity for arguing with the teachers. Some of them, the older ones, were okay. The younger ones seemed to have been infected with the attitude that whatever the United States did, it was wrong. From his readings he knew that this was called the revisionist theory of history. While he knew that some history needed debunking, particularly that dealing with the Indian Wars, he doubted that all of it was untrue. And told the teachers so. They, being used to dealing with young, impressionistic students, were not happy with being called to task. So it reflected on his grade.

He often shared his frustrations with Alix, who laughed and called him an inveterate troublemaker. "Can't you see, darling," she said after one particularly nasty fight with a young man Jim suspected, rightly, of staying in college so that he could avoid the war, "that it's a matter of cooperate and graduate? None of this matters. You're not going to change their minds. Nothing could do that. They may or may not believe strongly in their positions, but it would be too embarrassing to admit they're wrong. So you're only hurting yourself."

"So what I should do is just nod my head like one of those plastic puppies in the rear window of a redneck's car, and agree to this bullshit?"

She nodded. "And they'll go away, and you'll have your degree, and make major like you should. Ow!" she said as the baby gave her a particularly vicious kick.

"See there, he agrees with me." Jim laughed. "You're raising another little troublemaker."

"God help us," she sighed. She flipped over, her signal for a massage. He kneaded the tight muscles in her neck until they relaxed, moved down to the shoulders. He loved giving her a massage, feeling her soft skin move beneath his fingers, hearing the soft grunts of pleasure. She had told him once that it was what had decided her that she should marry him, the massage he gave her on the almost deserted beach at Big Sur, long before there was anything else physical going on between them. They'd had such fun then. Few responsibilities, going to class and studying Russian during the day and then practicing it on her at night, loving the faces she made when he mispronounced the words, long nights of love in her apartment in Carmel overlooking the sea. Now it was all career, and work, and worry.

"I *do* love you," she said, her voice muffled in the pillow.

God, I hope that's always true, he thought. Because I don't know what I'd do if it weren't.

CHAPTER 4

He and his team had been on a scuba recovery mission, retrieving the bodies of two helicopter pilots who'd crashed into Lake Falkensee, when he got a radio message. Report back to Bad Tölz. Immediately. He jumped in the BMW and tore up the roads, wondering the entire time what had gone wrong. Was something the matter with Alix? His mind, always fertile, had dreamed up all sorts of scenarios, each worse than the last, by the time he got back to the Kaserne.

When he got there he was surprised and alarmed to see Colonel Casey waiting for him. Oh, Lord, he thought, what the hell has gone wrong?

"We'll be driving to Stuttgart," the colonel peremptorily told him. "The staff car is right outside."

He thought it better to hold his questions until they were out of the Kaserne. He was beginning to think that at least he wasn't in trouble. Otherwise he would have been met by MPs instead of the group commander.

"I don't know," Colonel Casey said to his questions as they threaded their way through the German traffic. "All I know is that we got a message, said to have you at EUCOM as soon as possible. That I was to personally make sure you got there. I thought maybe you could shed some light on it."

"Not me, sir." Jim was baffled. EUCOM, European Command, was the Special Forces Detachment (Europe) higher headquarters. At least in matters dealing with tactics. Administratively they came under USAREUR, a fragmentation of lines of command that led to no end of confusion. But, again, this told him that he wasn't in trouble. If they were setting him up for a court-martial he would be going to Heidelberg, not Stuttgart.

The colonel had obviously come to the same conclusion, and further, that the captain beside him was more important than he had suspected. He hadn't really had to accompany the young officer to Stuttgart; he could have delegated the mission to any one of the staff officers. But he was consumed with curiosity. And determined that if anything good came out of it, he was going to be one of the beneficiaries.

He set the task for himself of being pleasant to the captain. He asked about the mission at Lake Falkensee, told him that he had gone to see the captain's wife just before picking him up at the airport and made sure she wanted for nothing, wanted to know if the captain wanted anything to eat or drink along the way.

Jim was amused. Other than ass-chewings, this was the most the colonel had spoken to him since he had arrived at Bad Tölz. It might have been a pleasant drive, had it not been for the fact that he was going crazy, trying to figure out what it was all about.

He had done nothing in the last three years to either distinguish himself or get into any major trouble. After Vietnam there had been that one more mission, the one he still had nightmares about, then the Infantry Officers' Advanced Course at Fort Benning, Russian Language School at Monterey, and finally assignment at Bad Tölz. He was, he knew, an adequate team leader, better than some of the others but about equal to a few. So it had to date back before that. Well, he would know soon enough. Best to sit back and enjoy the attention. It would end soon enough, he knew, and it would be back to normal. What the hell, he thought. This way I'll get to see Alix sooner. That ought to make her happy.

"Imagine my surprise," General Edward D. "Tink" Miller, chief of staff for Intelligence, U.S. Army, said, "when the first name to come out of the computer was yours."

Jim sat in silence, wondering even more now what was going on. Upon arrival at Patch Barracks they were told to report immediately to the bubble. This room, buried a hundred feet underground and shielded from any sort of electromagnetic radiation, was the most secure structure in Europe. From here the war would be conducted, if it ever came to that. In the meantime it served admirably as a secure briefing room, ensuring that even the most intrepid and resourceful intelligence service would get no hint of what went on inside.

Colonel Casey had been stopped at the door by an armed officer, who paid no attention to his argument that since Captain Carmichael was a member of his command, he was entitled to know what was going on. Jim had been fingerprinted, his prints compared with a card he knew must have come from his records in Washington, searched, and allowed to pass through. Inside were only General Miller and his aide, who, Jim saw, was wearing the starred blue ribbon indicating he had been awarded the Medal of Honor.

"I'd just told someone," the general continued, "about a young captain who thought he had a better way of running things. Then this thing came up, we fed in the parameters of the person we had to have for it, and voilà! There you were."

"I don't know if I should be grateful or frightened," Jim ventured.

"The captain has a sense of humor." General Miller chuckled. "Isn't that nice, Captain Sloane?"

Sloane, Jim thought. Bentley Sloane. I've heard of him. Sloane shifted and he caught a glimpse of the captain's right shoulder. He was wearing the combat patch of the Special Forces. Boun Tlak, Jim thought. He won the big blue at Boun Tlak. Something funny about the whole thing, I hear.

"Captain Carmichael, everything I've learned about you, and the experience we had at the debriefing in England, leads me to believe that you are an intelligent, brave, and dedicated young officer. Would you agree with that assessment of yourself?" the general asked. He went on without waiting for a reply. "We have a mission for which you are, among all the officers in the United States Army, uniquely qualified. I'm sure you're going to like it."

Jim Carmichael felt his testicles draw up, a sure sign of apprehension. Nothing about this boded well. When a three-star general started giving you a pep talk, you were about to get screwed. With or without the benefit of a kiss.

"Do you remember a fellow by the name of Y Buon Sarpa?" the general asked.

Good God, Jim thought, I haven't heard that name in eight years. He nodded, reluctantly. "I thought he was dead," he said.

"No, not quite. Not the fault of the Vietnamese. They certainly tried hard enough to kill him. Both the Saigon government and the boys from Hanoi. Didn't have many friends, did Y Buon Sarpa? You know the reason well enough, don't you, Captain?"

Indeed I do, Jim thought. Y Buon Sarpa had been one of the founding members of FULRO, acronym of the French term for the Unified Front for the Liberation of Oppressed Races. FULRO represented the aspiration of the hill peoples of Southeast Asia for freedom. The Montagnards were regarded by the Vietnamese, both North and South, as primitives, little better than animals. Before the war in Indochina they had been left alone. There were few things in the rugged mountains the Viets needed. The terrain they occupied was, however, strategic. Control the Central Highlands and you controlled Vietnam.

The South Vietnamese government, before the Americans came, practiced near genocide, bombing at will the Montagnard villages. The North Vietnamese entered those same villages and disemboweled anyone who would not support them, then carried the young men off to serve as pack animals. Little wonder, then, that the Montagnards got fed up with the whole thing.

Perhaps it was the Special Forces teams that showed them the way. Jim didn't know. The Special Forces had also recognized the strategic value of the Montagnards, but had taken a different course than the Vietnamese. Teams were inserted into the hills, made contact with the 'Yards, as they called them, and won their trust. The 'Yards were trained, equipped, and led by the men in the Green Berets, becoming a potent fighting force.

They also gained an appreciation of their own potential power. While the Montagnards lived the life of the hunter/gatherer and thus appeared to the outsider as primitives, they were anything but. All the 'Yards Jim had met were keenly intelligent, quick to learn, and possessed tribal knowledge that was often of far more use than the so-called civilized skills.

The Special Forces border camps became hotbeds of FULRO organizing. And, if the truth be known, most of the SF were in full agreement with their aims, though it was the official policy of the U.S. government to support official South Vietnamese policy. At first the organization was political, the Montagnards wanting to take their rightful place in the supposed democracy that was South Vietnam. But when those aims were thwarted, and FULRO was banned, the policy became one of clandestine organization with a view toward armed struggle.

It was into one of these border camps that young Lieutenant James NMI Carmichael had been thrust, on his second tour to Vietnam. He'd been warned that unrest among the Montagnards was building, that something was likely to happen. But no one had expected the extent to which it happened.

"Sarpa was, what? Your interpreter?" the general asked.

"Yes, sir," Jim replied. "At the time we had no idea of his rank within FULRO. The Saigon government thought the company commander, Y Buon Tlieng, was the leader. The Vietnamese Special Forces were keeping a close eye on him. 'Yards were pretty smart. They knew that would happen, so they let the Viets think what they wanted. All the time Sarpa was organizing things right under their noses."

"And you got to know Sarpa pretty well." It was a statement, not a question.

Jim nodded. "He was with me on every patrol. Probably saved my life more than once. Taught me how to speak Bahnar. We became good friends."

And more, Jim thought. They'd had that closeness that only combat veterans can have, men who have depended upon one another for their very existence. He didn't know if he could explain that to the general, or if he should even try. If the general was capable of understanding, he would know what Jim was saying without explanation. If he was not, no amount of words would make it so.

"So much so that you broke Army regulations and defied the policy of both the U.S. and South Vietnamese governments," General Miller said.

"Guilty, sir," Jim replied. Was that what all this was about? Had the actions he had taken as a young lieutenant come back to haunt him? He knew very well what the general was talking about, though he didn't know how the man had found out about it. He had thought it all buried in the years since. *Should have known better.*

It had come to a head one evening in August 1965. The Montagnards had been getting more and more disturbed over what they regarded as promises broken by the Saigon government. One of the conditions under which the 'Yards had agreed to support Saigon had been that they would gain autonomy over their areas in the Central Highlands; have their own provincial governors, representation in parliament. The generals who ran the country had, of course, no intention of following through; thought instead to bleed the Montagnards dry and then repopulate the hills with lowland Vietnamese who were regarded as more reliable.

Rumors of an uprising had been flying about for months, but when nothing happened the government relaxed. It was what FULRO had been waiting for.

The team leader had been absent that night, off on R&R to Hawaii, leaving Jim in charge. Intelligence had indicated that there were no specific threats against the camp, so normal watch procedures were in effect. Two of the Americans were awake at any given time, one in the radio room and one roaming the perimeter. Jim had just finished his watch and was drifting off to sleep when the team sergeant, who had just replaced him on watch, shook him roughly.

"We got problems, *Trung Uy,*" Master Sergeant Ed Miller said, his familiar Bostonian twang making him recognizable even in the dark. "You better come."

Jim struggled back into his pants, still unpleasantly wet from the day's sweat, grabbed his M-16, and started to follow the team sergeant.

"You better leave that here, sir," Ed said, referring to the weapon. "You'll see why."

They walked out of the team house and were immediately surrounded by Montagnard soldiers, all fully armed. Hands searched him quickly but thoroughly. All around him were familiar faces, men alongside whom he had fought. Their features were set and angry, yet somehow not threatening. A few carried torches. It looked, he thought, like a scene out of some old B movie. The other members of the team were coming out of their bunkers, those with weapons being roughly disarmed.

"What the hell is going on!" he demanded. He saw Y Buon Sarpa, standing with the others. "Where is the company commander?" he asked.

Sarpa smiled, exposing several gold teeth. "I regret to have to inform you that you are now our prisoners," he said. "Please don't make things difficult."

Their hands were tied behind them, and they were marched to the edge of camp, near the latrines. Exactly twenty-four holes had been dug there, in neat rows. In twelve were the bodies of the Vietnamese Special Forces team. Each had been shot through the head.

"We do not wish to do the same to you," Sarpa said. "We realize that you cannot go against the wishes of your government. You are soldiers, and must follow orders. We do not expect you to join us. We do expect that you will stay out of our way. Please do not try to resist us. You will be given free run of the camp. You will not try to contact the outside, unless it is at our direction. If you will give me your word as a soldier that this will be so, you will be released. May I have your word?"

Jim looked into his eyes. There was a pleading look written plainly on the Montagnard's features. At the same time he had no illusions that his former interpreter would hesitate to shoot him if it was necessary.

He considered the choices. I can demand that they lay down their arms, surrender, he thought. And almost certainly join the LLDB in the holes. They've gone too far by killing the Viets. They can't back up now. Or I can try to bluff my way out, give them my word and then when the chance comes try to get the team out of here, E&E until we can get to some friendlies. The chances of that were not great. Even if they could get out they had a hundred miles of enemy territory to cross before they got to the next American camp, and it was likely it had been taken over too.

"I give you my word," he said. "But you must realize how futile this is."

"The futility is in listening to the lies of the men in Saigon," Sarpa said. "We are finished with that. Better to die like men than to perish one by one like hunted animals." In Bahnar he gave the command for the Americans to be cut loose.

"Now we wish you to send a radio message," he said. "We will list our demands. I am glad that you came to this decision, Jim. You are our friends. We would not want to kill you."

"Plus that would leave you without any hostages," Jim said.

"Yes," Sarpa replied. "That too."

The Montagnard uprising of 1965 lasted less than a week. The enraged Vietnamese threatened to bomb the camps off the map, had to be restrained by the Americans, who, in a rare show of concern for the trapped Special Forces teams, told Saigon they would cut off all aid. But the end was a foregone conclusion. Saigon advanced troops on the camps; regular army supported by artillery and tanks. Cynics among the Americans said that had Saigon shown that much resolve against the Viet Cong the war would long since have been over.

The Montagnards were promised, once again, that their demands would be considered. Which meant absolutely nothing, as everyone knew. In the end the ringleaders faded across the border into Cambodia and Laos, hoping someday to fight again.

One of those to escape had been Sarpa, and that had been at the urging of Lieutenant James Carmichael.

Jim had learned more about the history of Vietnamese-Montagnard relations in the week of captivity than he could ever have imagined. He'd already been a sympathizer; now he became an outright supporter. The anger he had felt at being taken captive had faded away. What else could they have done?

The Vietnamese had demanded that Sarpa give himself up. No other demands were to be met until that happened. Sarpa was ready to do so, if it would help his countrymen.

"You do that, and they're gonna kill you for sure," Jim said.

The little Montagnard shrugged eloquently. "If it will serve my people," he said.

"I don't know what service your death is going to render to your people," Jim replied. "Seems to me you could do a hell of a lot more for them alive."

"So you are suggesting that I run away?"

Now it was Jim's turn to shrug.

Sarpa considered. "And what will you do?" he asked. "When we give the camp back over to you, you are supposed to arrest us. They will expect to find me."

"Hell, all you guys look alike to me," Jim said. "How can I pick out one in four hundred? Mistakes get made. And I'm just a dumb lieutenant. The army has the opinion that lieutenants can't be trusted anyway. But if I was you, I wouldn't be around here after tonight."

And Sarpa, with some of his followers, had slipped away. The Vietnamese had been enraged, had demanded that the officer responsible be punished. Had it been left up to the high command in Saigon that probably would have happened. But the 5th Special Forces Group commander in Nha Trang had argued persuasively that Lieutenant James NMI Carmichael had been responsible for the safe resolution of the incident in Camp Buon Dang and should have been commended rather than punished.

In the end the two recommendations had canceled each other. Or so he had thought up until now, anyway.

"Just as well," General Miller said. "At least with Y Buon Sarpa we know the one with whom we're dealing. And we have a man to whom he owes his life. That should count for something, shouldn't it, Bentley?"

"Don't know if it will or not, General," said Sloane. "But it's worth a shot."

Thought he was just an aide-de-camp, Jim mused. General almost sounds like he's deferring to him. Better watch my ass. And what shot were they talking about? Whatever it was, it was not likely to be pleasant. More likely it would be dangerous as hell.

He felt the old familiar tingling at the pit of his stomach. It felt good.

"What's this all about, General?"

"You follow the news, I'm sure," Sloane answered, effectively taking over the briefing. "You know that Saigon has at most a few weeks left. The whole damn country is collapsing. We won't have any presence at all left in that part of the world. Likelihood is that the North Vietnamese will consolidate for a while, then start to move on other countries. Our information says that the first target will be their erstwhile allies, the Khmer Rouge. They already control most of Laos. After that, probably Thailand, then Burma, Malaysia."

"I thought we had given up on the domino theory," Jim said.

"Some of us haven't. The people who think, anyway. The North Vietnamese are an expansionist bunch. Somebody once called them the Prussians of Southeast Asia." Sloane laughed. There wasn't a great deal of humor in it.

"In any case," he continued, "the Communists aren't likely to be any more supportive of the Montagnards than were the South Vietnamese. We have fairly good evidence that already the massacres are taking place. Whole villages wiped out, anyone who served in the Civilian Irregular Defense Group formations sent to 're-education camps,' the principals of FULRO hunted down and killed."

"Big surprise," Jim said, earning a look of reproof from the general. The hell with him, Jim thought. The hell with the lot of them. "The poor bastards. The French used them, then left them to the tender mercies of Saigon. We used them, told them we'd always be there, then we take off and let them fend for themselves. They've been betrayed by everyone. And now they're probably all going to die."

"Yes, well, that seems to be their conclusion as well. They certainly don't trust anyone, anymore. Especially not us. Yet it's in our best interests to keep them fighting. The more the Vietnamese are held down trying to pacify them, the more time we can give Thailand and the other countries in the region to get ready to resist."

"And what makes you think they'll want to?"

"They really don't have a great deal of choice. And besides, they've told us they do. We got a message last month from one of the contacts we still have in place. It came from your old friend Sarpa, who is now leading what's left of the Bahnar, plus some of the other tribes who've allied themselves with him. He's asking for help: arms, ammunition, medical supplies. Says they can hold out forever if we just give him what he wants."

"So why don't you do it?"

"It's not that easy. Suppose instead of fighting the Communists they decide they want to carve out a place for themselves somewhere else, like the Nationalist Chinese did in the Thai-Burmese border region? More practically, we don't have any idea of their capabilities. Would we be sending in a great deal of material to someone who can't use it? We would be running a hell of a risk, you know, making those air drops. Oh, we'd do it using black assets; Nationalist Chinese pilots, probably, but still it's going to take a lot of time, effort, and money. No, we can't just send it in blind. Against every principle of covert ops."

"What you mean is that the politicians won't let you," Jim said, earning another disapproving look from General Miller.

"Got quite a mouth on you, don't you, Captain?" the general said. "I suppose I should have expected it, from someone of your background. But that's essentially correct. We need someone who can make sure the stuff gets to the right people, and that it's used correctly. We think that man is you. Sarpa is unlikely to trust anyone else. You're an essential part of this plan."

"Begging your pardon, sir, but I don't buy it," Jim said. "Yeah, possibly Sarpa will listen to me. That's not to say he's going to agree with what I have to say; almost certainly isn't going to follow any orders I give."

"He will if it's in his best interests," Sloane replied. "Our plan is to send you in with a couple of other people. A radio man for sure, a medic, possibly a demolitionist. Full half of an A-team if you want it. No more than that, though. Too many people would attract too much attention. The general tells me you have some pretty strong ideas about guerrilla warfare. This will give you a chance to put them into effect. You stay with them a month or two, see if they really have the capability to do some good. Help them out with some of their tactical operations, set up the procedures for resupply. Once they start depending upon us for their support, they'll do what we ask."

"I'm sure it's occurred to you what would happen if the North Vietnamese capture or kill one of us," Jim said, knowing what the answer would be.

Sloane looked at the general, who nodded his assent. "You'll be going in sterile, of course. No attributability. Your records will be taken out of the personnel center and kept in a special file. Only the general and myself will have access."

"So, let me guess. If something happens, we'll be called rogue. Freelancers who got themselves into the wrong place at the right time. The U.S. government will be shocked that any of its citizens would be doing such a thing." Such things were not all that uncommon in the Special Forces. Hell of a deal, Jim mused. Not only does your government ask you to go get your ass shot off for God and country, but they deny knowing you when you do.

"Close," Sloane said. "Actually, we'll deny that you were even American."

"That does it," Jim said. He felt like laughing. This was just too much. "You want us to go in and make a man who, if in his right mind, would never have anything to do with you, follow your orders. You want to control a movement you abandoned, and a people you left to the dogs. You want to do it with American soldiers, who you will promptly abandon as well. You want a lightly armed force of tribesmen to take on the largest, most battleworthy, and now best-armed force outside the three superpowers. And you expect me to agree to it.

"With all due respect, gentlemen, are you out of your fucking minds?"

God, he thought, how could they even ask? Maybe, back in the old days, when the only person he had to care about was himself, he might have done it. It was just crazy enough to appeal to him, but then he had been accused of having a death wish a mile wide anyway.

But they had to know he was married, that his wife was expecting a baby. Did they care? How can you even ask, Jim? You know goddamned well they don't.

Well screw them! They could go find someone else to do their dirty work for a change. Yeah, he knew Sarpa, and that would have been a help. But it could be done by others. If it needed to be done at all.

Actually, it would probably be better in the long run if it wasn't. They had abandoned the Montagnards before; they would again. A new administration, new policy, and the men who were fighting at such cost to themselves and their families would again be given away. Better to let them go now. Perhaps they could come to some accommodation with the new rulers. And if they couldn't, they wouldn't be any worse off.

He took comfort in the thought that they couldn't just order him to do it. Such a mission required a volunteer. Otherwise it would be easy to blow the whistle. A phone call to the *New York Times* and the plan would be all over. Nice to deal from a position of strength, for a change.

No, he would go back to Bad Tölz, be with Alix and the new baby, become the husband and father he knew he could be. Hell, maybe he'd even make a serious attempt at the S-4 job. And if he couldn't get it, there was always the option of leaving the Special Forces. He was suddenly very angry. How could they ask it of him? Because, Jim, the answer came, they know they can. They'll use the guilt you feel, the sense of hopelessness, the sudden spurt of feeling of being once again useful, and manipulate you. Well the hell with that! I'm tired of carrying this thing around with me. Time to get rid of it.

"There's one other thing," Sloane said, seeing how it was going. "One part of the message we haven't yet told you about. Sarpa said his forces overran a jungle prison camp. And that he's holding two American POWs. People the North Vietnamese didn't send back with the others in 1973. And that he's not going to give them back unless we help him."

"And you believe him?"

Sloane nodded. "He sent evidence." He opened a folder, took out some documents and a photo. "Fingerprints, detailed descriptions of the men," he said. "It all checks out."

"And our goddamned government's official position is that there are no more POWs in Southeast Asia," Jim cursed. "I knew that was a fucking lie. Who are these guys?"

Sloane passed him a photo.

Staring out, older now, bearded, but unmistakably him,

was Major Willi Korhonen, U.S. Army Special Forces. Listed as missing in action on December 7, 1968, and declared dead two years thereafter. The newspaper he was holding in the photo made it clear that, as Mark Twain had said, the news of his demise was somewhat exaggerated. The date on the newspaper was barely six months ago.

CHAPTER 5

"I suspect you remember the incident in which Major Korhonen was lost," Sloane said. Indeed I do, Jim thought. Major Willi Korhonen had been flying Covey on an SOG team insertion across the border in the Prairie Fire area. The team had been hit shortly after insertion, had declared Prairie Fire emergency. Such calls were not casually made. It meant you were in imminent danger of being overrun, you had exhausted all your own options, and unless you got some outside help you were going to die. Probably within a very few minutes. All assets were supposed to drop everything and rush to the aid of the team. It sounded good in theory, but in practice there were precious few assets upon whom you could call. If you were lucky there were fighter-bombers who were in the area to pound traffic on the Ho Chi Minh Trail, or helicopters infiltrating or exfiltrating another team. Maybe, if there was time, you could get a Spike team from CCN headquarters in Danang, or FOB-1 in Phu Bai. There was seldom enough time.

Jim knew the drill well, having had to call a couple of Prairie Fire emergencies himself. He also remembered the gut-watering fear as the enemy closed the circle around you, the knowledge that you were going to die, probably within the next few seconds, then the overwhelming relief and gratitude you felt when, after all hope was gone and you had resigned yourself to death, help came from an unexpected quarter.

Needless to say, those who had been in the same situation were the ones who would move heaven and earth to come to the aid of the ones in trouble. Willi Korhonen had been there many times.

In a unit filled with legends, Major Korhonen was one of the most celebrated. Sixteen years old and a student in the military academy when the Soviets invaded Finland in the Winter War of 1939, he had led his fellow cadets in a slashing campaign through the Russian rear that had killed hundreds of the Red invaders and tied down thousands more. Dressed in white, moving cross-country on the skis they had used since childhood, they would pop up and destroy an ammunition dump one day, and the next ambush a supply column fifty or sixty miles away. He'd made such a name for himself that the Russians, finally made victorious by the tactic of piling hundreds of thousands of troops against the numerically inferior Finns, had demanded as a part of the truce that he be jailed by the newly installed puppet government.

Korhonen had escaped that jail, made his way alone across the frozen land all the way to East Prussia, where he had made his services available to the Germans. While he hadn't particularly cared for the Nazis, he saw that they were the only ones ready to fight the hated Reds. He'd risen to the rank of captain by the end of the war, having taken part in most of the campaigns in the east.

At the end of the war he had returned to his native Finland. The Finnish government, again at the behest of the Soviets, had arrested him once more. Again he escaped, this time making his way to distant South America. He became a moderately successful businessman in Venezuela, but his purpose in life was not being fulfilled. His enemies were the Communists, the men who had raped his land and even now held Eastern Europe in thrall. He bided his time, and when the United States opened its doors to those who would help fight its erstwhile ally he was one of the first to apply.

He entered the United States Army in 1952, quickly joined the newly formed Special Forces. His combat experience, tactical knowledge, and field savvy were invaluable in the training of this highly specialized unit.

He took part in most of the campaigns conducted by the Special Forces in the 1950s, and when they became involved in Southeast Asia went there as well. There were no pine forests, no skis, no snow, but there were Reds, and that was good enough. Wounded more times than one cared to count, decorated for valor on numerous occasions, he was a mainstay for the unit.

Thus it was no surprise when, after the team called Prairie Fire emergency, he chose to go back in to direct the effort to get them out. The weather was closing in; there were those who said the team should not have been inserted in the first place under such marginal conditions. He'd directed the pilot of the small plane down through holes in the clouds again and again, trying to find the team, trying to get helicopters in to them.

Then radio signals from the plane had abruptly ceased. Nothing was heard from them again. The team fought on for a little while. The last message heard was of the one-

one, the assistant patrol leader. Everyone is dead, he said, except me. Good-bye.

It was assumed that the light plane carrying Korhonen and the pilot had crashed into a mountain. Old-timers in the Special Forces had predicted for years that sooner or later Korhonen would come walking out of the jungle. He was indestructible, they said. He's gone through entirely too much to die this way.

Now, it appeared, they had been right.

"How long have you known he was alive?" Jim asked.

"We didn't know for sure for a long time," General Miller said. "We heard rumors. Agent sightings, that sort of thing. Then some of the people who escaped by boat started bringing out stories. About camps across the line in Laos, where lots of the missing persons were kept. A lot of those stories were discounted. Some could not be. Such was the case of Major Korhonen."

"And how many more are there?" Jim demanded. "That can't be discounted?"

"A few," General Miller admitted. "We're checking them out, rest assured."

"Then how is it the U.S. government can come flat out and state that there are no more live Americans in Southeast Asia? When we know there are."

"Because the sons of bitches are trying to blackmail us!" the general exploded. "We were told, shortly after the prisoners came back in 1973, that if we wanted any more, we were going to have to pay for them. Oh, the cynical bastards said it wasn't for themselves; claimed that some of our folks were being held by independent groups, people they had no control over. You know what a line of bullshit that is. They damned well have control over the Pathet Lao, and that's where most of the sightings take place.

"They put a price on each man's head. One million dollars. Payable to numbered accounts in Hong Kong. For the bones of those who are dead, we get a real bargain. Half a million." The general was clearly disgusted with such venality.

"We spent a hell of a lot more than that, for less," Jim said. "And will be doing it again, if I agree to what you ask. I don't know what a mission of this sort is going to cost, but it has to be a hell of a lot more than a million dollars."

"The president, and very rightly so, I might add, set a policy at that time that we would not give in to blackmail. That policy continues in this administration. It's a policy that is likely to be continued, no matter who becomes president in the next election. Key senators support it as well, and they're not likely to let it be changed.

"Can't you see what would happen if we gave in?" the general asked, seeing that his argument was having little effect on the captain. "Americans become fair game for anyone in the world who needs a little money. Hell, it's almost that way now. Can't you see what it would be like if we didn't at least try to stand up to them? Would you want to be the politician who was responsible for the wholesale blackmail of the American people? No? And neither would anyone else.

"You ask about costs. Of course this will cost a hell of a lot more than a million dollars. But we will spend any amount of money, and make any sacrifice, to reclaim our people. We will do it so that the enemy knows they will not be rewarded for their crimes; will, in fact, suffer for them."

It was a good speech, Jim thought. I wonder how much of it is true.

Not that it mattered, he decided. Korhonen was a hero, and deserved to be rescued, but someone else could do it as well as he. There were probably hundreds of Special Forces officers who would jump at the chance—all of them feeling just about as useless as he did in this peacetime Army, and many who wouldn't have a pregnant wife. Or any family at all. As for his relationship with Y Buon Sarpa, obviously it would make such a mission easier. But not impossible for someone who had never met the man at all.

Time to give it all up. Resign himself to the reality of the situation. Become a responsible adult. Damn! What a thought.

A thought hit him.

"You said there were two," he said.

"Pardon?" The general looked puzzled.

"You said Sarpa was holding two Americans. Who's the other one?"

Sloane, who had been watching the play of emotions on Carmichael's face and sensing that his decision was likely to go against them, suppressed a smile of triumph. Time to play the hold card.

He passed over another photo.

"Son of a bitch!" Carmichael swore. He looked first at the general, then at Sloane. "I never really had a choice, did I?"

He looked at the photo again. Glenn Parker looked a great deal the worse for wear, but then that was to be expected after spending a couple of years in a POW camp.

I grieved for you, Glenn. Of all the people we lost over

there, all the friends, all the waste, your death was the worst of all.

He felt, at one and the same time, exultation and sorrow.

He was going to have to go.

But first he was going to lead them around by the nose a little bit.

"Since I'm to be the man on the ground—if I decide to go—there's going to have to be some things we get straight," Jim said.

Both the general and Sloane relaxed. Carmichael had decided to go, despite his qualifier. That was the important part. Now it was all negotiations.

"Begging your pardon again, gentlemen," he started, "but I've been the victim of intelligence lashups before. I don't know how you had command structure planned, but in my view, it has to be a special operations show all the way. I want an Army voice on the other end of the phone, and preferably someone who's done it before. That means a Special Forces type."

"I don't see that as a problem, do you, Captain Sloane?" General Miller asked. "The CIA will be involved, of course. Has to be. They're the only ones with assets still in place, meager though they are. And we're depending on them for ELINT, electronic intelligence."

"Good," Jim said. "Now, I don't see any need for a split A-team. Too many people, too much chance of something going wrong. Three people. I started out as a medic. I've kept up in cross-training over the years. I can handle that aspect. I need a good commo man. And since these people are armed with whatever they could capture, it's likely their weaponry is going to be in pretty bad shape. I know a weapons man who is also one of the best demolitionists around. That's it."

"You'll have the pick of who you want. They'll have to volunteer as well, of course," the general said.

"I don't think there'll be any problem with that. I also want to plan the entire operation, including infiltration and exfiltration. And I don't want to hear a bunch of shit about how we don't have the assets for whatever I come up with."

The general stiffened. Jim wondered if he had gone too far. It wasn't every day that a three-star general got talked to like that by a mere captain.

But then it wasn't every day that a mere captain was asked to do what they were asking, either.

General Miller relaxed. "Done," he said. "I suppose you're going to want a little time to take care of personal things? You've got three days."

Jesus Christ, Jim thought. Three days. How am I going to explain all this to Alix?

The mission itself looked easy by comparison.

Colonel Casey had been taken off to the side by General Miller and told that Captain Carmichael was going to be detached from his command for a short time, that the captain was on an extremely sensitive and highly important mission, and that he would not be at liberty to disclose what he was doing. This had been at Jim's suggestion. Otherwise, he knew, Casey's anger at being left out would have been hard to bear. As it was he was barely able to restrain his curiosity on the ride back to Bad Tölz, asking just enough questions to make things uncomfortable.

But that he could deal with.

Maybe it would just be easier to take off, let Colonel Casey deal with her?

Coward! You've got to face her, try to make her understand why you have to do this.

And why is it that you do, Jim? You were all set to turn them down, before they mentioned Glenn Parker. That's something to be proud of, I suppose. Back in the old days I would have jumped at it right away. Just the sort of thing I liked.

Like Alix has said, and others before her, you've done enough. There were few people who could have claimed to have done more. You've given copious amounts of blood, pieces of your body, and a large part of your younger life to that cause. It's over. Why can't you let it go?

Because my best friend is still there. I owe my ass to Glenn, wasn't for him my bones would be scattered all over a hillside in Cambodia.

He and Parker had started Special Forces Training Group together, way back when. They had become fast friends, sharing bar fights and drunken sprees and enough combat over the years to satisfy even the worst crazy. Their paths had diverged when Jim had decided to accept a direct commission, while Glenn made his feelings for dog-ass officers clearly known.

Then there was one very bad day in a place where neither of them should have been. Jim had already resigned himself to dying, not seeing any possible way of escaping the noose of North Vietnamese troops who had already killed everyone else on the team.

Thus he had looked up in absolute disbelief to see Glenn Parker's homely face hanging out the door of a Huey, the bird shuddering from the dozens of AK-47 hits.

Somehow he'd scrambled the last few feet, grabbing Glenn's hand and being pulled onboard, the chopper pulling pitch so steeply it looked like it was going to stall.

It hadn't, and they had limped back across the border.

"Thanks," was all he had been able to say when they landed.

Glenn had shrugged. "You'd a done it for me," he said.

I can't leave him behind. Not and stay sane, anyway.

Now all I have to do is convince Alix of that.

To avoid thinking about it he occupied his time by planning the mission. He'd already had EUCOM send a telex to Bad Tölz, telling SFC Jerry Hauck to stand by. Jerry wouldn't refuse him. And he could think of no better man to have at his back.

He had two good commo men on the team, but they had a common problem. They were married. He intended to carry no one with him who had such responsibilities. It was bad enough that he did. He would not screw up someone else's life as well.

He had the perfect candidate. SFC Ezekiel "Dirty Dick" Dickerson. SFC Dickerson had been divorced for years, had no children, and chafed under the restrictions of the peacetime Army as badly as did Jerry Hauck. He was also the best commo man Jim had ever known, and in a unit possessed of virtuosos in communications, that was something indeed. He was also cross-trained as a medic and a weapons man. He was HALO qualified, and Jim had already decided the only feasible method of infiltration would be by free-fall parachute.

Would he go?

Get serious, Jim. There's not a man in Bad Tölz, or indeed in the Special Forces as a whole, who wouldn't go.

It was probably a good thing the mission was so highly classified. If word ever got out he would be swamped with people.

And the wives of Bad Tölz would probably get together a lynch party. Why couldn't women understand how important such things were to their husbands?

Because they're women, Jim. And the day you think you start to understand how a woman thinks is the day you better check yourself into an insane asylum. Because you'll be clearly delusional.

Ah, shit. I'm not looking forward to this.

"I'll divorce you. I swear to God I will."

"Don't talk like that," he pleaded. "Can't you understand that I have to do this?"

"I understand only one thing. That you can't love me very much. How can you think of such a thing? Leave me here, alone, pregnant! My God, the baby may be born before you get back. I can't believe you'd even consider it."

This was not going well. Even worse than he had anticipated. He had gotten permission from General Miller to tell Alix at least the broad outline of the mission, knowing that she would be the last one to consider a security risk. He had hoped it would help.

It had not. Alix had brushed aside his justifications like cobwebs from a corner. She had homed in on the one thing that was critical.

Who was more important? The Army, or her? The fate of two men, or his family? Because, she assured him, if he did it, he wasn't going to have a family.

"That's not fair," he said, knowing as the words were uttered that fairness had nothing to do with this.

It was obvious how deep her anger ran. She was not throwing anything. Her little flashes of anger usually came and went like lightning, and the inevitable result was smashed crockery. Now she was ominously calm, only the heightened tone of her voice giving away what she felt inside.

And there was nothing he could do about it. He was caught between two imperatives, and was going to lose something no matter how it went.

He sank to the couch, a curious feeling of numbness spreading from his chest all the way to the fingertips. Ah, God. This was too hard.

"I have to do it, you know."

"You don't have to do anything. Admit it. You want to do it. You want to run back off to that war, even if it means leaving me behind. Even if it means you'll lose me, and your child."

"That's not true," he said, wondering all the while if it was. Was he that irresponsible? If so, perhaps she would be better off without him. Find herself someone who would stay home day after day, work in a nine-to-five job, give her all the things she deserved. Could he ever be that man? Probably not. He suddenly felt very sorry for himself, and at the same time cynically detached. *Yeah, go ahead and feel sorry for yourself, Jim. Blame the whole goddamned world for your problems. You've brought all this on yourself.*

And you don't know how to stop.

"You're very sick, Jim," she said, her voice surprisingly soft. "You need help, and you won't admit it, certainly won't make any effort to get it. So you're going to go on, until someone puts you out of your misery, and you don't even know why. I suppose I should hate you for what you're doing to me, to us. But I can't. There's nothing I can say or do that's going to stop you. I love you, James Carmichael. But I can't live with this. Never knowing from one day to the next whether you're going to be alive or not, never knowing what you're doing. I can't stand the pain.

"I guess I knew this would come, way back when you asked me to marry you," she said, sitting down beside him and taking his hand. "But I thought you would change; thought that I might be able to change you. Let you experience love, instead of war and hate, and you would see how much better it was. But I never had a chance, did I?"

Her eyes were luminous with unspilled tears. He loved her more at this moment than ever before, could not bear the thought of losing her.

But he knew he would.

The next three days passed between them as if nothing had happened. Alix resolutely refused to listen to anything he had to say about it, telling him that there was no use causing each other more pain. She went around with a faraway expression, already detaching herself from him. Nights she would stare off into space, her hands on her swelling abdomen, communing, he supposed, with the baby. Sometimes a mysterious smile played over her face. She was so beautiful. Ah, God, it was just too hard.

Thank God for the days, he thought. There was so much to do it kept him, for a little while at least, from thinking about it.

As anticipated, there was no problem with getting Dirty Dick Dickerson to volunteer. Jim told him only the barest outline of the mission, all that he would be able to impart before they went into isolation. It was enough.

"Goddamned right, sir," he said. "Things are gettin' a little sticky around here with the ladies, anyway." SFC Dickerson was well known around Bad Tölz for his abilities in the bedroom. More than once he'd left from the back window of someone's quarters as the husband came in the front door, unexpectedly coming home early from a mission. On one of those occasions the window had been three stories up, and there hadn't been the usual cushion of snow beneath. Despite a belated attempt at a PLF, Dickerson had fractured his ankle. Well-deserved, said many of the husbands, who suspected that their wives, too, had enjoyed the attention of Dirty Dick but could not prove it.

Thereafter Dickerson had confined his attention to the ladies downtown, and now had at least three frauleins who were determined to marry him. The father of one of the girls was a former SS *Hauptsturmfuhrer,* who was equally determined that his racially pure daughter was not going to marry an American black man, even if he had to kill him to prevent it.

"I thought you'd see it that way," Jim said. "You've got two days to clean up your personal affairs."

"Way I figure, that's about forty six hours too long," the sergeant said. "Who's goin' with us?"

"Jerry Hauck."

"Blanket-ass Jerry? That's good. Get him away from the bottle. Get me away from the women. What you gettin' away from, Cap'n?"

Not what I'm getting away from, Jim thought. It's what I'm getting back to. Aloud he said, "You don't need to take anything with you, even uniforms. Travel will be by commercial air, in civvies. Everything we need for the mission is supposed to be on site."

"An' you trust 'em to have it there?"

Jim smiled. The habitual distrust of every operator in the Special Forces for anyone outside the unit was something he also felt. He'd drawn up a list of needed equipment in Stuttgart, told them that those items absolutely must be there. He had been reassured when General Miller told him who the operational base commander was to be. Lieutenant Colonel Mark Petrillo, who had recruited him for the Phoenix Program so long ago, could be trusted to make sure the logistics for the operation were straight. Anything else was up for grabs. Jim still hadn't completely forgiven him for the way he had been treated in that assignment, but knew that Mark really hadn't had any choice.

"Yeah, they'll have it there," he said. "Mark Petrillo knows if they don't I'll cut his dick off."

SFC Dickerson looked at the captain speculatively. He didn't know if the officer was joking or not, thought that he only partly was. He'd never been in combat with Captain Carmichael, but had heard stories. He didn't think he would want the captain as an enemy.

He stood up, stretched. "An' I bet you were sure enough of me to have them stock uniforms in my size, weren't you?" SFC Dickerson was six feet four inches tall and very thin. Standing he looked wispy, almost insubstantial. But like most Special Forces men, what he lacked in muscle he made up for in endurance.

"I sort of figured you wouldn't be able to resist," Jim said. "Hope I'm not putting us into something we can't get out of."

"Yeah, well, it don't matter nohow. Now, if you'll excuse me, sir, I've got some serious partyin' to do. Some a these ladies, I've been sort of holdin' back on. You know, for safety's sake. Now it don't much matter. What are they gonna do if they catch me? Send me back to Vietnam?"

"Al, I've got a real big favor to ask of you," Jim said.

Al Dougherty took a hefty swig from his stein. They were sitting in the Woodshed, a tiny gasthaus in the town of Bad Tölz. There were only four tables, and at this hour of the day they were the only patrons. Jim had chosen it as a meeting place for precisely that reason. Besides, they had the best beer in Bavaria.

"Name it, Jimmy. Long as it doesn't have anything to do with sex, you're on. You're not my type."

Trust Al to come up with a joke for anything, Jim thought. Of course, you could trust him for a hell of a lot more, too. That was why he was going to ask. But it was a hell of a thing to ask of someone.

"You probably ought not say that until you find out what it is," Jim warned.

"Get serious!" Al said, slightly miffed. "I don't want to get all blubbery about this, but I do owe you my tired-ass life. Why don't you just cut through the bullshit and tell me what you want?"

"Okay. I'm gonna be out of town for a little while. Like maybe two or three months. Can't tell you where I'm going, so don't ask. Anyway, Alix is just real goddamn unhappy about it."

"I just imagine she is," Al interjected. "I'm surprised you're not walkin' funny. I would have expected her to kick your balls right up into your belly."

"That would have been a relief. It's got way past that, I'm afraid. Anyhow, I'd like you to sort of keep an eye on her, if you would. Colonel Casey has promised to appoint an assistance officer to make sure she gets taken care of, but you know how that shit goes."

"What you mean is, you want me to go to the commissary and PX for her, chauffeur her around, that kind of shit. Sort of act like a surrogate daddy. Is that it? A goddamned Special Forces, Ranger, Infantry, Baby-killing snake-eater, acting like some sort of fucking nanny?

"Of course I will. You don't even need to ask. *Herr Ober! Nach zwei, bitte,*" Al said, ordering two more beers. "Christ, Jimmy. You do get yourself in a load of shit."

"Tell me something I don't know," Jim said; rather sourly, Al thought. "Hell, with any luck at all I can piss away my entire life like this."

"I can't promise you anything," Alix said, the night before he left. "I've given it a lot of thought. I do understand, even though you still think I don't. But you've got to understand me, too. I just don't think I can live like this."

"This is the last time," he said. "I'll quit after this. Do what you want me to do."

"Hush," she said. "Don't go making promises you can't keep. You don't have it within you to make that kind of commitment. I don't think you'll ever change. Don't even, sometimes, know if I would want you to. I fell in love with you as you are. It's not your fault. I should have known better. Now I just have to decide if I can live with it or not."

"That's fair," he said after a moment. He was very aware of her weight there next to him on the bed, felt already the ache of being away from her. How could he be doing this? It was only going to cause misery and pain for the both of them.

Because if you don't, there will be more misery and

pain than you could ever imagine, the answer came. You'll hate yourself, knowing that you could have been the one to get those guys out of there. You'll blame yourself for their deaths, as you already blame yourself for the deaths of so many others.

And sooner or later that hate will spill over. You'll start to blame her. If it just hadn't been for her and the baby, you'll start to say, I would have done it. It's all their fault. And that will be worse, far worse, than having her leave you right now. As much pain as there is, it is nothing compared to what could be.

She turned her back to him, and he thought she was going to sleep. It would be a long night. Ah well, you can always sleep when you die.

He felt her little bottom pressing into his groin, at first so softly he thought he was imagining it, then with more and more insistence. He kissed her hair, ran his hand down her flank, softly pulled up her nightgown. The feel of her bare flesh against him was heady, erotic. She pressed against him, harder, reaching down between her legs and touching his hardness.

He cupped her breast as he entered her warm softness, felt the groan as it rose like a prayer from her chest. Was glad that her head was turned, so she could not see his tears.

"Jesus, Captain, you look like shit," Jerry Hauck said.

Jim looked at the NCO, whose face was bruised and battered. Apparently Jerry had figured that all bets were off, had gone to the club and made up for all the time he had been off the bottle. And he's telling me I look like shit. Must be the truth.

Sergeant Dickerson wisely kept his silence. The captain didn't look like he would welcome a hell of a lot of conversation. He wondered, briefly, why the captain's lady had not come to see him off, then dismissed it, thinking it was none of his business. For himself, he was just as glad no one had come to say good-bye to him. Likelihood was that they would have been accompanied by a husband or father, and that the escort would have been armed. What a waste that would be! Getting killed before the NVA got another shot at it.

It was barely dawn when they left. The heavy fall mist cloaked everything, making the old Kaserne seem insubstantial, as if it was made of clouds instead of stone. Each man wondered if he would see it again. They did not fool themselves. This was a mission that stood an excellent chance of getting one or all of them killed. They had understood that from the start.

The headlights of the staff car bored through the fog, carrying them from the life they had known for the last couple of years toward an earlier, more harsh existence. An existence more primitive, depending upon reflexes, skill, and most of all, luck.

And within each man's soul, no matter what else they might have felt, was the sharp quick joy of life reduced to its most elemental parts; a life as primitive as the cave, and as old as man's first urge to kill his fellow man.

God, it was great to be alive.

CHAPTER 6

Bentley Sloane was headed back to Southeast Asia. Last time it had been aboard a chartered jet, surrounded by sweating, farting young men like himself. Young men whose bravado couldn't mask the fear that coursed through them, the fear of heading off into the unknown, where every man's hand would be turned against you. The fear of coming back in sealed metal coffins, like the ones they'd seen being offloaded from a cargo plane at Travis Air Force Base. Endless rows of them, moving down rollers in a long line, as they moved in their own long line to board the plane.

Now it was first class on Air France. The very pretty stewardess offered him yet another glass of champagne, insisted he try the foie gras, promised him a meal to remember, and hinted at something even more memorable, if he was but in the mood.

He kept his expression remote, noncommittal. It added, he thought, to the air of mystery with which he liked to surround himself. And when, slightly disappointed, she retreated, he smiled at her trim little rump. She'd be back. And perhaps there would be a little free time in Bangkok . . .

After all, look at what else she had to choose from. Middle-aged businessmen, the occasional diplomat, a faded film star on his way to a week's worth of debauchery in the fleshpots of Patpong Street. He was younger than any of them by a twenty-year margin. He was fit, handsome, and best of all, wore the blue rosette of the medal in the lapel of his well-cut suit. Ah, the medal! It had done so much for him. And would do a great deal more.

He fetched his briefcase from beneath the seat in front of him, opened it, and took out the folder the top cover of which bore the words TOP SECRET—LIMDIS. He ostentatiously folded the cover back, studied the first page. The man sitting two seats over was, he was sure, suitably impressed. He'd tried to engage Sloane in conversation shortly after takeoff, asking him if he was perhaps a student, and Sloane had rudely cut him off. Not hardly, he had said, and had refused to talk more.

A student! Look at this, he silently told the man. Would a student be carrying top secret documents around with him? Sit there and wonder, you turd!

Inside the folder was the file on Captain James NMI Carmichael. Sloane smiled. An inspired choice. It was he who had suggested Carmichael to General Miller after finding out that the captain and one of the POWs had a long relationship. They'd been together in Special Forces training company, then branch training, and even the first tour in Vietnam. That, in itself, might not have been enough to recommend Carmichael for the job. After all, there were dozens, perhaps hundreds, of Special Forces men who would have jumped at the chance for the mission. They'd had to leave far too many of their comrades behind to pass up a chance at rescuing two of them.

Sloane turned the page and reread the accounts of Carmichael's last tour in Vietnam. There were telegrams from someone named Eliot Danforth, an official in the CIA, who was demanding Carmichael's immediate withdrawal. Letters of commendation from Carmichael's immediate boss, who scoffed at Danforth's concerns and stated that the captain was the most efficient Provincial Reconnaissance Unit officer he had ever known, that his actions were directly responsible for the decimation of the Viet Cong infrastructure in Thua Thien Province.

Sloane turned to the page that described the investigation into the death of the province chief of Thua Thien, a man long suspected of Viet Cong sympathizing, who might have himself been an agent of the Communists. He had been found with an eight inch spike jammed through his face into the brain. Captain Carmichael had been known to use just such an instrument.

A psychiatric report on the captain. The shrink had obviously been fascinated and repelled by the man. He was described as "a coldly efficient killer who has no compunction about his actions."

And that was, in the final analysis, why he had been chosen. They needed a killer. Carmichael was one. He would do what was necessary, if it ever came to that. The mission might require it.

And the mission could not be allowed to fail. His plans depended upon it.

Lieutenant Sloane had returned to the States after a long shuttle through evacuation hospitals. His wounds had been serious, but not regarded as life-threatening, so he hadn't gotten the priority of evacuation that other soldiers had.

That had been fine with him. It gave him time to think about what was to come next. How to arrange his thoughts, his actions, his appearance for the next stage.

He'd already been told that he was being recommended for the Medal of Honor. An Army investigator, a lieutenant colonel, had caught up with him in the hospital in Japan, had taken his statement to add to the growing file, had allowed him to see the recommendation made by the man who'd initiated the whole process in the first place.

That man had been Finn McCulloden.

It had surprised him. From the moment Captain McCulloden had arrived with his Mike Force company to reinforce the beleaguered A camp, he had shown Lieutenant Sloane only barely disguised contempt.

Not that he hadn't deserved it, he had to admit. He had allowed the camp defenses to deteriorate to an alarming degree, had stopped all patrolling outside the wire, had made it easy for the North Vietnamese to stage their attack. To an outside eye, it must have appeared the height of incompetence.

Of course neither McCulloden nor anyone else had been privy to the plan.

He had decided well before being deployed to the war zone that achieving decorations for valor was largely a matter of luck. Every man had it within him to be a hero or a coward, and he suspected he had the capacity to be the former in full measure. But to be a hero, you had to have a fight. You could go for a full year in Vietnam and never get into a fight big enough to get you a Bronze Star with V device, much less the Medal of Honor.

Ergo, you sought out the fight. He'd volunteered for Special Forces in the first place because the conventional units, by the time he'd finished West Point and the officers' course at Fort Benning, were already beginning to stand down. He'd simply been born too late to get in on the big fights, the ones that were going down in the history books. But the A camps, especially along the border, still had plenty going.

Once in the camp, it had simply been a matter of luck that the team commander had been killed, leaving the inexperienced Lieutenant Sloane in charge. A matter of very good luck. Not that he had anything against the captain—he was simply in the way of the plan.

And no one thought it strange that he had neglected the defenses. *After all, he's just a wet-behind-the-ears second lieutenant! What the hell does he know?*

But McCulloden had to know now. Had to know that Sloane had deliberately neglected to set off a bank of claymore mines that would have stopped a North Vietnamese assault in its tracks. After all, he had been there, had seen Lieutenant Sloane rise up from his hole like some fire-breathing dragon, slaying all those who dared to stand before him. Had watched while the heroic lieutenant expended hundreds, perhaps thousands of machine-gun bullets into the ranks of the hapless troops, stalling their rush, bunching them up where they could be defeated in detail. Who had, moreover, repeatedly exposed himself to enemy fire as he moved from one position to another.

At which positions he had earlier stashed spare weapons, ammunition, grenades; all in preparation for exactly the thing that was happening. Heroic he was, but not stupid. Wouldn't have done much good to have stood up there waving nothing more than his pecker at the onrushing troops.

So McCulloden had to know, and had recommended him for the medal anyway.

He owed the captain. It would be nice to pay him back. After all, he didn't want to get the reputation of being ungrateful.

But that was for the future. Right now the mission was all that mattered. The mission that would enhance his career just as surely as had the medal. The mission that would once and for all set him on the path for rapid advancement. He would advance. Oh, yes he would. To the highest possible rank.

He just hoped his father—the old bastard!—would live long enough to see it.

They were in one of the cocktail lounges in John F. Kennedy International Airport when news came of the fall of Saigon. At Jerry Hauck's behest the bartender turned the television to a station that was covering it, earning scowls and a few comments from the other patrons, who were far more interested in watching a football game.

When Jerry told one of the larger ones that he was going to rip his head off and shit down his neck if he didn't shut up, the rest of them quieted down as well. Most of them got up and left, leaving the bar to the three ex-soldiers, who were obviously suffering post-traumatic stress disorder and who were probably very dangerous. People like that should be locked up, some of them said. They said it, of course, out of earshot of the three men.

"You ever think you'd see this day?" Jerry asked of no one in particular as they watched, spellbound, the tanks roaring down the familiar roads.

"No," Jim admitted. "Not even when I knew we were

going to give it up. I guess I wouldn't let myself believe it."

"Guess it shoots the shit out of option two," Sergeant Dickerson observed. They had been making plans during the long journey, drafting up the broad outline of the operation. Option two had involved, if everything went to hell, getting to Saigon, turning themselves in at the Embassy, and being evacuated. Now there was no Embassy. What was left was climbing onto helicopters from the roof.

"Poor bastards," Jerry whispered as they saw thousands of Vietnamese civilians desperately trying to escape. "Christ, they should have evacuated those people weeks ago. You can't tell me they didn't know this was coming. Hell, we could tell that, and we're half a world away."

"You think our people give a shit?" Jim asked, his cynicism even deeper than usual. "Hell, those guys only worked for us. Believed us when we told them we'd take care of them. Their own damned fault for listening." He slugged down the last of his drink, ordered another round.

"Damn fools," he added.

He looked over at Jerry, saw the tears gathering in his eyes. Goddamn, he thought, trying to stifle his own. Dick Dickerson was noisily blowing his nose into a napkin.

"Don't mean nothin', nohow," he said, raising his glass in a toast to all those who had given their lives in preparation for this moment.

"Don't mean nothin', nohow," they agreed. The clink of glasses drowned out the droning of the announcer, at least for a second.

"I've been meaning to ask you," he said to Dickerson, more to take their minds off the events on the television than from any real interest, "where you got your nickname."

Dickerson scowled. It was not something he liked to talk about. Rather embarrassing, he thought.

Jerry Hauck saved him the trouble of answering. "Hell, *Dai Uy*, you didn't know? Christ, I thought everyone in SF did." Jerry was very glad for the interruption. A little humor. That's what we need here, he thought. Else I'm gonna start blubberin', and then somebody is gonna say somethin', and I'm gonna have to rearrange his face.

"Spec-4 Ezekiel Dickerson was on White Star," he continued, referring to the Special Forces effort in Laos in the early 1960s. "Weren't many black men in SF in those days, as you'll remember. Dick was on one of the teams that went to work with the Meos. You know how those guys are, a lot like the Montagnards. Same ethnic group, anyway. They were way the hell up in the hills above Tchepone, with a group that had seen very damn few white men, and no blacks, before. Dick, here, was quite a novelty."

"Don't know why I should have been," Dickerson interjected, getting into the spirit of the tale. There is nothing a Special Forces man likes quite as well as a good story. Even when he's the butt of it.

"Anyway," he continued, "they were always touchin' me, feelin' my hair, rubbin' to see if the color would come off."

"And, if I understand right, wanting to see if it went underneath your clothes?" Jerry asked, already knowing the answer.

If Dickerson could have blushed, he would have. "Yeah," he said. "Spied on me, they did! I was takin' a bath down at the stream, thought I was by myself. Next thing I know, I look up and there's about a hundred of 'em—men, women, and kids too—all around me. Chatterin' about a thousand miles an hour. I say, fuck it, and go on washin'. Later on, I ask the interpreter what they were sayin'."

"What they were saying," Jerry said triumphantly, "is that he obviously needed to wash very carefully, because his genitals were even more black than the rest of him. And the team, because they didn't want to hurt his feelings just because he was black, explained that, yes, his genitals were very dirty. That was why he was called Dirty Dick Dickerson."

Those remaining in the bar wondered why the men who had just a few minutes ago been so hostile were now laughing uproariously, despite the news on the TV getting worse and worse. Just went to show how disturbed they were, one of them, a psychiatrist, thought. Mood swings like that were obviously indicative of severe mental problems. He wisely kept that thought to himself.

Last time I made this trip, Jim thought as the jetliner took off from California, I really didn't know what I was getting myself into. Course, I was a lot younger then, and considerably more stupid. Gonna save the world, I was. He laughed inwardly at the thought. It felt like bile.

I could do it then, though. No responsibilities, no hope for anything other than continued war, a quick death, and an end to it all. Who cared? Nobody. Not even me.

Two things changed that. I met Alix, and I made thirty. Of the two events, one had been joyous, and the other traumatic.

I never expected to live to be thirty years old. It was sort of a talisman; why worry about the rest of your life when you knew you wouldn't live very long anyway? It allowed you to do all sorts of silly things. Piss away your youth on one lost cause or another. Pass the days you weren't in combat in a haze of alcohol. Pop amphetamines to chase away the dark until you become so jangled you hallucinated. Go through women like a damned herd bull going through the cows, carefully avoiding the entanglements.

Then the thirtieth birthday came and went, and I was still here. Alix made a lot of it, calling me old man, telling me that I could no longer be trusted. Throwing a party at the club, the decorations all in black. Being toasted by friends and acquaintances, all of them laughing and joking, only one knowing that the morbid jokes had a basis in reality. Only one knowing how long and terrifyingly empty the years stretched ahead. Al Dougherty knew. Al had gone through it himself, only a year before.

Is that really why I'm here? Have I fooled myself yet again? Yeah, the answer came, you probably did, Jim. Oh, you justify it by saying you have to go in there and bring those guys out. How could you live with yourself if you didn't? Knowing that you were responsible for yet two more deaths?

Is that the real reason? Or is this just one more escape, a running away? From responsibility, from being a husband, a father, from the long boring years stretching out before you?

I don't know. I do know that if I keep thinking about it I'm going to go crazy. Best to try to get some sleep, like Jerry and Dick are doing. It's going to be a long, boring flight. No sense in hoping for a breakdown in Honolulu this time. Mark Petrillo isn't aboard to arrange it. Strange how that man keeps popping up. And why, when I think about it, I get this foreboding feeling.

Give it up, Jim. The die is cast, as the cliché runs. And

you sure as hell can't change anything now. Get this thing done, get it out of your system, and maybe you can go back and be the husband and father you should be.

If there's anything there to be a husband and father to.

Bangkok. It hadn't changed much over the years. Hot, dirty, incredibly crowded. The ride from Don Muang airport to the hotel just off Patpong Street took well over an hour, though it was only twenty miles. The exhaust fumes from thousands of vehicles hung blue in the air, almost obscuring the jungle that still pressed in to the sides of the road. Unlike traffic jams in every other place in the world, there was no sign of impatience in the unfailingly polite and cheerful people. Thailand was a world unto itself. Jim had almost forgotten how much he loved it.

But he really knew he was back in Southeast Asia when he got into the room in the distinctly spartan hotel. The Army certainly wasn't paying for frills on this one, he thought. The walls were of plaster over concrete block, green in places with the ever-present mold of the tropics. An air-conditioner in the window blasted away, raising a chill where the sweat had popped out on the ride from the airport. The bed was of cheap, unpainted teakwood, with a thin cotton pallet serving as a mattress. There was a free-standing sink in one corner, and in another a concrete partition hiding the toilet and shower. He looked in, could visualize the various fungi and bacteria waiting there to jump onto his feet, was glad he had remembered to bring shower clogs.

It felt like home.

By the time he had taken a shower to rid himself of the fatigue of travel, Jerry was banging on the door. "You feel like takin' a little walk down Patpong, just for old times' sake?" he asked.

"Hell, why not," Jim replied. They had the remainder of the evening and night free, before having to report in to the military mission at the Embassy in the morning. "Might be just what I need. How about Dick? He want to go too?"

Dickerson came down the hallway dressed in a very loud shirt, shorts exposing legs as skinny as those of a black stork, and Ho Chi Minh sandals. That answered the question.

"You're about an ugly motherfucker," Jerry told him.

"Yeah, well, the gals on Patpong ain't gonna give a shit about that, are they?" Dick laughed. "Especially when I got a pocketful of beauty and personality right here." He flashed a roll of greenbacks.

"Gets right to the heart of the matter, don't he?" Jerry said, joining in the laughter. Clearly Jim's two sergeants were in high spirits, looking forward to once again living the good old days. And what days they had been!

"*En avant, mes enfants,*" the captain said. "Probably gonna be the last chance you'll get."

Their first stop was Lucy's Tiger Den bar, just off Patpong. Lucy's had been a hangout for servicemen, expatriates, hangers-on, and other such riffraff for more years than anyone could remember. A sign on the wall grandiosely announced it as VFW Post Number One, the Claire Chennault Chapter. You wanted to find a particular American in Bangkok, you went to Lucy's. Sooner or later he would turn up there.

Lucy's was also one of the few serious drinking places around. It had bargirls, of course; tiny vivacious things who tried to finagle you into buying bogus drinks off which they got a percentage; girls who, given the right circumstances and an appropriate amount of money, would accompany you back to your hotel room for a couple of hours, a night, a week. But at Lucy's they weren't persistent. If you told them you weren't interested, they left you alone, went off to find a more likely prospect. Not like the places on Patpong where they would harass you all night, or until you gave up and in surrender ordered them a Bangkok Tea.

"Goddamn, muthafuck, you!" said the bartender upon seeing Dickerson. "Long time, no see, Dirty Dick. You still love me too much, you sumbitch?"

"Of course I do, Annie," Dick said, leaning across the bar and giving her a big kiss. Annie, also, had been a fixture of the bar as long as anyone could remember. Once she had probably been very pretty. That beauty had departed long ago, along with youth. But everyone still loved her, not least for what was probably the foulest mouth in Southeast Asia. Of course, she had learned it from the best.

"Three Singha, Annie," Jerry Hauck ordered. "And anything anybody else is drinkin'."

"I know you," she said, peering at him closely. "You crazy muthafuck. Alla time fight-fight. Like get nose bloody more than get pussy. You no fight tonight, okay? Or I shoot you ass." She displayed an ancient sawed-off shotgun, which to anyone's knowledge hadn't been loaded since World War II.

"No sweat, Annie," Jerry declared. "I no fight nobody. No like to fight anymore. I'm a lover now."

Annie's expression showed just what she thought of that lie, but she let Jerry kiss her anyway. "I think I see you too, long time ago," she said to Jim. "You Special Force, right? Alla you crazy muthafucks Special Force."

"Not anymore, Annie," Jim lied easily. "Out of the Army now. Workin' the oilfields down in Indonesia." It was a cover story that wouldn't hold up too well if anyone started asking too many questions, but that shouldn't be a problem. The patrons of Lucy's Tiger Den studiously avoided asking too many questions. Such things could be dangerous.

"Hokay," Annie said, mollified. Three frosty Singha beers were procured, and quickly drunk. With the sharp tang of the beer even more memories flooded back. Jim had only been in Bangkok once during the war, and that by a mistake of the Army. He and his team had been scheduled to launch into Laos from the base at Nakhon Phanom, Thailand, but had been weathered out. It was a policy of the Thai government that no indigenous personnel from Vietnam could spend the night in Thailand, so the Montagnard members of the team had been flown back to Danang. The weather had stayed bad, and the mission had been scrubbed. Air assets were at a premium at the time, so the two American members of the team, he and Jerry Hauck, had been told to make it back to Vietnam any way they could. It was an opportunity not to be missed. The two men caught a helicopter going to Bangkok, and of course could find absolutely no way to get back to Vietnam until they were both so sick of the debauchery that going back into combat seemed infinitely preferable.

As expected, three bargirls came up and tried to make conversation. They were quickly sent away. Jim had no intention of availing himself of their services, and the two sergeants were saving such things for later in the evening.

The girls were disappointed, but not too much. It was early, and there would be more marks coming in. They got enough income off the regulars to support themselves, anyway.

"Welcome home," Jerry said, clinking his bottle to theirs.

"Seems like we never left," Dick agreed. "Caught in a goddamn time warp or something."

Jim looked at his companions, saw the sadness that underlay their present high spirits. This was where they belonged, and they knew it. Why had they left? they were wondering. He knew that, because he was wondering too.

Am I the same way they are? Can I define myself only in war? Jesus Christ, Jim, are you going to keep asking yourself these same questions? Does it do a damn bit of good? Tomorrow you go back into the black hole, it sucking you in as surely as they say the ones in outer space do any matter unlucky enough to get close. Tonight you damn well better enjoy yourself. It's the last chance you may ever have.

"You guys about ready for another?" he asked after draining half the bottle in one long gulp. "I feel like gettin' shitfaced tonight."

They drank enough in Lucy's to get that pleasant fuzzy glow that makes everything, if not all right, at least bearable, then went back to Patpong. The street was lined with bars, barkers outside extolling the beauty of the women inside, neon signs bright as the sapphires and rubies you could buy for next to nothing in the hundreds of jewelry stores around the city. In the bars girls dressed in little more than smiles gyrated to the beat of rock and roll songs, standing on the tables and waving almost hairless pudenda at the eye level of jaded patrons. The only change from the sixties that Jim could see was that most of these patrons were now from Germany, Japan, or Saudi Arabia, replacing the GIs on R&R who had formerly filled the bars.

As soon as you went in you were surrounded by girls, each vying for your attention, each coyly asking if you would like to talk with them, if they could sit at your table, if you would buy them a drink. Jim didn't mind, even bought a couple of drinks. They were all beautiful, with that delicate grace only Thai women seem to have. All desirable, all available for the right price. In the old days he would have done as Jerry and Dick were doing, scanning the group, selecting the one or ones he would have for the night. On the last trip he and Jerry had bought all the girls in one bar, took them to the huge suite they occupied in a hotel not unlike the one in which they were now staying. Had run them back and forth between the beds, vainly attempting to enjoy them all. But that was in the old days.

I'm married now, and can't do that, he told himself.

Wonder how long that will last?

Through tonight, anyway. Have another beer, Jim. And keep your dick in your pants. You've got enough guilt without adding to it.

The evening got more and more hazy. Soon he lost count of the number of bars they'd been to, far less the number of beers he'd consumed. Jerry and Dick had rejected this girl and that, searching for something that only they knew of, that perhaps didn't exist.

At one point Jerry had gotten incensed that the few patrons didn't seem to be paying enough attention to the dancers. He had gotten up on the bar and joined them, stripping off clothes to wild applause. Soon people were coming in off the street to see the crazy American who was taking off his clothes. He gave, Jim thought, a very credible performance. The Mama-san thought so too, congratulating him on his dancing after he had stripped down to the buff. Jerry was visibly pleased.

"Only one thing wrong," she said. "You have good body, but very old balls."

Later, after the two sergeants had finally found a couple of girls that satisfied them, they went back to the hotel. It was past midnight, just the time, they thought, for a swim in the hotel pool. Everyone stripped off and jumped in, the girls at first shy, then visibly enjoying the frolic. They ordered more beer, added shots of tequila. Jim realized he was getting very, very drunk. But who gives a shit?

The waiter who brought them the drinks was very worried that Jim didn't have a girl.

"I can get you very pretty one," he said. "Maybe you want virgin? Or very young? Black? You tell me, I get."

This went on through several rounds of drinks, the offerings getting more and more exotic as the man ran through every variation known to man, and some that Jim had never even heard of.

Finally, tired of it, Jim growled "I don't like girls. I like fat little boys."

The waiter's face broke into a smile. "You wait right here, I get," he said, turning to leave.

"No! Shit! I was just jokin'," Jim said, panicked. Christ, that's all I need. "How about you just bringin' us another round, and shuttin' the fuck up?"

The man, disappointed, finally left him alone. "Damn,

Dai Uy," Dickerson said, "I thought maybe you'd decided to change your luck there. You know how the story goes. Rather hear a fat boy fart than a pretty girl sing."

"Yeah," Jerry chipped in. "Always did wonder about him. Sleeps real close to you out in the jungle, he does. Try not to bend over in front of him."

"And fuck both of you very much too," Jim said. "Buncha assholes." He took a shot of tequila, chased it with the beer. Was aware of a wave of affection for the two men. *It's gotta be done, I couldn't do it with anybody better.*

And I better get to bed, before I get maudlin with it. Must be like they say, you get more emotional in your old age.

"You guys have fun," he said, getting out of the pool. "Just be ready at 0800."

"No sweat, *Dai Uy,*" Dickerson said. "I'm probably gonna be up all night anyway."

"Yeah," Jim said. "I'll just bet you are."

CHAPTER 7

Captain (P) Finn McCulloden sat on a small knoll and watched the candidates for admission to the Thai Border Police go through their graduation exercise, and thought that for a bunch of raggedy-ass recruits they weren't doing all that badly. Not that they were great, far from it. But they'd made a good start.

The current exercise had them assaulting a dug-in position. Live fire. One squad was laying down a base of fire—Finn noted approvingly that they were applying very good fire discipline—while the other maneuvered into position, then took up the base of fire while the first squad jumped up and ran, ducking and dodging the imaginary return fire, until they flopped down into whatever slight cover the terrain allowed, whereupon the whole process was repeated.

The idea was that you kept the enemy's head down, degraded his ability to direct effective fire on your troops while you maneuvered close enough for the final assault. The truth was that, absent a very good artillery barrage, it was damned difficult to push someone out of a good defensive position. They had all the advantages—good fields of fire, overhead cover, little exposure of their bodies to the direct fire you tried to use against them. Usually you had to have a numerical advantage of at least ten to one when assaulting a fortified position. The Thai Border Police would never have such an advantage.

And why would a Border Police unit have to use such tactics? one might very well ask (and a congressional delegation had asked just such a question not more than a month ago).

Because you weren't facing a few refugees, Finn had told them, with an expression on his face that had clearly said, *What a dumb-ass question to ask.* (That expression had earned him a truly inspired ass-chewing from his commander, Lieutenant Colonel (P) Sam Gutierrez.

"You don't fuck with the congressmen," Gutierrez had said. "You say, yes sir, no sir, three bags full, and continue mission. Haven't worked this hard to make you a general someday, have you fuck it up now."

Both he and Gutierrez had been equally amazed when their names came out on the promotion list, hence the (P). Someday, probably in the far distant future, they would be promoted, Finn to major, Gutierrez to full bird. Given their proclivity for staying in special operations units far past the time they should have, neither of them expected to go much beyond what they had. Finn had, in fact, rather expected to be RIFFED (Reduced In Force) back to his permanent enlisted rank.

It hadn't helped that, after a short stint in the United States after his last tour in Vietnam, Finn had volunteered to "advise" the Thai Border Police—clearly a special operations assignment. The Border Police were a paramilitary outfit—had to be, given the situation—and as such bore little resemblance to police forces one might run into anywhere else. Thailand shared a common border with Burma, China, Laos, Cambodia, and Malaysia. As Finn had told the congressmen, they lived in a bad neighborhood. Jewel and drug smugglers from Burma regarded the border as nothing more than an arbitrary line that meant little or nothing. China was actively supporting the insurgency that smoldered in the northern provinces. Refugees from the wars in Laos and Cambodia flooded the camps just to the other side of the respective borders, and not a few of these were either common criminals or infiltrators also interested in assuring the downfall of one of the last remaining free countries in the region. Malaysia, back when it had been Malaya, had suppressed, with British help, a Communist insurrection, and large numbers of the hard-core supporters had taken up residence in southern Thailand.

"Why are they being trained as military?" Finn had answered the congressmen. "Because they're fucking well fighting people who damned well are military. You send someone out, tries to 'reason' with these folks, as you suggest, he's going to be found in pieces. If he's found at all. With all due respect, you don't understand this neighborhood. I do."

That he had not yet been relieved and sent home was a constant source of amazement for both him and Sam Gutierrez.

Special Forces had been working with the Thai Border Police for a long time. Way back in 1965 the Thai government had struggled with insurgencies along the border with northeastern Laos and on the southern border with Malaysia. The insurgents called themselves various names, but there was no doubt they were Communist-inspired. Hence the Thais called them CTs, Communist terrorists.

The Thai government had asked for help, specifically, Special Forces help. They didn't want massive numbers of U.S. troops—far from it. The government understood, as perhaps few other governments have, that the deployment of a division or two of Army or Marine Corps would do more harm than good. Sure, you could flood an area, suppress the insurgency for a while, but the very fact that the troops were there was a flash point in itself. One little incident and the populace would be turned against you. You lost legitimacy, were subject to the Communist label of lackeys of the imperialists, and before long things were worse than they were when you started.

Special Forces, on the other hand, kept a low profile. There were few of them—the initial deployment was a temporary 128-man group that arrived in April 1966, their assignment only to last for the traditional six-month TDY tour most often used when you didn't want to send people over for assignments lasting a year or longer. The Army, in its infinite wisdom, had decided that you could pay temporary duty pay—that is, reimburse the soldiers for the money they had to put out for lodging and rations—for six months. Not a day more. After that it was a permanent change of station (PCS), which meant that the Army had to provide all of the above, something it was manifestly not prepared to do at this early stage. It also meant that the dependents of the SF soldiers, who came from the 1st Special Forces Group in Okinawa, would lose their government quarters and have to be transported back to their homes of record in the United States.

It was, the troopers agreed, a hell of a state of affairs. Six months just about got you used to the place. You learned the terrain, established relationships with your counterparts, ideally got enough of the language to get by, and then you were gone. It had been the same in the early days of Vietnam. The Army had finally wised up and had sent the 5th Special Forces Group in its entirety to Vietnam for PCS tours starting in 1965. They'd also started the policy of allowing SF troops to "extend" their tours—many of them staying far longer than they probably should have. Many of them would never go home. At least, not under their own power. You can only go to the well so many times.

And so the same happened for Thailand, largely, the cynics among them said, and cynics are part and parcel of the Special Forces, because it cost too much money to pay them TDY. A new company was formed at Fort Bragg, designated D Company of the 1st Special Forces Group and, after pre-mission training, was sent to a place called Lopburi, the ancient Thai capital, located ninety-three miles north of Bangkok.

The new company quickly found itself in combat. If any trooper had volunteered for D Company expecting to find himself in a paradise (Bangkok was at that moment a destination for R&R for troops from Vietnam), he was in for a surprise. The CTs fought, and fought hard. It was an unsung war, and the SF troopers liked it that way. You didn't have to worry about some sorry-ass journalist showing up at your camp and demanding to be taken out on patrol.

Still later the SF troops, who had now been designated the separate 46th Special Forces Company, trained the Thai contingent to Vietnam, and some of them accompanied the unit, now known as the Royal Thai Volunteer Regiment, in-country. Others remained behind to advise and train the Border Police who were now fighting infiltrators from Laos and Cambodia.

The effort was so successful that the 46th Company was disbanded in 1974, most of the troopers—much against their will—returning to the land of the big PX.

But the war was still on. The North Vietnamese, emboldened by their successes in South Vietnam, were now casting their eyes toward the only nation in the region that had the audacity to reject the dictatorship of the proletariat.

Forty-sixth Company was gone. Official Special Forces involvement in the training of Thai troops was gone. Nobody believed it was time to quit. Hence the very quiet program of which Captain (P) Finn McCulloden was a primary member. Lieutenant Colonel (P) Sam Gutierrez had been appointed an assistant military attaché at the Embassy in Bangkok, and as his first act he had recruited McCulloden as the primary trainer for the Thai Border Police.

It was, Finn had thought, a damned nice assignment. The CT threat was largely gone, due to the actions of his predecessors. Gutierrez had called him up shortly after he had been assigned to the Infantry Officers' Advanced Course at Fort Benning and had asked him if he would take it. A year of Thai language training at Monterey. A short stint in Washington, where he'd learn the diplomatic skills necessary to a member of the military mission, assigned to the State Department, in Thailand.

Not much getting shot at.

The last part was okay, and not okay. The peacetime Army was, he concluded, a hell of a boring place.

The exercise ended with the recruits swarming over the objective, firing down at the silhouette targets inside, dropping grenades into the deeper holes. Finn noted that most of the troops just pulled the pin and dropped the grenade. That would have to come out as a part of the critique. The grenades had a four-second delay, plenty of time for someone inside to scoop it up and throw it back at you. Accepted procedure was to pull the pin, let the spoon fly, count one-one-thousand, two-one-thousand, then drop it. All the while your mind was whirling with the possibility that instead of a four-second delay you might have far less, and the 'nade would go off in your hand.

The only good thing about that, if you could call it anything like good, was that there was absolutely no chance you'd be maimed. Finn had seen the results of one such incident when one of his Mike Force troopers back in Vietnam had picked up a grenade and had tried to throw it back at the enemy. It had gone off the instant it left his fingertips, blowing his arm off at the shoulder, laying open his chest as neatly as would have a coroner's scalpel at autopsy.

Finn fired the green star cluster that signified end of exercise, and the formerly grim assault group immediately turned into a happy, chattering group of teenagers. Grinning, slapping each other on the back, laughing at and harassing one of their group who had fallen on the final assault and had torn a gaping hole in his pants.

Won't be that way if they ever have to do the real thing, Finn thought sourly. They'll be looking back down the hill at the ones who didn't make it, hear the wounded calling for help, seeing the torn-apart bodies in the holes. Bodies of kids a lot like them. Smelling the blood and shit and explosives smoke and the retch-inducing odor of those who had died hours or days before and had been left to rot because to expose yourself to try to bury them was to assure you'd join them.

His assistant advisor, who had been following the group closely to assure no one pointed a weapon in the wrong direction or otherwise endangered his comrades, evidently shared his opinions. With a few sharply worded commands in Thai he had them clearing their weapons, assuming something like a military formation, and marching back down the hill to the waiting trucks that would take them back to base camp.

Finn walked that way too, reaching the trucks just as Lieutenant Benjamin "Bucky" Epstein was slamming the last tailgate shut.

"Good job, B," he said.

Epstein acknowledged the compliment with a nod, signaled the truck driver to start up, walked back with Finn to their waiting Jeep.

"They'll do, I guess," he finally said as Finn started the Jeep and, staying well back to avoid the choking cloud of dust thrown up by the deuce-and-a-half truck, followed it back into camp.

Finn knew that his subordinate was probably mentally comparing the Thais with the Montagnard troops of the Mike Force and the strikers of Camp Boun Tlak, and was finding the comparison unfavorable. Of course those troops had been left behind by the abandonment of the country by the Americans, a constant source of mental pain for the both of them.

Bucky Epstein had been a staff sergeant during the epic twenty-four hour battle for Boun Tlak and had been instrumental in staving off the attack by elements of two North Vietnamese infantry regiments, with an NVA artillery regiment in support. For those actions he had been awarded the Silver Star and had, at the recommendation of Captain Finn McCulloden, been offered a direct commission as lieutenant of infantry.

Epstein had been openly contemptuous of the offer. He'd been exposed to entirely too much of the dog-ass officer corps, he told the startled general who'd made the offer. He sure as hell didn't want to be one.

It had taken the combined efforts of Finn and Sam Gutierrez to convince him otherwise.

"You're goddamned right there are some sorry-ass officers in the corps," Sam had said. Everyone knew, without it being said openly, that one of them had certainly been a lieutenant at Boun Tlak who had endangered and then probably saved the camp. "That's why we've got to have some good ones. There are going to be other wars, and troops who are just babies now are going to have to go out there and fight them. You want them to be led by a bunch of people who can't pour piss out of a boot, even if the directions are on the heel? Because that's sure as hell what'll happen. The good people will leave, the bad ones will be promoted, and someday, when the stakes are higher than they are in this pissy little war, we'll reap the results."

Epstein had finally, reluctantly, come around to their way of thinking. Then it had been another major task to convince the insulted general to reissue the rejected offer.

It had taken even more effort on the part of Finn McCulloden to keep Epstein in the Army later. Both had been assigned to the U.S. Army Infantry School at Fort Benning, Finn to the Infantry Officers' Advanced Course, Bucky to the Infantry Officers' Basic Course. The latter was where, according to the Army, you learned to be an officer. As such it was filled with newly graduated Reserve Officer Training Course (ROTC) lieutenants coming out of college.

Many, if not most of them had been thoroughly contaminated by the slant of what was being taught in the schools. Some thought the sputtering war in Vietnam not only immoral, but illegal. Others who at least accepted what we were doing there thought that it was being fought badly, being lost by the very ones who were fighting it. Their only commonality was that they looked with deep suspicion at the second lieutenant whose uniform bore the weight of several rows of ribbons, some from the American Army and others from the Israeli, where he had fought with distinction as a sergeant in the Israeli Defense Forces during the Six Day War.

The Special Forces combat patch on his right arm didn't help. Nobody was foolish enough to call him a baby-killer, but you could tell, he said to Finn one night at happy hour at the club where both had gone to drown their sorrows, that the thought was there.

Finn had it somewhat easier, in that his classmates were fairly senior captains and a few majors, all of whom had at least one tour in Vietnam. Some of them were facing another tour immediately after graduation, as district and regional advisors to the Vietnamese army under Nixon's Vietnamization Program.

And many of them would later die or be severely wounded in the 1972 Easter Offensive, when the NVA came perilously close to cutting the country in two.

Finn might have joined them, had it not been for Sam Gutierrez's offer. It hadn't been a hard sell to convince the colonel that the mission would be immeasurably improved by the inclusion of a certain lieutenant.

Finn and Bucky had often been joined in their Friday-night sessions at the Benning O Club by Finn's old friend, Jim Carmichael, who if anything had an even worse attitude than they did. They'd get riotously, uproariously drunk, hazard the ever-present Military Police to drive to one or another of their favorite hangouts, and try without too much seriousness to get laid.

Since the choices downtown were either professional girls or local talent who saw a wedding ring slipped onto their fingers as a path out of dead-end jobs in Columbus, they more often gravitated to the club annex, located in the middle of an officers' housing area.

There the choices were often worse. Women whose finger showed the tell-tale dent of absent wedding rings, their husbands either still in Vietnam or away on exercises or temporary duty. Sad-eyed girls whose former husbands were now residents of one or the other national cemetery, looking to get back to a life they'd once known, and loved. Women whose husbands were neither absent nor dead, but were probably out on a quest of their own.

Thus they often ended up in one or the other of their bachelor officer quarter (BOQ) rooms, drinking until drinking no longer had any real effect, seeming to get more and more sober with each shot.

The pattern continued into the weekends, ending finally on Sundays when they'd collapse of exhaustion, the only uninterrupted sleep any of them ever got. Back to class on Monday, a few beers at lunch to take care of the raging hangover, later in the week the beers augmented by a few shots, until by Friday afternoon all semblance of discipline, reason, and motivation had disappeared. Whereupon the entire cycle would repeat itself.

It hadn't been much better in Monterey, where Finn and Bucky had gone to study Thai and Jim to take Russian, except they'd had to study much harder to pass. At least there they only drank heavily on the weekends.

And the choice of ladies had been considerably upgraded. Jim, lucky bastard that he was, Finn thought, had met and married a beautiful girl who not only put up with his foibles, but seemed genuinely to love him.

Neither Finn nor Bucky had been so lucky, but they hadn't wanted for companionship, either. Finn still corresponded with a flight attendant he'd met on a trip to San Francisco, and was planning to meet and spend a weekend with her the next time he got down to Bangkok.

Bucky preferred to not get even close to serious. His needs at Monterey were taken care of by the increasing number of female soldiers now attending language training, girls who would leave on their own assignments and who he knew he'd never see again. Here in Thailand he made the occasional trip down to Bangkok, happily sampling the smorgasbord that was Patpong Street.

They wheeled up into camp and Bucky went to supervise weapons cleaning. Finn entered the headquarters building, intending to get started on the paperwork that always accompanied efforts of this sort. He was surprised to see Sam Gutierrez, up from the Embassy in Bangkok, sitting at his desk.

"We've got a problem," Sam said without preamble. "We just got reports the NVA is moving troops toward the border. SIGINT says regimental and divisional support units are following them."

"Shit!" Finn said.

"To say the least," Sam said.

It looked like the long-expected invasion of Northern Thailand was about to begin.

CHAPTER 8

His sergeants were present at 0800; pale, sweaty, looking as if dying would be infinitely preferable, but there. Of course, he didn't feel much better himself.

"Doesn't look like you've changed much, Jim," Mark Petrillo said. Mark was clad in comfortable-looking civilian clothes and sported a gold Rolex President on one wrist and a heavy gold ID bracelet on the other. He'd gained weight since Jim had last seen him in Vietnam, now had a substantial pot belly.

"You either, Mark," Jim said. "How've you been?"

Mark shrugged. "Bored, mostly," he said. "Not much shakin' in this part of the world."

"Yeah, I'll bet," Jim said. Mark, he knew, had continued his liaison with the CIA after the Phoenix fiasco; he had been in on many of the clandestine programs that proliferated like toadstools after a rainstorm in the last days of Vietnam in a desperate attempt to stave off the inevitable. For all he knew, Mark was one of those officers who held dual commissions in the Army and the Agency. There had always been a very close association between the two. Too close, to Jim's thinking.

"Put your stuff in the van," Mark said, indicating a plain black Ford with no windows in the back. "We're going to be catching a helicopter over at the Thai army headquarters. It'll take us to Nakhon Phanom."

Dick and Jerry did so, then stretched themselves out on the cool floor with their suitcases as pillows and tried to get some sleep. Jim rode up front with Mark Petrillo.

"Congratulations on the promotion," he said.

Mark glanced at him quickly to see if he was being sarcastic. Seeing nothing in Jim's face, he took it as it was said. "Thanks. Just goes to show if you sit around long enough and do nothing, sooner or later they'll reward you for it. Always been convinced that if you were to lock a new lieutenant in a wall locker just as soon as he's commissioned, and not let him out for twenty years, he'll come out a general. Only guys like you, want to change the world, who get in all the trouble."

"I'd wanted to take a bunch of shit, I could have stayed home with my wife," Jim said, a sour expression on his face.

"No," Mark said, "you haven't changed a bit. Good to know there are some constants in this world. Birds fly. Fish swim. James NMI Carmichael has absolutely no respect for those whom Congress and the Army, in their infinite wisdom, have appointed over him. Going to be good working with you again, Jim. How'd they get you to volunteer for this rat-fuck, anyway?"

Jim explained about what he had been told in Stuttgart, ending with the presence of the two American prisoners of war. "I asked the general why the government is still sticking to the story that no American POWs were left in Vietnam after the war," he concluded. "He never did bother to answer."

"I can't give you an answer to that, either," Mark said, expertly steering the van through the jammed Bangkok traffic. "All I know is, we'd had rumors about them for years. Lots of sightings, some of which might even have been real. Some con men showing up with bones, claimed they were from some of the people who died. Turned out to be animal bones, most of them, and the ones that were human were of Asians. So we had no hard evidence. This is the first time we knew for sure. That's why such an all-out effort is being mounted."

Jim wondered how much of what Mark said was true. Or if Mark even knew what the difference between truth and fantasy was anymore. Probably no way he would ever know, but he resolved to not trust his former comrade in arms. A hard lesson, he thought. Maybe you're getting smarter, after all.

"You'll get the full story at NKP," Mark continued. "We've got all the equipment stockpiled there; all the stuff you asked for and quite a bit more. Sarpa wants to go on fighting the Viets, we'll sure as hell give him the stuff to do it with." He pulled in to the Army compound, where an Air Force CH-3 stood with its rotor already turning.

"Get on board," he shouted over the whine of the engine. "Got a lot of people looking forward to meeting you crazies."

The jungle took over once they left Bangkok itself. Flying over the smooth canopy of trees brought back even more memories. Only thing that's different, Jim thought, is that there aren't any bomb craters. The Thais have been spared that, so far. Maybe, if things go right, it will stay that way.

There you go again, Messiah. Thinking that you can

really do something that makes a difference. Didn't that get you in trouble once before?

Disgusted with himself, he lay out on the web seat and followed the example of his sergeants. Good idea to get a lot of sleep. It might come at a premium where they were going.

Nakhon Phanom seemed different somehow. The same buildings were there, even the command bunker from which they had gone on some of the hairier missions in Northern Laos. The runways were, of course, still shimmering in the heat. The trees still crowded close to the perimeter wire.

Then he realized what it was. It was entirely too quiet. Almost deserted. A few years ago the air was constantly filled with the roar of jet engines, the whop of helicopter blades. Scores of jets took off at all hours, to streak their way across the jungle below and drop their loads of death on largely uninhabited forest. Those who went north came back with pieces hanging from them as the most concentrated antiaircraft fire ever known took its toll. There would be the occasional one limping in, trailing smoke and hydraulic fluid, barely making the runway. Ambulances wailing their way to pick up the wounded, and the dead.

Now there were only a couple of Jolly Greens, and a black C-130 with the strange antennae on its nose that told Jim it was one of the Air Commando birds. The appendages weren't antennae at all, but guides for the Skyhook. Skyhook was a system in which a man on the ground tethered himself to a large balloon and the plane came by and snatched the rope connecting him to the balloon, whereby he was reeled up into the rear of the aircraft. Ideally, that is. Sometimes the rope broke, usually just as the man attached to it was at the highest point, and he had a very long and fatal ride down.

The Blackbird, as the C-130 was called, would be their ride into the operational area. It was jam-packed with electronic gear and could confuse and blind enemy radar, making it highly unlikely they could fix on it long enough to guide a missile to it. Jim hoped the patrons of the North Vietnamese, the Soviets, had not had enough time to analyze the electronics of the one they had captured and had not devised countermeasures. Otherwise this might be the shortest mission on record.

It was also equipped with transponders capable of mimicking those of the commercial airliners that had, even in the days of the heaviest fighting, flown serenely overhead, leaving contrails that mocked with their very remoteness the struggles of those on the ground.

"Come on," Mark said, motioning toward the bunker. "Russian spy satellite comes by here in a little while. They say it takes good enough pictures to read your nametags. If you were wearing any."

"Lovely," Jim said. "What about the birds out on the runway?"

"Oh, they know we're up to something," Mark replied, waving it off as if it wasn't important. "But they don't know what."

Jim glanced at Jerry, whose frown eloquently spoke of what he thought of such slipshod operational security. "Jesus, *Dai Uy*," he said in a whisper, "these fuckheads never learn, do they?"

Inside the bunker were a number of people Jim didn't know, and one he did: Bentley Sloane. He didn't have a good feeling about that. Sloane might be a bona-fide hero, but what did he know of operations like this? Too often amateurs got their fingers into the pie, to disastrous effect. The fact that you'd gone to the Special Forces Officers' Qualification Course did not automatically make you an accomplished clandestine warrior. It took years of experience, a great deal of listening to those who had gone before you, a certain amount of humility. Captain Sloane had not impressed him as having any of the above.

He shook it off. Nothing he could do about it at this point. If he raised an objection they would just tell him that he was full of shit; that Sloane was there as an official observer, that was all.

Besides, he'd come this far, and he wasn't going to stop now. Too late for that.

The briefing started immediately, officer after officer going to the situation map and providing information in his specialty. Weather, climatic conditions, terrain, enemy, concept of operations, logistics, communications, medical, command and control; each item of the familiar litany tolled by. The team had listened to hundreds of such briefings, each preparatory to going out and once again risking their lives for a cause in which no one really believed anymore.

At least the briefers were professional. It was obvious, though they wore no insignia of rank or unit, that they were military men, and probably Special Forces. Jim didn't recognize any of them, but that didn't mean anything. In the heyday of Special Forces there had been over twelve thousand active members.

At the end Mark Petrillo again took the podium and asked for questions and comments.

Jim looked at the two sergeants, who shrugged. "I've got one," he said.

"Shoot."

"A few years ago, SOG was having a hell of a time getting anyone on the ground," he said. "Teams shot out as soon as they touched down, lots of folks getting killed, some teams never heard from again."

"And your point is?" Captain Sloane spoke up.

"My point, *Captain*," Carmichael said, putting into the word a twist of tone that said you're just a junior shithead who probably doesn't know a goddamn thing, and you should keep your mouth shut until you do, "is that the operations were compromised. Someone was telling the bad guys exactly where the teams were going to put down. And we never found out who it was. What makes you think the same thing won't happen now?"

Sloane flushed in anger, started to say something, was stopped by a gesture from Mark Petrillo.

"There's no more of the old command and control structure from SOG," he said. "All gone. Viets are either captured or on their way to the States. None of the guys here," and he gestured to the men around the room, "were in it. No chance for leaks. Whole new slate."

Jim looked at the two sergeants again. Once again they shrugged.

"Have to do, I guess," he said. "We'd like to get to the equipment, take a look at what we've got, get it rigged. I'm sure there will be something that will come up. I assume that your staff will stand by in case we need them?"

"Absolutely," Mark averred. "They're completely at your disposal."

Yeah, Jim thought, until I ask something embarrassing or something I shouldn't know. Then we'll see just how much at my disposal they are. Aloud he thanked them for a

professional presentation and told them it would be a pleasure to work with them. Everyone knew just how much
bullshit it was.

In truth, the preparations for the mission were giving
him no trouble at all. Everything had been covered; they
had taken the sketchy operational plan he and the NCOs
had worked out back in Germany and made it real. He had
no doubt that when they checked the gear they would find
all the things they had requested, and probably a lot more.
It was the mark of a good operations officer to anticipate
problems and come up with alternative courses of action,
and the equipment to support those alternatives. And these
men were certainly good. Mark Petrillo would surround
himself with nothing less than the very best.

No, no trouble with the preparations. The only problem
was with the mission itself. It was a muddle typical of so
many that had gone wrong, back when they had been fighting the war. There were essentially two missions: support
Y Buon Sarpa and FULRO, keeping the North Vietnamese
tied down in a guerrilla war within their own borders; and
rescue two American POWs being held as bargaining chips
by that same guerrilla movement. Which was the more
important? No one had bothered to specify that. What
would they do if Sarpa refused to give up the Americans?
Were they expected to take them out by force? That would
be a hell of a trick; rescuing two Americans who could be
expected to be in terrible shape from their years of captivity, fighting off not only the Montagnard guerrillas but also
the North Vietnamese, who would be more than happy to
recapture the two and add to their stocks by getting three
more.

Or, and the sudden thought horrified him, were they to

sacrifice the two Americans to the cause? Leave them there, to be used again and again? He knew he couldn't do that, no matter what directives he might receive from Operational Base. No, the Americans would come out, one way or the other. I'll just have to call in my markers with Sarpa, he thought. He owes me his life. And if he won't go along with it, maybe I'll have to kill him, and damn the U.S. government.

After all, it wouldn't be the first time he had disobeyed orders. Probably wouldn't be the last. As long as he lived through it.

"Tiger Six," Dickerson said. "That used to be his callsign. Kept it, no matter where he went. Drove the communications security people crazy. The enemy will know who you are, they used to tell him. You need to change callsigns every once in a while, throw 'em off. And he used to tell them, hell, why would I want to throw them off? I want 'em to know the name, know who they're up against. Want 'em to be afraid, know that they're gonna die. Major Korhonen was big on that psychological stuff," he concluded.

Jim looked up from where he was taping a knife to the left shoulder strap of a STABO rig. There had been a selection of knives in the supplies: Air Force survival knives with heavy handles and sawtooth backs suitable for cutting through the skin of aircraft, Marine Corps K-Bars, even a couple of World War II era Commando knives. The one he had selected had been made especially for SOG during the war; a gray-blue blade shaped in the classical Bowie fashion, beautifully worked leather handle, wrist thong, brass pommel with a space in the blade for the index finger. It was made for only one thing—fighting. While he hoped he would never have to get close enough to anyone to have to use a blade, you never knew. Besides, it had a certain sentimental appeal.

"You knew him well, then?" he asked.

"Real well," Dickerson said. "I was his radio operator back in White Star, in Laos. Later on he requested I be assigned to him in an A camp in the Delta. Everybody was scared shitless of him. Our side and theirs. Any battle you got in, you could be sure Tiger Six was going to be there, even if he might have been on R&R when the thing started. Wouldn't exactly say he was fearless, but he was close enough it didn't count. Smart motherfucker too. Knew just what to do. Never lost his head, found a way out of anything you got into."

"Till he got caught," Jerry offered.

"Yeah, and that's the one thing I can't figure. I would never have expected him to stay a POW all that time. Either he'd break out, or they'd kill him. Always expected him to come walkin' out of the jungle sometime. And when he didn't, everyone said he must have been killed in an aircraft crash like the Army decided. Now we find out he's not only been a POW, but is being held by another group? Real strange." Dickerson finished packing the ANGRC-109 radio into his rucksack. The old radio was of World War II vintage, extremely heavy, well-built, and utterly reliable. It was for those qualities Dickerson had chosen it over the more modern equipment available. Besides, he had said, we're gonna leave this stuff for the guerrillas, anyway. Best to have something they can work, and more important, repair.

Jim, who knew he was going to have to carry the hand-cranked generator in his own rucksack, was less enthusiastic about it, but kept his silence. It was the job of the officers to carry the generators, which weighed about thirty pounds, from the time Special Forces had been organized. It pretty quickly weeded out the summer help from those who were serious about staying in Group.

Besides, the Angry 109, as it was called, could make communications with anyplace in the world, given the right antenna and atmospherics. No reason to tamper with success. And Dickerson was the commo man, and what he decided was what was done. No Special Forces officer in his right mind argued with the expert.

The only new piece of equipment that was worth a shit, in the mind of most commo men, was the burst device. It allowed you to key the message into a tiny tape recorder, which then spat it out at high speed when the station on the other end came up. A similar recorder on the other side took the message and slowed it down so it could be decoded. That way you didn't have to stay on the air too long, and the enemy stood almost no chance of applying triangulation intercept on you. Two of these devices were to go along.

"Who knows what happened to him?" Jim said, shrugging. "Maybe he did crash, had some bad injuries. The pictures don't show much. Maybe he can't do anything about it. Hell, maybe he doesn't even know what's going on." He finished taping the knife, started attaching the ammunition pouches to the belt. Four of them, enough to hold sixteen magazines of twenty rounds of 5.56mm ammunition. Bandoleers containing another twenty magazines would go in the rucksacks. They'd been offered a selection of weapons and had been gently pushed toward the AK-47 that the opponents would be carrying. Each man had chosen, instead, a CAR-15; the short version of the M-16. For all of them it was almost an extension of themselves, they had used it so much. Besides, the ammunition was much less heavy than the 7.62 x 39mm the AK-47 used. It was more ammunition, by several orders of magnitude, than the normal basic load of the soldier. But they weren't ordinary soldiers, couldn't expect to be resupplied when their ammunition ran out. And they had learned, in firefights throughout Southeast Asia, that ammunition ran out very quickly when you were trying to get away from someone.

The magazines were loaded with regular ball ammo, except for the last two rounds, which were tracers. Impossible to count your rounds when you were firing on full auto; the two tracers told you your magazine was empty and you'd better damn well be getting another one in, as quickly as possible. Besides, the immediate action drills devised after a hell of a lot of trial and error depended upon the visual signal. One man fired his magazine in the direction of the enemy, whereupon he ran to the rear of the formation while reloading, taking up a new position. The next man, when he saw the second tracer leave, opened up, then did the same thing. This way there was never a time when a stream of fire was not eating up the terrain around the enemy, which tended to make them keep their heads down. You had to have that steady stream of fire. The people they were fighting were professionals. The moment the fire stopped, they would once again be in pursuit. Nothing more deadly than a long pause while a group that had fired all its ammunition at once stopped to reload.

"That's the case, we're gonna have a hell of a time walkin' him out of there," Jerry offered. Jerry was busy checking one of the Browning Hi-Power 9mm pistols they had chosen to carry as backup weapons.

"That's why one of the first resupply drops we're gonna get is gonna include a couple of Skyhook rigs," Jim replied. "It becomes necessary, we'll hook 'em both out of there. Situation on the ground allowing," he amended. They would have to get to an area with no real air defense facilities to make the Skyhook mission possible. The Blackbird had to fly low and slow to hook the balloon and was a sitting duck to anyone on the ground. Failing that there were always the Jolly Greens flying nap-of-the-earth, using jungle penetrators if no LZs were available. Failing both, there was a hell of a long walk all the way across Laos, back to Thailand. Jim didn't look forward to the last alternative.

Jerry finished checking the Hi-Power, slipped it into the holster clipped to the web belt, then attached two canteens to the same. Contrary to what most people believed, water was at a premium in the jungle. They would carry not only the two one-quart canteens on the belt, but a two-quart bladder in the rucksack. He then put a couple of claymore mines into his rucksack.

"You ever feel like a fuckin' pack horse?" he asked, his expression implying that he didn't find the prospect all that dismaying.

"Shit," Jim said. "Break down a goddamn packhorse, this would." In addition to all the ammunition, mines, radio gear, and water, they also had to carry rations, emergency radio equipment, penflare launchers and the flares to go with them, smoke grenades, first-aid kits, serum albumin for restoring blood volume in case of wounds, compasses, maps, fragmentation grenades, 40mm grenades for the

M-79 launcher Jerry insisted on carrying, and extra medical supplies for the M-3 Aid Kit Jim had chosen to take with them. In short, it was very similar to every recon mission they had been on; seventy to eighty pounds of extra weight. And that only after they had cut away every single thing that they might not need until after the first resupply drop.

They'd already rigged the resupply: fifty more CAR-15s, PRC-77 radios for squad and platoon communications, several hundred pounds of C-4 plastic explosives, claymores, M-21 mines, thousands of pounds of ammunition, enough medical supplies to equip a small dispensary, M-60 machine guns, more M-79 grenade launchers, and a couple of sniper rifles with scopes. It would only be the tip of what was needed, but enough to give the enemy fits if it could all be used against him. If everything turned out all right there would be many more of these resupplies, dropped in the middle of the night from an aircraft flying at least thirty thousand feet overhead and guided into drop zones by very sophisticated homing systems.

If everything went right. Hell, Jim thought, if it doesn't, we're not going to have to worry about it too much. Still, might as well get it right in the first place.

"I understand you knew Glenn Parker pretty well," Jerry said. "I heard he's a pretty good guy."

"The best," Jim said.

"How did he get caught?"

"Stayed after the truce, went to the JPRC," Jim replied. The JPRC, Joint Personnel Recovery Center, was the unit designated to locate MIAs, the thousands of troops listed as missing in action, after the 1973 truce and subsequent return of prisoners of war. The JPRC excavated crash sites, investigated sightings, dug up graves, did everything possible to resolve the fate of those who had simply disappeared.

"In '74, according to an NCO who overheard it, he got a phone call, said he had word of an American deserter hiding out in Cholon. Went to check it out. NCO asked him if he needed any help, he said no, didn't think bringing in some deserter would be all that much of a problem. He didn't come back, and within twenty-four hours they were searching for him. White Mice found his jeep, parked next to the Saigon River. He wasn't in it. No sign of a struggle. Nothing at all, in fact. Big investigation, inconclusive. Some said the deserter, or his friends, killed Glenn, threw his body in the river. Of course, nothing could be proved. So he joined the ranks of the missing he was pledged to recover."

"Hell of a thing," Dickerson said.

"Yeah. Hell of a thing."

"Took one too many chances, sounds like," Jerry said. "Sounds like other people I know."

"You wouldn't, of course, be speaking about me?" Jim asked.

"Heaven forbid," Jerry replied, assuming an expression of innocence. "Why would a lowly enlisted swine like myself presume to comment upon the psychological makeup of a person who would give up a perfectly good career as a pecker-checker to become a sorry-ass motherfuckin' officer? Not that all officers are sorry-ass motherfuckers, you understand. Just most of them." Jerry shook his head in sorrow.

Next came the parachutes. Standard MC-1-1s with black canopies, as requested, with LOPO reserves in a piggyback configuration. Each man popped the chute, checking the ripcord very carefully for burrs or kinks. Finding nothing there, they spread the canopies out, checked them for holes and tears, followed the shroud lines to make sure they were clear and not twisted, opened and refolded the spring-loaded pilot chute, made sure the light canvas sleeve would slip off the canopy. Finding nothing amiss they assisted one another in repacking, being careful to flake the canopy properly, folding it more carefully than they would have a baby's diaper. Each of them had been a rope jumper—everyone in Special Forces had started out with static line opening systems—in which someone else packed your parachute. There had been stories going around, probably since the first time someone had jumped out of an airplane, about the rigger who was drunk, or was mad at someone, and rigged the canopy so it would be sure to fail. Everyone with the confidence born of bravado and the sense that it couldn't really be true—could it?—had shrugged off such stories and jumped anyway. But all, once they had started freefalling, had liked the idea of making sure, by packing it yourself, that if something went wrong it was your own damned fault.

Finally, all was in readiness. Two hours before deadline, Jim thought.

Ah shit, what the hell am I doing here?

"Weather's not looking too good," Mark Petrillo said. "We may have to scrub tonight."

Jim had been watching the thunderheads gathering for the last couple of hours and was not surprised. He had no great desire to try to freefall into a thunderstorm. More than enough things could go wrong on a drop of this sort; you didn't need to add to them.

"When's the decision?" he asked.

"Right now," Petrillo said. He looked outside the bunker, obviously didn't like what he saw. Off in the distance thunder could be heard. The nearest thunderhead was suddenly backlit, a flash outlining the black/blue like a stage set designed by Picasso. "We'll try it again tomorrow. We got a small club here. Want a drink?"

"For everyone?" Jim asked.

Mark looked offended. "What the hell do you think we are here" he demanded, "the regular Army? Thought you'd have known me better by now, Jim."

Jim, smiling, didn't say anything.

"Look, I know you're probably still pissed off about how you were treated in Vietnam," Mark said. "But I didn't have a hell of a lot of choice in that. You had to be vetted." Mark was referring to an occasion when he'd introduced Jim Carmichael to a young woman who later turned out to be a member of the same unit controlling the Phoenix Program, a woman who had done her best to see that Captain James NMI Carmichael had a very short lifespan.

"You'd have done the same thing," Mark concluded, lamely.

"Sure I would have, Mark," Jim replied, not meaning a word of it. You never treat friends like that, he was thinking. Of course, what ever made me think you were a friend?

"Jerry, Dick," he called, "come on. Happy hour. Unless you object?"

"Shit, *Dai Uy,* thought you'd never ask," Dickerson said. "I been smellin' beer for at least an hour."

The club, a pale imitation of the one that had been there

when the base was filled with fighter pilots, was still relatively merry when they got there. The pilots and crews of the Jolly Greens were there, as were the Blackbird people. Evidently they had been watching the weather even more closely, had come to the decision at least an hour ago that the mission would be delayed. Stacks of beer cans on the table testified to their pleasure at being allowed to live at least one more day.

"Give these men a drink!" commanded a man in a flight suit with the wings of a master aviator and the shoulder insignia of a full colonel. "Gentlemen," he said, sticking out his hand, "I'm Ben Jaworski, and I fly that big black motherfucker out on the runway."

Jim shook his hand, accepted the proffered beer. San Miguel, he noticed. It had been a long time since he'd had a San Magoo. The sharp bite of the Philippine beer was welcome on his tongue.

"Thank'ee, Colonel," he said. "Lookin' forward to flying with you."

"You're a lying motherfucker, your feet stink, and you don't love Jesus," Jaworski said, laughing. "You ain't looking forward to flying worth a shit. You're looking forward to getting out of it. Though why anyone in their right mind would want to jump out of a perfectly good aircraft is beyond me. Still, you snake-eaters are okay in my book."

"First of all, Colonel, ain't nothin' perfect. Second, damned few people been killed flyin' in an airplane. It's that hard landing that gets you. So we just avoid that part." Jim took another swig of the beer, beginning to enjoy himself.

Colonel Jaworski roared with laughter, ordered up another round of beers. Twenty-four hours of bottle to throttle was clearly not operative here. Just like the old days. Shit, Jim thought, why can't life always be like this?

Because, you asshole, you have to grow up sooner or later, the answer came, unbidden.

Yeah, well, in the meantime I might as well enjoy it. May not be any later, anyway. Damned irresponsible, aren't you, Jim?

Yep. Sure am. What the fuck's it to you, anyway?

Ah, Alix, you never did really have a chance, did you? There is a mistress that is older than you, one I've loved longer than I can remember. And I can't stay away.

I'm so sorry.

Ah well, hell. Might as well make the best of it. The younger officers were crowding around, eager to hear the stories they knew would come from this group. Jaworski didn't disappoint them, telling of a time when he'd been flying Sandys—prop-driven aircraft that were the first line of defense for downed airmen—and had himself been shot down. He'd escaped and evaded—E&E in the jargon—for a few hours, then found himself face to face with an apparition. A camouflage-suited, face-painted Caucasian leading a group of tribesmen who had grabbed him up, told him to shut up if he wanted to live, and led him miles away to an LZ where a Jolly Green was called in. One of those goddamned snake-eaters, you know. Just like this mother-fucker here.

Jerry, not to be outdone, told about one of the recon missions he'd been on, one that involved being backed up against a cliff by at least a hundred North Vietnamese, calling for somebody, anybody, to come and help. And how a Spectre gunship had diverted, come in and hosed down the entire area with minigun fire, killing people, rocks, trees;

making what had been jungle look like a football field. And then how they'd been pulled out by the Air Force.

Christ, Jim thought, don't we sound like a mutual admiration society. Maybe we are. For good reason. He'd been the one-one on the mission of which Jerry spoke, remembered the things that Jerry didn't talk about. Like how they had discussed mutual suicide, should the choice be that or capture. The feeling of absolute desperation, knowing that they were about to die. The almost giddy sense of irresponsibility that feeling gave. You're going to die, might as well go out with flair.

At one point a rocket-propelled grenade had come in, exploded on the radio, filling both men with small pieces of shrapnel. That radio, equipped with the new KY-38 encryption device, had been giving them trouble the entire time they'd been out. Jerry had stood up in the middle of the firefight, shouted "Ha, ha, ha, you motherfuckers, it didn't work anyway!" Jim had pulled him back down, threatened him with a voice that continually had to struggle against laughter, that if he ever did something like that again, the NVA wouldn't get the chance to kill him, because he would himself.

Godalmighty. Here we go again. "Give everybody here another beer," he ordered. "Even these Air Force motherfuckers."

CHAPTER 9

Two days later the weather, remarkably bad even for the early monsoon season, finally cleared. The team had used the time to constantly refine the plan. Still, the hours went slowly. Even Jerry Hauck got tired of the drinking, deciding instead to go through the library left behind by the departed Americans. He settled on Proust, *Remembrance of Things Past,* noticing that the spine looked unbroken.

Jim wrote three letters to Alix and tore two of them up. The first, he decided, had a distinct tone of "I feel sorry for me," and the second sounded entirely too casual about the whole thing. He felt anything but casual. In the last he just told the truth. That he loved her, missed her, and hoped she would be there when he got back. It was a short letter.

Sergeant Dickerson came into the room just as he was folding it into an envelope. "Mind if I ask you something, sir?" he said, uncharacteristically formal.

"Siddown, Dick. What's on your mind?" He had noticed that Dickerson had become a little withdrawn in the last couple of days, not his normal cheerful self.

The sergeant sat for a moment in silence, his brown face

impassive. Then he flashed a smile. "I gotta tell ya, *Dai Uy,*
I think we're gonna get in some real shit here."

"No bullshit. Whatever gave you the first clue? You
having second thoughts?"

"No way!" Dickerson was horrified at the thought. He
wouldn't let down the other men now, even if he wanted to.
And he didn't.

"Nah, it's just that I want to ask you to do something, if
I bite it. Not too many people know this, but I got a couple
of kids back in the States. I know we did wills and all, but
you know how things get screwed up. 'Specially since they
don't have my name and all. The lady and I never did quite
see our way clear to getting married. You mind?"

"Kiss my ass," Jim said. "You seriously think I'd turn you
down? Course I'll take care of it. Not that I'll need to. I plan
to bring everybody back, and that includes your sorry ass."

"Thanks, *Dai Uy,*" Dickerson said, looking relieved. He
handed the captain a piece of paper upon which he had
written the names and addresses of his two children, a boy
of six and a girl of three. He had seen them only a few
times in between assignments, something he now deeply
regretted. And there might not be any more chances to
remedy that now. Despite what Captain Carmichael said,
and he had every faith in the captain's abilities, he had a
strong hunch that this might be the one that gave him what
he had been looking for for so long.

Jim sat for a little while after the sergeant left, once
again thinking about his own life. Christ, am I so different?
I've pissed away everyone who ever loved me. I have a
brother I haven't seen for six years, a father I've stayed
away from a hell of a lot longer, women who have loved
me and whom I've abandoned, and a wife and unborn child

I just ran away from. Maybe I ought to have asked for the same favor.

No, goddamn it. I meant what I said. Everyone is coming back this time. I won't leave anyone else behind. No matter what.

His thoughts were interrupted by the weather officer, who told him that they had a window of at least four hours that night, and that it didn't look like there would be any more for at least a week. Did they want to try it? The look the captain gave him told him better than words that he had asked a stupid question.

They dressed carefully, slowly, like knights getting ready for the joust. Every piece of equipment was stowed properly; a place for everything and everything in its place. Camouflage jungle fatigues, made in Korea, no labels speaking of their origin. Jungle boots, same source. No socks or underwear. Fabric staying next to the skin kept it moist, made it an ideal home for the bacteria and fungi that teemed in the jungle, lying in wait for their next host. A couple of days and you would have a spectacular case of crotch rot and athlete's foot. A couple days more and you were out of action, unable to move without screaming in agony as the skin flaked off in sheets.

Next came the Air Force–type mesh survival vest with the strobe light, penflares, mini smoke grenades, URC-10 ground/air survival radio and extra battery, first-aid kit, and survival packet containing matches, fishhooks and line, cable saw, malaria suppressants, antidiarrheal tablets, razor blades, and signal mirror. Every single pocket of the vest was taken up with something important. The vest was the last thing you lost, because without it you were truly alone.

Atop the vest was the STABO harness and pistol belt

containing all the things you would need to fight. Over all this were the rough-terrain coveralls, a loose-fitting garment of tough canvas with extra padding on shoulders, elbows, knees, and buttocks. They would be jumping into the trees; could not depend upon finding a clear landing zone. Besides, there was too much chance the clear zones would be occupied by someone else. The coveralls and a tough plastic helmet with a mesh faceguard made it possible to land in the canopy without hurting yourself too much if you kept your feet together and didn't get one snagged in the vee of a branch and rip it off.

Already the men could hardly move. Next came the parachute, shrugged into and clipped together with quick releases in the front. The CAR-15 was slipped over the shoulder and tied down with string and a canvas band. Wouldn't need it coming down—shooting at someone while you were hanging underneath a parachute canopy was strictly for the movies—but you wanted quick access as soon as you got on the ground. The heavily laden rucksacks had already been carried to the plane, as had the bundles they would be kicking. The rucksack would be attached to the rear of the harness just before jumping, where it would ride on the backs of the legs. No use being more uncomfortable than necessary. This was quite bad enough, thank you. Each man was sweating heavily even in the air-conditioned bunker, and when they waddled outside to get in the van they felt like they were in a steambath. Though, as Jerry was quick to point out, without some LBFM to give them a blowjob.

The driver of the van, a young Air Force sergeant, asked him what an LBFM was. Jerry rolled his eyes.

"Christ, where do they get these guys?" he asked

rhetorically. "Little Brown Fucking Machine, of course."

Once on the C-130 they connected their facemasks to the oxygen console, started breathing pure oxygen. The cool dry gas was pleasant on the lungs, produced its usual slight euphoria. Jim settled onto one of the webbed seats, relaxed. There would be at least an hour of this as the system was scrubbed of nitrogen. Nothing much to do except sit back and look around.

In the front of the cargo compartment, behind curtains beyond which mere mortals were not supposed to go, the technicians checked their magic machines. This one here would alert them to the presence of enemy radar. That one would tell them if they had been "painted"—locked on to by fire-control systems that would guide the guns or missiles to them. Yet another would blank out those fire-control systems, fill the screens with static, cause the missiles to fly out of control. If all else failed there were chaff dispensers to confuse the radar, flares to release to attract heat seekers. And if all that failed? he had asked one day while being briefed on just such an aircraft.

Then you die, the pilot had said.

The bundles with the equipment they would not be able to carry on their backs were strapped to the tailgate, parachutes attached, ready to go. The rucksacks were next to them. The crew chief was busy checking his baby. Every crew chief believed that the aircraft under his care belonged to him and him alone. The pilots were only the drivers, and not to be trusted. The crew chief knew the sounds she made, was alerted to problems and even the location of the problem by the slightest difference in hum or rattle. Could repair anything on the aircraft, at least long enough to get it back where it came from, with nothing much more than a crescent wrench, copper wire, and hundred-mile-an-hour tape. Woe be unto the unwary, treating the plane in a less than respectful manner, if the crew chief was around.

Jim let his mind slip into cruise control. How many times have I done this? My life is made up of the smells of avgas and hydraulic fluid, cordite and TNT smoke, shit and blood. Instants of peace, snatched where you can, before once again throwing yourself into the shitstorm. Colors of olive drab, camouflage, jungle green, melding into nothingness. And each time you ask yourself, will it be the last? Promise that if God will just allow you to get through it one more time it will be. That you'll quit, never again allow yourself to be talked into such foolishness by anyone. Or by yourself. Resist the seductive talk of country and the cause—the devil's temptations, all. Find another line of work, one that stands a bit better chance of allowing you to live longer than just the next few hours.

And each time, after it is over, you think, that's it! I'm free.

And in a few days, or at the worst a couple of weeks, the bad parts start to fade. Increasingly, you think about the sheer exhilaration of danger, the adrenaline-fed battle euphoria that allows you to do amazing things. The indescribable joy of sharing a desperate cause with worthy companions. The pleasure of being just a little bit quicker, or smarter, or just luckier than your opponents.

And you're ready to go again; start to chafe when you can't. And it goes on and on.

Until, as the man said, you're dead.

With a hydraulic whine the tailgate closes. Another whine, the engines are starting. Out the window, should you care to look, the props are starting to turn. The vibrations possess the aircraft, inhabit the soul.

The hums and pops of the machine, familiar from so many times before, feel like old friends. There is anticipation; the airplane is clearly struggling against staying, wanting to flee to the realm that is its home.

Physical release; the brakes slip; movement. Gathering force, irresistible, though it is nothing more than air itself being pushed. Rumble across the pocked runway, unkept by the magic of technology since the Americans departed. Trees outside the perimeter shaking, small birds once again in fear scattering.

Brake at the end of the runway. Run the engines up to full power; technicians worshiping the gauges, alert as any acolyte to the slightest fluctuation, whims of their god.

Forward. Gathering speed, the engines run up to full. Roar that fills the ears, even through the helmet. Long run out; no need to get a combat takeoff here. Nobody shooting at you, for a change.

In the sky, climbing hard. Long way up to thirty thou. Up where the airliners cross the sky, their passengers blissfully oblivious. Follow just behind an Air France jet out of Bangkok, so close they can't tell you're there—one blip for the radar downstairs.

Couple of minutes now. The crew chief gives the signal. You've heard it anyway, through the earphones you insisted on wearing. Give the signal to the two people with you. Get smiles in return. Ready.

Help each other attach the rucksacks behind the legs. Added weight makes it damned difficult to move. Shuffle about like an old humpbacked woman. Help the crew chief and aircraftsmen free the bundles. Hit the strobe atop each bundle; the light flashes through the airplane like a dance hall gone mad. The tailgate yawns open. Outside is dark eternity.

Watch the lights just to the side of the hydraulic shaft of the tailgate. Red now. Crew chief gives the signal for just a few more seconds. Disconnect from the console. Crack the bailout bottle attached to the harness. The familiar free flow of oxygen rushes into the lungs. Let it flap out the cheeks of the mask as you breathe out. At this point you have only one decision to make. It is a jump, or it isn't. There are no turnarounds. You don't have enough capacity in the bailout bottle to play.

Green light. Push the bundles out the tailgate, watch them disappear into the night. Clasp hands with the others, out into the great dark, slipstream catching, flip once, down fall.

Fall free and clear, catch sight of the strobe on the bundle, follow it down. Thirty-six thousand feet upon release; cold, damn cold. Fly close. No desire to play games up here. Now you follow the flashing light of the bundle as if it was the godlight itself.

Altimeter winding through thirty, twenty, ten. Fly so close you can feel the presence of the others. You, who have felt yourself such a solitary, want the closeness of brotherhood, of blood. Push away from each other only enough to get freedom for the canopy. Watch for the opening of the bundle; now, pull.

Full canopy. Pull one toggle line, then the other to make sure they're free. To either side, dimly seen, are the others. Shadows in the moonlight. Follow the bundle down; nothing fancy here. At least there's no one shooting. Of course, what would they shoot at? Ghosts, clouds?

Nothing to see below; smooth blackness. You've been dependent upon the navigational skills of the Air Force, now for a moment you're seized with doubt. Suppose something went wrong, you got seriously off course? Instead of jungle you're about to drop into the ocean, or a major lake. With all the equipment you're carrying you'll be dragged to the bottom long before you can get free. Such things have happened before.

There is a crackling of branches as the bundle crashes down, and you breathe a sigh of relief. Cross the legs, point the toes down, cross your arms in front of your face; poor protection against the branches but better than nothing. The rucksack will not be let out on a lowering line this time—in its position on the rear it will protect your backside. There is always the fear, crashing through the trees like this, that a broken branch will jam through the tough canvas jumpsuit like tissue, run right up your ass. Of all the things that could happen that seems somehow to be the worst.

Contact and the foliage whips by, grasping, clawing, trying to shred the intruder. Don't let it pry your feet apart! You'll straddle a branch and likely get caught that way, break a leg at best. At worst, rip one off. Bounce heavily against the bole of a tree, knocking the breath from your lungs. The canopy above catches, rips loose, catches again. Now is the time of the greatest danger. If it collapses completely and doesn't catch anything on the way down you will fall free to the ground. And the ground is a long way down here in the triple canopy. Still falling, it seems faster now. Try to catch hold of something? No, that's a fool's errand. All you'll do is break something, and probably not be able to grasp anything to break your fall anyway.

The canopy catches again, rips, the noise agonizingly loud. Bounce at the end of the risers like a puppet, ripping again, a little more drop, then it holds. Sway slightly at the end, finally allowing yourself to breathe. Bounce experimentally, just a little. There is no more ripping. Caught firmly, thank God.

Rest there for a second in the harness, listening. Another ripping sound as one of the other men comes in, a heavy thud, a loudly whispered "Shit!" Jerry. You hope he's okay. No groaning in pain, and that's encouraging.

Look down, into the inky black. No way of telling how far down the ground is. Pull the quick releases on the rucksack, let it fall to the end of the lowering line. It bounces against more foliage a couple of times, then stops, pulling the line taut. More than thirty-five feet to the ground, at least you know that much.

Pull a mountaineering snap link from the pocket, hook it into the front of the parachute harness. The hundred-foot length of flat nylon strapping is already hooked into the risers just above the quick release. Pull it loose, wrap it twice through the snap link, hold it tight against the hip with the right hand as with the other you unfasten the quick releases. Slight drop, and you are free. Rappel down the strap until you feel the rucksack hit the ground, followed very quickly by your feet. Good thing. There is only about another ten feet of free strap left. Trees were damn high.

First thing to come loose is the rifle; chamber a round, listen carefully for sounds. Nothing to indicate the crashing of pursuit; relax a little. Take off the parachute harness, strip out of the coveralls and helmet. Wait again, still no sounds.

Over to the right comes the dim flashing of the strobe still attached to the bundle. You'll rally there. Move slowly, cautiously through the jungle. Back in the familiar triple canopy. Lots of stuff down at the bottom level to trip you up, make it damn difficult to move. Wait-a-minute vines covered with tiny thorns, low-growing creepers to catch the feet, the thousands, millions of branches fallen from the trees above making a natural abatis. Phosphorescence from the rotting vegetation makes an unearthly glow down close to the ground, almost but not quite bright enough to see by. Makes the imagination go wild: Is that something moving over there? Perhaps just one more of the legions of the dead forever condemned to walk this unholy ground.

Jesus Christ, Jim. Get a hold of yourself.

The bundle, heavy as it is, has crashed through all the way to the ground. That's both a relief and a burden. If it had hung up in the trees they would just have left it, depending upon possible passersby not seeing it. The area in which they had dropped had been chosen deliberately for its remoteness. No trails or rivers came anywhere close; there was no real reason for anyone to come here.

Now they would have to cache it; carry it some distance away from the parachutes still caught in the trees and bury it. Find some distinctive terrain feature from which they could take polar coordinates so they could, they hoped, someday once again find it.

"That you, Captain?" Jim heard, raising the hackles at the back of his neck. *Christ, have I been away from this for too long? I would have heard his approach back in the old days.*

"Yeah, Jerry, come on in," he whispered back. A dark form detached itself from the rest of the inky blackness, came forward. By the light of the still-flashing strobe Jim saw that his sergeant had suffered a few problems in his ride through the trees. The coveralls he was still wearing were torn and slashed, and there was a dark stain on one leg.

"Branch got me," he explained. "Fuckin' thing was like a razor. I'm okay, though. Put a pressure bandage on it, got the bleeding stopped, I think."

"Siddown," Jim commanded, hearing Jerry's sigh of relief as he took the pressure off the injured leg. He took out his flashlight, in the red filtered light looked at the injury. The pressure bandage was already leaking through. Jerry had obviously lost quite a lot of blood.

"Damn, what happened to you?" Dickerson said, startling Jim once again. Either his two sergeants could move soundlessly, or his combat skills had suffered a severe degradation.

"Gonna need your help," he told Dickerson. "Hold this light." He cut away the pressure bandage, saw the heavy ooze of blood, black in the red light. Nothing squirting, anyway. That was a relief.

He got the aid kit out of his rucksack, flipped open the canvas instrument holder. "Morphine?" he asked.

Jerry shook his head.

"Let me know if you change your mind. This is gonna hurt."

He tore open a package of sterile surgical sponges, daubed the wound to clear the blood away. It was quickly filled again, but it appeared that there were no major blood vessels involved. Only a couple of not terribly important veins. He selected a hemostat from among the instruments, daubed the blood away once again. There. He caught the severed vessel in the jaws of the hemostat, clamped down to shut off the flow. Leaving the instrument clipped in place he took another, performed the same action again. In a few minutes there were four hemostats protruding from the hole, and the only bleeding a slight ooze from the capillaries.

Jerry had kept his teeth clenched so tightly throughout the ordeal he had chipped one. Only a soft moan escaped his lips when the last hemostat was clipped into place.

"Easy part's over," Jim said, earning himself a muffled curse. He next selected a forceps and some surgical gut, tied off each of the bleeders just above the hemostats. The gut would hold the flesh long enough for the blood to clot and the wound to scarify, then dissolve in the body. Then he chose another length of the gut and sewed the muscle back together where it had been cut almost in two.

As a last act he chose some surgical silk and closed the skin together. Gut usually wasn't strong enough to hold the skin; the silk would be removed as soon as the flesh had grown back together. He left a small space at the bottom for drainage. Likelihood was that the wound would get infected; though it had been relatively clean you never knew what kind of Southeast Asian pathogen might have been hanging around on the tree branch. He would keep Jerry full of antibiotics, check the wound every day, open it up again and debride it should it become necessary.

He hoped it wasn't. There would be no evacuations on this mission; no Dustoffs to come in and get the injured man, fly him to a field hospital where sterile conditions could be maintained.

He had not realized how much he had counted on the immense machine supporting their efforts during the war. No matter what happened, you could always count on someone coming in to get you, take you away from all the blood and filth and terror. Now they were on their own.

It was a terribly lonely feeling.

He and Dickerson busied themselves with the bundle while Jerry rested. Jim had already come to the decision that they would not be able to carry it very far with only two people. As it was they would have to take on most of Jerry's gear as they moved.

"We'll bury it here," he said. "Hope nobody finds the chutes." He shrugged. "We have to, we can do without it, anyway." The bundle contained duplicates of almost everything they carried, and since nothing had been lost in the drop, was not essential to their operation.

"They ain't gonna find the chutes," Dickerson said. He rigged a couple of short pieces of nylon strap into Prusik knots, slipped them over the lowering line on which Jim had come down. The Prusik, a mountaineering knot, allowed you to slip it freely upward, but when you put weight on it caught the rope around which it was tied and refused to slip downward. Dickerson stood in the loop of one while he pushed the other up the lowering line, then put his weight on the other and repeated the process, slowly making his way upward until he could finally reach the first branches. After that it was a short shinny up to where the chute was hung—a few tugs in the right direction and it came slipping down. Two more times—luckily neither his nor Jerry's chute had caught up quite so high— and he had all the evidence of their jump piled with the bundle.

They dug a deep hole with the entrenching tools included in the package, cursing and sweating as they made their way through the tough roots of the trees and vines. Luckily the roots didn't go very deep; the jungle soil everyone thought so rich because of the rank growth that sprang from it was actually very thin. Beneath it was hard-packed clay, tough to dig through but much easier than cutting through the roots.

It was almost dawn before they finished. They shoved the bundle, still wrapped, into the hole, followed by the coveralls and parachutes, then covered it all back up, spreading the leaves and rotten limbs over the area as well as possible. It would have to do. Wouldn't fool anyone right now, but with a couple of days of rain it would fade into invisibility.

"You guys hungry?" Jerry asked. He had reconstituted three of the LRRP dehydrated rations with canteen water, offered them to the two dirt-covered men. Gratefully they sank down beside him and dug into the food. Jerry had jazzed it up slightly with the inevitable Tabasco sauce; only thing that gave the cardboardlike mess any flavor.

Still, it filled a hole. One hundred percent of your daily requirement of vitamins and nutrients, all served in one almost indigestible mass.

"You gonna be able to move?" Jim asked the sergeant.

"Don't have a hell of a lot of choice, do I?" Jerry replied. "It's a little stiff right now, but I'm gonna be okay. Hope you didn't think you'd be leaving me behind."

No, Jim thought, but we were afraid we'd have to carry you. And that wouldn't be a hell of a lot of fun. The rendezvous point specified by Y Buon Sarpa was a river junction over twenty kilometers away.

Jim stuffed the empty food bag into the side pocket of his fatigues, got up, and stretched. His shoulders ached from the digging, there was dull pain from the bruises he had suffered on his way down through the trees, and he was looking forward to a hell of a long walk through thick jungle.

It felt right. He smiled.

There was only one more task. Dickerson once again climbed the trees and rigged an antenna while Jim broke out the radio and generator. Dick then tuned the ancient machine, tapped out a code word on the key he'd attached to his thigh. No need for the burst device this time—the code word was the approved signal that they'd made it in and were ready to continue the mission.

If the radio operator had been transmitting under duress he would have tapped out another code word and, back in the old days, waited for the air strike that would have blown both him and his captors to rags. Of the two, captivity or death, Dickerson figured the latter was the far better choice.

Jerry resolutely refused to let them carry any of his gear. The only concession to his injury was to allow them to help him into his rucksack. He moved, limping, forward. "Hell," he said, "time's a wastin'. You fuckers want to take a nap or something?"

"Pain in the ass little shithead, ain't he?" Dickerson said, bowed under the weight of his own ruck. He grinned, teeth flashing in the early light of dawn filtering weakly through the trees in the eternal twilight of triple canopy.

"Wouldn't know him if he wasn't," Jim agreed, and moved off in point. Ordinarily that would have been Jerry Hauck's position, but even the tough little sergeant recognized that to do all he had to do and break trail too would have been just a little beyond his abilities.

They'd landed almost atop a ridge line—at least they didn't have to climb. Not yet, anyway. For it is an immutable law of the infantry; for every hill you go down there is another one you will have to go up.

Jim followed a general compass heading; didn't try to be exact. As long as the navigator had put them anywhere close to where they should have been dropped there was no chance they would get lost. There was a river somewhere to the northeast of them, and another to the southeast. As long as they kept moving in a general easterly direction they would sooner or later run into the junction.

This method allowed him to follow contour lines, rather than a straight line up and down the hills. Far easier to move. Also allowed them to avoid the open areas. Even here, as far away from civilization as man had probably ever been, there were the scars from the slash-and-burn agriculture practiced by the H'Mong, a people of the same ethnic stock as the Montagnards. Though there was no sign of those people. They'd long since moved out, tired of being bombed by both sides.

The few trails they came across were totally unused, almost overgrown. Jim felt better and better about the whole thing. Unlikely anyone would have seen the drop, unlikely the parachutes would be discovered. With any luck they would be able to perform the mission and be out of there without the Communists being any the wiser.

They took frequent breaks. Jerry, despite his determination to keep up, was limping badly. No hurry, Jim told him. We don't get there today, we'll make it tomorrow. Or the next day. Not as if we're on schedule or anything. Sarpa said they'd come to the rendezvous point every day for the next three months. That still leaves us a month.

In truth, he wasn't feeling all that well himself; welcomed the breaks. It was the heat, he supposed. Certainly he was in good enough physical shape; they all were. The rucksack marches and runs through the mountains of Bavaria had made sure of that. But the wet oven they were going through bore no resemblance to the crisp mountain air of the Alps. It sucked the energy out of you, gone with the sweat running in rivulets down your sides. All of them drank as much water as they could; dehydration was a very real danger here. Fortunately there were a few streams along the route in which to replenish the canteens. A couple of iodine tablets to kill the bugs, and you were good to go. Never mind that it felt like you were drinking medicine. Better than the worms, spirochetes, bacteria, amoebas, and pathogens as yet unknown with which the brown liquid was undoubtedly filled.

At the noon break Jim checked beneath Jerry's bandage, was pleased to see no more blood leakage. Haven't lost my touch there yet, he thought. He gave the sergeant a couple more tetracycline pills, watched as he took them. What he was doing would be frowned upon by a surgeon. Giving antibiotics as a prophylaxis, they said, would make future generations of bacteria that much more resistant.

Of course, those surgeons had sterile operating rooms, access to critical-care facilities, and the staffs of huge hospitals to back them up should the patient develop an infection. He intended to keep so many antibiotics in Jerry that the bacteria would have no chance to take hold.

By nightfall they were all exhausted, and still at least eight kilometers from the objective. Jim started looking for a place to Remain Over-Night, RON as they called it back during the recon days. Someplace easily defensible, with escape routes should it become necessary. He finally found it in a slight depression between the trunks of three giant trees.

Despite there having been no sign of any followers, he and Dickerson set out claymore mines to cover the avenues of approach. No use taking chances. They set out tripwires attached to flares to the outside of the mines. Anyone coming in would light up the area, whereupon the men inside the RON would blow them away with the claymores. No way for the survivors to pinpoint their position that way, and they could make good their escape. It was a technique worked out by recon leaders long ago, and had always worked well. No use tampering with success.

They ate again, once more cold rations. Probably could have chanced heating some water over a piece of C-4, Jim thought. The burning explosive gave off tremendous heat and very little light, warmed a canteen cup of water in almost no time. Still, you never knew, and old habits died hard.

Be as a ghost; move across the land like a wraith, leaving no trace of your passage. Not light, nor heat, nor smell, nor noise. Not for nothing had the NVA called the recon teams the black ghosts. You weren't, you became a ghost for real.

Just before dropping off to sleep Jim heard the monkeys howling above; even they were oblivious to the presence of the humans below. That's the way it should be, he thought. Maybe I'm not totally out of practice, after all.

CHAPTER 10

He woke to a sound that brought him scrambling out of his poncho liner, weapon at the ready, eyes anxiously scanning the dank foliage. A quick glance over each shoulder showed Jerry and Dirty Dick similarly alert, weapons pointed outward, the three so close in a triangle their feet were touching.

Jim cocked his head, looking up. There it was again.

The unmistakable whop of the blades of a Huey.

It passed over them, the sound fading now, reverberating through the trees.

"After us, you reckon?" Jerry whispered.

"Far as I know, there ain't no friendly choppers around here these days," Dickerson said.

It had come to a hell of a pass, Jim thought, that the sound of a Huey, ordinarily something to be welcomed, was now feared. Must be how Charlie used to feel, he mused.

"Whatcha think, *Dai Uy?*" Jerry asked.

"Not necessarily looking for us," he replied. "But we're not too far from the rendezvous, which indicates our friend Sarpa may have a problem. This far over the border, that chopper must be almost at the limit of his fuel. Unless, of course, they're using some of our old support sites for re-fueling stations." The thought, and others, brought him up short. The NVA wouldn't be operating under the restrictions the Americans had to suffer during the war. They could be damn near anyplace.

Including on their trail.

"Saddle up," he said. "The sooner we get this done, the better."

They ate a hurried breakfast, this time using a couple of rolled-up pills of C-4 to heat water in canteen cups. Some things you can do without, Jim reflected. Hot coffee isn't one of them.

Just before leaving, Jim uncovered Jerry's wound, was pleased to see that none of the stitches had broken loose. He wiped it with sterile gauze, inspected the cloth, and found only clear serum. The surrounding flesh was red, as it should have been, but not overly hot to the touch. So far, so good. He rebandaged the wound, gave Jerry a couple more tetracycline pills, watched carefully as the sergeant downed them. Within days the flesh would granulate, each side of the wound reaching for the other, and in a few days more would close off on its own. It would leave a hell of a scar, but somehow he didn't think Jerry Hauck was overly worried about how he would look in a bathing suit.

He buried the old bandage deep enough to discourage the forest scavengers from digging it up. Unlikely anyone would find it anyway, but you didn't leave anything to chance. The minute you thought you were safe from some-thing like that the fates played their cosmic crap shoot and you came up snake eyes.

Dickerson had in the meantime been rolling up the

claymore wires, removing the blasting caps and stowing mines and caps in separate pockets in the rucksacks. Again a precaution, but a necessary one. If a bullet hit the blasting cap it would explode it, producing a nasty little wound, particularly if it was close to your back. But if it was still in the mine and it went off there wouldn't be enough left of you to provide positive identification.

To the extent possible they sterilized the RON site, making sure there were no little scraps of paper, pieces of foil from the rations packets, anything that might tell someone that a team had recently stayed here. It wouldn't stop a skilled tracker, but if they had a skilled tracker on their trail they were pretty much screwed anyway.

Finally satisfied, they shouldered rucksacks, grabbed weapons, took a quick azimuth, and slipped back into the jungle. As nearly as Jim could figure they were about eight kilometers away from the rendezvous site and at the rate of travel they'd maintained the day before it would take slightly more than half a day to cover it. If no one was there the plan was to once again RON, wait twenty-four hours, then head for the alternate site. The alternate was almost thirty kilometers away from the primary—a hump none of them were looking forward to, particularly when it involved the crossing of a fairly major river.

Just had to hope someone was going to be at the primary.

By noon they were once again exhausted. The terrain closer to the river was cut up by ravines and washes, making for much harder going. Some of them they could cross, sliding down one side and scrambling up the other, the first man up pulling the others by main force. Others were far too deeply cut, the bottoms a jumble of rocks that made sure you weren't going to follow them to the water. A simple solution would have been to follow alongside, but the lay of the land would, according to Jim's calculations, have led them downstream from the RV site at least six or seven klicks. For one major ravine they had to backtrack almost two klicks until they could find a crossing point, then box back to where they would have been, only then once again taking up the correct azimuth. The eight kilometers to the RV site were quickly becoming more like ten or twelve.

The one good thing was that they hadn't heard the helicopter again. Maybe it was just a passover, Jim told himself, wishing he believed it.

They flopped down, still maintaining some semblance of a defensive perimeter, but didn't bother to put out claymores.

The meal was once again reconstituted Long Range Reconnaissance Patrol, LRRP, rations, eaten cold. Recon men called them lurps when they were feeling particularly charitable, ever increasingly obscenity-filled names when they weren't. If you were out with the 'Yards you could always depend upon them to come up with the odd animal or plant to supplement the unappetizing mess, and Jim supposed that if he wanted to put himself out, he could do the same.

But right now he was just too goddamn tired.

Why shouldn't he be tired? he asked himself. After all, he was getting to be an old man. Thirty-three years old. Five more years and he would be eligible to retire. Half pay at the rate of a major. That was, if the Army ever again unfroze the promotions. He'd been a captain for eight years now. Back during the war captains were making major with two to three years in grade.

Goddamn peacetime Army, he said for only about the millionth time.

Although it wasn't all that peaceful here, was it? The fact that it was quiet didn't mean anything. At any moment an enemy platoon could come bursting from the jungle and they would once again be in a fight for their lives. With very damned little chance of survival, now that they couldn't call air, artillery, evacuation, or any damned thing else.

Gotta stop volunteering for this kind of shit, he told himself, again for about the millionth time.

A few minutes later and an uncomfortable heaviness in the pit of his stomach told him it was time. He gritted his teeth. God, he hated to shit in the field! You were so goddamn exposed, so vulnerable, your butt hanging out to the breeze while you strained to get just one little turd out. Yeah, the others would be maintaining watch and you probably weren't a damned bit more vulnerable than you were right now.

Still, it seemed like it. He knew he wasn't alone in his aversion. Back in the war it had come to such a pass that the SOG recon teams had been issued a special pill. Something with an impossibly technical name, but which came to be known, quite naturally, as the no-shit pill. Take one of those little hummers and it tightened you up so close you couldn't drive a tenpenny nail up your butt with a ten-pound sledge. Of course, when they finally wore off your intestines were so packed with hardened feces it felt like you were having a baby when you finally did go to the latrine.

No use putting it off, he told himself. He told Dickerson what he was going to do, left the rest site, going only a few meters away and downwind, quickly scratched out a cathole, dropped trousers, and, holding his carbine across his lap, eyes anxiously scanning the jungle, took care of business. A quick wipe with the toilet paper included in the lurp ration bag, cover it all, and scrape leaves over the disturbed earth. Gratefully return to the rest site, secure in the knowledge that this particular task was taken care of for one more day at least. Next time it would be within the FULRO camp, the exposure factor far lower.

That afternoon, luckily, because Jim didn't think they would have made the RV site otherwise, the terrain cooperated. By four o'clock they were in the general area, confirmed by a quick terrain analysis.

"Let's find a hidey-hole," Jim said. "Now we wait."

"Any word from the team yet?" Bentley Sloane asked Mark Petrillo.

"Aside from the initial contact? No. Nothing."

Sloane frowned. "You don't have them on a regular contact schedule?"

"Nope."

"How come?"

Now it was Petrillo's turn to frown. What he wanted to say was, it's none of your business, you freaking straphanger. But you had to be careful, very careful, when dealing with people like this. You never knew who had the real power. After all, the chief of staff for Intelligence hadn't sent him here just to watch and learn.

"Carmichael wanted it that way," he said. "Said he didn't have time to stop and set up an antenna every time somebody in the rear felt lonely. He'd contact us when he had something to report, and not before."

"And you let a field operative set the rules?" Sloane was acutely aware of his inexperience in matters of this sort, but still . . . if you let someone like Carmichael, who by his record was a notorious rule breaker, do as he wanted, how could you control him?

"When the field operative is Jim Carmichael, yes," Petrillo answered. "He knows what he's doing. Besides, if he doesn't want to make contact, how are you going to force him? What are you going to threaten him with? A bad OER? Send him back to Vietnam?"

Petrillo was now smiling, and it infuriated Sloane. It wasn't bad enough that someone was right, as he recognized the lieutenant colonel to be. But they always had to rub it in.

"Speaking of something to report," he said, "shouldn't they have made contact with Sarpa's people by now?"

"We don't even know if they've made the RV point," Petrillo said, tired of the conversation and wanting to get back to work. "That's some shitty terrain out there. Hard to move cross-country, especially when you're snoopin' and poopin'—not exactly as if they can call in an arclight if they get tumbled now, is it?"

Privately he was thinking, bet you've never had to do that, have you, you little shit? He knew, of course, about Bentley Sloane's war record. Had made the necessary phone calls to friends in the Pentagon who were happy to forward anything they could on the young captain. The fact that Sloane had been an A team executive officer, and that he had during the course of a very bad day won the Medal of Honor, didn't really mean a lot when it came to things like this. The fact that you could be incredibly brave during a single action didn't mean that you were automatically a good field soldier.

Since he had been, of course, pulled out of active field service after winning the big blue, it was unlikely that he would ever get the chance to prove himself either. The Army didn't like to risk its certified heroes. People like Lew Millett, who had won the medal in Korea by leading the last bayonet charge ever conducted by a unit of the U.S. Army, had been forced to fight the entire military establishment to get the opportunity to lead a combat unit in Vietnam. The people he'd pissed off during that effort had made certain that Millett would never reach flag rank. That, as Millett had once confessed to Petrillo during a long, liquor-filled evening, and the fact that he had a desertion on his military record. He'd been in the Army in 1940, had been so pissed off at our neutralism that he'd gone AWOL, crossed the border, and joined the Canadian Army, where he got the combat he was seeking. After Pearl Harbor he had returned home to an Army grateful enough to get anyone with any combat experience that his sins were forgiven. But the Army never really forgot.

"I suppose," Sloane said, barely willing to concede the point. Still, if he'd been running things it would have been vastly different.

"Besides," Petrillo said, "we've got more things to worry about than Carmichael not making contact. Signals intercept is picking up a hell of a lot of chatter from the NVA headquarters for that area. Coded, so we don't know what they're talkin' about, but it's worrisome."

"Any other explanation for it?" Sloane asked.

"Not that I can think of."

"So you think the mission might be compromised?"

"Yeah," Petrillo answered. "Just like the old days."

Just like the old days indeed, Sloane thought. With one big difference.

They'd taken turns on watch—Jerry had the first shift from eight to twelve, Dickerson to four in the morning, now it was Jim Carmichael's turn. Dick had woken him from a particularly good dream, where he and Alix were in a huge bed under a down coverlet as soft as a cloud, and she was touching him, and . . .

Shit! he muttered, rolling out of the poncho liner and feeling the dampness and chill that characterized early morning in the mountains of Laos. Kept you awake, this. Stay rolled up in the warm poncho liner and likelihood was that you'd drift back off, easy prey for someone with a little bit of stealth and a sharp knife.

It was still quite dark, wouldn't be light for another couple of hours at the least. He dug in a side pocket of the rucksack, took out an infrared scope, scanned the surrounding jungle. The scope was obsolete, deservedly so. It put out a beam of infrared light that could easily be picked up by anyone with a passive infrared scope, but he had calculated that any North Vietnamese unit in this area wouldn't be so equipped. Besides, the instrument had a couple of advantages. It was lighter and far less bulky than the AN-PVS 2 Starlight scope he had left in the equipment bundle. And, since it was obsolete, it could be obtained in any well-equipped army surplus store. Deniability, General Miller had said. Above all, we must have deniability. Your cover story, should you be caught, is that you're on a private rescue mission, much like that already being run by a few veterans out of Thailand.

Personally, Jim didn't think the cover story would hold up worth a shit, and even if it did, the likelihood that the NVA would take any more kindly to civilians in their rear areas than they would to a military unit was slight.

But it would allow the U.S. government to say, Who, us? Of course we didn't authorize any such mission. Now, if you would, please return these people to our control, and we'll make sure they're prosecuted.

Features jumped out in the eerie reddish light. The lump that might have been someone slowly making his way into the RON site resolved itself into a big rock. The crackle of noise was a very large civet cat, snuffling at the jungle floor in an unending search for food. Easy to get spooked out here. Nerves were on edge anyway, and imagination if let loose would conjure up demons, ghosts, and sprites—or NVA sappers making their inexorable way into your perimeter.

He'd tucked himself against the trunk of a banyan tree, sat hunched with the carbine upright between his knees. That way if he did go to sleep, the moment his head nodded he would smack his forehead on the muzzle. Many was the time he'd returned from patrol with a big bruise right between his eyes.

No problem with that this morning. His mind was far too active. Overactive. No one had been at the RV site when they arrived the evening before. What did that mean? Supposedly someone was going to occupy it for a month. Were they, in fact, somewhere around, observing, making sure that the people that came in were the ones who were supposed to be there?

Worse, had they abandoned the site? There were many reasons for such an action. Enemy pressure was only one.

If so, that might mean that the enemy was still in the area, hence the need to be even more careful.

Or it could be, Jim, that you're in entirely the wrong spot. Such things had happened before. No matter how good your navigation you could be off by several kilometers. One bend in a river looked very much like any other bend in a river. If the Air Force navigator had been off in his calculations they could have been dropped all the hell and gone away from where they were supposed to be, and without the right start point it didn't really matter how good your navigation was after that.

A few years ago he would have been able to call Covey, the light plane that maintained communications with the recon teams, and have had him overfly the correct spot. Thus, if you didn't hear the plane you knew damned well you were in the wrong place.

There would be no Covey plane in this mission. He just had to hope his doubts were nothing more than the slight mist that started to fall, causing him to wipe the lens of the scope again and again, soaking through his fatigues, making him long for a warm room somewhere, preferably in a big bed under a down cover . . .

Whack! He came suddenly awake again, his forehead burning from the strike against the muzzle of the carbine. "Shit!" he muttered.

From the poncho-wrapped form of Jerry Hauck he heard a low chuckle.

They made first contact just after dawn, when the light was still wavery and insubstantial, what little bit of it managed to filter down through the canopy. Two of them, both armed with AK-47 rifles, dressed in camouflage that had clearly seen better days—there seemed to be more patches than there was original material.

But the brightly colored scarves around their necks were anything but ratty. Jim recognized them as II Corps Mike Force scarves. Kept somewhere safe, he supposed, and only brought out for special occasions.

That did not mean, however, that he could just let them walk right up on the team. Mike Force scarves wouldn't have been hard to come by in the aftermath of the war and the collapse of South Vietnamese resistance. And the fact that they were quite obviously 'Yards didn't mean a whole hell of a lot either. Even during the war some Montagnard tribes had actively cooperated with the VC.

"Halt," he commanded, so quietly only they could have heard it.

The two soldiers stopped instantly, looking around to see whence the command had come. Jim had, at the break of dawn, camouflaged his position, now lay beneath several branches with a scattering of moss on the top. Wouldn't stand intensive scrutiny for long, he knew, but in this business the matter of life and death was decided in instants.

Out of the corner of his eye he saw Dickerson move, achingly slowly, into a position where they could put any assault into a crossfire. Jerry would, he knew, now be covering their rear.

Jim scanned the area behind the two soldiers, didn't see anything out of place, but that didn't mean a lot. Could be a whole damned platoon of them concealed out there and unless someone screwed up he wouldn't know it.

"Oklahoma," he said.

The two 'Yards relaxed visibly. Obviously they had recognized the challenge.

"Sooners," one of them said, grinning widely enough to show a mouthful of gold teeth with brightly colored enamel inserts.

The challenge and password procedure they had just gone through was for the protection of both sides. After all, the Montagnards could very well have been running up against a North Vietnamese squad, and the Americans could have been being sucked into a trick. It wasn't foolproof, either side could have given up the key words under duress, so you had to maintain alertness, but at least it was something.

"Come forward," Jim said, this time in Bahnar. "Sling your weapons."

The soldiers obeyed his instructions, walking slowly forward until they were almost on top of him before they finally saw the muzzle of his carbine.

"*Commandant* Sarpa said you were good," one of them said in only slightly accented English. Jim saw that he was wearing the two rosettes of a lieutenant. "*Le commandant* would like to see you. Will you accompany us?"

Jim rose from the ground, shedding branches and moss, shouldered his rucksack. "Lead on," he said.

"And the others?" the lieutenant asked.

"What others?"

"You came alone?" The lieutenant clearly thought this improbable.

"Why would I need more?" Jim wished he felt as confident as he sounded.

The lieutenant shrugged. "We had hoped for at least a team," he said. "Like in the old days."

"The old days are over," Jim replied. "Now, shall we go?"

He followed them as they slipped back into the jungle, down a trail that was little more than an animal track. There was little or no sign of their passing.

Behind him Dickerson and Hauck waited five minutes, then followed.

CHAPTER 11

"No air?" Finn asked.

"Nothing more than what the Thais themselves can provide," Gutierrez replied.

Finn shook his head in disgust. They had been discussing the plan to insert Thai recon teams across the border, some as far as the Plain of Jars, to determine the true extent of the North Vietnamese buildup.

The Thais had ranged widely throughout Laos during the war. Some of them had fought as CIA-sponsored "mercenaries" providing artillery support and infantry stiffeners in the seesaw battles that had characterized the annual struggle for the Bolovens plateau. Still others had been trained as recon teams and had been accompanied by the American advisors of 46th Company, covering the areas to the west of the Prairie Fire operational area of the MACV SOG teams operating out of Vietnam. At one time there had even been a serious proposal to have the Thai army invade across the Mekong and meet Americans coming in from just below the Demilitarized Zone, the purpose being to cut the infamous Ho Chi Minh trail, denying the enemy the supplies without which he could not have continued the war. Only the very real threat of the Chinese entering the war to support their fraternal socialist comrades had stopped that gambit.

Thus the government had at its disposal a corps of battle-hardened and competent troops. Much higher quality, in Finn's opinion, than had been the regular South Vietnamese army.

The problem was that there were just too few of them. A couple of regiments to throw against an army that now numbered in the multiples of divisions. An army, moreover, that was now the best-equipped military force, absent the Chinese (and since the effects of the Cultural Revolution, probably better in many ways than the Red Army) in the entire region. The collapse of the South Vietnamese government had left the spoils of fifteen years of American support—tanks, artillery, helicopters, fighters and transport planes, millions of rounds of ammunition. About the only thing they were short on was fuel, and that only because the U.S. Congress had, in a fit of pique, voted to stop providing its South Vietnamese allies with the wherewithal to fight the war at its most critical juncture.

And now there would be no air support, despite the presence of an aircraft carrier group in the Gulf of Thailand.

Finn often wondered if the people in Washington were active supporters of the Communists, or just plain stupid.

"So if one of the teams gets into trouble, we're going to have to depend on a few obsolete choppers, maybe a couple of flights of F-5 fighters." Finn shook his head again.

"And no Americans on the ground," he continued.

"Absolutely no Americans," Gutierrez replied. "I'll restate that in the strongest possible terms, just as it was

given to me. Any violation of that direct order will be met
with the full choices of punishment under the Uniformed
Code of Military Justice. Which means, to dumb-asses like
you and me, you'd be subject to court-martial and confinement to hard labor in Fort Leavenworth."

"You know what happened when we stopped sending
out Americans with the recon teams from SOG."

"Obviously," Sam replied. What had happened was that
some of the recon teams had continued to do an outstand-
ing job. Others had been inserted, had hunkered down and
sent in reports that were increasingly fabulous. The problem was, you didn't know which ones to believe.

"But these are good troops," Sam continued. "They've
been doing this for years, often without Americans along.
Besides, with no air, you don't need an American voice on
the other end of the radio."

"I don't like it," Finn said.

"I don't recall anyone asking you to like it," Sam
replied, somewhat brusquely. There was a time for arguments and a time to go out and do your job. It was that
time. Finn would go on and achieve results that would
often appear impossible. He always had. But he always
had to bitch about it.

That was why, when CINCPAC had assigned him the
responsibility of doing everything possible to help the
Thais, absent actually supporting them, he'd called Finn
McCulloden into the planning center and had assigned him
the task of monitoring the reconnaissance effort. He was to
do so from the old Air Force base at Udorn, familiar to a
generation of U.S. pilots.

"And I don't suppose the powers that be are going to
change their minds?"

"The Joint Chiefs are doing everything they can. They've suggested an air wing be moved back in, that we mount operations from carriers, even that we deploy a division of Marines. But you need to understand the politics. The president is up for re-election next year and he's already not looking too good, what with the Nixon pardon and all. He's afraid that if we go back to war there'll be massive protests, demonstrations in the street—hell, some people are even talking about civil war."

"So we'll let some dickhead demonstrators set national policy. Abandon the only ally we still have in the region. Let them make the Gulf of Thailand a Vietnamese lake. Then what? Malaysia, Indonesia, Australia?"

"There's no such thing as the domino theory, haven't you heard?"

That brought a small, although bitter smile to Finn's lips.

"Yeah," he said. "So I've heard. But did anyone tell the Vietnamese that?"

"They told us we couldn't cross the border, and we won't," Finn told Bucky Epstein in a later planning session. "But they didn't tell us how close we could get to it. Udorn is too far away. We'll run the support section out of there. But we'll use the Border Police base at That Phanom for the FOB."

"You do realize that if the NVA come, it's going to be right about there," Bucky said.

Finn smiled back at the small grin that was starting to play on Bucky's lips.

"Hadn't really thought about it," he lied. "But just in case, I've got Billy Craig working on some supplies for us."

Master Sergeant Craig was another of those NCOs who would probably not have survived outside Special Forces. His grateful SF compatriots called him the greatest scrounger who'd ever worn the Green Beret. The people from whom he'd obtained impossible-to-get items called him a notorious thief, con artist, and other names far less complimentary.

Craig had been a team sergeant in an A camp in the Delta when ambushed by the Viet Cong. He'd taken a burst of machine-gun fire in the stomach and upper legs, had very nearly bled to death before the team medic could get to him, but had still enough spirit to keep fighting long enough for the rest of his patrol to mount a counterattack and drive off the ambushers.

He'd spent well over two years in various hospitals. The doctors had been forced to remove several feet of his intestines, shorten one leg by two inches where the bone had been shot away, and combat the raging infections that were inevitably the result of intestinal contents' being scattered throughout the abdominal cavity.

He'd gone from a strapping six-foot, two-hundred-pound fighting machine into a rail-thin, limping figure who no one figured would ever be the same again. He'd had to fight the disability discharge they'd wanted to give him all the way up to the highest levels of command, had succeeded in the end only because his Tennessee-born mother had been a high-school girlfriend of the current senator from that state.

But leading men into combat was obviously out of the question. He had the will. He simply didn't have the endurance, and very well knew it.

He'd decided that if he couldn't be with the troops, he

could damned well support them. He wangled an assignment to the MACV-SOG support activity in Taiwan, and from there had mounted the operations that would make him legendary. A team wanted Chinese Communist RPD machine guns because they were a lot lighter and more reliable than the American-made M-60 (and besides, if you ran out of ammunition you could pick up some more from the people you'd killed), and they'd soon be delivered, still packed in the People's Army cases. Unable to get the brass in Saigon to give up any of the captured weapons, Craig had gone to Hong Kong, made contact with a People's Army representative, and bought them.

British Intelligence had learned of the deal, informed Washington about it, and there had been a move afoot to court-martial the NCO for dealing with the enemy. A lawyer at the Pentagon had tactfully pointed out that Craig couldn't be guilty of dealing with the enemy, as technically we weren't at war with the Chinese.

From there it went on. What he couldn't get by barter, buying outright, or applying the appropriate incentives to the supply systems of any and all armed forces U.S. and foreign, he would steal. And if it didn't exist, he'd finance the effort to build it.

Had he chosen, with the connections he'd developed he could have become a very rich man. Instead he got by on his sergeant's pay.

"I've asked Billy to get us a few things to strengthen the defenses," Finn continued. "Antitank mines. Antiaircraft guns. Redeye missiles. He thinks he can lay his hands on some TOWs and launchers."

Bucky gave a low whistle of amazement. The TOW, the acronym standing for Tube-launched, Optically-guided,

Wire-controlled missile, was fairly new even to the U.S. Army inventory. No current Soviet tank could stand up to its warhead. And given a good operator the missile would unerringly hit even a fast-moving target out to the maximum extent of its trailing wire, some three thousand meters. Way past the range of the cannons of the T-34s and T-55s with which the Vietnamese would most likely stage an attack.

"Won't completely stop 'em," Finn conceded. "But it'll give 'em fits for a while. Maybe long enough to get some reinforcements."

"Don't suppose Billy could come up with a SADM," Bucky suggested.

SADM, another acronym from an Army queer for them, stood for Small Atomic Demolition Munition, the so-called backpack nuke. About a half-kiloton in yield, it would very effectively blunt an enemy assault.

"Wouldn't be surprised," Finn replied. "Only problem is, he got 'em, we couldn't use 'em. We'll have to stick to the conventional stuff. Hold out long enough, maybe our leaders will come to their senses."

"You really think that?"

Finn pretended to consider the question for a moment.

"Nah," he said finally. "Not a chance."

CHAPTER 12

Y Buon Sarpa looked not a day older than he'd looked ten years ago. An almost childish, open face, a countenance that had stood him in good stead in conspiracies and plots that dated back at least twenty years. Who could believe that this kid was the brains behind a major element of FULRO?

"Carmichael, my old friend," he said, coming forward and enveloping Jim in a heartfelt embrace. "What should I call you? You must at least be a colonel by now."

"Still a captain," Jim said, a trifle sourly. The message that Jim would be the one coming must have mentioned that. Sarpa was trying to flatter him. It put his hackles up.

"No!" Sarpa said, releasing him to arm's length and looking him directly in the eyes. "Then the American Army is even more foolish than I thought. You look tired, my old friend. Would you like to rest? You are safe here. At least, as safe as any of the rest of us."

Jim felt himself relaxing almost in spite of himself. Sarpa had that effect on him. You might think him the lyingest little sonofabich on earth, but at least he was good at it.

It had been a hard little hump over another four kilometers and he was, in truth, damn near reaching the exhaustion point. And he'd noted the layout of the camp as he was coming in, and had approved. It was atop a knoll high enough to make any enemy assault have to come uphill, but not so high that it was obvious dominant terrain. Fields of fire had been cleared out to the maximum effective range of the motley assortment of machine guns he spotted in well-camouflaged bunkers around the perimeter. The defenders had, wisely in his opinion, given the fact that air superiority now belonged to the other side, not cut down any of the overarching jungle canopy to get these cleared fields of fire. Anyone overflying it would see only unbroken jungle.

They'd been challenged twice on their way in, both times by sentries he hadn't seen. And the route in had been reasonably complicated, with a couple of right-angle turns and one damn near one-eighty—bespeaking a path through a minefield. Jim would have bet there were also claymores artfully placed to do the most good.

Perhaps he could relax.

But not yet.

"Lieutenant Drot tells me you came alone," Sarpa said.

"Did he, now?"

"I didn't think so," Sarpa said, grinning widely. "You are as careful as always. That is good. One never knows when or where the traitors will strike."

"I learned from an expert," Jim replied. "Seems you've managed to survive quite well too."

Sarpa chose to take the comment as a compliment, nodding his head in seeming modesty. "Against all odds," he said. "But you know all about that."

"Where are the others?" Jim asked. There were no women, no children, none of the dogs that inevitably hung around the Montagnard villages. This was a fighting position, pure and simple.

"Safely hidden away," Sarpa said. "Deeper in the jungle, where the Viets never go."

The word, Viets, was spoken as an expletive. Not too much of a surprise there, since the Han Chinese–descended Vietnamese had been trying to wipe out the Indo-Malayan–descended mountain people for the last fifty years.

Now, of course, there was only one side. Made it simpler, as far as the Montagnards were concerned.

"And the Americans," Jim asked. "Where are they?"

"Waiting for you," Sarpa said. "Come. We will celebrate your arrival."

Hauck and Dickerson were in a good overwatch position just out of the range of the direct-fire weapons guarding the Montagnard position. Jerry traced Captain Carmichael's path through the minefield using battered Zeiss binoculars that had once belonged to an SS captain, liberated shortly after D-Day by Corporal Daniel Hauck of the 101st Airborne Division and passed down to his son as Dan Hauck's only worthwhile possession when he died of alcoholism.

He counted paces and estimated azimuths as the group made its complicated way through the minefield, providing a running commentary to Dickerson, who wrote it all down. He hoped they'd never have to use the information to try to infiltrate the camp—the minefield was one of the least of their worries—but you used anything you got and left nothing to some dreamy hoped-for outcome.

"He's in," Jerry said. "And I think the guy coming to meet him is Sarpa."

"You see any of the roundeyes?"

Jerry swept the area through the still crystal-clear lenses. He had, over the years, tried all sorts of other types of binoculars, both issued and purchased, and had found none that matched the Zeiss. Germans might be assholes, he said to anyone who asked why he still carried the scarred and outdated piece of equipment, but they sure as hell know how to make good stuff.

"Not a sign of them," he finally said. "Place is thoroughly bunkered in, they could be in any one of them. It was me, I'd have 'em hid out and separated. Maybe not even in this position at all. Keep some smart guys, like us, from comin' in, tryin' a rescue."

Dickerson grunted, thinking that he wouldn't particularly like to be on a team that tried to get into this particular target. It looked like a tough nut to crack.

"I'll get an antenna up," he said. "Let the SFOB know we made contact, and that Sarpa is here."

Jerry agreed. "And after that," he said, "you want to go on a little scout?"

Back in Nakhon Phanom the radio operator heard the keyed code that indicated message traffic was on the way, quickly tapped out Send, and was rewarded with a stream of code transmitted so fast it sounded like a short Blurrrrt! He tapped out the receipt code, and the radio went silent.

The burst transmission had been automatically recorded. Now it was slowed down sufficiently for the operator to recognize the code. He quickly noted the corresponding letters in five-letter groups, then turned to his one-time pad. The first group would have noted the correct page on the corresponding pad of the sender, and the group of random letters that would have been used to start the text. X then became C, B turned into O, V into N, and so forth until the word Contact was spelled out, then made, then with. The entire decoded message was written contactmadewithsarpacoordinatesKX706245nosignofamericanhostagesstandingby. It was up to the radio operator to separate out the words into a coherent message—not too difficult in this case, but in long and detailed messages a complicated task.

He tore the used page out of the one-time pad, unlocked the burn bag, put it in, locked the bag back up. The bag would be under constant visual surveillance until its contents were thrust into a burn barrel and set afire. The burn barrel was just that, a fifty-five-gallon drum with air holes drilled into it, the entire rig set up on a spit and equipped with a turning handle. You constantly turned it as the contents burned, making sure combustion was complete as well as mixing the ashes so thoroughly nothing could be used to reconstitute the contents. All the procedures were observed and documented by at least one other person, and the resulting log kept in a classified safe. It might not have been a perfect system, but it was as close as you could get in a field situation.

Besides, even if someone got hold of the used page from the one-time pad, it would be all they had. Yes, they could decode that particular message, but no other. The pad's code groups had been randomly generated in a giant computer somewhere in the state of Maryland, and no page remotely resembled any other. It was as nearly unbreakable as any system had ever been, the only danger being that the enemy might somehow get a copy of one of the pads and be able to decipher any message that used the same pad. That was why the radio operators protected the pads with their lives, and also why there were procedures to signal the receiver that the sender was operating under duress.

The final safeguard was the fact that each radio operator had a unique characteristic in keying code. His "hand." It was as identifiable to someone who was used to it as was handwriting. It couldn't be faked.

Using the computer to generate random code eliminated one of the early faults of one-time pads. The first ones had to actually be written by hand, using great numbers of specially trained experts. It worked okay until, as in the case of the Soviets just before the outbreak of World War II, you just had too much demand for pages. The Soviets had thought that, as long as the pages were inserted randomly into various codebooks, they could get away with using duplicate pages.

They were wrong. Codebreakers from Army Intelligence cracked the code in a project that came to be known as Venona. The result was the pinpointing of various Soviet espionage agents infesting the U.S. government, academia, and industry. The Rosenbergs went to the electric chair still unaware that their own side had tripped them up with faulty tradecraft.

All this was unknown to the radio operator, who had a certain set of procedures to follow and by God was going to follow them, no matter what.

He signed out of the code room, leaving his assistant in charge of the radios until his return, and carried the deciphered message to Lieutenant Colonel Petrillo. The colonel breathed a sigh of relief.

"Wait one," he told the operator. "We'll need to send this to CINCPAC. Reformat and send."

CINCPAC, the acronym for Commander-in-Chief, Pacific, was the intermediate command between operations in Southeast Asia and the Chiefs of Staff in the Pentagon. Ordinarily the command was run by a Navy admiral, and most of the staff was Navy as well, reflecting the fact that the Pacific was regarded as a U.S. Navy lake. It had been thus during the war in Vietnam and the decisionmakers found little reason to change it. After all, the command was still fully staffed, the channels were open, the procedures in place. Reorganizing would take a lot of time and money, and there was little of the latter to be had now that the administration and Congress had decided that America didn't need the large military establishment that had grown up during the war.

Transmission to CINCPAC was an entirely different matter. There was simply too much traffic to use the one-time pads that were so useful in the field. Some of the reports that had come in from Tan Son Nhut, the headquarters of the commander of the U.S. forces in Vietnam, had run to the hundreds of pages, and there were hundreds of other messages coming in from various commands throughout Southeast Asia.

These messages were sent via coded teletype machines, which generated their own random code for each letter or number. It was a system similar to that used by the Germans in their Enigma machine, but incredibly more sophisticated. It was a simple, albeit elegant system. You typed in the message, the machine did all the work, it was sent to a similar machine somewhere else, and that machine translated the code back into the original message. These machines could only talk to each other, using a coded key system that unlocked a particular routine. That way if someone captured a system, as the British did with an Enigma, all you had to do was change the coded key and that particular system was useless.

Thus the radio operator was secure in the knowledge that while he tapped the message into his teletype the team's information was as secure as the resources of the most powerful nation on earth could make it.

"They've made contact," Petrillo told the assembled group in the operations room.

There were no cheers; just a few grunted expressions of satisfaction at the news that at least one of the hurdles had been passed. After a moment the S-4 sergeant went back to planning with the air liaison officer the details of the first air drop of supplies, the weather officer continued to consult his meteorological charts, and the operations sergeant, once again, went over alternate courses of action for a hundred different scenarios.

Petrillo handed the report to Sloane, who read it quickly and then cocked an eyebrow in question.

"Pretty sketchy, isn't it?" he said after Petrillo showed no sign of responding to his unasked question.

"Short and sweet," Petrillo said. "Just like the book says."

"Wouldn't it have been better to wait, get more details before transmitting?"

"You havin' a little trouble making up your mind, Captain? First you wanted them to transmit every stop, now you want 'em to wait. Which is it?"

Sloane flushed in embarrassment. Petrillo was right, of course, but that didn't make it any less irritating.

Petrillo decided to take pity on the young captain. After all, this was probably his first experience at matters of this sort, where Mark had been doing it in one assignment or another for over ten years. Problem was, you always had the tendency to second-guess everyone, including yourself. Wasn't exactly as if there was a Field Manual on it. Let's see, FM 2742 dash 14, Subject: *Trying to Run an SFOB when you have troops in the field and they don't damned well want to talk to you.* Maybe he should write one.

"We've got the first supply drop ready to go," he said, changing the subject slightly and letting the matter pass. "Soon as we get the word from Carmichael, we'll get it going."

Grateful to talk of matters far less nebulous than the actions of a team in the field, a team moreover that was run by a man notorious for his independence of action, Sloane asked what the bundles would contain.

"Sustainment stuff," Petrillo replied. "Medicine, some rations, radio equipment and batteries, both ground-ground and air-ground. Some light weapons, all Chicom manufacture. Got an agent in Hong Kong, gets all that kind of stuff we need from the Reds. Becoming regular little capitalists, they are."

"SAM-7s?" asked Sloane. The SAM-7, code named Grail by the Soviets, was a hand-held antiaircraft missile system. Introduced late in the war in Vietnam, it had made life even more interesting for American and South Vietnamese pilots. Its heat-seeking guidance system homed in on the exhaust of the aircraft and the five pounds of high explosive set off when it impacted would shred an engine. It wasn't terribly effective against the fast movers, but could be devastating when used against helicopters.

"Yep," Petrillo replied. "Though so far the communications from Sarpa haven't indicated too much problem with NVA air assets. Suspect that's more because they can't find his people than it is unwillingness to use them. After all, by now they have the biggest air force in Southeast Asia. All those choppers and planes we left sitting on the runways? We're gonna see them again."

So, Sloane thought. We wait, once again. It was driving him crazy. If this was what intelligence work was going to be like he wasn't sure he was cut out for it.

"I'm going to go for a run," he announced. There was still a pretty decent dirt track left over from when the Air Force had maintained this base, and right now physical exertion seemed to be the best way to work off his frustration. It had taken a long time to recover enough from his wounds to be able to run again, and he wasn't going to let that ability get away from him.

"Good idea," Petrillo said. "But by the way, you might want to watch for the cobras. They like to get out there and sun themselves early in the morning. Ran over three of them yesterday."

Shit! Sloane thought as he changed into his running shorts a little later. Problem was, he didn't know if Petrillo was jacking with him, or actually warning of danger. Either way he was screwed. If he didn't run the story was sure to get out of how well and thoroughly he'd been spooked.

And if he did, he was going to have to do it very carefully. Just in case he tucked a little Browning .25 semiautomatic into his waistband.

A little later he almost had a heart attack when a crooked

stick lying at the side of the trail suddenly moved into the grass.

"Jesus Christ!" Jerry Hauck exclaimed. "I do believe that's Willie Korhonen." He made a minute adjustment to the Zeiss binoculars.

"Yep," he said. "It's him, all right. I'd know that square-headed motherfucker anywhere." He passed the glasses to Dickerson.

Dick focused the lenses for his own eyes, pointed them toward where Jerry had been looking. Captain Carmichael was talking to a Caucasian male, and from the looks of it, the talk wasn't going very well. That it was Korhonen he had no doubt. He had only passing acquaintance with the officer, but the block-built Finn was unmistakable.

Only thing Dickerson couldn't figure was, why were Carmichael and Korhonen yelling at each other?

"You'd think he'd be grateful, us coming in to get him like this," he said as he passed the glasses back to Hauck.

"Or maybe pissed off because it took so long?" Jerry offered.

"Well, hell, that ain't our fault."

"Maybe not. Alls I know is, I'd spent a few years in a bamboo cage, I might be a little perturbed too. Especially if it took a bunch of 'Yard renegades to get me out, instead of my own people."

Dickerson was silent for a moment. Then, making up his mind, said, "Well, fuck him if he can't take a joke."

Carmichael and Korhonen were indeed screaming at each other, and it had nothing to do with what the two NCOs were thinking.

It had started when Sarpa had led him to a bunker and had told him that Korhonen was inside. Then he had left.

Jim had braced himself for what he might find. It was likely that the man inside would look nothing like his memories. Seven years a POW, in the worst possible conditions a man could endure? What would that do to you?

The guys who had finally come home from their stay in the Hanoi Hilton had looked bad enough. Had undergone torture of the type most people would think medieval. Had starved and suffered from injuries and diseases, and had, worst of all, been horribly, terribly alone. At least until as a result of the Son Tay raid the NVA had gotten spooked and had brought them all together out of the outlying POW camps where conditions were even worse that those at the Hilton.

But in the scheme of things these men had it easy, compared to the ones being held in the South, and in Laos and Cambodia. Nick Rowe, held in such conditions for five years until finally escaping, had written a book describing his experiences, and in reading it Jim had once again vowed never to be taken alive. There were some things worse than dying.

Thus he was quite taken by surprise when Korhonen himself walked out of the bunker, and to Jim's eyes looked little different than he had the last time Carmichael had seen him at Fort Bragg, nearly ten years ago. The hair that he always kept cut short was a little more gray, and there was less of it. He had another scar on his face, this one starting just beneath the left eye and continuing up into the eyebrow, the puckered flesh making it look like he always had one eye cocked in question. That and the old one, where he had taken a Russian bayonet slash across one cheek, down across the corner of his mouth and into his chin, and that turned that side of his mouth into a permanent frown, made for quite a picture.

"I know you, I think," he said, his accent after all these years still heavy with the intonations of his native Finland.

"We've met," Carmichael confirmed. "Back at Bragg."

"You volunteer for this, gonna be some kind of big hero?"

Jim bristled. He sure as hell hadn't come all this way to be insulted. He opened his mouth to speak, thought better of it, fought his anger down.

"You look well enough to walk," he said. "Let's talk about how we're gonna get you out of here."

Korhonen grinned. "I'm not fuckin' gonna go nowhere."

And that was when the argument started.

"I've got orders to get you out of here," he said, aware that his voice was rising but unable to do anything about it.

"Your orders ain't my orders," Korhonen replied.

"Last I heard, you were an officer in the United States Army," Jim replied. "And I'm in charge of this mission, hence, rank or not, you're to follow my lead. Now, if you want me to get hold of the people back in Thailand to give you specific orders, I will."

"Yah, and where were you and the fucking people behind you when I was waiting for you to come get me, huh? You weren't too worried about it then. Why now?"

"Because everyone thought you were dead. Nobody had heard anything from you or about you since the crash. You were declared Missing in Action, and after the proper time, Killed in Action—Body Not Recovered. You know the drill. How the hell were we supposed to know they'd captured you? Hell, Glenn is bound to have told you that—he was in the JPRC. Where is he, anyway?"

"Sick," Korhonen replied. "I'll take you to him in a moment. And as for not knowing I was alive, bullshit! The Viets told me they'd notified the Red Cross they had me. They also told me that, after all the rest of the POWs were returned in '73, it was obvious the Americans didn't want me. So, they said, we can keep you forever. What you know about that, hah?"

"And you believed them?"

"I never believed a goddamn thing they said. But I also know you got radio intercepts, agents, *chieu hois* that tell you all about the prisoner of war camps. Makes me not believe you either."

Jim didn't have an answer, and it infuriated him the more. He'd had his own experiences with treachery at higher levels, and couldn't for sure tell Korhonen he was wrong.

He decided to change tack. He and Korhonen had gotten so close in shouting at each other that their noses were almost touching. The Finn's breath was foul from rotten teeth and God knew what other ailments. He took a step back.

"I don't know about all that," he said. "What I do know is that we can get you back. Don't you want to go home?"

"Home?" Korhonen made a sweeping gesture. "This is my home now. These are my people."

"People who blackmail us, tell us they're not going to let you go until we do as they say? Hell, you're just as much a prisoner here as you were in the tiger cages."

Now Korhonen smiled. "Hah," he said. "I told Sarpa you could be fooled."

A light seemed to go on inside Jim's head.

"They're not keeping you prisoner at all, are they?"

"These are my friends. They save me from the Communists. They need help. I tell them how they can get help. Would you even be here, if it were not for that?"

Jim had to admit that, no, he would not. The Montagnards had been left to their own devices, despite their sacrifices during the war. He would himself not be alive had it not been for the 'Yards. His bones would have long since been bleaching white on a hillside somewhere.

And he couldn't force Korhonen to go if he didn't want to. It would be dicey enough getting a willing subject out, particularly if they had to use Skyhook.

"So," he said. "What's your plan of action?"

Korhonen grinned again. "We kill some more goddamn Communists," he said. "You gonna help?"

Wouldn't be as if I hadn't done it before, Jim thought.

"Right now, take me to Glenn," he said. "What kind of sick?"

"Don't exactly think they're gonna kiss and make up," Jerry said. "But at least it don't look like it'll come to blows."

"What're they doin' now?"

"Went into one of the bunkers—big enough it looks like it might be the headquarters. Or maybe a dispensary. Saw a guy comin' out of it earlier, had a bandage on his leg."

"Still no sign of Parker?"

"Not yet. I reckon they may be holdin' him back, won't give us both of 'em until we do what we say we're gonna do."

Dickerson thought for a moment. Looked around the little shelter they'd made for themselves in the rocks. It wasn't exactly the Ritz, but it would do. They'd stretched a poncho out over the top to shed the rains that were coming with more and more frequency, and were, generally, dry most of the time. The position had good visibility on all sides, plenty enough to warn them if someone was coming, anyway, and they'd strung tripflares for nighttime intruders. They'd positioned claymores close in, backing them up against the massive tree trunks that surrounded them. That way they'd be shielded from backblast if they had to use them, if not the blast overpressure. But both of them figured that shattered eardrums were a small price to pay if it got that serious.

About the only thing they didn't have was a nearby source of water, and that bothered Dick. One of them had to make a run to a stream nearly two hundred yards away at least once a day. It was the only time either was exposed.

"We'll stay here for now," Dickerson finally said. "I know the captain, he ain't gonna put up with a bunch of bullshit. Glenn Parker is in that compound, he's gonna find him. Then we'll see."

The plan, worked out at the last moment, was for the two NCOs to remain in hide positions outside the Montagnard position until Jim Carmichael gave them the signal to come on in. Pitifully small as a backup, but better than risking everyone if the whole thing had been a trap.

"I'll tell SFOB about Korhonen tonight, when I make commo," he said. "'Bout your turn to make the water run, ain't it?"

Lieutenant Tan Vanh Trinh scoped the American position yet once again. He grunted in grudging admiration.

Of course, in the old days their preparations would have done them little good. Trinh had led an anti-infiltration group working against the recon teams the Americans kept sending into Laos, and had been very good at his job. He had four American kills and at least two probables to his record, and he had lost count of the Nung and Montagnard team members. For this he had been highly decorated, promoted, and when the war finally ended, promised repatriation to his farm east of Hanoi, there to live in relative ease.

He and his team had, in fact, been in a truck headed that way when the message came. He was told to report to the regional commander near Tchepone, and to waste no time.

Not that it was a problem getting there. No longer did they have to travel the bumpy roads at night, always fearful when they heard the drone of an airplane. It felt strange, not having to look always to the sky. Not right, somehow. He often wondered if he'd ever be able to hear a plane again without cowering as deep as he could get in a hole, waiting for the rain of fire and steel that had swept away so many of his comrades.

But Lieutenant Trinh was nothing if not obedient. He informed the driver of the change, ignored the protests of his men, and within a day was at Tchepone.

"The Americans are coming back," he was told. "And you are to find them."

He cursed. Back in the old days he would simply have called for reinforcements, surrounded the position, and under covering fire from mortars and B-40 rockets, assaulted. Antiaircraft guns would have been positioned all around to take care of any would-be rescuers.

There would have been casualties, of course. The recon

teams fought like tigers when they were cornered. But the result would have been foreordained. A team of six to eight men, no matter how good, could not defeat two or three hundred. Not without a lot of help, and increasingly in the days when the war wound down, that help did not come.

Now, however, he could not attack the position. Not without giving himself away, and he'd seen enough of the Montagnard position on the knoll across the way to know that the moment a shot was fired they'd come swarming out, and the chase would be on. This time he would be the quarry, and that wasn't something he was used to or that he would have looked forward to.

The commander in Tchepone had promised him backup in the form of at least a seasoned battalion, but they would be at least two days away. He could have his mission done and be away long before their arrival. Then there would be more medals.

Wait for the right moment, he told himself. It will always come.

CHAPTER 13

Jim Carmichael walked down the steps to the indicated bunker, opened the door, and was hit with a smell of putrefying flesh so strong he had to swallow hard to avoid gagging. It took a moment for his eyes to adjust from the sunlight outside, but he didn't need eyes to tell him what was in the bunker.

Dead people, and those about to be.

Some of the men lying in the cots had obviously suffered combat wounds. Legs and arms were missing, one man had a great gaping hole in his stomach, yet another was swathed in bandages from chin to the crown of his head, the bandage leaking pinkish red.

That he could deal with. Combat wounds were an accustomed sight. He'd treated enough of them himself over the years. You performed the lifesaving steps, stabilized the patient, and got him evacuated.

There would be no evacuation here, but the Montagnard medics moving around taking care of the patients were calm, competent, and would do the best they could. Some of the men would die, some would not. He'd be able to improve their survival chances once he got the first resupply bundle and its load of antibiotics. He recognized one of the medics from a camp in II Corps, older now, but then so was everyone. He'd thought then that the young man, given different circumstances, would have made a hell of a doctor.

Now it looked like he was, of a sort.

But the combat wounded were the least of it. At the other end of the bunker lay the source of the smell. He moved closer. The man lying on the cot was in obvious agony, twisting and turning and trying to find some method of taking the pressure off skin that looked like someone had hit it with a flamethrower. Blisters covered his legs and lower trunk, and from the neck up bright red petechiae bloomed. His lips were covered with blisters and from the sound of his breathing Jim knew that his lungs were filling up with liquid.

The others were, in varying degrees of seriousness, like him. And it wasn't just young men of combat age, like the wounded at the other end. There were several women and, worst of all, at least three children.

As he watched, a couple of the medics picked up one of the bodies, obviously now relieved of his pain, and started to carry it toward the rear door. A black, leathery chunk of skin slipped off from where one of them had grasped him and the body dropped to the floor. It made a curious thunk, like a full watermelon.

He stepped around the corpse, looking for Glenn Parker. Was this what Korhonen had meant, when he said Glenn was sick?

If so, it was a hell of a lot worse than being sick.

"What the hell happened here?" he asked, aware that Korhonen was close behind him and glad to hear that the other man was having as much trouble with the smell as he was. It was almost as if you were afraid to take a deep breath, fearful that whatever had afflicted these people would find its way into your lungs as well.

"The Communists," Korhonen said. "They did it."

The jungle is an unforgiving place. Leave a scratch unattended and it is likely to become the home of pathogens yet unknown to modern medicine. For many years the tribespeople had depended upon their own healers, men and women who knew what fungus or chunk of bark or plant was good for what ailment. And the system had worked reasonably well. Sometimes you got healed, sometimes you didn't. If you didn't, it must mean that the gods that inhabited the rocks and trees were angry with you.

Then the French had come, and after them the Americans. Bringing ampoules and pills and injections that cured the infections like magic. No longer did you have to worry about malaria—it could be cured, or better yet, prevented. Children stopped dying of diarrhea. Women were more likely to survive childbirth than not.

So the old ways went away, were remembered only dimly by the eldest of the tribe. Why search for magical bark when you could go to the dispensary and come away with all the pills you needed?

Then the Americans left, and the diseases came back even worse than before, because in the intervening years the tribespeople lost the immunity gained from having the various diseases in lesser degrees of seriousness, and surviving.

Parker had been visiting one of the outlying villages, Korhonen explained. Since his rescue he had made it a practice to make the rounds of the places where the dependents of Sarpa's group hid away in the jungle, providing what help he could, using the drugs left over from the camps from which the Montagnards had fled in advance of the North Vietnamese final assault.

"They heard a plane flying over," Korhonen said. "Didn't worry too much about it. They were well concealed, just like this place. Had bunkers to get into if there was any sign of an attack.

"Then the rain started to fall. They were surprised. It was the middle of dry season, no rains for weeks, and none expected. Still, they didn't think much of it. The drops hit the trees above, came wafting down through the leaves, and they put their pots out to catch it.

"But it wasn't like any rain they'd ever seen. The drops were yellow, sticky. What is this? some of them said. One man took a bit of it onto his finger, tasted it.

"By then they were burning. It felt like someone had poured acid on his skin, Glenn said. He had sense enough to cover his head, pull his shirtsleeves down, try to get to shelter.

"What you're seeing here are the survivors of a village of over two hundred people," Korhonen said. "Most of the others died on the spot. Throwing up and shitting, all at the same time. Skin falling off in sheets. Some of them went crazy, running around until they were exhausted, then falling down to die. The man who had put a drop on his tongue choked to death, his tongue so big he couldn't get air around it.

"And they continued to die, the survivors. Each day there are fewer. Some will make it—not many."

No wonder he wants to kill them all, Jim thought of

Willi Korhonen. Anyone who could do this, deserves to die.

And I think I might just help him.

"Where's Parker?" he asked, steeling himself for the sight of his old friend.

"Down here," Korhonen replied, throwing aside a mosquito net to reveal the figure on the cot.

Jim's first thought was that Glenn didn't look so bad. Certainly not like the others on the ward.

Then he saw the burns at the corners of his friend's mouth, the redness around his nostrils, the great patch of hair that had fallen from his head and was now lying beside him on the pillow.

Oh, shit, he thought. Where he had worried about getting a resisting Korhonen into a Skyhook rig, he knew now that it would have been an easy task compared to getting Parker out of here. There was no way he would survive the shock.

"They've been keeping him sedated," Korhonen said. "If we had enough drugs, we would do them all."

"I'll get you the drugs, and anything else you want," Jim replied. "Where are my quarters? We'll take him there. I'll take care of him myself."

He felt helpless. There wasn't a great deal he could do for Glenn Parker, other than try to keep him comfortable and treat the symptoms. It wasn't as if there was some wonder drug, some antibiotic that he could administer that would suddenly, almost magically, cure him.

He racked his brain for dimly remembered treatments for chemical burns, because that was obviously what he had here. Like the mustard gas used in the First World War, it blistered wherever it touched, burned the lungs, and when it was ingested, burned the intestinal tract as well.

Keep him hydrated—that was the first and probably most important step. He'd already given Parker one of the two bags of serum albumin he carried in his rucksack, would give the other before the night was out. He wished he had some way of intubating the patient—getting liquids down past an obviously damaged esophagus—but didn't have the equipment.

He'd already administered a quarter-grain of morphine when Glenn showed signs of coming up out of the drug-induced coma the Montagnards had put him in. It just showed, Jim thought, how much they valued the Americans, that they would expend precious morphine on an American and leave their own people to suffer.

Tomorrow he'd summon Dickerson and Hauck in, get the resupply drops ordered, request special items to take care of the casualties. Knowing that Korhonen was an active part of Sarpa's plan had at least removed one of his worries. He'd kept the team split in case of double-cross, but that seemed to be the least of the problems at the moment.

That the NVA, or someone, was using chemical warfare was beyond doubt. Against all international norms, but then the Viets had never worried too much about various conventions and treaties.

But who was supplying it to them? Jim didn't know a lot about chem/bio—only the very sketchy briefing all the officers had received in the Advanced Course—but was fairly certain it required a fairly sophisticated laboratory and well-developed expertise. The NVA were unlikely sources of the substance.

Russians? Chinese?

Did it matter?

He watched the hissing flame of the Coleman lantern.

Alix would say you've gotten yourself in way beyond your depth, he thought.

And I'm not sure she's wrong.

Jimmy Hauck made his slow, careful way down to the stream to fill the canteens. Every few moments he stopped, intently scanned the terrain, listened for any noise that shouldn't be there. He paid particular attention to the jungle floor—few people were good enough to walk through it without leaving at least some sign.

Satisfied finally, he would walk a little farther.

Though there was no outward sign, he couldn't shake the feeling that something was wrong. The hackles at the back of his neck stood up, and often he thought that if he could just stare through the foliage a little farther he would see someone.

If he was the point man on a patrol he would have halted them, they would have spread out and would have made an area recon. If someone made contact they would instantly execute an IAD, an immediate action drill. Whoever made the contact would let loose with a burst on full automatic, somewhere in the area of where he thought the enemy to be. No aimed fire—the purpose wasn't to kill anyone. It was to make them keep their heads down.

IADs made someone think twice about following you. Especially when they'd know from experience that you were probably also sowing toe-popper mines on your backtrack.

But he wasn't point man, and there was no one to back

him up, and they needed the water. You could get by without food for a long time, but the jungle heat dehydrated you so quickly that if you didn't get at least a quart every two hours, even at rest, you'd soon lose all effectiveness. You'd be stumbling and running into things and given enough time would drop from heat exhaustion. Or worse, heatstroke.

He'd emptied his rucksack back at the hide site, now had it full of collapsible canteens. Easy moving at the moment. Only weight was the irreplaceable weapons belt and the rifle. Wouldn't be that way on the way back, with the rucksack full of water. And it was all uphill.

Not for the first time he thanked Captain Carmichael for the punishing physical training they'd done as a matter of course back in Bad Tölz. Oh, he'd hated it then. A couple of years at Bragg after the last tour in Vietnam, not a lot to do except go to the Sport Parachute Club and drink beer, and his formerly whip-thin frame had filled out so much he'd had to get his fatigues let out. The only PT he'd gotten had been trying to outrun the MPs on his infrequent trips down to Combat Alley—Fayetteville's notorious bar section. And, he admitted, he hadn't done very well at that. Mostly he'd ended up in back of the patrol car, new lumps on his head.

He sure as hell wouldn't have been able to make the last few days if he'd stayed like that. Bad enough that his ankle still hurt like hell.

He stopped again, watched for foliage that moved in a direction other than that determined by the slight breeze that came through the trees. Nothing. The only sounds were those of the denizens of the jungle. The far-off howls of a tribe of monkeys. Closer in the clacking of the mandibles of a swarm of leaf-cutter ants, steadily reducing a bush to nothing more than branches, then bearing the leaves like conquering heroes on their way back to the den.

He moved forward. Another forty or so yards to the stream. He approached it from a different angle each time, never setting a pattern. If they stayed where they were much longer it was his intention to search out another water source. It might be farther away than this one, but the more you went to one spot, the more likely it was that someone could find you. He knew he was leaving sign as well, careful as he was. Any skilled tracker could find it.

Close to the edge of the water he stopped once again. He hadn't had a drink in the last half hour and the smell of water was tempting. Too tempting. Never rush into anything, one of his team sergeants had beaten into his head. That's what they count on.

He crouched behind a wait-a-minute vine, listened and looked for another half hour.

Not completely satisfied, but deciding that if he was to get the water he was going to have to take a chance, he moved the last few feet to the edge of the stream.

He never heard the explosion.

Jim Carmichael was almost asleep when he heard the beeping from inside his rucksack. He pawed through it, finally finding the Motorola two-way radio he'd insisted the mission director provide them with. Why? Petrillo had wanted to know. You can't make commo with us with these damned things.

No, but we can sure as hell make commo with each other, Jim had said. The Motorolas were light-years ahead of the old squad radios he'd tried to use in his tours in Vietnam. The squad radios, some wag had said, were truly essential equipment. They made wonderful substitutes for bricks when you wanted to whack someone in the head.

The only other radio that would have worked would have been the PRC-77, and it weighed at least fifteen pounds without battery. The battery not only added another five pounds of weight, it would have taken at least half a dozen of them to keep the radios going before they could be resupplied. With the weight the team was already carrying no one wanted the additional thirty or so pounds the PRC-77 would have represented.

The Motorola was not authorized in the Army supply chain, of course. It was lightweight, relatively weatherproof, utterly reliable, and, if you didn't have a lot of terrain between you and the recipient, made commo. The Army would adopt it, Jim was sure, after it had been re-engineered, had so many bells and whistles the Field Manual would weigh as much as the radio, and after it had long since been replaced by a model half the size, twice the range, and powered by sunlight.

He pressed the push-to-talk switch, said, "Go ahead."

"We got a problem," Dickerson replied.

"Nature?"

"Two-zero hasn't come back from the water run. And I heard an explosion in that direction."

Jim swore under his breath. There could have been a number of explanations for Jimmy Hauck's absence. None of them were good. He could have stepped on a piece of unexploded ordnance. God knew there were enough of those around. This section of Laos had been heavily bombed for a number of years. A number of those bombs had been cluster bomb units, CBUs. Some of them exploded like they were supposed to, but a heavy percentage didn't. Weatherproof, virtually indestructible, they lay in wait for the unwary. Oftentimes you could pick one up, throw it, and it wouldn't go off. Jim had come back to camp one day in 1966 to see one of the Vietnamese LLDB shooting at one he'd stuck up on a rock. Luckily he was a terrible shot.

All too often, however, the slightest jar and they would explode. The exterior was constructed of a thin metal shell; inside was a matrix of steel balls embedded in resin surrounding a chunk of military explosive. The bursting radius, the circle in which anyone unshielded would suffer at the very least a debilitating wound, was twenty-five meters. So you didn't stand much chance if you kicked one.

Or it could have been a toe-popper, left there by some long-forgotten recon team, in which case Jimmy would be lying there badly wounded.

Or it could be that they hadn't been as lucky avoiding the enemy as they'd thought.

Whatever it was, he had to get out there.

"Roger," he said. "I'm gonna send somebody out to guide you into the camp. You need to take care of Glenn." He quickly described the condition of the patient, told the sergeant what to do in his absence.

"Set up the radio, get SFOB, get an operational immediate resupply. Coordinate with Sarpa as to the drop zone." He reeled off a list of medicines and equipment they would need to treat not only Parker but the other victims of the yellow rain.

"Then stand by," he said.

After a moment he added, "And by the way. I don't come back, you continue the mission. Do you roger?"

Dickerson, who had intended to protest that it was he, instead of the captain, who should have been going after Hauck, recognized the tone in his commander's voice. His arguments would have fallen on deaf ears.

He rogered the last transmission.

And God be with you, he breathed.

Jim shrugged back into his web gear, grabbed the CAR-15, and headed out of the bunker, to see Willi Korhonen standing there with a squad of Montagnards.

"We heard an explosion," Korhonen said. "Getting ready to go check."

"May be one of mine. I know where he's supposed to be. I'll lead."

"With all due respect, Captain," one of the Montagnards said, in English that would have done a teacher proud, "we know the area. I was on RT Texas, out of CCN." He pointed to two others in the squad. One was armed with a cut-down RPD machine gun, the other had an M-16 with an M-203 40mm grenade launcher mounted beneath the handguard.

"These men, also, RT Texas. All that is left. The others here were II Corps Mike Force."

Jim grinned. "Then I'm in good company," he said. "Let's go."

They headed back out the way Jim had been escorted in. The troops maintained a healthy distance between men, alternated weapons from side to side, and once they entered the jungle outside the perimeter the drag man started walking backward, covering their rear.

"They're good," Jim said to Korhonen, who walked right behind him. The major was carrying an old Swedish K submachinegun—not a weapon Jim would have chosen to go up against someone who was armed with AK-47s, but that was his choice, wasn't it? He had a feeling that Korhonen would more than hold up his end in any firefight.

"I thought you came alone," Korhonen replied.

"I lied."

"Yah," Korhonen said after a moment. "I would have too."

If there was such a thing as perfect patrol movement the Montagnards were achieving it. They had assumed the attitude of what Jim often thought of as relaxed alertness. If you stayed too tense you got tired too quickly, and your performance suffered. If you were too relaxed you didn't catch the small signs that might mean the difference between life and death.

They moved quickly and surely, through areas that, although they showed no signs of being well traveled, were clear enough of obstacles that Jim realized they were used as normal avenues of approach. Took a hell of a lot of work to do this, he thought. His appreciation of Korhonen and Sarpa went up a notch.

Dickerson had given him an approximate coordinate where he had figured the explosion to be. As they moved Jim wondered how Jerry Hauck could have been taken by surprise, if indeed that was what happened. Jerry was one of the finest field soldiers he'd ever known. It wasn't like him to fall into an ambush.

Maybe we've just been away from it too long, he thought, and not for the first time. When you lived on the edge you developed senses that often defied logical explanation. Some called it gut feeling, a few of the newer guys had attributed it to extrasensory perception. Whatever it was, some had it and some didn't. The ones who did tended to survive. The others were shipped out in body bags.

He just hoped he wasn't going to have to put another friend in one.

Jerry Hauck stumbled and fell, only to be prodded back to his feet with the point of the triangular bayonet affixed to the barrel of the AK-47. He got up as quickly as he could, given the fact that his elbows were tied so far behind his back they touched, and his wrists were similarly bound.

He was falling less and less now, indicating that at least some of the equilibrium thrown off kilter by the explosion was coming back.

He hadn't expected to wake up. Had been terribly disappointed when figures swam into view, all of them pointing rifles at him. By that time he was already trussed like a hog, eliminating any thoughts of resistance. They'd stripped him of his rucksack, web gear, and weapon, and had obviously searched him quite thoroughly. One of them, Jerry figured him to be the officer, was examining the snub-nose .38 Special revolver he had carried concealed in an ankle holster.

"Get up!" the officer had said.

Jerry flailed his legs, acted even more addled than he actually was. Delay, he was thinking. Take as long as you possibly can. Make it a shorter chase for the people you know are coming after you.

The bayonets disabused him of that idea. The one wielded by an NCO with the face of an ascetic drew blood, and Jerry knew he was scant inches from being run through. Yeah, they wanted a prisoner, but not bad enough to die for it.

Professionals, these. He got up.

Still, he'd had trouble walking, and they seemed to understand he would. For the first couple of hundred meters two of them had flanked him, supporting him when he stumbled, pulling him to his feet when he fell.

But at last their patience had run thin, or perhaps they just knew he was faking it now. Now it was the bayonet again.

They were moving at almost a trot. The tactician in him disapproved. Easy to walk into an ambush like this. He just had to hope that if someone was setting up somewhere down the trail they would recognize him as an American and at least attempt to avoid hitting him.

More than likely a claymore would kick it off, and those were notoriously indiscriminate.

This is what you've been looking for, all this time, ain't it?

Might have been, he told himself. But now that he was faced with the probability of his imminent demise, he found that he wanted very much to live.

He only hoped that one thing or another happened, either he died or someone rescued him, before the torture started. He vowed that before that happened he would attempt an escape, as hopeless as that might be. Better a bullet than hours and hours of more pain than anyone could possibly endure.

He stumbled again.

The point man came across Jerry's sign, held up a closed fist in signal to stop, dropped to the ground and inspected the faint prints, and then waved an open hand forward. He changed track slightly, now going at a forty-five-degree angle from their original azimuth.

Everyone tensed slightly, knowing they were getting close. For all we know, Jim thought, they could be up there lying in ambush. A whole hell of a lot of them. And good as these folks are, we can't go up against a whole hell of a lot of them. A squad-sized element fighting its way out of a battalion ambush might be a good scene for the movies, but John Wayne was nowhere around.

Another hundred meters and the point man signaled a stop again. Then he waved the patrol leader forward. Carmichael and Korhonen followed.

The leaves that covered this part of the jungle floor were churned by a number of feet. And close to the edge of the stream the patrol leader pointed out a scorched spot. There was no blood to be found.

"Concussion grenade, I figure," said Korhonen. "Knocked him out, took him, and they're gone."

"How the hell did they know where to set the grenade?" Jim wondered.

"I expect if you were to search this stream you'd find where they set them every twenty-five yards or so. We used to do the same thing to the Russians. No matter where they go, you can get them. They probably watched your guys, took a chance that they were going to keep coming to this stream, even if in different spots, laid it all out."

"Shall we follow?" the patrol leader asked.

Korhonen glanced at Jim, who already had his mind made up. If the patrol didn't follow, he was going to. By himself. What he'd do when he found them, he didn't know. What he did know was that he couldn't leave Jerry Hauck in their hands.

The people back at NKP had made it quite clear. The one thing the U.S. government couldn't afford was to have the NVA waving a new prisoner of war, crowing about how it proved that the war wasn't over, that the new administration was just as bad as the old.

Not that he cared what the people who were running things wanted. He wasn't going to leave Jerry Hauck. He'd left far too many people behind. Wasn't going to happen again.

Korhonen gave an exaggerated sigh. "I suppose so," he said. Then he grinned.

"Looks like about the same number of people we have," he said, looking at the footprints. "Unfair. To them."

They quickly formed up again, the patrol members who had fanned out to form a hasty perimeter assuming their former positions and heading out. The trail wasn't hard to follow—Jim thought that, even as rusty as his skills were, he could have done it. Their quarry was making haste, doing little to hide their sign.

It was a battle between impatience and caution. On the one hand he wanted to get to them as quickly as possible, preferably before they linked up with a larger unit. On the other, it would do no one any good if they ran up on a booby-trapped claymore. He would have put one out to discourage any followers, couldn't see why they wouldn't too.

At the moment Jim was almost glad that he wasn't the patrol leader. He was far too emotionally invested in it. The thought of what they might be doing to his old friend would keep him pushing, perhaps far more than he should have.

Not that they were going slowly. The point man was pushing out as quickly as prudence would allow. Jim sensed an eagerness in the men. It was almost palpable; perhaps a mixture of excitement, sweat, and testosterone. So must the earliest ancestors of man have felt, he thought, when they sighted the enemy.

They came to a cleared area, all that was left of some Montagnard or H'Mong slash-and-burn farmstead, skirted around the edge of it, just as their quarry had done. The setting sun was just now touching the tops of the trees on the other side. It cast crimson rays into the sky.

Like bayonets, Jim thought. Bloody fucking bayonets.

Now he was stumbling again, and this time he wasn't faking it. The man behind him pushed him, hard, and he fell face forward. With his arms bound he had no chance to break the fall and he felt a great whoosh of air as his chest hit the ground. For a moment he lay there choking, and then he heard laughter. The bastards thought it was funny!

The lieutenant came back to see what was causing the commotion, spat a few angry words at the guards, who sheepishly picked Jerry up and set him on his feet again.

The lieutenant started to turn away, then jerked his head, noticing something. He put out a tentative finger, touched Jerry's neck.

The finger came away coated with blood.

The lieutenant again spat a few words, and this time Jerry caught most of it.

He's bleeding from the ears, the officer had said. He

could die. We cannot allow that. Hurry! And if he falls again, carry him.

Was wondering how come my neck felt wet, Jerry thought. Now I know. He concentrated on his head, trying to feel for anything other than the dizziness that spoke of inner-ear damage.

Nothing. But that didn't mean a hell of a lot.

Had my head beat in more times than I can count, he thought. And now I'm gonna croak because of a goddamn concussion grenade?

Didn't seem fair somehow.

CHAPTER 14

It was well after dark when the point man stopped again. They had closed the column considerably—even with the strips of luminous tape affixed to the backs of their hats it was easy to lose contact. A momentary bit of inattention and half the patrol would be going one way and the other part a completely different direction. Getting lost could be dealt with. Stumbling into one another and getting into a friendly firefight couldn't.

After a moment a whisper passed down the line summoned Jim to the front. The point man and patrol leader were waiting for him.

"Smell it?" the patrol leader asked.

Jim sniffed. Sure enough he could smell something. Smoke.

It could, of course, be the cooking fire of a H'Mong family that had somehow escaped the devastation that had been wrought on this area. Jim didn't think so. Those natives who hadn't fled the bombing had been herded up and moved by the NVA, afraid that they would provide assistance to the recon teams.

Jim tested the wind with a wet finger. The smoke was

coming from their left front at about ten o'clock. The smell was faint—either it was quite some distance away or it was a very small fire. Or both.

"They've stopped," he whispered to the patrol leader.

Korhonen, who had soundlessly slipped up to join them, nodded in agreement.

"They're used to this being their backyard," he said. "They were always chasing us, instead of the other way around. Makes for bad habits."

"Can you send a man to scout it out?" Jim asked the patrol leader. "All of us go up there, likely we'll make too much noise."

He'd thought to go himself, then realized that even in his best days he couldn't move through the foliage as silently as could one of the 'Yards.

The Montagnard nodded, then held a whispered conversation with the point man, who quickly shed everything he was carrying, taking only a pistol. He slipped into the underbrush, and it was as if he had never been there.

The rest of them assumed a close defensive perimeter as they waited. They didn't bother to put out tripflares or claymores. The last thing they wanted was to alert any reserve force the NVA might have to their presence. If they were compromised they would simply melt into the jungle, to link up later at a predesignated rally point.

Half an hour later the point man was back. He whispered to the patrol leader, who translated as fast as the scout could talk.

"About two hundred meters away," he said. "Ten men. Half are asleep, the other half on sentry duty. Very alert. He had to be special careful."

Ten. That was slightly more than they had figured.

Maybe Korhonen will think it's more of a fair fight now, Jim thought.

Nah. Probably won't.

"Did he see the American?"

The patrol leader posed the question, then translated as the scout answered. "Yes. He is in center of perimeter. Couldn't see if he's okay or not, but they wouldn't be guarding a dead man. One more thing. Says that one of the guards has AK roped to your friend's neck. He tries to get away, or we try to rescue him, all he's got to do is pull the rope tight and pull the trigger. Can't miss."

Shit, Jim thought. That ruined his hoped-for plan. He'd been thinking about trying to infiltrate the camp, get close enough to kiss them with the knife. But all it would take would be a small mistake and Jerry would be dead. If they'd only posted one or two sentries he might still have tried it. But five? No way.

"Ideas?" he asked.

Korhonen looked at the patrol leader, who nodded in agreement.

"We wait," he said. "Find out which way they're headed tomorrow, get in front of them."

Jim didn't see how that was going to work any better than trying to get in there at night. Probably even worse during the daytime. Set up an ambush? You'd have to make damned sure the guy holding the AK was dead before he could pull the trigger. How were you going to guarantee that? Even dead weight as he fell would be enough.

He voiced his concern.

"Bobby, here, has a neat trick," Korhonen replied. "He can do it."

The patrol leader nodded in confirmation. "Something I learned at CCN," he said. "I'll tell you how we used to do it."

The enemy patrol broke camp just before dawn, when the false light coming through the triple canopy made visibility tricky. Sometimes, Jim thought, I'd rather have it still dark.

The moisture that had collected as dew during the night softened the leaves underfoot, and that was good. Made it much easier to walk without making a lot of noise.

Bobby had stationed men all around the enemy campsite, making sure they knew in what direction the patrol was going to travel. Within moments of the start of movement the man covering the west side of the site came back to the patrol to tell them the enemy was going that way.

Bobby quickly made his deployments. The man who had spotted them would trail behind, making sure they didn't change direction. Jim gave him a spare Motorola with which to make contact.

The remainder of the group swung out into a circle, moving fast. They had to get ahead of the enemy, and thus would take the chance that there might be someone else out there. Someone who bore them no goodwill at all.

They had dropped rucksacks, carried only their web gear with plenty of ammunition, grenades, and a couple of canteens of water. And, of course, their weapons.

Two men carried claymore bags.

Jim had to hope this was going to work. If not, he was going to have a very dead friend.

*   *   *

Jerry woke only after being prodded so hard the bayonet brought blood. Goddamn them! Couldn't they just let him lie there and die?

He sat up and was rewarded with such dizziness he realized he was swaying. He wished he could reach up and touch his ears. Was he still bleeding? If so, it probably meant the explosion had ruptured something more than his eardrums. He thought it unlikely. He hadn't been particularly good at remembering the signs and symptoms of brain damage, or any other medical phenomenon, for that matter, during cross-training, but was fairly sure that if the covering around his brain was torn he would probably be dead by now.

Too bad. Wouldn't that have pissed them off! He almost smiled.

The officer spoke to his guard, who looked like he didn't care for what he was hearing. Then after a moment he roughly shoved a rice ball under Jerry's nose. It stank of *nouc mam,* the fermented fish sauce of which the Vietnamese were so fond, and, in Jerry's experience, was probably filled with insects of various kinds.

He wolfed it down. One of the primary tenets of E&E, escape and evasion, was to keep your strength up. That meant eating whatever was offered, as often as possible.

He made a choking sound, meant to inform them that he was thirsty. Reluctantly the guard unscrewed the cap off his canteen—an American plastic model, Jerry noted—and poured water in his mouth.

Jerry swallowed as much as the guard would allow— not much, but it was better than nothing, and for the first time he felt just the slightest tinge of hope. They weren't going to take him somewhere and shoot him, of that he was sure. If they wanted him dead he would already be. And they couldn't keep him tied up like this forever.

To test that theory he said aloud, "Shit."

The guard looked at him in askance.

"I need to take a shit," he said, although he didn't.

The guard obviously didn't understand English, and Jerry wasn't willing to tip his hand to how much Vietnamese he knew, so he repeated what he'd already said.

The officer, who obviously did understand, came over.

"Later," he said. "We go now."

Bobby had picked the site well, Jim conceded. There were very few chokepoints in the Laotian jungle, but this was one of them.

An outcropping of karst, the rotted granite of which the Annamese cordillera was largely made up, would make for hard going if they tried to climb it. To the other side was a swiftly flowing stream. Also not easy going. If the patrol kept on the same track they would have to come through here. And it seemed that they were—he'd gotten no transmissions on the Motorola to indicate they'd changed directions.

The team was lying in well-camouflaged ambush. The two RPD gunners had the flanks, both to contain the enemy within the kill zone and to take care of any possible outside response.

He and Korhonen were lying about five meters from each other near the middle. The others were scattered at about the same distance—just far enough apart that a grenade couldn't kill more than one, and close enough to support one another.

Bobby and another man had just come back in from where they'd been emplacing the claymores. They had taken a long time, sighting and resighting the mines until they were completely satisfied. Now Bobby held the clacker in his hand, ready to send the spurt of electricity down the lines that would detonate the explosives in the deadly little weapons.

Jim hoped Bobby knew what he was doing. The mines sprayed a fan of steel balls that totally annihilated anything in their path. They were excellent in an ambush if you wanted to slaughter everyone in the kill zone. Not so good otherwise.

The sweat was starting to run in rivulets down his sides even though it wasn't all that warm yet. He had his head cocked forward enough that the drops collecting in his eyebrows fell to the ground without getting into his eyes. He stifled the urge to get a drink of water. If you moved at all while in ambush position it was achingly slowly—the eye picked up movement before it did shapes—or you didn't move at all.

Best not to move at all.

The best measure of how well you were doing in a situation of this sort was the animals. They generally fled at your approach, at least those in visual range. If you were quiet enough the ones that didn't catch actual sight of you went on with their daily business.

It was after you settled down and remained motionless that the true effectiveness could be judged. They returned, tentatively at first and then with increasing frequency and casualness, heartened by the fact that the lumps lying on the jungle floor offered them no danger.

Above him a chittering flock of black and gold birds of

a type he hadn't seen before happily pecked away at the insects that infested the foliage, occasionally letting go with foul-smelling droppings that pelted his back. Some time later a krait slithered by about a foot from his nose, flicked a tongue out to feel his heat and then, finding him far too big to be prey, went on its way. Jim was glad that it was already quite warm. Occasionally the deadly little snakes would come up into your sleeping position to share your warmth.

A large bug of some kind crawled up his back and danced across his unprotected neck. He had to hope it wasn't a scorpion.

One night back in '66 he had made the mistake of lying on a bed of termites during an ambush like this. He hadn't known about them until they'd chewed through the poncho he'd laid down to protect against the ground moisture, whereupon they started trying to chew through his skin.

That was one night he'd had to abort the mission. When they'd gotten back to the patrol base he'd inspected himself by flashlight to find a hundred bleeding wounds where the bugs had torn pieces of flesh out of him with mandibles designed for tearing down trees.

Nothing like that today. It was pleasantly warm, speaking of the heat that would follow in the afternoon. Not too bad, though. Here high in the cordillera it never got as warm as it had in the lowlands back in Vietnam. What little sunlight made its way through the trees felt good on his back. It was easy to drift off into uncaring drowsiness when you were out here. No matter what your physical condition you were always tired when you were on patrol. Part of it was due to tension, part to the physical exertion, and a major part to the fact that you never really slept. Each sound brought you instantly awake, clutching your rifle and hoping the crackle of brush was an elephant, rather than a platoon of searchers resolutely looking for your position.

He was jerked back into alertness by a tug of the thread tied to his little finger. He in turn tugged the one connected to the man on his left. Each man in the position was thus linked.

They were coming, the unspoken message said. Get ready.

Jerry was feeling better and better, something he hid from his captors. The dizziness had gone away, but he still stumbled as often as he thought he could get away with. Make them think you're helpless, he strategized. That way they'll be all the more dumbfounded when you make your move.

They'd already become far more relaxed. The farther away from help from his side the more, he suspected, they believed they'd gotten away with their audacious move. He also suspected that there were reinforcements not too far away. That made his plans all the more urgent. If he waited to try to escape until he was surrounded by a battalion, rather than a small patrol, the likelihood he could get away would be so minuscule as to not be worth counting.

He'd repeated, several times, his need to take care of nature's call. The lieutenant kept telling him to wait. He'd considered just going in his pants to force the issue. There were few people who could stand the smell of feces from another person. Only the individual whose shit it was thought his shit didn't stink.

He glanced up to see the karst on his right, the rotted

granite so full of holes you could hide in there forever. Yep. It's time.

He also smelled water and realized once again just how thirsty he was. He wanted to ask for a drink again, remembered the guard who had so reluctantly given up his canteen. The lieutenant was well forward in the patrol, would not likely hear his request, and the guard damned sure wouldn't give him anything without a direct order.

Give it time, Jerry, he told himself. You'll either be drinking water a free man, or you'll soon be dead. Either way it was better than what he had.

He looked ahead, saw a small space where the vines and underbrush were thinner than the area in which they'd been traveling.

Right there, he told himself. That's where we're gonna do it.

Jim Carmichael saw the point man pass his position and tried to make himself even more a part of the ground than he was. He thought that the eager glitter of his eyes must give him away, shining like a beacon in the morning sun.

Number two, scarce a few feet behind the point. Bad tactics, he told them. Thank you very much.

Four and five, and finally he caught sight of Jerry Hauck. Stumbling and reeling. Making the Viet who was obviously his personal guard, who still had the AK tied to a rope around Jerry's neck, very pissed off.

Don't make him kill you, he silently told the NCO. All we need is a couple more seconds.

He'd noted the piece of brush that Jerry would have to pass before Bobby kicked off the ambush. He aimed at the guard, centering the front post of his sights on the man's head, then moving it slightly forward, to about the base of the nose. Sometimes it didn't seem like you'd need much lead when people were moving that slowly, but it could be deceptive. By the time your brain told your finger to pull the trigger, and then your nerve endings actually performed the act, a center of mass target could be moved a few inches. Just enough to make a brain shot a clear miss.

Almost there. His finger tightened on the trigger, taking up the slight amount of slack. Two more pounds of trigger pressure and the bullet would be on its way. Give it just a couple more seconds and . . .

There were no words to describe the actual deflagration of high explosive. He'd read comic books, so avidly his parents had despaired of his ever getting out of a fantasy world, as a kid. WHOOM! CRAAAK! BLAM!

If only they knew. It was a cataclysmic event, something you simply had to experience. And having done so, even as many times as he had, it still came as a surprise.

The claymores went off simultaneously, and where there had been living men was only empty space. Lying on the ground, he knew from experience, would only be shattered flesh and bone where there had once been hopes and dreams and the knowledge only a life could contain.

His target had disappeared.

So had Jerry.

Fuck!

Then came the familiar voice. "Sonofabitch. Motherfuck. Goddamn pricks!"

Jim grinned with relief. Leave it to Jerry Hauck to be pissed off when someone saved his life. He jumped up, ignoring the single-round reports as one or another of the Montagnards finished off the wounded. Ran to where Jerry was still lying on the ground, struggling to get to his feet. He ignored the NCO's loudly voiced protests, checked for wounds, and finding none extracted his survival knife from the sheath on his harness and cut Jerry's bonds away.

Hauck's arms fell uselessly to his sides. The tingling of blood returning told him that soon he was going to be suffering full-flood agony.

"Claymores?" he said. "You fucking crazy?"

"Only way we could figure we could get you out without their blowing your brains out," Jim said. He was already searching the dead guard for anything of value. "Guy who runs this patrol said that was how they used to get prisoners. Set up the claymores to take out everybody else, a chunk of C-4 to stun the target. Worked like a charm, he said. Had to hope he was right."

"Ain't doin' my hearing a goddamn bit of good," Jerry said. "Blow out my friggin' eardrums twice in twenty-four hours. We get back, I'm gonna claim disability."

Jim grinned. "You do just that," he said. "Hell, I'll even sign the papers. Right now, however, we might want to think about how we're gonna get back home so's you can do that."

Bobby was already signaling withdrawal. His team had thoroughly searched the dead, were carrying away anything of value. The weapons that hadn't been destroyed in the mine attack were a first priority. After that it was papers, diaries, pictures, maps. You never knew what someone might be carrying.

"Can you walk?" he asked Jerry.

"Goddamn right. Only one thing."

"What's that?"

"I really need to take a dump!"

"That's gonna have to wait. We be gone."

"Mighta known," Jerry said. He grabbed his CAR-15 from the guard who had carried it, cursed once again at the sight of a claymore pellet hole through the receiver. "Shit," he said, tossing it away. He grabbed one of the undamaged AKs, jacked the bolt back, put it on safe. The AK fired from the open-bolt position—that is, when the trigger was pulled it released the bolt, picking up a cartridge from the magazine, inserting it into the chamber and striking the primer with a fixed firing pin. Not the most reliable or the most accurate system in the world, but it had the advantage of not leaving a live round in the chamber when the barrel got hot enough from automatic-weapons fire to cause the bullet to go off all on its own.

Satisfied, he assumed the port-arms position and a loose, very loose, position of attention.

"Okay, fearless leader," he said. "We want to get the fuck out of here?"

Two hours later they took their first break. Even the 'Yards were sweating profusely. They'd been moving hard, putting as much distance between themselves and the ambush site as possible.

Jim took the opportunity to check Jerry's ankle, was happy to see that the flesh was granulating nicely. He replaced the filthy bandage with a fresh one, gave the NCO another couple of tetracycline tablets and a drink from his own canteen.

"Sorry, *Dai Uy*," Jerry said.

"About what? Close as I can tell, they had that whole damned stream rigged. Wasn't a place you could have gone, you wouldn't have run into something."

"Which means that . . ."

"Which means they had plenty of time," Jim answered for him. "They knew about us right from the beginning."

"And I think I know why," Korhonen said, waving the map he had taken from the NVA lieutenant. "What were your jump coordinates?"

Jim gave them to him. Korhonen showed him the map.

There was a clearly marked red X on exactly those coordinates.

"They were waiting for you on the DZ," he said. "Followed you the entire way. Now, how is it the NVA knew exactly where you were going to be?"

"Dunno," Jim said. "But I sure as hell intend to find out."

CHAPTER 15

The Thai recon team spilled out of the helicopter, dragging a bound and blindfolded prisoner with them. Finn noted in approval that they looked matter-of-fact, didn't have that wild-eyed fear-generated look so many of the Vietnamese STD teams had come back with after Saigon had started restricting cross-border operations to Vietnamese only.

They were armed and equipped much as the recon teams from SOG had been, CAR-15 carbines, some of which had the M-203 40mm grenade launcher slung beneath the front handguard, web gear loaded down with extra magazines and grenades, various signaling and survival gear stashed away in various pockets and pouches. Of course, they'd been trained and equipped by 46th Special Forces Company, so why wouldn't they have been? You messed with the tried and true only after something else had been well and truly proven.

This particular team had used little of their ammunition and few grenades. Their mission had been prisoner snatch, a task they'd accomplished with remarkably little fanfare. They'd moved as close as they dared to a large encampment, determined the patterns, looked for weaknesses, and finally decided on grabbing a member of one of the watering parties that left the perimeter carrying big plastic jugs down to the network of streams that fed the Mekong. Such parties usually consisted of six to eight soldiers, with only two of them serving as guards.

The Thais had ambushed them near the stream, killing the two guards with sound-suppressed M-3 Greaseguns firing the well-tested .45 ACP cartridge. Earlier uses of sound-suppressed weapons had shown them not to be all that useful—the suppressor bled off so much of the propellant gases that smaller rounds depending upon speed for their effect had proved not so effective after all. The .45 with its greater mass than the 9mm (over twice the weight of bullet), and orders of magnitude greater mass than the other choice, the .22, still had enough lethality to give one-shot stops even after the bullet had been slowed by one-third. It was like getting hit with a good-sized rock, a rock moving at seven hundred feet per second. Inasmuch as the old .45s and .44s used in the American West hadn't been moving much faster than that, and had proved themselves in hundreds of gunfights, it didn't seem like much of a sacrifice to give up a little bit of speed.

The ambushers had then set their sights on the other members of the watering party, killing all but one. The mathematics of it was implacable. A recon team of six men couldn't control more than one prisoner and maintain its own security.

They'd then evacuated the ambush site, moved several hundred yards away, and had called for extraction. The Hueys, flown by crews who had also been trained by the Americans and who had, during the campaigns in Laos during the war, gained invaluable experience in just such operations, had them picked up and back over the border within minutes.

They'd radioed ahead, alerting the FOB to the presence of the prisoner, giving Finn time to roust the Vietnamese interpreter he'd managed to recruit from one of the many refugee camps that were increasingly a feature of the Thai border area.

Finn took possession of the prisoner, telling Bucky to get him into the interrogation tent, and turned to congratulate the team. In Thai he praised their performance, told them that the beer was on him at the club they'd hastily reactivated, and dismissed them to their own debriefing. They'd be getting good and drunk tonight, he knew. Trying to chase away, for a little while, the thought that although this mission had gone exceptionally smoothly, there would be others. And they couldn't all be like that.

He'd done the same thing, many times.

In the interrogation tent Finn told the interpreter, a Mr. Quan who had last worked in an A camp in the Delta, to take the prisoner's blindfold off.

The young Vietnamese, a baby really, Finn thought, physically recoiled at the sight of the Americans. He would, Finn knew, have been told all sorts of stories about how the Americans butchered their prisoners, cutting off various portions of their anatomies and force-feeding them to the unfortunate men.

Such tactics, ironically, worked in favor of the questioners. The interviewee had to be convinced that his situation was hopeless, that to resist was only to bring unnecessary pain before inevitable death.

Then when, instead of the beatings he was expecting, you acted like a human being, the gratitude was such that you wanted to do just about anything to please your surprisingly kind captors.

"Ask him if he's thirsty," Finn told Quan, who translated it quickly into Vietnamese.

Bucky Epstein, who spoke Vietnamese so well that when he'd used it over a captured radio the Viet Cong had thought him one of their own, nodded to Finn. The interpreter was saying exactly what he was supposed to. Not adding or subtracting, not putting in his own fillips. Interpreters always had to be checked, first for accuracy (since being an interpreter for the Americans had carried such financial benefits, anyone who spoke even a few words of English advertised himself as a linguistic expert), and then for reliability. The fact that someone spoke good English didn't necessarily mean that he was your friend. Far from it. The VC had even run their own language school, attempting to put their graduates into positions from which they could report back everything they learned. After all, the interpreter was always going to be in on any planning sessions and briefings, and would learn far more than even the commanders of Vietnamese units working with the Americans.

When their prisoner registered first surprise at the question, then hesitant gratitude, Finn untied his bonds and Bucky gave him a canteen cup full of water. The North Vietnamese sat for a moment rubbing his wrists, looking at the water, clearly longing for it, but afraid to take it.

Bucky took a sip, then offered it again. The young man grabbed it, his throat working frantically as he downed it to the last drop.

Fear and adrenaline always had that effect, the body telling the brain that it needed water, and needed it badly.

Even if you'd filled your belly with it only moments before.

The Vietnamese handed the cup back to Bucky, who signaled, More? The Vietnamese nodded and Bucky filled the cup again. This time he only drank about half of it.

The Vietnamese looked longingly at the tent flap, then at the men around him, and Finn thought he could almost see his mind work. Try for an escape? After all, he had his hands and feet free.

There was absolutely no chance of that, and the prisoner would recognize it for himself. None of the men in the tent were armed, eliminating the chance to snatch a weapon. The two Americans outweighed him by at least fifty pounds. Even if he managed to get out of the tent he was still in enemy territory, surrounded by hundreds of Thai troops who would, unlike those in the tent, be armed and would be positively happy to shoot a fleeing prisoner.

Seeing his shoulders slump in resignation, Finn started the questioning. He started from the simple: name, rank, unit. Under the Geneva Accords the prisoner didn't have to answer the last question, but Geneva didn't say you couldn't ask it. Besides, though the United States honored the provisions of the accords it had never been a signatory. The Vietnamese had been signatories, but had never honored it.

Within just a few moments they had the information that they were in possession of one Dinh Thuan, private soldier of the Vietnamese People's Army (VPA), and that he belonged to the 328th Infantry Regiment. Private Dinh had absolutely no combat experience, being a new draftee and having undergone basic training only a few weeks before being transported by truck through the Mu Gia

Pass, down the Ho Chi Minh Trail (which was now achieving the status of near-superhighway) and joining the 328th.

The combat-hardened sergeants, corporals, and senior privates that made up the 328th had given the new draftees pure hell. Impugning their patriotism for not joining sooner, although Dinh was barely seventeen. Putting them through endless drills that Dinh and his comrades privately thought were designed more to make them miserable than to serve any real tactical purpose. Assigning them the shit details, one of which had been the water party. And horrifying them with their tales of combat, of having to live in muddy caves for months while the American bombers prowled overhead, of being wounded and having to depend upon maggots to clean the wound out because there was no medical help, of watching comrades die in agony.

Something the new recruits would never have to experience, the older men said. Because the victorious VPA would sweep away all opponents, and the Americans were afraid to come back because their own people wouldn't stand for it. Implying that the young men would be the less for not having experienced the true horrors of war.

The unit had been, as far as Dinh knew, brought up to full strength, replacing the casualties suffered on the victorious march through the Central Highlands all the way down to the city now known as Ho Chi Minh. It had also been re-equipped, with the weapons modern, the transportation sufficient, the artillery taken from the South Vietnamese puppet army refurbished and repaired with the spare parts of which there had been warehouses full.

They were, Private Dinh told them, not without a certain amount of pride, fully ready for combat.

*   *   *

When finally Finn had decided they'd gotten all out of the prisoner they could, he summoned the Thai guards and had them take Private Dinh away. Within an hour he'd be on a plane to Bangkok, there to undergo yet more interrogation, this time by some true professionals. After that, who knew? After all, Thailand and Vietnam weren't at war. What the Thai recon team had done was, technically, illegal by international norms. Finn would bet that the Viets would claim they were in Laos at the invitation of the Laotian government.

That was, if the Viets made a protest. Somehow Finn didn't think they would. They had bigger fish to fry.

Thailand and Vietnam weren't at war. Yet.

"You find 'em?" he asked Bucky, who was going through the North Vietnamese army order of battle book.

"Yep," Bucky replied, slamming the book shut. "Thought I recognized the designation. The 328th is a part of the 2nd VPA Division. The Yellow Star."

Finn, who had been fairly certain he'd recognized the designation as well, was dismayed to hear he had been right. The Yellow Star was one of the NVA's best. Bloodied in numerous battles with American and Vietnamese troops, the most notable battle of which had been the operation called Crazy Horse, the 2nd VPA was first-rate.

"Wanna bet a bottle of good scotch the Yellow Star isn't the only one out there?" Finn said.

"You oughta know by now I don't do fool's bets," Bucky replied.

"Didn't think so. Let's go see if any of the other teams have come in yet."

CHAPTER 16

The walk back into camp was nerve-wracking. They took a roundabout route, avoiding any chokepoints and trails, but still the thought that the enemy had a pretty good fix on them was bothersome. Not to mention the fact that the claymore ambush could have been heard for several kilometers, and they had no idea how close the NVA patrol had been to their link-up point.

Still, after a number of alerts that caused them to change direction again and again, fading back and splitting up at one point only to link back up at a predesignated rally point later, the trip was uneventful. Or as uneventful as it could be here where the fantastic shapes of the weathered karst formations gave vent to over-vivid imaginations.

After seeing what he'd thought might have been a tank, which turned out to be nothing more than a rock outcropping with a fallen tree braced against it, Jim decided that he was getting entirely too old for this shit. Occasionally he liked to torment himself with the fantasy of lying with Alix under their down comforter, feeling her warmth, touching the softly growing belly that hid their child.

Could have been there, he thought. Dumb-ass.

Better concentrate, he told himself after stumbling over a root. That could have been a tripwire. His first Purple Heart had been acquired thus. At least it hadn't been he who had tripped the mine. Had it been, he wouldn't be here now. As it was the first four people in front of him had been mangled beyond recognition, and the point man who had done the deed had been virtually vaporized.

He'd only had his eardrums blown out, and had been the unhappy recipient of some twenty to twenty-five pieces of shrapnel—the doctors had never been really sure just how many—some of which had pierced his stomach wall and lodged in his intestines.

Three others had transfixed his penis to his thigh. Later, at the field evac hospital to which he had been evacuated, the nurses had found it vastly amusing to come in and throw back the sheet to show their friends his enormous, swollen, blackened appendage.

And of course, Special Forces men being the sensitive, caring individuals they are, they had given him a nickname he'd spent years living down.

"Hey, Piccolo," the greeting went. "How do you piss out of that thing? Play it like a flute?"

His thoughts were suddenly jerked back to the present. The point man was signaling a halt.

The 'Yards faded into the underbrush, becoming as one with the leaves and branches. Someone could walk within inches of them and never see anything more than, perhaps, their glittering eyes. Of course, if you were close enough to see their eyes, you were moments away from dying.

Korhonen, ahead of him, signaled "Look," forked fingers to the eyes, then the same fingers pointing in the appropriate direction.

Just to the other side of an abandoned slash-and-burn field, he saw them. Moving casually, weapons slung. Why not, he thought. It's their backyard, after all. And they're sure as hell not worried about the likes of us.

Had to be at least a battalion of troops. Marching in a column of twos. As at ease as they might have been back in Hanoi.

They waited a good half-hour for the troops to pass, then took a slight dogleg and proceeded. Once safely out of range, the patrol leader called another halt. At his signal Jim and Willi Korhonen joined him.

"I think they look for our camp," he said.

Korhonen nodded in agreement. "We have big problem," he said. "When they didn't know where we were, we could ambush them, draw them away, keep them confused. Never let them mass enough troops to attack." He looked at Jim Carmichael, and the look was clearly accusatory.

Not my fault, Jim thought. But try and explain that. Right now he was longing for the support upon which he could once have called. Put a B-52 arclight strike on those assholes and we wouldn't have to worry about it.

They'd taken several FM radios from the ambushed NVA patrol and had tuned their own radios to the frequencies they'd found. The traffic had indicated that the patrol had been very efficient at passing on the information they'd found. Sarpa's camp had been well and thoroughly compromised.

"You have ideas, Captain?" Korhonen demanded.

"Pretty simple," Jim said. "Get back to Sarpa, warn him, get that place evacuated. He can't stand against the entire goddamn North Vietnamese army, because that's what he's going to get, once they get their people in place.

Split up, regroup somewhere else. Get our resupplies, take the time to build up your forces, fight them at a time and place of your own choosing."

Korhonen thought for a moment. "I agree," he finally said. "But you're going to have a hell of a time selling that to Y Buon Sarpa."

"Doesn't believe in living to fight another day?" Jim asked.

"Quite the opposite," Korhonen replied. "Sarpa believes in fighting to live another day."

Sarpa had a simple answer.

"We attack," he said.

Jim looked at him in question, wondering if the pressure had finally gotten to the Montagnard leader. Clearly he'd lost his mind.

"We sit here, they come with more and more people," Sarpa explained. "The one battalion becomes two, then a regiment. With artillery. Aircraft. Do you think we can survive that?"

"There's another answer," Jim replied.

Sarpa snorted. "I know your answer before you say it. We move, right? Give up this position, find another. How long do you think it will take them to find it? And what happens to the villagers who depend on us? You want them to move too?" He shook his head.

"We've moved enough. It is time to fight."

"You're going to lose, you know," Jim said.

Sarpa smiled, and it was a smile of resignation.

"If we lose, we die. If we win, maybe we die too. But we die with honor. Your country once understood honor. I have read much of your Civil War. I think your General Lee, he knew he was going to lose. But he fought, anyway. Now what do you do? You declare 'Peace with Honor,' and you leave. Do not tell me what I must do, Captain. You do not have the right."

Sarpa turned on his heel and walked away.

"You've got to talk some sense into him," Jim said to Willi Korhonen.

Now it was Korhonen's turn to snort in derision.

"Even if I could," he said, "I wouldn't. Let them come." He was silent for a moment, perhaps thinking of all the combat he'd seen, the lives lost, the honor of which Sarpa had so eloquently spoken given away by politicians far away. Men who would never really know what the word meant.

"Maybe I've lived too long anyway," he said. "If it's time, it's time."

Jim shook his head. Sarpa's words had stung. But they'd been nothing more than he'd once said, himself.

In truth there was little he would have liked better than to join in the fight. But he had other responsibilities. He'd come to get Korhonen and Parker out. Korhonen refused to go. So be it. That didn't end the mission.

Besides, he had two NCOs to think of, and while they too would probably like nothing better than a good fight, that was a decision they'd have to make on their own. He would get them out, back home. Just as he'd promised— God, was it only three days ago!—in Thailand.

And last, but certainly not least, there was Alix. Ruefully he admitted to himself that what he'd said so many times— that a warrior should never take a wife, never become hostage to family and the responsibilities it entailed—was undoubtedly true.

But he had, and there it was. Nothing for it now.

Except continue the mission, and try to survive it. Glenn Parker was in no shape to travel, so getting him out before things turned thoroughly to shit was out of the question. So much for the mission. It would have to wait.

As to surviving, well, the options were limited. But not nonexistent.

"Shit," he said to Korhonen. "We're gonna do this, let's do it right. I've got a couple of ideas.

The Finn broke into a smile. "You young guys always have ideas," he said. "Sometimes they're even good. Let's hear it."

Lieutenant Colonel Duong Tri Minh was getting impatient. He'd wanted to attack the Montagnard position immediately, but had been told to wait for reinforcements. Reinforcements! As if he needed them to annihilate the savages. Little did he care what his scouts had told him, that the position was well defended and that it was likely they'd lose half their number before they got through the first layer of the defenses. Defeatism! These men had been at war too long. Now all they wanted to do was go home, see the wives who probably had long since given them up for dead, embrace the children who would be children no longer. Who would probably not recognize the gaunt man in his ragged uniform as the plump young father who had left so long ago.

The colonel was not tired of the war. Far from it. He'd had very little chance to see it up close, an omission he intended to rectify.

Instead he'd been assigned to one of the many prisoner of war camps that dotted North Vietnam, where he had probably been more safe than anyone else in the country. The Americans knew where the camps were—it seemed like they knew practically everything. Not that it did them a great deal of good.

But they wouldn't bomb their own people. So when the jets came sweeping across the compound he had often walked outside, showing his utter contempt for the roundeyes. And then he would go back inside and thoroughly beat one or more of the prisoners.

Punishment, he told them. For what you are doing to my country.

In truth, and he barely admitted this even to himself, he rather liked the beatings. Such power over another human being is seldom given. And if they died, as they sometimes did, well, that was just too bad. His reports would tell of the disease that had swept the camp. And of his heroic efforts to keep the valuable prisoners alive.

Then the Son Tay raid, and the prisoners had suddenly been shipped to Hanoi, leaving him without a job. He'd been reassigned to a coastal artillery unit, and suspected it was because his superiors didn't really believe his stories. He'd been promoted regularly over the years, but now the promotions had stopped. Was it to be his fate to suffer in the middle ranks while the combat veterans, wearing the medals he knew he would also have earned, given the chance, came back and became full colonels and generals?

He had friends in Hanoi, people for whom he'd done little favors, like shipping them the expensive watches the pilots often wore. He campaigned tirelessly for a combat command. Few were available in the waning days of the war, and those went to experienced officers.

And when the command finally came it was to this backwater. Where nothing ever happened, where the extent of his combat was to overrun H'Mong villages whose men were all gone.

Now this chance. He would distinguish himself, that he knew. If only given the opportunity. Pull back and wait, indeed! Let the savages kill his men, as they had the unfortunate Lieutenant Trinh? And let the Americans get away?

He allowed himself to imagine the praise that would be heaped upon him when he returned to Hanoi with the prisoners trussed like so many pigs being taken to market. And the news conferences where he would be displayed prominently, perhaps even being allowed to tell the world about the lies of the Americans.

Still, he wasn't going to disobey a direct order. To do so was tantamount to suicide. He would not attack. But if the enemy did something, he would have to protect his men, wouldn't he?

Any good commander would. And he was a very good commander. Hadn't the men who had served under him told him so?

Jim Carmichael wasn't aware of the mettle of the men he would have to face, and it wouldn't have mattered if he had been. The way he saw it, there was only one answer.

You had to draw them into a battle of your own choosing. On favorable terrain. And hit them with such force that they would become disorganized, fearful. A rabble.

A rabble was easy to fight. A cohesive unit wasn't.

He could only hope what he'd seen when he'd been out

with Bobby and Korhonen was typical of the enemy battalion. They'd been entirely too casual about their security. After all, the war was over, wasn't it? What did they have to worry about here?

Besides, they'd won. Victors are often complacent.

A lot depended upon that attitude. The entire plan, in fact. He'd argued it out first with Korhonen, and after the old veteran had finally come around to his way of thinking, with Y Buon Sarpa.

Now it was on his shoulders. If it didn't work, it was likely he'd never see another sunrise. If it did he still stood an excellent chance of getting killed.

But it was better than waiting there in the camp, knowing that at any moment the yellow rain might once again fall. Several more of the afflicted had died. Glenn was barely hanging on. He shuddered, thinking of the pain the ones still living had to endure.

Nope. This was it.

Talked yourself into it one more time, didn't you?

Shut up, he told himself. Last thing I need is you giving me a ration of shit right now.

Lieutenant Colonel Minh was seething. Insubordination! He thought of himself as a tolerant man, but one thing he could not abide. How dare one of his junior officers question his decisions!

And it was a very good decision. The troops had to have water, did they not? Why, then, should they encamp far from a good stream? It was a lovely spot, reminding him of his home back in Vietnam. A cleared area suitable for the command post. Hills rising off in the distance, the tops wreathed in the clouds that told of the impending rainy season. Not only was the stream within easy walking distance, the sound it made as it tumbled over the rocks was immensely soothing.

And the commander of his First Company had the effrontery to tell him the position wasn't tactically sound! That they should be seeking the high ground and avoiding any cleared areas.

Why? The enemy didn't have aircraft. And the savages who were their only possible opponents couldn't stand up to his battalion—one rush and they'd run away like the cowards they were.

No, the captain had spent too much time fighting the Americans. Such things might have been important then. They were not now. It was only that the man was so highly decorated that kept him from being relieved on the spot. Perhaps in chains.

He settled in for the evening. His tent had already been erected and his aide had gathered enough moss to make a very nice mattress for his bed. His belly was full.

As he drifted off to sleep he could, he thought, faintly hear the cheers of the crowd in Hanoi when he brought back the captives.

CHAPTER 17

No more recon teams came in that day, nor on the second. On the face of it that wasn't necessarily a bad thing. The prisoner snatch had been planned as a quick in-and-out, where most of the other teams had been given road watch and area recon missions. You carried enough supplies to last you six to ten days, and sometimes you even got to stay in that long.

Far more often you were compromised and the mission was scrubbed, the extraction helicopters coming in to snatch you from the jaws of the troops enclosing your team. And sometimes the choppers didn't come, or if they did were shot down and you not only had to worry about your team, but the survivors of the crash. Oftentimes SOG missions had grown into battalion-sized operations as troops and aircraft kept being thrown into the fight.

Finn had to hope that wouldn't be the case here. The Thais were good troops, tough fighters, but simply didn't have the wherewithal to fight a pitched battle across the border. Close air support was limited to a few helicopter gunships and Northrop F-5 fighter planes, the "Freedom Fighter" the U.S. government was fond of forcing its allies to take. It was a good bird, very maneuverable, easy to fly, but simply didn't have the ordnance capacity or loiter time to make it an efficient close-air-support vehicle.

At least there was only one team with which they'd lost contact. That could have been due to any number of factors: failure of both radio and backup, the team being so close to the enemy they didn't dare make contact, the team leader simply exercising his option not to get on the radio but to wait to be fully debriefed once safely back at the FOB.

Or it could be that they were being chased. Or that they'd been detected upon insertion, the NVA choosing to wait until the helicopters were back over the horizon before attacking.

Such things had happened all too often to the SOG teams. RT Idaho had simply disappeared, and it was as if the world had swallowed it. A recon team sent into the point of insertion of Idaho had found exactly nothing, and the team had never been heard from again. Neither of the two Americans had been turned over during Operation Homecoming, either. But then, no one had expected it. The NVA troops hated the recon teams who could bring down death and destruction with a simple call on the radio, and weren't likely to let any of them survive.

The other teams were sending in a wealth of information, and none of the news was good. The Vietnamese had massed at least two divisions in addition to the troops of the Yellow Star. One team had almost stumbled across an artillery emplacement equipped with 105mm howitzers, within easy reach of targets across the border.

Another team had affixed a wiretap device to a landline they'd come across, the device now transmitting a stream of information that was being translated as quickly as possible. The people using the phones were speaking in code, but given the fact that the military attaché was transmitting the information back to the National Security Agency as quickly as it came in, there was no doubt the code would soon be broken.

Finn could only hope that it wouldn't be moot. It was obvious from the reports coming in that the Viets could mount a major attack within days, if not hours.

Finn chafed at his own inactivity, but supposed that the orders to stay put were, all in all, correct. Across the border he'd be just another team member. Here he could at least coordinate, or try to, the support the teams would need if they got into trouble.

Sam Gutierrez had been up that morning, getting firsthand the reports that flowed in.

"Any word from Disneyland East?" Finn had asked him.

"Secretary of state's trying to get together a meeting of the SEATO nations," Sam replied. SEATO stood for the South East Asia Treaty Organization, conceived as a counterpart to NATO. It committed its signatories to come to the mutual aid of any one of their number attacked by an outside power. SEATO was intended as a bulwark against Red China, as NATO was against the Russians. But where NATO had helped deter the Soviet threat, SEATO had dissolved into a fractious forum where the only thing that got done was an endless round of meetings.

"Bet they'll have some really good lunches," Finn said.

"And a nice dinner at the end where they'll all drink champagne and congratulate themselves on the strong warning they'll deliver to Hanoi," Sam confirmed. As the military attaché, he'd gone to any number of meetings of the sort.

"Which will be written on really soft paper so Le Duc Tho won't hurt his hemorrhoids when he wipes his ass with it."

"Probably," Sam said. "More to the point, the Joint Chiefs have decided to send a battalion of Marines to 'exercise' with the Thais down at Pattaya."

"Where they'll be easy to evacuate when the NVA overruns the country."

"Gotta send a signal, you know," Sam said, his smile not very successfully hiding the bitterness of his tone.

Washington was famous for "sending signals." We'll bomb 'em, that'll send a signal. Of course, don't hit anything vital, wouldn't want to piss them off too badly, now would we? Okay, that didn't send the signal we wanted. Let's stop bombing, that'll show 'em we're reasonable men. Maybe they'll come to the negotiating table. They didn't? Screw 'em, we'll bomb 'em again. This time we'll hurt 'em worse.

And the enemy regularly paid no attention whatsoever to the signals, unless it fit within his own strategic plan to do so.

"Be a better signal, they dropped the 82nd Airborne on Udorn," Finn said.

"And you and I both know that's not gonna happen," Sam replied. In truth, he wasn't all that sure how much good the 82nd would do, other than serve as a so-called tripwire, much as the 2nd Infantry Division was just behind the demilitarized zone in Korea. The thinking in higher government circles was that the American people wouldn't stand for their sons being slaughtered wholesale, that before that happened they'd demand the really hard solutions. Which might or might not include the use of tactical nuclear weapons.

The paratroops of the 82nd were very lightly armed, certainly not suited for going up against the tanks and artillery massing across the border. Besides, the rot that had set into the Army as a whole hadn't skipped even the elite airborne unit. Drug use was common, officers and NCOs who tried to enforce discipline were often threatened with "fragging," the desertion rate was twice what it had been back in the early sixties.

The truth was that the United States no longer had a lot of options in Southeast Asia. Armored units would take far too long to move. Besides, the planners and strategists in the Pentagon would be saying, What if this is just a feint? Intended to distract us, cause us to pull our reserves out of the States. Then the Warsaw Pact comes rolling through the Fulda Gap and we've got nothing to stop them with.

Such a doomsday scenario was by no means impossible. In such a case it would have to be met with nuclear weapons. You nuke us, we nuke you, and before long there's nothing but radioactive glass where Moscow and New York used to be.

Sam had said as much to Finn.

"So we're out here on the front line of the free world with nothing much more than our dicks in our hands," Finn had replied.

"That's about the size of it, if you'll excuse the pun."

"Why is it I suddenly feel the urge for a strong drink?"

But having even one drink was out of the question when you were running an FOB and had teams in the field.

Someone had once compared it to conducting an orchestra. Finn thought it more like a ballet, with a stage measuring hundreds of square kilometers, including both the ground and the air above it, with stagehands sabotaging your every move and the audience throwing rocks.

It was later that afternoon when he got his first taste of it. It started with a radio message from an unknown source, but the voice was unmistakably American. The message came in on the secure band.

"You got some folks over across the fence?" the voice asked.

Finn was immediately on guard. No one except the military attachés' office was supposed to have his frequency. Moreover, to be talking on this band at all meant that you must have similar equipment on the other end. But stranger things had happened. The NVA must have been able to capture any amount of secure radio equipment when Saigon fell, and an American accent wasn't too hard to come by. And for all he knew one of the news networks might have invested in the gear and be even now looking for the scoop that would be career building for the reporter and career ruining for the interviewee. He could almost hear Walter Cronkite's mellifluous tones announcing that evidence gathered by intrepid CBS staff proved that the Thai government was running illegal cross-border operations into a neutral county, and that the Americans were heavily involved in it.

"*Cabrón* said you might be a little suspicious," the voice said.

Finn relaxed slightly. With his usual warped sense of humor Sam Gutierrez had assigned code names. Finn's was *Chingador*.

"What you got?" he asked, knowing better than to press the man on the other end as to exactly who he was and from whence he was transmitting. Somewhere in-country at least. The secure radios they were using didn't have enough range otherwise. CIA? Possibly. They still had plenty of assets in Thailand, and perhaps a few left across the border. DEA? An even greater possibility. The so-called Golden Triangle where Thailand, China, and Burma met was a drug hotspot.

"We heard something on the emergency freq," the voice said. "Garbled, but what we got out of it was a team calling for emergency extraction. Speaker would switch back and forth between Thai and English, but what we could understand indicated they're in deep shit. Team name is Mongoose. You got anybody out there like that?"

Finn indicated that they did, thinking furiously as he did so. Mongoose was the team that hadn't reported in. That they'd fallen back on the emergency radio, an URC-10 handheld, meant that either the primary had failed, or the radio operator and equipment had been killed or captured. The URC-10 was air-ground exclusively, used only in last resort and with a lot of sometimes unrequited hope. It had been okay back in the days when the skies were filled with American airplanes—likelihood was somebody, somewhere would finally hear you.

That meant that whoever was on the other end of the line had air assets, and that they were fairly close.

And whoever it was would have the information necessary to contact Sam Gutierrez, get the code word and the frequency, and the clearance to talk to the FOB. Gutierrez would also obviously know who it was at the other end of the line.

Finn wondered what else his boss had neglected to share with him.

That was something he could take up with Sam later. Right now he had more important things to do.

"Don't suppose you've got a fix on them?" he asked.

"As a matter of fact, we do. At least the coordinates where they were an hour ago. Took that long to get through to you."

The anonymous voice rattled off a set of coordinates. Bucky, who had been listening over Finn's shoulder, quickly checked them against the area in which Mongoose had been inserted, quickly nodded that they were feasible.

"And I don't suppose we could get you to keep your bird up there, try to make contact again while we organize and extract?"

The voice at the other end was silent, someone obviously asking the question of someone else.

Another voice came out of the radio, one Finn thought he vaguely recognized.

"Ah, what the fuck," it said. "In for a penny, in for a pound. Get your shit together, call me back when you're ready. Out."

In Nakhon Phanom Mark Petrillo turned from the silent radio to face a coldly furious Bentley Sloane.

"You do realize you could be compromising this entire operation," Sloane said.

"And how's that, Captain? We've got a radio relay plane up twenty-four hours a day. It orbits over Thailand, never gets more than ten miles from the border. We've got air clearance from the Thai government."

"No one is supposed to know we're here!"

"If you think they don't, you've been smoking Thai weed. Soviet recon satellites cover this area twice a day. You think they're not seeing that big black motherfucking C-130 out on the runway? They know we're here, all right. They just don't know what we're doing."

Sloane started to say something again, was cut off by Petrillo. "And if you think I'm going to sit by while a team gets its ass chewed up, when we could do something to help, you're outta your fucking mind.

"Besides," he said, a small smile playing on his lips, "what your people can do is ruin my career, and it ain't all that great, anyway. What Sam Gutierrez can and will do is cut my balls off and stuff them down my throat. Of the two, I think I prefer the former."

He turned back to the radio, his broad shoulders an effective dismissal of Captain Bentley Sloane.

Left to stew about it, with few options other than reporting back to the Pentagon, and Sloane wasn't really sure he wanted to do that, he reflected on the irony of it all.

Fate had brought a man back into his life, a man who had once told him he thought he was one of the sorriest officers he'd ever met, but who had nonetheless endorsed the recommendation that led to his being awarded the Medal of Honor.

If he was a superstitious type, he told himself, he would have seen something sinister behind this.

As it was, it must be purely coincidence.

He went back to writing his daily journal, reporting fully the tactical and perhaps strategic mistake he thought Mark Petrillo was making. Petrillo was right. His career was going to be torn to ribbons. Captain Bentley Sloane would make sure of that.

*   *   *

In Bangkok, Sam Gutierrez sat in the tiny room where the secure radio was kept, staring at a gecko lizard on the wall, idly wondering how the little lizard had managed to get into the most tightly guarded and sealed-off room in the Embassy complex.

Gonna starve to death in here, little fella, he told the tiny reptile. The room was sprayed with insecticide at least once a day. If flies and other bugs, of which Thailand had a multitude, got in here they'd head for the radio, get inside, short it out. Not for nothing was a glitch in a computer called a bug. The very first failure of a computer system had involved exactly that.

He opened the door, herded the gecko out. You didn't try to grab them—all you'd be left with was the tail as they shed it to get away.

As the little lizard scurried away to better hunting grounds, Sam thought that it was a good analogy to a team in trouble. You shed whatever wasn't absolutely necessary to your survival.

He could only hope that rescuing Team Mongoose would be as easy as saving the gecko.

CHAPTER 18

If you want to suck somebody in, you have to give them something they can't resist.

Those words from a long-ago team sergeant reverberated through Jim Carmichael's brain.

They want an American, here one is, he thought as he and the Montagnard platoon took position. It was just before dawn, in the false light that made things seem even more insubstantial than they were. When men's minds played tricks on them; when eyesight that could be so sharp later in the day was fooled by the shifting and imperfect light.

They were almost in position. Just a few more moments before the flank would report, then all hell was going to break loose.

Even worse odds than usual, he told himself. Last time you went up against a battalion you got your butt shot, didn't you? And lost half a company in the process. How many are going to die today, and all because of your bright idea that all of a sudden doesn't seem so bright anymore?

That old familiar jangling at the pit of his stomach.

Wish I'd eaten when I had the chance. Too late to worry about it now.

Anyhow, I'd probably puke it up. Wouldn't do so much good for the confidence of the troops, see their fearless leader hurling up his guts.

The feeling would, he knew, disappear when the first shots were fired, but right now it was well-nigh unbearable.

Both Hauck and Dickerson had tried to talk him out of it. "Hell," Jimmy had said, "I already been caught once. Probably want me back worse than they'd want to get some ugly sumbitch like you."

In truth, any American face would have done for what they were planning. Not that it mattered. It was his plan. It was therefore his ass to risk.

There it was, the clicks on the radio that signified readiness.

Too late to worry about it now. He flicked the selector switch off his CAR-15, all the way past single shot to full automatic.

Even as his finger squeezed the trigger he wondered if he was doing the right thing.

Lieutenant Colonel Minh woke to the sound of heavy automatic-weapons fire somewhere to his south. Cursing, he pulled his boots on and exited the tent.

Only to be pulled to the ground by his aide as bullets ripped through the canvas at just about the point his head would have been. "What?" he asked. "Who . . ."

The First Company commander came rushing up. "We are being attacked," he said.

Colonel Minh would have sworn that the captain was about to say, "Just as I said we would be," when another burst of fire caused him to dive to the ground and lie there beside the colonel and his aide.

"Stupid!" the colonel spat. "They must know they cannot win. Why would they attack?"

"Perhaps they *are* stupid," the captain said dryly. "They don't know. My second platoon is fixing them by fire while the first and third are maneuvering to their flanks. I believe it is but a probe. We must remain ready for the main attack."

"Of course, of course," Minh replied. "Exactly as I would have ordered. Keep me informed."

The captain ran off to rejoin his men. Minh's aide was busy scraping a hole in the rich soil, into which the colonel tumbled in some relief. He could now hear the heavier reports of the AK-47s with which his men were armed, interspersed with the blast of B-40 rockets. He allowed himself a smile. His first taste of combat, and he was doing rather well, he thought. No fear, at least not any that showed. And that was all that was important. He was already considering how he would write the action up. It all depended upon how many bodies they stacked up. The more the better.

He would wait here until the firing died down, then go forward and inspect the damage. Show the troops just how fearless their commander was, to risk himself so. He fingered the pistol his aide had just brought him out of the tent. Maybe there would be wounded. His finger jerked almost of its own volition, just as it would as he put a bullet into the head of the one who had dared attack them.

A runner—from his collar tabs the colonel recognized him as a member of Second Company—came tumbling down next to his hole. The man was so breathless he could barely get out the message.

"Calm down, man!" the colonel commanded. "What is it?"

"*My!*" (American), the man said. "I saw him myself. Leading the assault. We were told the *My Lo* (Long Noses) had all gone!"

So that was it, the colonel thought. The savages were once again being led by the Americans. No wonder they thought they could take on the victorious People's Army.

He would teach them just how mistaken they were.

"Bring me my rifle," he commanded his aide. "Come," he said to the runner. "Show me this American. We cannot allow him to escape."

Jim's platoon broke contact after assaulting only as far as the first line of pickets. They'd killed perhaps ten or twenty men, something that wouldn't have happened back in the old days. Then the NVA would have been well dug in, would have had ambushes out on all the trails, would have maintained enough men on alert to have told them of danger long before he could have gotten his platoon into position.

It was a nice benefit, but it really didn't make much difference. They could afford to lose the men. There were plenty more where they came from.

The important thing was, he had heard several of the survivors screaming about the sighting of the American. Cursing and swearing, shooting wildly in his direction. A couple coming close enough he'd decided that part of the plan was at least achieved.

No use risking your ass now, he told himself. You've got more work to do.

He reached the rally point just after the last squad made

it there. Took a quick head count. As many men as he'd started with. They were grinning, happy. They'd bitten the enemy. Hard. That was all that mattered.

Not yet, boys, he told them in passable Bahnar. We've still got work to do.

Petrillo handed Captain Sloane the deciphered message, waited for his reaction. He wasn't disappointed.

"Is he out of his goddamned mind?" Sloane demanded.

"Some people have said that," Petrillo replied. "Me, I just think it's another case of Jim Carmichael doing what he thinks is right."

"At the cost of the mission?"

Petrillo shook his head. "You've read the message," he said. "He can't get Parker out—too sick. And Korhonen isn't willing to come. He's got to buy some time. He figures this is the way to do it. Bloody their noses, maybe they'll not be so eager to take on the buzzsaw. Knowing Jim, I'd say it's the only way he thinks the mission can be done."

"Bullshit! He just wants to go out and kill people again. As I remember from his file, he's pretty goddamn good at it."

Petrillo started to say something, stopped, and swallowed the words that had threatened to scorch this goddamn wet-behind-the-ears captain who, by the way, just happened to be the aide of one of the most powerful men in the Pentagon. He hadn't gotten as far as he had in the Army by making such mistakes.

When he did speak his voice was mild. "You probably need to understand a little something about James NMI Carmichael," he said. "He has something that most people lack. Including me, and I suspect, you. A moral compass.

He believes in what he's doing—otherwise he wouldn't be doing it. Now, that compass may point him in directions you don't like. Sure as hell did back when we worked together in Vietnam, for me. But it's there, and by God he's going to follow it no matter what. Sure he's a killer. An extremely good one." Petrillo smiled.

"Mutual friend of ours, Al Dougherty, used to say Jim Carmichael has killed more people than cancer. Slight exaggeration, of course.

"But when he kills, it's for a very good reason. Then he does it without remorse or maybe even thinking about it twice."

"And following orders," Sloane said. "What about that?"

"Best make sure the orders are right," Petrillo replied. "Then stand out of the way. He'll get it done."

"He'd better. He gets caught, we're in worse shape than we were before he went in."

"How do you figure that, Captain? He's a rogue. Isn't that your cover story? Went in on his own to check out the rumors of POWs still being held. What are they calling it these days? Post-traumatic stress disorder? In spades. Hell, you could use him for the poster child. Hanoi trots him out, denounces the warmongering dogs of the U.S.A., we tell them we don't know what the hell they're talking about. Carmichael sure as hell isn't going to tell them any different."

Sloane calmed down, if only slightly.

"I suppose that's true," he said. "You're sure they can't turn him?"

"Now that's telling me you really don't know this guy," Petrillo replied. "They might kill him, but they aren't going to turn him. Stake my career on it."

You are. You just don't know it, Sloane thought, but did not say.

"Anyway, I've gotta get going on this supply request," Petrillo said. "We'll get a bird up tonight. Weather looks halfway decent for a change. Don't know how long that will last."

Sloane nodded, dismissing the senior officer as if he were nothing more than a mere lieutenant. After all, despite ranks, one really knew who was important in this little venture.

Which, of course, thoroughly pissed Mark Petrillo off. "By the way," he said, fully intending the dig, "you do have a Plan B, don't you? In case everything else turns to shit."

"Of course," Sloane replied. *But God help me if I have to use it.*

"You might think about sharing that with me, sometime. Inasmuch as I seem to be the one in charge here. For the moment, anyway."

"In due time," Sloane said, enjoying the look on Petrillo's face. "Need to know, you understand."

Lieutenant Colonel Minh, red-faced and sweating, wanted to call a halt to the chase. It had been going on for an hour now, and what they had seen was no more substantial than the fog that raised off the paddies of his home village. His battalion was hopelessly strung out. First Company and its insufferable commander off to the right flank somewhere. Second Company with him, along with half his battalion staff. Third Company back at the original bivouac site, guarding their food stores and the rucksacks he had made the pursuit companies leave behind.

"We can move faster that way," he had told the assembled company commanders, earning a frankly incredulous look from First Company's captain.

"We won't be gone that long," he had felt obligated to say. Which infuriated him the more. He should not have to explain himself to a mere captain! No matter what experience the man had.

Now he was wondering if he had done the right thing. He had long since finished the water in his single canteen, and they hadn't run across any streams for a long time now. He could always demand that of his aide, but feared the news of it would get back to the men.

No, he must remain stoic. The leader they all wanted to emulate. A man to be respected. And feared.

Still, would just a small rest be such a bad thing?

His thoughts were interrupted by a huge explosion somewhere to his front, followed shortly thereafter by the cries of the wounded and dying. He forgot his fatigue, rushed forward, and was stopped short by the scene of carnage.

At least a half dozen of his men were dead, their bodies shredded. Another ten or so were down, and even to his untrained eye they looked like they had an appointment with a higher god. The smell of explosives, blood, and torn-apart intestines assaulted his nose and it was only through major effort that he stifled a gag.

"Claymore," one of the squad leaders said, using the American word like a curse. "They set a claymore mine!"

The sons of dogs! Minh raged. They would suffer for this.

"Find them!" he screamed. "Track them down."

His mind was already working on what he would do to the American if, Buddha willing, he managed to take him alive. The sufferings of his countrymen in the camps Minh had run would be nothing in comparison.

After all, his superiors wanted the American alive. They didn't say in what kind of condition.

"Call Third Company," he instructed. "Have them come forward and take care of these men. The rest of you, go!"

He ignored their stares, their unspoken importunity. He knew that it was like a blow to them, to leave men behind. Even the dead.

That was not important right now. Worry about what they think of you later.

For now, find the American. He fancied that the surrounding foliage had taken on a blood-red hue. And not just from the splatter the mine had caused.

Rage, he realized. The feeling was good.

The problem, Jim thought, is that you have to run fast enough they can't catch you, but not so fast they give up. Neither was easy in the jungle. You could break contact in a matter of a few meters—something he was used to doing. Scatter. Cause them to split their forces smaller and smaller, until, if you desired, you could pick them off. Making the survivors even less eager to chase you down.

That was why he'd planted the tripwired claymore. Ordinarily you wouldn't do that—even though it had eliminated a few of the pursuers, it had pointed as surely as a finger to where he and his men must have been, thus focusing the search.

He tucked behind the bole of a banyan tree, scanning the jungle behind him for movement. Around him the

Montagnards also took cover, some of them grinning, some of them obviously fearful.

He smiled, more to try to show how confident he was than out of joy. He wasn't joyful. He was just as scared as they were. Just thought it wouldn't be a good idea to show it.

Panic is a strange thing. Men who just a few moments before had been fighting for their lives, holding position no matter what, would be seized with unreasoning fear, and that fear would spread quicker than any disease. One man would break, and then another, and it was soon a flood. Battles had been lost for less reason.

So you sucked it up, projected confidence you didn't feel.

A WHANG! as a round snicked off the tree just above his head, warbling now as it tumbled end over end into the jungle.

Shit, he thought. That's a little too close. Time to move on.

Several hundred meters ahead Y Buon Sarpa and Willi Korhonen finished emplacing their heavy weapons, then took their places in a hastily dug hole that would serve well enough for a command post. Their weapons were a hopeless hodge-podge, firing a dozen different cartridges. Some of the boxes the bullets had come in were so old they still bore the markings of the World War II antagonists who had first used the weapons—7.92 Mauser for the KAR-98s with which a long-ago CIA program had armed village defense forces, 7.65mm for the MAS-49 rifles left over from the French, 9mm Parabellum for the Schmeisser submachineguns and MAS-38s, .30 M1 carbine, .30–06 for

M1 rifles and 1919A-6 machine guns, 7.62 NATO for the M-60s, 7.62x39 Kalashnikov for the AK-47s and RPDs, .45 ACP for the Thompson submachineguns and M-3 Greaseguns, 5.56mm for the M-16s and CAR-15s. And that didn't count the pistols.

Going up against a modern, well-armed and homogeneous force. A force, moreover, that had been hardened and tested in a dozen years of war. And which, by the way, outnumbered them.

Korhonen, at least, was happy. "Just like when we fought the Russians," he told Sarpa, for perhaps the tenth time. The Montagnard commander was getting heartily tired of the speech, but didn't see a way, absent shooting the big Finn, to stop it.

"Always outnumbered," Willi continued. "But we hit them in the rear, on their flanks, confused them. Took out their leaders. They don't fight well without leaders. Neither do the Vietnamese."

Neither, particularly, do we, Sarpa thought. Years of training under the Americans hadn't completely erased the tribesman's tendency to defer to the chief in all things. Even when the chief was wrong.

Sarpa wondered if he was. Perhaps he should have been taking his people to refuge in Thailand, as so many others had, rather than sticking in his homeland. Becoming a thorn in the side of the enemy. Was it just that he hated them so much? Would not rest until the last of them was chased back to the lowlands where they belonged?

He shook his head, almost imperceptibly, at his own thought. No. His people belonged here. They had been in this place longer than recounted in the tales told late at night by the old ones who were heirs to the tales told at night by generations of others. He knew, with a knowledge that came from the very core of him, that he would surely pine away and die should he be taken from this place. As would most of the others.

Korhonen noted the tiny movement of Sarpa's head. "You don't think we can win?" he asked.

"Of course I do," Sarpa replied. "We must. We have no other choice."

And that's just the problem, he thought. We have no other choice.

They heard a burst of fire, muffled by the trees but still fairly close.

"Jim Carmichael is still alive, then," Sarpa said. He allowed himself a small smile.

"Or was until just then," Korhonen said, somewhat grudgingly. He thought it should have been him who led the Viets into the ambush.

"Sometimes I think he is the only one who will survive this whole war," Sarpa said. "Look!"

Breaking through the trees by ones and twos were the Montagnards who had accompanied Carmichael. They were now at a dead run. Only open area ahead. Channeled by the river on one side and a field so overgrown by secondary growth that trying to move through it would take machetes and more time than anyone had. Such a place was a killing field. Only fools would try to make it through.

Sarpa smiled again. Only fools, and a crazy American, who was just now emerging from the trees, taking a moment to turn and fire a magazine into his unseen pursuers.

Lieutenant Colonel Minh heard heavy firing to his rear and had a moment of doubt about the wisdom of this course of action. It was hard to tell exactly, but it sounded like where he had left his headquarters.

No matter, he told himself. Third Company can handle itself without me. Probably only a diversion to make me stop the chase.

As if it would work! Up ahead he could see the quarry, trying to make their way across the open ground. Not a chance. They would be cut down long before they reached the next treeline. Already his men were steadying themselves, some in the kneeling position, others braced against trees to better their aim. The AK-47 was not particularly accurate, being meant more for volume of fire than preciseness, but at this range his men could hardly miss.

"Don't shoot the American," he screamed. "I want him alive."

His shout was lost in the burst of fire. One by one they went down, dropping like stones and not rising again. He was shouting now, CEASE FIRE, CEASE FIRE! but it was doing absolutely no good.

Then the American dropped, and his heart dropped as well. The idiots! He had not come this far only to fail because of a bunch of fools disobeying orders. For a moment he thought to take the pistol and shoot a few of them. That would show them the folly of disobeying.

Then the last of them was down, at least a hundred meters away from the nearest treeline. The firing slowed, slackened, finally stopped except for a few stray shots.

He was seething. "Go, go," he screamed. "Maybe one or two of them is still alive. If the American is alive, and someone hurts him further, I will personally blow his brains out on the grass. Do you understand me?"

The men closest to him nodded that they did. The ones

farther away rolled their eyes at his foolishness. These men had killed their friends. Of course they had to die too.

He strolled out into the open, squinted up at the sun. Was it still so early? It seemed a lifetime since the chase had begun. Ahead of him the men were moving cautiously, angering him the more.

"Go, go," he said. He was thinking that, if they let him bleed to death . . .

The next thing to go through his mind was a match-grade .30–06 round fired through an M-1 Garand sniper rifle equipped with an M-82 scope. A weapon hopelessly obsolete, used extensively by the U.S. Army in World War II and Korea, long since superseded by the M-21 sniper system based on the accurized M-14 rifle.

But it still did the job, Korhonen thought as he watched the Vietnamese commander's head disappear in a pink mist. He sighted on the radio operator.

The shot was the signal for the initiation of the two-hundred-meter-long ambush. A roar of fire as a hundred weapons opened up, each shooter having taken his aim at a specific individual. The exposed troops were cut down like wheat before a combine, those surviving the first burst of fire trying frantically to hide, find cover, return fire.

Only to be caught by the crossfire of the men they thought safely dead, now emerging from the predug holes into which they'd dropped when the bullets from the tree-line had gotten too close.

Jim Carmichael methodically worked the M-60 machine gun that had been sited specifically for the purpose. Three-round bursts into one man, already moving to the next before the last round had time to hit. They flopped back, or dropped where they stood, or twisted as if they

were trying to bore a hole in the ground. No theatrical flying through the air, even when grenade bursts from the
40mm M-79 rounds fired by the little Montagnard in the
next hole over landed at their feet.

They died, that was all. If you were to ask Jim
Carmichael what he was feeling at the moment he would
have looked at you like you were from another world. A
world where it meant something to kill a man. Here it
meant nothing at all. It was a job that had to be done, that
was all.

The ambush was set up in the form of a Z, if you
straightened the upright. His troops were at the bottom leg
where they could sweep the kill zone with enfilade fire.
The main force was on the upright, pouring flanking fire
into the enemy. At the top a holding force guarded against
the enemy trying to flank the flankers.

The kill zone had been picked with special care. The
ground was almost perfectly flat and level, courtesy of
some long-ago farmer who had undoubtedly spent years
working on his fields. There were no folds, no dips, no
hillocks behind which you could take shelter.

You stood up, you died. You lay down, you died. The
flanking machine guns were positioned to sweep the kill
zone with interlocking fire about six inches high.

A few of the brave ones tried to assault into the
ambush. They got no more than twenty feet before being
cut down.

And as quickly as it had begun it was over. The lack of
sound was somehow shattering. Where before there had
been chaos, now there was only the snap and creak of
slowly cooling guns and somewhere out there the moans of
someone not yet quite dead.

Jim maintained position as the recovery teams swept the area, grabbing anything of value. Guns, ammunition, grenades, documents, maps.

There was no more shooting. The wounded would stay that way. Jim had insisted on it, back when he'd laid out the plan to Sarpa and Korhonen. Not out of any particular sense of mercy—as badly as some of those out there were suffering it would probably have been a kindness to put them out of their misery.

"Kill someone, and they bury him," he'd said. "Half-dozen grave diggers can do that for any number of people. Wound someone and it takes at least two people to carry him. Maybe four. And they've got to get him treated, which takes up medicine I suspect they don't have a lot of. Then they've got to keep him in a field hospital, or evacuate him. Anybody up and down the line, they look at him and think, that could be me. Dead people they can forget about. Wounded ones, they've got to look at every day."

Korhonen had looked at him in new respect.

"You've learned your lessons well," he'd said.

"I was taught by the best," he'd replied. And now he looked at the carnage and thought that perhaps he'd learned a little too well.

Worry about that later. Sarpa was giving the signal for withdrawal.

They faded back into the jungle, the only sign they'd been there the empty brass littering the firing positions and the bodies left behind.

CHAPTER 19

Finn McCulloden surveyed his assets for the extraction of the team and reflected that, for a country not at war, Thailand wasn't in bad shape. There were three Huey "slicks," troop-carrying choppers armed only with M-60 machine guns on each door. One would act as the extraction chopper, one would be in reserve in case the first one got in trouble, and the third would act as command and control.

Two Cobra gunships, armed with 2.75-inch rocket pods and miniguns mounted in a swiveling ball under the nose. The Cobras' mission would be to suppress ground fire that might endanger the slicks. Long, skinny birds, they provided as little surface as possible at which to aim.

Orbiting overhead would be a flight of F-5 fighters. The F-5s would provide bombing and gun support for the extraction, taking out targets that offered too much threat to the slower-moving Cobras. Two of the four fighters would be carrying napalm and the other two had 250-pound bombs. All had gun pods for close air support. Their dwell time was minimal and they had no midair refueling capability, so they'd be on hold until just before the actual extraction, then would take to the air. Inasmuch as the team's position was only ten miles across the border, it wouldn't take the subsonic fighters long to get there.

Back in the old days the fighter support would have been "Sandys," the A1E prop-driven fighter planes first used in the Korean War. Dump trucks of the air, some people called them. They carried an unbelievable amount of ordnance, could loiter over the objective for hours, and had pilots who loved to get down and dirty. But the A1Es were all gone.

Except for those the Viets might have captured, Finn found himself amending. Be a hell of a thing, to find them on the other side.

Of course, there would also have been a Covey, a light plane containing a pilot and a rider, the latter of which would have been a recon man himself. Covey would have been directing the action, communicating with everyone concerned, controlling the aircraft in a hugely complicated aerial ballet.

No Covey. The Thais didn't have anyone trained in the technique, even though they had a few of the older-model O-1 Birddog planes that Covey had used until they'd been replaced by the newer push-pull prop O-2s.

No, command and control of this operation would have to be done from the Huey. And it would be done by Finn McCulloden and his Thai counterpart, Captain Tienchai.

Finn had rationalized that he had been restricted from going on the ground in Laos, but no one had said anything about his being in the air. The idea had actually been posed by Lieutenant Bucky Epstein, who had of course intended to ride the C&C ship himself.

And had been highly pissed when Captain McCulloden had pulled rank and had taken the mission himself.

"Then why can't I ride chase?" he'd asked.

"Because we need someone here to take care of the rest of the teams," Finn had said, reasonably, in his estimation. "Besides, I get shot down over there, I'd sure like an American voice on the other end of the radio. That would be you."

"Shit!" Bucky had said. He was even now sulking in the command center.

The choppers were spooling up, the whine of the turbines filling the air, scattering a flock of birds at the end of the runway. They rose squawking into the sky, the red and gold of their wings beautiful in the sunlight.

Finn looked to the east, saw the thunderclouds that had been worrying him all morning moving closer. The air weather officer in Bangkok had forecast a probability of rain, starting today and perhaps continuing through the near future. A typhoon was building somewhere out in the South China Sea.

It was now or never. The weather closed in and the team would be well and truly screwed.

He and Captain Tienchai had already made arrangements to extract the few teams that hadn't already crossed the border to safety. Those teams had moved to safe areas where the extractions should be relatively routine.

The only wild card was this one. Their as-yet-unknown benefactors had been providing a steady stream of information through the URC-10 radio contact they continued to maintain. The team had broken contact a half-dozen times, only to be found again and again. Two team members had suffered wounds, though both could still function.

They were down to no more than two magazines of ammo each, and very few grenades. One or two more contacts and it would all be over. The team leader had vowed never to be taken alive. It was get them now or try to recover bodies at some later date.

That wasn't going to happen. Not if Finn McCulloden could help it.

He and Tienchai ran to the helicopter, fitted on the headsets connected to the big radio console mounted just behind the pilots, made commo check first to the pilots and the crew chiefs, then to the other choppers. Tienchai would do the work necessary for close air support; Finn would control the actual extraction. It was a division of labor that had worked in earlier field problems, Finn finding Tienchai to be a consummate professional. Never rattled, at least not in the exercises. Only time could tell what would happen when the bullets started flying.

He didn't think he had anything to worry about. The Thai captain spoke excellent English and had attended a number of schools in America, including the Infantry Officers' Advanced Course just a couple of classes behind Finn.

His only problem, as far as Finn was concerned, was that he seemed terribly worried that Finn remained unmarried. Tienchai had fixed him up a half-dozen times with what he called very nice Thai girls; no hookers, he insisted. One of them had been his sister, another a cousin.

Not that Finn minded all that much. He wasn't immune to the charms of the tiny girls with the merry brown eyes, had done his share of sampling the delights of Patpong Street while in Bangkok. But he thought that marriage, whether to a Thai girl or to anyone else, just wasn't in the cards. He'd seen too much of the results of wives left at home while their husbands wandered the world, wanted no part of it for himself.

Someday, he told himself, when I get tired of this shit and decide to settle down, then maybe.

In the off-chance I'll ever make it that far.

"Feen," Tienchai said, his voice tinny over the radio. "What you think?"

Finn looked out to see the blades whirling on all the choppers, the Cobras beginning to hover. Indications of readiness came over the radio.

"Let's do it," he said. Tienchai keyed his mike and within seconds they were airborne, leaving the clouds of red dust where the rotor wash had churned it up looking like storm clouds below them.

The door gunners flipped belts of ammunition into the feed trays of the M-60 machine guns, closed and locked the trays, put the weapons on safe. Ran their fingers down the belts to make sure there were no kinks, no bullets that had slipped either forward or back in the links, that the path of the belts would be smooth no matter which way the guns were pointed. The guns had full range of movement outside the doors, stopped only in the rear by the masking of the back of the doorway, in the front by a fabricated post that kept them from pointing at the back of the pilot or copilot's head. Fliers did tend to get a little testy when they looked to the rear and saw the muzzle of a loaded machine gun staring at them.

Finn inserted a magazine into his CAR-15, pulled back the charging handle, and let it go, chambering a round. He put it on safe, let it hang from the sling he'd fabricated from one that had come with an M-60. Long enough to allow him to bring the weapon to his shoulder, short enough to keep the gun from banging into things it shouldn't. Like his knee when he tried to jump from the chopper, as had once happened. He'd spent a very long four days on patrol, limping on a knee that looked like a baseball and was very nearly as hard.

Tienchai charged his own weapon, a FN-FAL 7.62mm assault rifle that was very nearly as long as he was tall. The Thai scorned the 5.56mm cartridge of the M-16s or CAR-15s carried by most of his countrymen. Little bitty bullet, little bitty hole, he said. Big bullet, big hole.

The surprising thing was how well he shot it. The FN's recoil was ferocious, particularly when fired on full automatic. Finn, who could in no way be called a small person, had trouble controlling it, seldom able to keep it in the target zone for more than a three-round burst.

Tienchai had no such problems.

The choppers formed up and headed back toward the west. Although it was only a short hop across the Mekong into Laos, it would have been foolish to take that route. By now the NVA, through a spy network that had been established during the war and was undoubtedly still operational, would have been watching the camp and the approaches quite carefully. The spies would alert the air defenses and the flight would likely have run into a whole hornet's nest of guns, everything from the AK-47s of individual troops up through the 37mm and 54mm radar-guided batteries that had proven so effective against air power on the Trail.

Instead the choppers flew to a training area they'd used before, and the lead settled down into a small clearing while the Cobras made dry-fire practice runs. The hope was that any observers would think this just another training exercise and not pay a lot of attention when, after the lead picked up from the LZ and tucked in behind the follow bird, they flew north.

A half-hour of this and the birds turned back to the east. They dropped altitude, flying right down on the deck.

SMACK! Jesus, Finn thought, are we being shot at already?

A bout of nervous laughter came over the intercom, followed by a burst of Thai, only a little of which he caught.

"Bird," Tienchai said, pointing at the windscreen. Their flight had scattered a flock of lorikeets, one of which had impacted the windscreen. Luckily the Perspex had held. Finn had been the passenger on a Huey back on an exercise in Louisiana when a duck had made a similar hard landing. It had ended up plastered to the chest of the copilot.

He barely saw the glimmer of the Mekong before they were over it. Indian country now. The door gunners were anxiously scanning the foliage below, ready at an instant's notice to return fire against any muzzle flashes. Not that it did a lot of good, generally. They were moving entirely too fast for effective fire, but at least it might suppress the gunners below long enough for the other choppers to get through.

That was the theory, anyway.

It was only minutes until they were in the area from where the team had last made contact. Tienchai already had his URC unlimbered and was attempting contact. For the first few moments there was nothing, and it showed on his face. Frustration, fear for their safety, anger at the men who might even now be rifling their bodies.

Then a voice, very faint and broken. Batteries dying, Finn thought, listening in on his own emergency radio. A series of numbers he recognized as coordinates. Tienchai quickly checked the map he had unfolded on his lap, located the site, gave instructions to the pilots. The pickup ship broke formation, heading south, followed quickly by the chase. The Cobras assumed flanking positions.

The pilot of the command ship, following Tienchai's instructions, climbed up to a position where they could see what was going on. It was a far more dangerous spot, but you couldn't very well influence the action down there on the deck. All you'd see would be the tail ends of the other choppers.

Finn watched as the pickup chopper suddenly flared out, the pilot bringing it from an air speed of over a hundred miles an hour to a near dead stop. Finn could see no clearing beneath, no place to land, certainly no place to pick up a team in trouble.

Then bundles came tumbling out the doors, one to each side, each quickly paying out line.

Shit! he thought. Rope extraction.

Down below the team, or what might be left of it by now, would be grabbing the nylon ropes, each of which would have four snap links attached, and would be hooking up the corresponding link on the STABO rigs they wore. The STABO rig had been invented by a couple of Special Forces NCOs in Vietnam. It consisted of a harness designed much like that worn by freefall parachutists. You wore the leg straps folded up in the back, it being a sure way of getting chafed half to death should they be kept in the ready position between your legs. When ready to go you unsnapped them, brought them up between your legs, and snapped them into the front of the harness.

On the shoulders was an inverted V-shaped harness, the

legs of which attached to the main body of the harness, the V part with another snap link. Snap in, give the signal, and the chopper would lift you straight off the ground, above the trees, then assume forward speed. You dangled beneath the bird until you reached a relatively safe area, whereupon you would be let down, the ropes would be pulled in, and you could board the chopper for the next part of the ride.

The STABO rig had been designed to replace the McGuire rig, nothing more than a loop of canvas in which you sat, with a smaller loop you were supposed to put your hand and wrist through to hold on to. It had worked well enough, had saved any number of recon teams in trouble, but the problem was that if you were wounded you stood an excellent chance of falling out of it when you lost your grip. After a couple times watching helplessly as a team member made the long trip to the ground, the inventive SF men had decided that, clearly, something needed to be done.

The STABO rig even allowed you to bring out the dead. You could also, at least theoretically, return fire at people shooting at you from below. In reality, since you were probably spinning out of control as the wind buffeted you, it was likely all you really wanted to do was hang on.

The system worked great in training. In practice, when all too often the only time you would call for rope extraction was when you were in deep shit and couldn't get to a cleared area for extraction, you were likely to be under fire. And helicopter pilots, when under fire, tended to try to exit the area as soon as possible. A bird slowly lifting until the people underneath were clear of the trees was an irresistible target.

Back in the Advanced Course Jim Carmichael had told the story of one such extraction, when the pilots had dragged him through the trees for at least a hundred meters (though with each telling the distance got longer and longer), and how he'd been stripped of everything but the rig itself.

Finn had laughed, along with the others, at the thought of Carmichael's skinny white ass being displayed for all the world to see, but suddenly the thought didn't seem nearly so funny.

Still no firing from below. Had the team managed to break contact well enough that they'd gotten away? Didn't seem likely, them calling for a rope extraction and all.

He was just on the point of calling for the backup F-5s, thinking it possible that this was the setup for a giant ambush, when the copilot let out a string of oaths and dived toward the deck. Finn was on the cusp of asking "What the fuck?" when he heard a Whoosh!

Dirty gray trails of smoke suddenly appeared outside the open door, followed moments thereafter by twin explosions as two rockets hit the jungle below. Finn craned his neck to look behind them, saw something that chilled his blood.

Two helicopter gunships jockeying for position, and even as he watched the lead let go two more rockets.

Down on the ground the team leader had just snapped in when he heard the explosions. He swore. He knew it was all going too smoothly. They'd been compromised shortly after insertion, and it had been a mad chase ever since. The radio man had been killed in the second firefight and there had been no chance to salvage their only contact with the FOB. They'd broken contact, only to be discovered again by a team of NVA beaters, who, it appeared, were trying to channel them into a kill zone. He'd surprised them by attacking, bursting through the lines in a hail of fire that took out one more of the team. There had been no chance to determine if he had been killed or was just wounded.

Each of them had known at the outset that this would be the way of it. They had committed their lives to the cause, and hoped it would be enough for the Buddha.

Two more days until he'd finally made contact with an unknown station, which had told them to hunker down, avoid contact, and that they'd call for extraction.

Another day of hiding, wondering if he was doing the right thing, or if he should take his surviving soldiers back to the west and attempt to cross the Mekong into safety. He knew the likelihood was that the NVA would have a cordon in that direction, that the chances of fighting his way through it again were slim to none, but it had seemed preferable to just sitting there and waiting for someone to come kill them.

Then the call on the radio. He'd recognized Tienchai's voice, and hope sprang up again. And when everything had gone so smoothly up to now the hope had increased to near-certainty that he was going to live.

Fool! he told himself.

They were ignoring the lift ship, and that was, Finn supposed, good. It would have been nothing more than a big, fat target. The 2.75-inch rockets weren't really intended for precision, served more as aerial artillery, and when the warhead landed anywhere within fifty meters it was considered good. But at the ranges the attack choppers could get—just outside standoff distance so the explosion wouldn't take them out as well—they really couldn't have missed.

As it was the pilot of the command ship was applying all the maneuvers he'd learned in flight school and several years of flying thereafter. He was, Finn knew, a graduate of the U.S. Army flight school at Fort Rucker, had received advanced training as a member of the Cobra Division in Vietnam, and had another five years of practice under his belt since.

Still, it was everything he could do to evade the rockets. And now the other gunship was jockeying into position, trying to triangulate them, thus cutting down his room for maneuver even more.

They knew what they were doing. They wanted the command ship specifically, knowing that the high-value targets would be inside, hoping that the operation would collapse into chaos without command and control. Then they could pick off the lift ship and possibly the chase as well, somewhat at leisure.

Even if the lift got the troops off the ground and past the trees it would still be an easy target. It couldn't very well maneuver with the team on strings down below. The crew chief and pilot would then be faced with a stark choice—wait for the rockets to hit, as they surely would, and lose everyone, or cut the team loose to fall screaming into the jungle below. Every time you went out on a rope extraction the crew chief maintained a very sharp machete close at hand. All too often someone below would get caught up in the trees, and the chopper would be straining to lift him and a two-hundred-foot-high banyan tree as well. A quick swipe with the machete, and it would be over.

Finn saw a glimmer of a chance when the second chopper swept around to their left, crabbing suddenly into firing position. "Shoot!" he screamed to the door gunner.

The gunner, just a kid, was frozen into position, undoubtedly praying to Buddha to keep him safe and forgetting completely about the M-60 machine gun he was clutching so tight Finn had to muscle him away from the spade grips.

Now if this sonofabitch will just work, Finn thought as he pressed the butterfly triggers with his thumbs. And they kept it lubed, and didn't put the belt in upside down, and there's no missing parts, or any of a dozen other things that would keep the temperamental gun from working. Back in the old days they would have test-fired both weapons as soon as they'd reached a free fire zone, but there were no free fire zones inside Thailand, and by the time they'd crossed the border they hadn't dared attract the attention the chatter of the guns would bring.

The gun roared into action, the sound deafening even through the headphones. Brass clattered on the floor, the disintegrating links of the belt falling with them, powder smoke quickly filling the air.

Too low and left. The tracers were falling below the enemy chopper. Finn directed the gun like a fire hose, watching as the arc of bullets moved up toward the front windscreen of the Huey, seeing the mouths of the Vietnamese pilots inside suddenly working.

The chopper veered away, the two rockets they'd managed to punch out shooting harmlessly wide. Finn followed it with the tracer stream, was rewarded with the sight of at least a few of the rounds impacting into the tail boom.

His own pilot, seeing the action and a small chance of at least stinging the enemy, swung their own chopper around, clearing the field of fire of the crew chief on the other side. The chief, a grizzled old veteran of perhaps thirty, needed no prodding. His gun roared, tracers reaching out for the following chopper, forcing it to also break off its rocket run.

The enemy choppers, obviously communicating, suddenly changed tactics. Fed up with the inaccuracy of the rockets, they decided any number could play the same game. The chopper Finn had been shooting at suddenly pulled pitch and rose while the chase machine slewed sideways. Finn saw green tracers flash by, heard even over the roar of his own machine gun the heavier boom of the enemy weapon.

Shit, he thought. They've mounted 12.7s on the pintle mounts. The 12.7mm was the Soviet bloc equivalent of the .50-caliber Browning Machine Gun. As his chopper was armed with 7.62mm M-60s they were seriously outgunned.

Just aside from being outnumbered.

And if the other chopper got above them they were seriously screwed. The M-60 mounts were intended for ground support. There was no way they'd elevate enough to shoot at someone above them.

Shit!

The Thai team leader was amazed to feel the lift of the chopper, his feet leaving the ground so abruptly he almost dropped his weapon. He gave a moment of thanks to the pilots above, and another to the Buddha. He was pulled steadily upward, glancing over at surviving members of his team to make sure everyone was properly hooked up, that no one stood in any danger of getting snagged on the trees. All clear.

He looked up to see the face of the crew chief, eyes

shielded by the smoked plastic visor of his helmet, grinning down at him. The chief raised a thumb in question. He returned the gesture. All clear.

Now they were in the upper canopy. A few more feet and they'd be clear. Procedure was to get them a few more meters above the tallest of the trees around them, then pull pitch and assume forward speed. The inertia of the bodies below would cause the ropes to swing backward, raising them even higher.

Then it was a straightforward ride to the border. Once across they would be safe. Or at least he assumed so. As many troops as he'd seen on this side, he couldn't be sure they hadn't already crossed into his own country.

They'll get a proper welcome, he thought.

They cleared the trees and the sight that greeted him was such that he hung there stunned. Three helicopters in an intricate aerial ballet, the long fingers of tracers reaching out for each other.

This doesn't look good.

"Better get him to climb," Finn shouted to Tienchai. "That guy gets on top of us, we're well and truly fucked."

As Tienchai passed on the information Finn fired another burst at the following chopper, this time seeing the bullets pass right through the opened door from which the 12.7mm bullet were coming. Suddenly the enemy fire stopped.

Got your ass! There was grim satisfaction in the thought. *You might have the better gun, asshole, but I'm the better shot.*

The lull lasted, at most, a few seconds and then the tracers came again.

Damnit! Either they put a replacement on the gun, or the guy I just shot, I didn't shoot good enough.

They had balls, anyway. He felt a grudging respect even as he sent the bullets their way that would, he hoped, take those balls off right at the stomach.

The pilot pulled pitch, clawing for altitude. Too late, Finn thought. He chanced a look outside, saw the enemy chopper at least twenty-five meters above them and moving fast to block their ascent.

Always wondered how it would end. About to find out.

Another burst from the chase chopper and this time the bullets found their mark. The Whang! as they punched through the thin skin of his bird was deafening. Imagine your head inside a five-gallon bucket and someone beating on the outside of it with a hammer and you still won't even come close to the noise.

The pilot had swung the bird around again to allow the crew chief a clear field of fire. Finn looked behind him when he didn't hear any noise, only to see the chief dangling from his safety harness outside the door. The smear of blood and brains he'd left behind told Finn that he'd be wasting his time trying to get the man back in.

The young door gunner Finn had pushed away was staring at the smear in horror. The horror was soon replaced by determination as he got up, unclipped the safety harness that would keep him away from the crew chief's gun, and grabbed the weapon. The enemy chopper was still slewed to the side, a momentary air pocket caus-ing the 12.7mm rounds to go wide. The Thai gunner opened up, spraying rounds from nearly the cockpit door all the way to the tail boom. Sparks struck off the metal as the rounds punched through the thin aluminum skin and the chopper suddenly veered away.

It would be only a momentary respite. Finn was desperately trying to elevate his gun enough to take the chopper above them under fire, finally gave up, flipped the release and pulled the M-60 off the pintle mount. He leaned as far as he dared out the door and let off a burst that came close enough to the enemy to cause him to veer away as well. The Thai pilot jinked suddenly as yet more rockets came whooshing by and Finn lost balance, forcing him to let go the gun and grab hold, barely, of the chopper. His feet started slipping as the chopper banked hard left and he watched as the gun slid out the door, the belt trailing as it fell to the jungle below.

He pulled himself back from eternity, clawed his way back to where he'd left the CAR-15. Not much of a weapon at these distances, but he didn't really have much of a choice, did he?

Tienchai had abandoned the radio and was now unlimbering his own weapon. He ran through a magazine of 7.62mm, firing once again at the chase chopper, which was now maneuvering slightly to the left rear, the better to allow its gunners to take them out. Without tracer he had no idea if he was hitting anything or not. The gesture was more one of defiance than one with any real tactical purpose.

The chopper above them was once again maneuvering into position. If it got atop them it would be a simple matter to fire down into the cockpit, the heavy bullets making short work of pilot and copilot. Both sat on folded flak vests, and the floor of the bird was armored with steel plate, but the only thing above them was thin Perspex.

Finn leaned out the door again, fired a magazine of 5.56mm at the bird above, thought he was probably hitting it, but the little bullets seemed to have no effect.

He dropped the empty magazine, pulled another from its pouch and slammed it home so hard the bolt released on its own, chambering another round. He took careful aim at a point ten feet ahead of the bubble nose, pulled the trigger.

The chopper shuddered as if it was in the grasp of a giant animal, pieces of it flying away, bullets striking sparks that quickly turned into flames as the fuel tank took multiple punctures. For a second Finn could only watch in wonder. Had he done that? It seemed impossible.

He quickly saw that it had been as he watched the Cobra gunship maneuver into position for another gun run. The nose-mounted minigun spat fire again, raking the enemy chopper from stem to stern. The tail boom cracked, separated, flung itself away from the bird. Absent the stabilization the chopper went into a spin, the pilot obviously fighting the controls trying to keep it stable.

It was a hopeless exercise. It went into the trees and moments later a great gout of flame marked its final resting place. Dirty black smoke rose to the skies.

Where the hell have you been? Finn soundlessly asked the Cobra. Not that we don't appreciate your showing up when you did.

The other Cobra was having a little more trouble with the bird that had been chasing them. Its nose mount contained a forty-millimeter cannon, devastating in its effect but of a shorter range than the minigun, and firing much slower. It had to get closer, much closer to the target, exposing itself to the fire of the enemy machine-gunners. The enemy chopper once again slewed sideways to give its gunner better fields of fire, and that was its final mistake. The Cobra was a very thin target head-on like this, and the bouncing of the chopper in the air made for extremely difficult target acquisition. On the other hand, the Cobra gunner could hardly miss the huge target the side of the enemy helicopter presented. A ten-round burst, the shells flying so slowly Finn could see them, the first impacting at just about where the copilot's head would be, the others smacking into engine, door gunner, fuel tank. One hit a rocket pod.

The enemy chopper suddenly exploded in midair, the force of the blast very nearly driving Finn out the door again. Where there had been a living, malevolent entity there was now only a cloud of dirty black smoke, pieces of the chopper spinning down into the canopy below.

Finn breathed a sigh of relief, realized he was trembling so hard his teeth were chattering. He looked out to see the lift chopper with the team riding on their strings off in the distance.

He keyed the mike. "How about we get the fuck out of here?"

Tienchai's voice came back, as calm as if nothing out of the ordinary had happened. "I think maybe so," he said. "Enough fun for one day."

CHAPTER 20

The jungle telegraph was, Jim Carmichael thought, alive and well. Word had quickly spread about their victory, and there had been a steady stream of volunteers coming into Sarpa's base camp. Montagnards from a half-dozen tribes, including those who had never before cooperated with one another, had sent representatives. Bahnar, Jarai, Rhade, Sedang, Stieng, Bru; all were there, speaking not only their own languages, barely comprehensible to anyone outside the tribe, but the bastard French they'd learned during the Indochina War and the English the Special Forces advisors had imparted.

All of them wanted to fight the Vietnamese, to carve out a homeland for themselves that would be free, for the first time in several hundred years, from outside interference. All they wanted was the instruments with which to do it.

Jim had organized a steady stream of resupply flights, the Blackbirds coming over in the dead of night dropping the freefall bundles full of weapons and ammunition, medical supplies and communications gear, mines and explosives upon which they would depend. He had been amused, upon breaking open the first bundle, to see that all of the gear bore the markings of Chinese manufacture. AKs, RPD machine guns, B-40 rockets, Semtex plastic explosive. Even the grenades were of foreign manufacture, though not the malfunction-prone stick grenades the VC and NVA had used. These were of Belgian manufacture, heavy as hell but, Jim suspected, quite reliable, as most of the things from that small but well-armed country tended to be.

The radio gear bore no U.S. markings, though, Jim noticed, it would net very well with anything the Americans had. German and U.K. manufacture, to NATO specs.

Some arms dealer was doing very well for himself, Jim thought. *Wonder who the Agency's got on contract these days.* Early in the Vietnam War they'd bought all their weapons from a former U.S. Army NCO who had, as a part of his official duties during the occupation of Germany, managed to secrete an entire trainload of Nazi weapons in a warehouse in Spain. Thus the weapons that had armed the village defense groups and Civilian Irregular Defense Groups run by the Special Forces had been KAR-98 Mausers, Schmeisser submachineguns, MG-42 light machine guns, and Walther P-38 pistols.

Jim didn't mind that the weapons were the same ones used by the enemy, thought it a good idea in fact. When the weapons reports sounded the same you didn't know if someone had perhaps ambushed one of your patrols, or if it was just some unit testing their weapons. It gave the advantage of surprise, particularly when you were the ones doing the ambushing.

Still, he thought the emphasis on avoiding U.S. equipment altogether was just a little overdone. Was it not likely that the Montagnards, if they were acquiring the weapons from whatever source would sell them, as the cover story was supposed to be, would not also accept M-16s if that was all the supplier had?

Not that he wanted M-16s. The cynic in him said that sooner or later this support would stop, probably about the time he managed to get the former POWs out of there, and the 'Yards would once again be on their own. Their only source of supply would then be what they took from the enemy, and the enemy wasn't using 5.56mm ammunition.

The drops were going exceptionally well. They'd lost only one bundle and that because it had fallen into the river. The enemy was avoiding the area after having lost several patrols to Montagnard ambushes, so the recovery parties could search for lost bundles without worrying about getting shot.

Sarpa had carved out a de facto homeland, into which the Vietnamese came only at their peril. He'd even made contact with the remnants of Vang Pao's H'Mong army, themselves abandoned by their CIA supporters after the NVA and Pathet Lao had overrun the country. There would be, he had announced in a joint communiqué, a republic of the native peoples of the highlands straddling Vietnam, Laos, and Cambodia. He was already asking for diplomatic recognition.

Jim smiled at the thought. There would be no such recognition, of that he was sure. And he was also sure that the NVA was simply biding its time. Hanoi could ill afford this thorn in its side.

The attack would be coming. Best use the time to get ready for it, rather than sending out useless communiqués.

The very first bundle had also contained all the items he'd requested to treat the yellow rain victims. There was, unfortunately, no antidote, no magic pill. All he could do was to treat the symptoms, try to maintain life force, allow the bodies to heal themselves. Some were beginning to show progress. Many, all too many, either had died or were going to.

Glenn Parker was one of those showing progress. He no longer wheezed when he breathed, a sign that his lungs were healing themselves. The bundle had contained a thoracentesis needle and syringe, which Jim had used, inserting the needle just above the floating rib into the lung, first on one side, then the other, and had drawn off several hundred CCs of yellowish pus. The improvement in Glenn's breathing had been almost immediate.

The skin lesions had been harder to treat. Areas of heavier concentration of the agent had formed huge blisters that broke and ran constantly. The skin then sloughed off, leaving patches of raw flesh that quickly got infected by the ever-present pathogens that infested this particular area of the highlands. Jim had to treat all the patients, not just Glenn, with a cocktail of antibiotics, as some of the pathogens responded well to the standard penicillin-tetracycline regimen, while others didn't. Chloramphenicol became the drug of choice. Of course, chloramphenicol had a number of undesirable side effects, not the least of which was bone marrow depression.

Inasmuch as one of the effects of the mycotoxins that formed the active part of the yellow rain also depressed bone marrow, too much chloramphenicol would throw the patient into irreversible loss of red blood cells. Wouldn't do too much good to cure the infections only to have the patient die of acute anemia.

The eyes he could do absolutely nothing about. Glenn

had regained consciousness two days after Jim's return from the ambush, only to stare at the ceiling in incomprehension.

Glenn Parker was going to be blind, and there was absolutely nothing to be done about it. The mycotoxins had attacked the retinas, literally searing them from his eyeballs. All Jim could see when he retracted Glenn's eyelids was a milky-white surface that bore no resemblance to a normal eyeball.

He'd bandaged the eyes and now kept them closed, telling Glenn during his increasingly longer periods of lucidity that it was just a precautionary measure. And when Glenn had asked if he would ever be able to see again, Jim had told him, somewhat truthfully, that he didn't know. After all, he wasn't up on the latest medical research. Maybe there was something out there that could replace retinas. He didn't think so, but there was no use making Glenn Parker's psychological state worse than it was already.

And though his patient was making progress, there was simply no way to get him evacuated. Jim had asked the FOB about helicopter evacuation, had been turned down flat. The directives straight from CINCPAC absolutely forbade it. They were not willing to risk having a CH-53, that being the only helicopter with the range necessary to get to them and make it back to Thailand without refueling, shot down over Laos. There was simply no cover story that could possibly hold up under such circumstances.

Glenn would, of course, not be able to stand the physical demands of a Skyhook extraction. As it was he could barely move enough to get off his soiled cot and make it to the chamber pot Jim had set up as his latrine. Many times he didn't. The little Montagnard nurses who provided his care and supervision uncomplainingly cleaned up the mess, paying absolutely no attention to the American's shame and distress.

Jim knew that he couldn't have done without the 'Yard medics and nurses. There simply weren't enough hours in the day for him to take care of Glenn and the other casualties and still supervise the air drops, the arming and training of the new recruits, and the construction of new fighting positions.

He'd suggested to Sarpa and Korhonen that, with the influx of volunteers, it would be best to design a defense-in-depth system, rather than depend upon the one camp. Reconnaissance of the surrounding hills had allowed them to pick out key terrain upon which to build other fighting positions, each mutually supporting the others. When they were finished any attacking force would have to take out several positions before they could make any headway at all, and stood an excellent chance of being channeled into killing zones covered by both direct and indirect fire.

Would it be enough? Jim had no illusions about that. When the North Vietnamese Army came, as it most certainly would, they would be there in such force that they would quickly sweep away the outposts, overrunning each in turn just as they had during the final assault through the Central Highlands that won, finally, the long war. They would take casualties, of course. Perhaps thousands of them. But they'd always seemed to be able to absorb horrendous casualties and keep coming. There simply was no point at which body count was going to be able to stop or even slow to any great extent their advance.

Jim had tried to convince Sarpa to abandon the fixed positions, to keep his army mobile. Keep the units small, no more than company size, stay to the jungle and the jumble of rock that made up the Laotian karst, coming together only to attack specific targets. Hit the enemy were he was the most vulnerable: his supply lines, headquarters, administrative and support staff. Without that support a modern army wouldn't be able to keep the combat battalions in the field. Unlike in Vietnam, where the Viet Cong guerrillas had been able to live off the populace, there were few people in this area upon which to subsist and those were barely able to feed themselves. Not to mention that they were implacably opposed to the Vietnamese invaders.

Sarpa had rejected the suggestion out of hand. How can I claim to have a homeland, he asked, if I don't have a homeland to point to? Just keep supporting us with supplies, and we'll do the rest.

There being no choice, Jim did what he could to help. But it would not be enough. That he also knew.

Still, so far they'd been successful. Another month or so and Parker might be well enough to travel. Jim's plan was to have Montagnard litter parties bear him west, getting close enough to Thailand over perhaps a month of travel to make it across the border.

No problem, he'd thought. I'll only have to make it through a hundred miles of the roughest terrain in the world, occupied by about half the North Vietnamese Army and all the Pathet Lao, find a boat and get across a major river, and then hope we don't get the hell shot out of us by the Thais.

At the moment that was probably the least of his worries. The North Vietnamese were building a road.

The information had first come to them courtesy of one of the H'Mong bands. This particular group had, during the war, operated as a CIA sponsored road watch team in the area west of Tchepone, Laos. Tchepone had been the nerve center for the Ho Chi Minh Trail, had been the objective of the disastrous Lam Son operation conducted by the South Vietnamese army, and had been the unattainable goal of any number of SOG recon teams. There had at one time been more antiaircraft artillery around Tchepone than around Hanoi. But then, the little Laotian town had been more vital to the North Vietnamese war effort than had the capital city of North Vietnam. After all, if Hanoi became uninhabitable there were lots of other places to locate the high command. On the other hand, if the Americans or South Vietnamese had managed to take Tchepone they would have exerted a stranglehold on the Trail that would have subjected the troops in the south to slow starvation and death.

Jim had, during a short stint with SOG back in the mid-sixties, been inserted into an LZ ten kilometers south of Tchepone. He'd lasted exactly fifteen minutes on the ground, the NVA spotter teams quickly warning the hunter-killer units that swarmed the LZ like a herd of angry ants. It had only been due to the efforts of a hell of a lot of aerial support that he and his team had gotten out with nothing more than a few flesh wounds.

Now the forces around Tchepone, the H'Mong reported, had been drawn down to a mere shadow of their former strength. There was little need for the Trail now that the South had been conquered. The victorious NVA divisions were being fed off the huge stocks of food left in the warehouses, arming themselves with captured weapons, firing the ammunition that remained in the armories of the defeated South Vietnamese army. Instead of guarding the

Trail, they were busy mopping up the last remnants of resistance, rounding up officials of the defeated government and shipping them off to re-education camps, pacifying a sometimes restive population.

All except the engineers and some skeleton guard forces, the H'Mong said. Who were busily working on an extension of Highway 9, the infamous road that passed through so many well-known battlegrounds—Khe Sanh, the Rockpile, Lang Vei, on across the border to Tchepone, and from there?

An arrow pointed right at the northern provinces of Thailand.

Jim hoped the Thais were getting ready for it. It didn't take a military genius to figure out that once the NVA finished with the South they were going to start the march west.

And it also didn't take much figuring to realize the only thing that stood in their way was a band of barely armed, ill-trained natives.

Sarpa not only wasn't going to get his homeland, he was going to be swatted away like the pest he was. Sure the Viets would take casualties. But they'd never seemed to worry too much about that before. Unlikely they would now.

The only thing he could do was make it expensive for them. In the long watches of the night he wondered if it would be enough.

Willi Korhonen, on the other hand, seemed not to worry at all. He'd thrown himself into the task with an energy that was a source of awe, particularly when you considered the fact that he was fifty-five years old, had suffered countless combat wounds, had been the host of tropical diseases known and unknown, and had for nearly ten years been a prisoner of war in the worst circumstances known to man. He'd been kept in a bamboo cage too short for him to stand upright for so long that he still walked with a hunched-over gait, much like the silverback gorillas Jim had once seen on a nature special.

Their initial antagonism dissipated through shared combat experience and a growing respect, Jim and he had started spending a lot of time together. During the day they trained the troops. At night they sat under the light of a hissing Coleman lantern and talked.

"They wanted me alive," Willi had said one night to Jim's question about how he'd survived.

"Not that I made it easy for them," he continued. "Not that I could do much at first. I had two broken legs and my chest was caved in on the left side in the crash. They got me to a hospital in a cave down in the Parrot's Beak, took care of me. As good care as they could give to their own, which wasn't much. I wondered then why they were taking so much trouble.

"Later a guard unit picked me up, moved me further into Cambodia. I tried to escape seven times. Each time they caught me, brought me back, beat me. But not so much I was in any danger of dying. Again I wondered why.

"Then the years in the cage. Moving at least once a week. They fed me as much as they got themselves. Not much. I'd look at myself in the streams we crossed. I looked like a skeleton. But so did they.

"Always we moved west and north. Crossed the border into Laos sometime in the early seventies. They started chaining me; short ankle chains during the moves, shackles at night. I asked why. The Americans are everywhere here, they told me. We have been told that to lose you would cost us our own lives.

"All the time I had hope. Surely my own people would be looking for me. Of course we would have intelligence, agents within the ranks. The information would get back, there would be a rescue mission, and even if I died, it would be among my own.

"It never came. Finally we came to the camp just south of the Plain of Jars. There were many others there. Pilots and crew shot down over Laos. Technicians from a radar site the Pathet Lao had overrun. Two SOG men. From them I learned what was actually happening in the war, not the propaganda my captors kept feeding me."

A wry smile had played on Korhonen's lips. "And you know what? The news from my countrymen wasn't much better. It was easy to see we were losing the war. It wasn't as easy to see why.

"And over the years many of them died. Starvation. Beatings. Executions. Diseases for which there were no medicines. At least none we were given. But I was never beaten, at least not badly. Sometimes the other prisoners became suspicious. Why is it, they asked, that you are being treated better than we? Why do you get a shred of meat in your rice, when the only meat we ever see are the weevils? Why, when you try to escape you are not caught and stood against a post to be used as target practice?

"I didn't have an answer. Not then."

Korhonen was silent for a moment. Jim took the opportunity to pump up the lantern, whose mantel had faded to a yellow glow. It brightened with the pressure, casting fantastic shadows on the inside of the bunker. The rats that had been coming ever closer under the cover of darkness scurried back to their burrows.

"But you do now?" he asked.

"I do now," Korhonen confirmed. "About six months ago the camp had a visitor. By then there were very few of us left alive. Only Glenn, an Air Force pilot named Radke, and me.

"The visitor was Caucasian. In civilian clothes. The clothes didn't hide the truth. I knew what he was the minute I saw him. And for the first time, I lost hope. If they're here, I thought, and know who I am, there is no chance.

"Russian?" Jim chanced.

Korhonen nodded. "Said he was happy to finally meet me. That he'd been following my travels with great interest. And that I should be prepared for another trip. That there were people very eager to meet me.

"Now I knew why I'd been kept alive, when so many more were dead. They never forget. And they never forgive. I was to be transported to Moscow."

"Don't suppose there was any chance of you being made a hero of the Soviet Union?"

Korhonen laughed, an unpleasant barking sound.

"Years before, I'd found a shard of metal buried where they placed my cage," he said. "Sharp. A chunk of shrapnel from one of the bombs. I hid it. It wasn't big enough to use as a weapon. It was my insurance policy. I always knew that if things got too bad, I could use it to open a vein. I already had picked the spot, had played it over and over in my mind. By the time they found me in the morning I would be past saving. How angry they'd be! To go to all that trouble, only to be cheated at the last moment.

"And always it never got bad enough to use it. Even in the worst times."

"But you wanted to then."

Korhonen nodded. "I was ready. The Russian left, telling the guards to get me ready to transport. He would come back in two days. And what of the others? the Viets asked him.

"I have no use for them," he said. "Do whatever you want."

"To this day I have no idea if the camp commander simply got lazy, or if he decided it wasn't worth it. When you live with someone so long, you stop thinking about them as the enemy. They are men, just as are you, suffering the same hardships, facing the same fears.

"In any case, when Sarpa's men came in the next night there were no guards around. We simply walked away from the camp."

Korhonen dug into a pocket, pulling out a cloth-wrapped piece of metal. He showed it to Jim.

"I keep it," he said. "You never know when you might need it again."

CHAPTER 21

After the near-debacle of the extraction Finn McCulloden was instructed to send recon teams no farther into Laos than they could be pulled out without air assets. This meant in practice that the teams could range no farther than five to ten kilometers, at the outside. It was anything but long-range patrolling, but Finn really couldn't fault the decision. Yes, they needed information about the North Vietnamese buildup, but at what cost? The few teams that did manage to get across the river and cover any distance at all reported that the NVA had massed antiaircraft guns so thickly there was simply no chance of getting a chopper there in one piece.

The teams reported that they'd seen huge, long-barreled cannon that, upon identification in the Order of Battle book, Finn adjudged to be the hundred-millimeter guns that had formerly only been encountered near the Mu Gia Pass coming out of North Vietnam. Radar-guided, they were formidable pieces. Even the fast movers of the U.S. Air Force got shot out of the sky with astounding regularity. The slower birds the Thais had to work with wouldn't stand a chance.

Could SAMs be far behind? He'd tasked the teams to find out, hadn't yet gotten any confirmed sightings, but that didn't mean they weren't there.

Most infuriating, he could often stand outside the command bunker and see helicopters flying all over the place over there. Former South Vietnamese, for the most part, the yellow and red colors replaced with yellow stars. But a good sprinkling of Russian birds, including the Mi-28 Hind—bristling with rocket pods and guns and, he had read in a classified report, the crew protected by a titanium bathtub proof against all small-arms fire.

Some bad shit coming down here, he often thought. He just couldn't figure why they were waiting so long. The recon team he'd rescued had identified elements of two more divisions, both first-class combat units.

He'd studied his Giap, and thought the wily general probably was just building up his forces, until such time as he had overwhelming combat power, able to overrun the entire country in a matter of days. Before the Americans could mount a response, even if they were inclined to.

Personally he didn't think they would. Certainly Sam Gutierrez hadn't been encouraging on that point. It was all still being debated by the administration, Sam had said. Which meant that some of the president's advisors would be adamantly against it, others for it, but probably not as adamantly. Meaning, of course, that the former would prevail. True believers always did.

Still, the delay had allowed him to emplace the equipment that had been coming through in a steady stream from God knew where (but Billy Craig obviously did). The FOB itself now had more M-60 7.62mm and M-2 .50-caliber machine guns than did most U.S. infantry battalions.

Finn had personally supervised their emplacement, bunkering them in so deeply it would take a series of direct hits with the heaviest artillery the Viets had to take one out.

Supplementing the machine guns were four 106mm recoilless rifles with stocks of high explosive (HE), high explosive antitank (HEAT), and beehive antipersonnel rounds. Bucky Epstein, for whom the 106 was a weapon so familiar Finn imagined it featured prominently in his dreams, had sited them for mutually supporting fire, each weapon being backed up by at least two others. The HE would be used against troop concentrations, thin-skinned vehicles, and the enemy's own direct fire weapons. The HEAT rounds would punch through the armor of the NVA T-55 tanks, immolating the crews inside. And the beehives would be held in reserve until the assault troops got close, whereupon they would be chewed up by the thousands of finned flechettes released by the rounds.

Craig had also managed to get them a TOW missile launcher and twenty rounds. Finn doubted that the American troops facing the mass of Soviet armor at the Fulda Gap in Germany had as many rounds for each weapon. The rounds were so expensive that only the honor graduate of each TOW class got to fire one. Finn had expended four, training his own Thai crews. The missile was wire-guided, responsive to the slightest correction of the gunner, who kept his sights trained on the target until impact. A good gunner could take out a tank moving laterally at maximum speed.

Finn didn't fool himself by thinking that it would be enough. They'd delay the enemy divisions, at most, a few hours. There were simply too many of them, the border with Laos was too long to effectively guard, and there would be no reserves upon which to call. Most of the Thai army was being concentrated around Bangkok and a few other major cities.

Not for the first time he wondered what he was doing, fighting other people's wars for them.

Because their wars are your wars, he told himself. Fight them here, fight them at home. Better here.

Now he just wished Bucky would get back. They had things to talk over.

First Lieutenant Epstein was, at that moment, wondering if he was engaged in a huge waste of time. They'd found exactly nothing, except several Thai woodcutters and a couple who had sneaked away from the nearby village to consummate their lust. His point man had come across them, had motioned the patrol forward where they watched for a while until the snickers of the troopers alerted the embarrassed lovers to their presence.

It had been Epstein's idea to patrol around the FOB to look for enemy reconnaissance units. Certainly he would have had his own patrols out to scout the target long before any planned attack. Grabbing up one of the enemy patrols might give them vital information on time and place for the assault.

Besides, he'd been going about half crazy sitting in the FOB. They'd done about all the work they could with regard to fortification and weapons siting. Now it was just endless days standing around, wondering if this was the day the troops would come storming through the cleared zone, the tanks and artillery on the other side of the river providing support, the sappers blasting holes through the wire.

He shuddered at the thought. He'd had that experience before, and had no desire to see it repeated.

Finn McCulloden had raised no objection to the idea, and hadn't even bothered to clear it with Bangkok. After all, the restriction was against Americans' accompanying patrols across the border into Laos. Why would anyone object to their going with the Thais in their own country? Hadn't they been doing just that while training the Border Police?

Now that mission seemed to be from another life, even though it had only been a few weeks before. Then he'd only had to worry about the stumbling and bumbling recruits they'd saddled him with. Even the graduation exercises, when they'd been transported to the far north of the country to patrol one of the few areas in which there was still a threat from remnants of the Communist terrorist organization that had once been so strong it had threatened to sweep the country, didn't offer much in the way of danger. A couple of firefights useful in acclimating the students to the feel of it, the occasional casualty on one side or the other—now it seemed like some game they'd played.

No games here. If they ran across a North Vietnamese recon unit the encounter was likely to be bloodier than anything they'd encountered in many a year.

Of course the troops he was out with now weren't barely trained Border Police. These were Thai special forces, initially trained by the 46th Special Forces Company in Lop Buri, then blooded in hundreds of encounters throughout the region. They'd been a vital, if unacknowledged, part of the Thai contingent in Vietnam, had conducted highly successful operations against the aforementioned Communist movement in Thailand, and had provided the backbone that had kept the campaign against the Pathet Lao alive long after it would otherwise have collapsed into a devastating shambles. Tough, hard little troopers, they were as good as or better than any he'd worked with in service with two armies.

They'd almost finished their area reconnaissance mission, searching for a sign, any sign, that the Viets had crossed the border and were wandering around in proximity to the FOB. Bucky was about ready to give it up and go back in. The thought of a warm shower and a cold beer after five days in the field was almost impossibly alluring.

Besides, it might be interesting to see what new goodies Sergeant Craig had managed to get his hands on. He supposed it would have been too much to ask to get a SADM. The Small Atomic Demolition Munition, the supposed backpack nuke that looked a lot more like a beer keg, had a yield of about a half-kiloton, would take out a half-mile or so, and could be transported and emplaced by one man.

Wouldn't that shock the hell out of the Yellow Star!

As well wish for a benevolent God to bring down targeted lightning.

They were running two-man teams out of a central patrol base, radiating out like the petals of a daisy. Two teams had already come back in, reporting that they'd seen nothing. As soon as the other six came in Bucky would form them up and they'd make the long march back to the FOB. Screw it, he thought. We're just wasting time.

Sam Gutierrez looked at the mass of information spread out on the conference table. Intercepts from the NSA. Agent reports from the few assets the CIA still had in place in Hanoi and Vientiane. Aerial photos taken by the high-flying U-2s and SR-71s. Radio messages from Finn McCulloden—most valuable of all. The conclusion was inescapable.

And yet the people in State were still in denial. The ambassador scoffed outright at the idea that the North Vietnamese might invade Thailand. Haven't you heard? he'd asked Gutierrez. The domino theory isn't valid anymore.

Domino theory my aching ass, Sam thought. That was the problem with the eggheads who seemed to control policy. They dealt in clichés, and when a cliché was no longer in fashion the idea behind it, in their minds, ceased to exist.

Even if faced with something like this. A show of force, the people back in Washington were saying. The Viets are having enough trouble consolidating their victory in Saigon, are still fighting in Cambodia. It would be foolish of them to take on another battle, at least right now.

Did they never look at a fucking map? Sam had raged to no one in particular, frightening at least two secretaries so badly they went to their bosses and told them they'd never go back into Colonel Gutierrez's office without escort.

Taking control of the kingdom would put them next to Burma, a country more ideologically close to them, a country with a laughable military, a country whose own internal problems would ensure its not being a threat. To the south there was Malaysia, with a very short border anchored on both sides by water. Easily defensible.

To the north there was only China, and China was supporting them. At least for the moment. Some of the reports coming back-channel to Gutierrez suggested that the wartime sponsors of the North Vietnamese weren't too happy with that country's evident lack of gratitude. That might be something that could be played, but not in the short term.

And the short term was what they had to deal with. About the only reason Sam could figure that the NVA divisions hadn't already poured across the border was that they hadn't secured their logistics. The piss-poor roads and trails leading from east to west weren't suitable for trucks and heavy equipment. Sure, they could do the same thing they had in the earlier days of the war in Vietnam and use an army of coolies to bring supplies across, using not much more than reinforced bicycles as heavy transport.

Such measures worked when you were fighting a guerrilla war and the heaviest weapons you used were mortars and rockets. You could feed yourself by taxing the peasants in your area. If you ran low on ammunition you could always take it from the enemy.

It would not work to support conventional operations. Any major assault had to be supported by artillery, to suppress enemy return fire, to eliminate fortified positions, to prevent reserves from being deployed. And heavy artillery required massive numbers of shells, not to mention the fact that the artillery itself couldn't be disassembled and moved by bicycle. They'd be using tanks, and tanks needed not only ammunition, but gas as well. The numbers of troops required for such an assault would quickly outstrip the local area's ability to support them with forage. There would be evacuation and hospitalization requirements, and so forth.

Anyone who thought that the logistics for such an operation were routine simply had no idea of what modern warfare required.

Hence trucks, and lots of them. The NVA had the trucks. Their sponsors in the PRC had made sure of that.

They just didn't have the roads to put them on. The Ho Chi Minh Trail, a massive undertaking, had taken ten years to construct. Now the NVA didn't have to worry about trail interdiction—at least not much of it—so the process could be considerably shortened.

But not done away with. That bought the Thais some time. How much, who could tell?

Maybe it would be enough. Sam Gutierrez had resisted bringing out his own big gun up to this point. You used it and there was no turning back. It would mark you for the rest of your career. Those whose heads you'd gone over would be furious, and they carried grudges.

What the hell, he thought. I didn't have much of a career anyway.

He left the room, triple-locking the door behind him. Were there spies within the Embassy?

There were spies everywhere. Anyone who thought his information was safe was an idiot.

Sam Gutierrez was many things, but an idiot wasn't one of them.

When he left the Embassy he drove to one of the few U.S. military installations left in Thailand, a secure communications site close to Don Muang airport. The gate guard checked his ID, peered closely at his face, made a call, and only then let the officer inside. A four-star general had come there one day, intending to make an unannounced visit, and had been left sputtering at the gate when the guard had refused him admittance. You didn't have an authorized reason to be in the facility, you didn't get to go in, and that was that.

Sam Gutierrez was allowed in, although by rights he should not have been, because he had befriended the major in charge of the installation, had cut through all the red tape that wound inexorably around the officer when he had tried to marry a Thai girl. Such things might be okay for the enlisted men, the higher brass thought, but not for an officer. Especially not for one whose security clearance had the code word Cosmic.

Major Bates met him outside the MARS station. "Don't suppose I can ask what this call is all about?" he said.

"Don't suppose you can, Sean," Sam replied. "But you know I wouldn't do it unless I had to."

Sean Bates nodded. He trusted the colonel more than he would his own brother. Of course, his brother was a goddamn war-resister hippie, so that might have had something to do with it.

"All warmed up," he said, leading Sam inside the Quonset hut. "You know the drill." He unlocked a door, ushered Sam inside, left, locking the door behind him.

On the table was an ordinary-looking telephone. But none of Ma Bell's phones had this capability. His voice would be routed to a transmitter that bounced signals off the troposphere, to be picked up by a receiver somewhere in the hills to the west of Washington, D.C., there to be shunted into the national telephone grid. Anyone intercepting the signals would get only a garbled jumble of syllables, the scrambling of which was done by a mainframe computer at the transmitting end and the unscrambling done by a similar unit in Virginia. Only when the words went into the phone lines would the text be clear.

And if someone intercepted that?

They might, Sam thought. And if they do, and the old

man finds out about it, there'll be more hell to pay than there would be for somebody simply going through back channels to get something done.

He picked up the phone, listened for a second, realized he was already connected.

"Senator?" he said.

The familiar voice, indelibly marked with the inflections of his native West Texas, came into the receiver. "Sam?" it said. "What kind of shit you got yourself into now?"

Senator Clyde Macallan had been a politician all his adult life, or at least all of it after a short stint in the Army during the Korean War. The Distinguished Service Cross he'd earned there had been a sure-fire credential for a young man running for office in patriotic West Texas. Elected to the House, where he'd served for twelve years, then to the Senate, Clyde Macallan had never aspired to the public leadership roles. There was no doubt that, had he chosen, he could have been Speaker of the House. His name was still being bandied as a candidate for Senate majority leader, though when interviewed the senator expressed his opinion that the position was worth about as much, as another old Texan had once said about the vice presidency, as a pitcher of warm spit.

Macallan had confided to Sam Gutierrez one night, after perhaps a few too many bourbon-and-branch, his secret to success.

"You get out front, you're a target," he said. "Done that. Won me a medal once, and more holes in my young body than I care to count. No more. Everybody's gunnin' for you. Reporters, they may love you for a while, but sooner or later it's just like their last girlfriend. That pussy they thought was sweeter than honey, suddenly it don't smell so sweet anymore. So they find more and more things wrong, and next thing you know, they can't figure out what it was they saw in her in the first place.

"Me, I like to let other people, the ones that like to see their pictures in *Life* magazine, get out there. Get to meet the ambassadors, go to all the big parties, have the corporations falling all over themselves to get them the right seats at whatever it is they want to go to.

"And when they get up there, they remember the ol' boy who helped 'em. Knew the right people, got this or that pet bill through. Could call up the chief of police in Podunk, Arkansas, and get that DUI ticket suppressed. Made sure the picture that some smart reporter took down at the Tidal Pool, two o'clock in the morning and the aide was doing something best described by a French word, never got in the paper. Then when I need something done, it gets done. My constituents need a new bridge, we get a highway bill passed. Army needs a new piece of equipment, we find the money somewhere in the budget. Everybody's happy. That's the best way to be, happy, ain't it?"

He'd known the Gutierrez family ever since he could remember. Everyone in Winkle, Texas, did. The Gutierrezes were the biggest landowners in that part of West Texas. Their holdings dated back to the sixteenth century, land grants from a grateful king to one of his favorite soldiers.

The martial tradition had continued. The Gutierrez family had fought Comanche raiders, had sent volunteer companies against the Navajo uprising in Santa Fe, had furnished soldiers for a dozen campaigns as far north as the

Red River, east to the Mississippi, west as far as California.

Unlike many of the other old land grant families, they'd welcomed the new immigrants from the United States, finding them to be hardy, frugal, and possessed of the fighting spirit the Gutierrezes so admired. The other families were largely absentee landlords, living in style in Mexico City or back in Spain, and had little feeling for how things were here on the frontier. These new people could be valuable allies, or enemies as fierce as the Comanche and Kiowa raiders. It just depended upon how you treated them.

And when more and more of them came, and the government in Mexico City decided they were undesirable, the Gutierrezes had fatefully decided to cast their lot with the Texicans. A Gutierrez had died at the Alamo, two others fought on Sam Houston's side at San Jacinto.

A grateful Republic of Texas had not only confirmed their claim to the land grants, but had offered them thousands more acres on the proviso that the Gutierrezes did all they could to develop the all-too-desolate countryside.

Over the years since the family had proved as adept at business as they were at war. Three-quarters of the people in the counties surrounding the Gutierrez ranch owed their jobs to one or another of the enterprises the family had started.

Not that it had always been easy. The land itself seemed sometimes more of an enemy than a whole army full of soldiers might have been. Rainfall in West Texas is, to put it mildly, inconsistent. Months would go by without a drop and the hardy buffalo grass would wilt and die. Then the clouds would roil and spin, the heavy drops for which they'd waited so long would begin to fall. And wouldn't

stop until the rivers overran their banks, cattle lowed pitifully on the little islands upon which they'd been stranded.
The whirling tubes of the tornados would rake the land like
the fingernails of the gods.

Still they hung on, stubbornly resisting selling off even
small pieces of the land they'd won at such cost. Sons left
to join the military, some never coming back. The ones
who did married into the local populace, so much so that
there were more blond-haired, blue-eyed Gutierrezes than
there were those who harkened back to their Castilian her-
itage.

It had paid off when the wildcatters came. The Gutierrez ranch was found to be sitting atop one of the biggest
pools of oil in West Texas.

The sudden wealth changed things not a great deal at
the Gutierrez ranch. Pickup trucks were still the vehicles of
choice. Old Antonio Gutierrez, Sam's father, was still to be
found perusing the racks at the local hardware store, his
worn jeans and boots that sadly needed resoling looking
just like those worn by everyone else.

The one thing they did do, and for this Clyde Macallan
was eternally grateful, was support their local politician, as
long as that politician reflected the values and desires of
the constituents of West Texas. Antonio Gutierrez had
financed his first campaign, and had been a reliable donor
ever since.

What he'd just done for Sam Gutierrez would in no way
pay the debt Clyde Macallan owed the family. But the family didn't deal in debts and payoffs.

They just expected you to do the right thing.

He was pretty sure he had.

CHAPTER 22

Mark Petrillo passed the just-received message to Bentley Sloane. Sloane glanced at the flash priority stamp. Operational immediate. Drop everything else you're doing and pay attention to this. Very few messages were flash priority. When they came through, you paid attention.

He read it quickly, glanced back at Petrillo. The latter's face was set in grave lines.

"This sure as hell changes things," he said.

Petrillo nodded. "Guess the POWs ain't high priority anymore," he said. "Big surprise."

Sloane stifled the reply that threatened to escape his lips, the one that said, "They never were." That part would have to remain secret.

Besides, why antagonize Petrillo? Over the last weeks they'd come to an accommodation—Sloane wouldn't question the tactical decisions the FOB commander made, and Petrillo in turn would keep him fully informed, including explaining the reasons for this or that.

Besides, he'd gotten a letter from his father, a letter in response to his asking questions about just who Mark

Petrillo was, that he seemed to have so many connections. Important connections.

Don't cross him, the answer had come back. The Petrillos are old money. Lots of old money. And old money buys power, political and otherwise.

Sloane's career objectives didn't include antagonizing someone who could bring such power to bear.

"So you're going to pass it on to Carmichael?" he said.

"You see any wiggle room in what they're saying?"

"None at all," Sloane replied. The message was quite succinct, and very specific.

Poor bastards, he thought. This is going to get them all killed.

Jim Carmichael had much the same reaction when he read the decoded message handed to him by Sergeant Dickerson.

Goddamn stupid, he thought. Sarpa, with his help, had carved out a nice little enclave where the NVA intruded only at their peril. For the last few days there had been no contact at all. The 'Yards and their H'Mong allies moved freely about the area, now not even worrying about the helicopter gunships that still overflew, albeit at altitudes that kept them safely above small-arms range.

And for just a little while Carmichael had allowed himself a little hope. That the area wasn't important enough to the Vietnamese to risk the casualties they'd take in winning it back. That he'd be able to finish his mission, get the former POWs out, though Korhonen was still saying he wasn't going anywhere. He had a plan even for that. One of the resupply drops had brought, among other medical supplies, a bottle of chloral hydrate. He or one of the sergeants would slip the knockout drops into Korhonen's food, bundle his unconscious ass up, and have him on the end of the string of a Fulton Recovery Rig before he woke up.

Now this.

Stupid.

Sarpa won't go for it anyway, he told himself. For a lot of reasons. Why should he sacrifice his people for us, again? We sure as hell haven't done right by them so far. We abandoned them in Vietnam, we won't even let the ones who made it into the refugee camps in Thailand come to the United States, and now they're being requested to bail us out again?

We do it, and there won't be such a thing as a Montagnard enclave. The NVA would never allow it. They'll come in here and kill every living thing.

Goddamn stupid.

"Sarpa in the camp?" he asked Dickerson.

Dick nodded. His brow was knotted in worry. "Saw him just a few minutes ago," he said. "Told him you might want to talk to him, once you got this message."

Carmichael sighed. Orders were orders. Even if they were stupid.

To Jim's complete surprise, Y Buon Sarpa not only accepted the mission sent down from the Pentagon, but seemed happy with it.

"I knew they would need allies in this region again," he said.

Jim wanted to say, but didn't, that yes, they'd want allies for this. And then they'd abandon them just as quickly once the mission was accomplished. If it could be accomplished at all.

He contented himself with protesting that they really didn't have sufficient assets. A couple of thousand able-bodied Montagnard soldiers, hampered by at least four times that many dependents. The heaviest weapons they had were mortars. There would be no air support, no artillery. They'd be attacking seasoned combat veterans. Surprise would only go so far.

"But don't you see, Jim, that the road must be stopped?" Sarpa replied. "If it is allowed to go through, there will be no place in this part of the world in which we can be safe. We will continually be fighting a rear-guard action, surviving only because they don't want to take the trouble to wipe us out. They must be stopped."

"I agree," Korhonen chimed in. "We allow them to do this, there will not be a base in Southeast Asia from which we can roll them back. They will be in full control."

We're never going to roll them back, Jim wanted to say. They've got Laos, Cambodia as soon as the Khmer Rouge finish consolidating, and they're going to have them from now on. Or at least as long as it takes for their system of government to fall of its own weight. There is going to be no D-Day, no Normandy, no allied army rolling them back.

His last hope that Sarpa would come to his senses was dashed when the Montagnard commander summoned his subordinates and started laying out plans.

"At least, let's get the dependents out of here," he said. "Send 'em south with an escort of soldiers. Right now the border between Laos and Cambodia is a no-man's-land. They can hide in the caves down there, be safer than anywhere around here."

Sarpa thought for a minute, looked at Korhonen, who nodded. "Good idea," he said. "It will free up some of the troops who now have to guard the villages. And we will need all the troops we can get."

Damned if you won't, Jim thought.

"You will help us, Jim?" Sarpa said.

Carmichael shrugged. "Might as well," he said. "Don't have anything better to do."

The first attack on a road-building crew took place two days later. The Montagnards had moved into position the night before, surprised to find that the Vietnamese had placed no outposts, had no patrols in the area. At first light they were ready. The attack was kicked off by a round from a 57mm recoilless rifle slamming into the engine of a Russian bulldozer. By the time the sleepy road crew got out of their hammocks and tried to return fire they were overwhelmed by the assault parties that swept through the construction site, leaving only death and destruction behind. Forty-two Vietnamese were killed in the assault, another half-dozen were tracked down and shot as they tried to escape into the jungle, and two were taken prisoner.

Besides the bulldozer, which was burning merrily, they destroyed three trucks, a road grader, and a communications van. In a bunker they found several hundred pounds of industrial dynamite—made in France, Jim couldn't help noticing—which they carried away for future use.

It was a small attack, but significant. It was followed by two others, equally successful. Road-building equipment that could be replaced only weeks, or perhaps months, later was being destroyed. The road-building crews were getting spooked. And after the Montagnards captured or killed three survey parties no surveys got done.

Road building stopped. The surviving crews pulled back to Tchepone.

It wouldn't last, Jim told himself.

He was right.

The attack came just after dawn, when the mist that perpetually shrouded the mountains was at its heaviest. Jim heard the whop of the helicopter blades just as one of the Montagnard sentries started banging on the suspended artillery shell that served as an alarm bell. He had time only to grab for the bag strapped to his leg before the olive-green form of the bird appeared over the southern edge of the camp.

All over the camp the others were doing the same thing. One of the first items Jim had requested be included in the resupply drops were sufficient M-17 gas masks for everyone in the camp. He and the NCOs had trained all the soldiers in their use, conducting drill after drill in which every soldier stopped whatever he was doing, ripped the mask from the bag strapped to his right leg, pulled it over his face, slapped a palm over the exhaust valve and blew any contaminated air out of the mask, then finally tightened all the straps. Sarpa had levied heavy fines on anyone caught without the mask, to the extent that all the soldiers carried them wherever they went, even if it was to the latrine, and had them close to hand when they crawled into their hammocks at night.

He was just clearing his own mask when the yellow mist started drifting down. He'd also insisted that the soldiers wear sleeves rolled down, as his own were now. The stuff acted as a blister agent on exposed flesh—too much of it and you'd show the same symptoms as someone with third-degree burns. The little places still exposed after putting the hat back on after masking—the hands and maybe a little flesh on the neck—would be painful but not incapacitating.

He could only hope that the men still in the bunkers had heard the alarm. The yellow rain would settle in the low places, contaminating them for days if not weeks. An unmasked individual had no chance at all in one of the bunkers.

The 'Yards out in the open, he was glad to see, were fully masked and even now running toward gun emplacements. Within seconds a stream of tracers was reaching from one of the machine-gun pits toward the chopper. The pilot banked sharply, disappeared behind a stand of trees. Good pilot, Jim thought. Probably trained him ourselves.

Suspecting that this would simply be a softening-up exercise, Jim ran to the bunker where he kept the SAM-7 handheld antiaircraft missiles, finding one of the Montagnard sergeants already there and handing out the deadly tubes. He grabbed one, ran to an open area where he could get a clear shot for long enough for the heat seeker on the nose of the missile to acquire the target.

Sure enough, he heard the whop of blades again, this time multiples. The heavily laden gunships, called Hogs by crews and ground troops alike during the Vietnam War, came in from the east, the first releasing a volley of rockets that impacted close to the machine-gun bunker that had fired at the chemical bird.

Gotcha, motherfucker, Jim mouthed as he pressed the acquisition button, heard the growl inside the missile that indicated target acquisition. He pressed the firing button, was rewarded with a spray of unspent, still-burning rocket fuel in his face as the missile jumped from the tube.

Glad I got this goddamn mask on, he thought. The Soviet missiles weren't as user-friendly as was the American Redeye.

It seemed impossible that the missile, its spent fuel showing a trajectory that spun like a bottle rocket, would hit anything. But at this range it simply couldn't miss. The heat seeker in the nose homed inexorably in on the hot turbine exhaust, the force of the rocket driving it deep before the explosives went off. Not much of a bang, really. Less explosive than was in a claymore mine.

It was enough. The wrecked engine seized, the rotor stopped turning, and the chopper had all the flyability of a large rock. Its forward momentum carried it into the trees at the edge of the perimeter where it burst into a fireball, the sounds of rockets and small-arms ammunition cooking off like a firefight all its own.

Jim dropped the useless tube, was ready to go back to the bunker to get another, saw that there was no need. The Montagnard gunners had fired at least six more missiles, four of which had found their targets. The surviving chopper, a command and control bird by the look of it, had turned tail and run.

Won't be the last of it, Jim thought. He turned to the sounds, clear even over the continuing explosions from the burning choppers, of someone in dire pain in one of the bunkers.

He dreaded what he would see.

"Glenn Parker's dead," Petrillo said.

Bentley Sloane shook his head in sorrow. Poor bastard, he thought.

At the same time he couldn't suppress a niggling sense

of relief. He ought to feel ashamed of himself, he knew, and maybe someday when the pressure was off and all this was just an unpleasant memory he would.

But right now it made the mission vastly less complicated. Ever since the message informing them of Parker's injuries from yellow rain he had wondered just how the hell they were going to get the injured NCO out of there. Even after Parker had recovered enough to walk he was still blind. Walking the dozens, or perhaps hundreds, of kilometers necessary to exfiltrate was hard enough for someone in good health, with all his faculties. You got hit by a superior force and you could always split up to join up again later. How was a blind man supposed to accomplish that?

"The chemical settled in the low places," Petrillo continued, choosing to ignore the conflicting play of emotions on Sloane's face. "Carmichael and his crew were busy fighting off the choppers, 'Yard nurse taking care of Parker managed to get a mask on him, but he tore it off. Apparently the yellow rain had some extra shit in it. VX, Sarin— we won't know until we get some samples. According to the nurse, he took a deep breath, next thing she knows he's drooling, goes into convulsions, stops breathing."

For a moment the two officers were silent, reflecting on a man who had known just how much of a burden he was to his friends, and who had chosen to remove that burden.

Greater love hath no man . . .

Sloane brushed the thought away angrily. What horseshit!

Carmichael and Dickerson stood over the freshly closed grave, Jim wishing he remembered more of the sermons to which he'd been subjected as a boy, before he'd become a thoroughgoing agnostic. A prayer seemed appropriate, but for the life of him he couldn't come up with one.

Dick was humming something, so softly Jim had to strain to hear. "Rock of Ages."

At the moment Jim couldn't even remember the words to the old hymn.

"Good sonofabitch," he finally said.

Dickerson cleared his throat. "Damn good," he agreed.

Jerry Hauck came back over. He had been busying himself with taking polar coordinates of the grave site. They'd picked a spot that would be easy to find again, with readily identifiable terrain features from which to take back azimuths and distances. An outcropping of karst that looked like a dog's head served as one marker—seventeen degrees at a walked-off distance of 753 meters.

The other feature was a characteristic bend in the river where it washed up against an outcropping of rock, forcing a change in direction. Two-five-oh degrees at a distance of 512 meters.

You tried to pick out features that would be there forever, or at least long enough for you to come back. Trees weren't good. They died, rotted. Or were vaporized in bomb blasts, as so many had been on the Trail. Hilltops looked much the same, particularly when the foliage took back over.

You also tried to get features that were neither too far apart nor too close together. Something 180 degrees out would result in a back azimuth that came close to paralleling, rather than intersecting at a sharp angle. Too close together and a thick pencil mark would blend together, again nearly paralleling.

The idea was that sometime in the future you, or some-body like you, would come back here. Take a map and pin-point the terrain features, draw lines on back azimuths, and where the lines intersected you would dig. If by some chance one of the terrain features had disappeared or couldn't be located you could still find the spot, simply by taking a back azimuth on the feature you could find, mark the distance, and there would be the spot.

You didn't want to leave anything to physically mark the spot. No cairn of stones, certainly no cross or other grave marker. Jim and Dick had spent some painstaking time in camouflaging the site as well as possible, depend-ing upon the weather to finish the job. An obvious spot would attract attention, perhaps causing the curious (or vindictive) to dig up the remains and move them.

Jerry came back over to where the others were stand-ing. "Too bad we ain't got no bourbon," he said. Bourbon had been Glenn Parker's favorite drink. Mixed, straight, over ice. He hadn't really cared. Nor had he cared about the quality, or lack thereof, of the drink. Glenn would drink Jack Daniel's Black or Four Roses with equal appre-ciation.

Jim saw Dickerson grinning, cocked an eyebrow in question.

"Remember when the SAS came to Fort Bragg, back in the early sixties?" Dick asked.

"Yeah," Jerry said, now smiling too. "Brits tried to get Glenn started on scotch. Said bourbon was some goddamn redneck potion, not fit for man nor beast."

"Parker takes a sip, hauls out his dick, pisses in the glass," Jerry continued, now laughing at the memory. "Takes a big slug.

"This regimental sergeant major, big sonofabitch, mean looking. Asks, 'What the fook did you do that for?'"

"Glenn says, 'Hell, sour mash that's been run through once is better than the shit you were trying to feed me,'" Dickerson finished.

They all laughed. Better this way. Special Forces funerals were often the scene of unrestrained hilarity as the good memories shoved away the bad.

Another moment of silence.

"Good sonofabitch," Dickerson said again.

"That he was," Jim agreed.

It was as fitting an epitaph as any.

CHAPTER 23

They got back to the camp, picked up their already packed rucksacks, and joined the last column to leave. The Montagnard position had to be abandoned. Not bad enough that the enemy knew exactly where it was, but the chemicals they'd dropped this time had lingering effects. This was shown when one of the 'Yards had picked up a weapon that looked perfectly dry, but which had thrown him into the same convulsions that had killed Glenn Parker.

They'd decontaminated the equipment as well as possible in the nearby stream, but of course couldn't be sure that the very ground they walked on wouldn't kill them, so the decision had been made to evacuate.

Carmichael avoided, barely, telling Sarpa and Korhonen that this was what he had recommended in the first place. They knew it, hence it didn't need to be said.

They were splitting up into smaller bands, each of no more than a hundred soldiers. Never again would they present such a big target. If a future target demanded more people than one band could supply they would rendezvous, hit the target, and once again split up.

On the face of it, it might have seemed a foolish plan.

How could you out-guerrilla the guerillas the rest of the world regarded as the best in the world, the ones that the entire might of the American army had not been able to smash?

In truth, most of the actual guerrillas, the Viet Cong, had been annihilated during the Tet Offensive of 1968 and the campaigns thereafter. They'd been replaced by North Vietnamese regulars who increasingly had fought a conventional war. South Vietnam had fallen not to indigenous forces fighting against the government, but to North Vietnamese divisions invading in an entirely conventional campaign.

The NVA troops they'd faced thus far, to Jim's mind at least, proved the validity of the Montagnard tactics. Kill the officers and senior NCOs and the rest of the troops were lost, showing none of the initiative that characterized a good guerrilla. They stayed to the trails and roads, the land navigation skills necessary to move cross-country entirely absent. Several of the captured soldiers being herded away by another band of Montagnards had been caught when they became hopelessly lost, so pathetically grateful when the 'Yards materialized out of the underbrush that they immediately surrendered their weapons in exchange for food and water.

Jim, Sarpa, and Korhonen had worked out a campaign wherein they would continue to harass the NVA supply lines, making life hell for the rear-echelon troops. The hope was that the campaign planners back in Hanoi would recognize the precariousness of the front-line soldiers out there at the end of a tenuous supply line and would pull them back from the border to secure the rear areas, at least in the short term.

More than likely, Jim recognized, they would just send in more troops from the North and from the units no longer needed to pacify the former South Vietnam. They'd move more antiaircraft artillery in and the resupply flights upon which the Montagnard guerrillas depended would become more and more hazardous, until inevitably one of the planes would be lost. At that point the planners in the Pentagon would decide that the program was costing entirely too much, was too subject to compromise (particularly if one or more of the airmen were caught alive), and would pull the plug.

Then the 'Yards would be left out there hanging, yet once again. They'd be slowly, inevitably whittled down. The survivors, if there were any, would be reduced to fleeing through the jungle, hoping they could reach Thailand.

That would be, of course, if Thailand offered any sanctuary at all. Which it wouldn't, if the North Vietnamese invaded.

Which was why, when Dickerson had come to him with an idea earlier in the day, he'd been all too willing to listen.

"Back during White Star," Dirty Dick had begun, referring to the Special Forces mission in Laos in the early sixties, "I was on the team that was based out of Tchepone. Working with the Royal Laotian Army. Buncha worthless turds, but that's neither here nor there.

"Anyway," he continued, "plan was back then that we'd cut the Trail by fortifying a corridor leading from the coast, up Highway 9, all the way to Attopeu. To do that we needed Nine for a supply road. Had the SVN repairing it up to the border, the Laotians were supposed to do the same thing on their side.

"Problem was the monsoons. You know what it's like. Little damn streams you could jump across become rivers eight feet deep and a hundred yards wide. Every time we'd get a section of the road done the rains would come and wash it out again. Lots of 'em got bridged, but some of 'em were so goddamn wide we couldn't."

Jim tried to maintain his patience, though for the life of him he couldn't see where this was going. What difference did it make that they'd had trouble with the rivers? That was true of all of Southeast Asia, particularly here where the streams started way up in the Annamese cordillera and came tumbling down the steep mountainsides, joining with other streams, and others, until finally they emptied into the mighty Mekong.

"Anyhow," Dick said, sensing Jim's impatience, "the biggest problem was where the Nam Kok and Xa Ba Nghiang rivers joined, just north of the road. One of 'em we might have been able to bridge. Two of 'em together, no way. Then some bright engineer got an idea. Dam one of 'em up, control the flow. Let the water out in the dry season, catch it when it rained. Wouldn't work completely when you got real big rains, but that only comes about once every ten to fifteen years. We figured we could live with that."

Over the last month the rains had steadily been increasing, to a degree Jim, even with all the time he'd spent in Southeast Asia, had never seen. The Montagnards had brought out the rope and bamboo bridges they'd stowed during the dry season, maintaining a network of trails that could be used to move quickly over and around the flooded rivers.

"And you think this is going to be one of those years?" Jim said.

"Looks like it," Dick replied. "But even in a normal year the lake they formed with the dam across the Nam Kok is gonna be pretty full by now."

"And just where is this dam?"

Dick produced a map, pointed to the spot with a twig.

"Holy shit," Jim breathed. "That's right on the edge of Tchepone itself."

Dick nodded. "Blow that dam and you're not only gonna take out the road and bridge, but about half the damn town itself. Including, if I don't miss my guess, the headquarters of the NVA unit that's building the road."

Jim grinned. "I like it," he said. "Infiltrate into probably the most closely guarded place in Southern Laos, sneak up to a dam, plant a shitload of explosives, which ain't gonna do the least bit of good."

Numerous field exercises in both the United States and Europe had convinced Jim of the futility of attacking anything like a dam. The amount of explosives you'd have to carry to make even a scratch in the structure would dwarf the capabilities of a guerrilla band. The Brits had shown, during the bombing of the dams on the Ruhr, the difficulty of the mission. Even huge bombs, skipped off the water until they hit the dam itself, had barely touched many of the giant concrete structures.

About the only way to successfully attack a concrete dam was to get down inside it, plant your explosives in a spot that would ensure their effectiveness through the tamping effect of the water outside, and blow it. The likelihood that his group could get into Tchepone, get inside the dam, and have time to blow it, without being discovered and annihilated by local security troops, was so small as to be nonexistent. It would truly be a suicide mission, and while Jim wasn't completely opposed to that, he was opposed to the idea of getting himself and all the others killed to no purpose.

He expressed as much to Dickerson.

"I'd agree with you, *Dai Uy*," Dick replied, "if the damned dam was concrete. It ain't. It's dirt."

Now Jim grinned for real. Get enough explosives into the waterline on an earthen dam and explode them and you'd cut a channel through which the water would come pouring. Within seconds it would cut a channel deep enough to collapse both sides, leading to a complete failure of the dam. The rush of mud and water would be irresistible. Jim mentally pictured the bridge being swept away, the terrified troops below seeing inexorable doom, trying pitifully to scramble out of the way of the onrushing flood.

There was no worry that innocents would be affected. The innocents had long since been driven away from Tchepone. Anybody who was there now chose to be there. So be it.

And that was why his group was now carrying, broken down into ten- and twenty-pound units, the eight hundred pounds of dynamite captured during the raid on the road crew.

"So, what's Carmichael's plan?" Sloane asked.

"The good Captain Carmichael is being quite coy," Petrillo replied. "Can you blame him?"

Sloane thought that, no, he could not. Particularly now that radio intercepts forwarded to the FOB by NSA scoops confirmed what the captured documents had indicated. The aerial attack on Sarpa's compound had been ordered before the Montagnards had initiated their campaign against the road crews. And the purpose of the attack was to keep them from doing exactly that.

Now, there were only three ways NVA intelligence could have known about the campaign in advance. One: Someone in Sarpa's camp gave them prior notice. Somehow Bentley Sloane didn't think that possible. The only people who had known about it were Y Buon Sarpa, Willi Korhonen, and Jim Carmichael. Carmichael had assured them of that fact.

Second: Someone in the FOB had alerted the Viets. That was flatly impossible. No one was allowed outside the compound, for any reason whatsoever. Besides, the only ones who had actually known about it were the radio operator who'd deciphered the original message, Petrillo, and himself. He damned well knew he hadn't done it. It was his nature to be suspicious of everyone, but the likelihood that one of the other two had managed it without his knowledge was remote. He'd taken his own security measures, put into place slowly and carefully, and there had been no triggers tripped.

That left only the third. Someone was reading the radio traffic back to CINCPAC. It could have been someone on the inside who was passing the information on, and since the info was so timely that was unlikely. Surreptitious communication with an agent handler was a necessarily lengthy process.

Meaning that the messages themselves were being read by an outside listener. To do that you needed the codes. Someone, somewhere, was passing on the codes and the codebooks.

General Miller had suspected as much, but had no

proof. And when he carried his suspicions to the chief of staff of the Army, and that individual had carried the information to the chief of staff of the Navy, he'd been laughed out of the room. Our codes are secure, he was told. Always have been. Always will be.

Hence the main purpose of Sloane's mission. Sure, they wanted to get the POWs out, particularly since their very presence gave the lie to the prior administration's assurances that all the prisoners had been returned during Homecoming in 1973—and subsequent administrations had been aware of the lie.

And of course it was in everyone's best interest that the victorious North Vietnamese have as much trouble with consolidation of their gains as possible. Particularly now that they were threatening Thailand.

But the fact that someone was reading our mail had ramifications far past Southeast Asia. If you could read the message traffic between Southeast Asia and CINCPAC in Hawaii, it followed that you could read the traffic all over the world. Such an advantage would be of inestimable value if the hot war everyone feared finally came to pass.

Worth, then, the sacrifice of a few soldiers fighting in the jungles of Laos, if it came to that. At least that was what Sloane told himself when he woke up in the middle of the night, covered with sweat, the dream of shattered bodies all too real.

"They've pulled some of their best troops back," Finn McCulloden told Sam Gutierrez. "And we can't figure out why."

He and Bucky Epstein had been closely monitoring the situation on the border, sending recon teams across the river when possible, gathering information from the fishermen and woodcutters trying to eke out a livelihood, who paid little attention to arbitrary lines drawn by strangers far away. The wads of baht pressed on them by the agent handlers loosened their tongues quite nicely.

"Artillery?" Gutierrez asked.

"Only the light stuff, the pieces they can break down and transport without trucks," Bucky replied. "No heavy pieces at all, and none of the big antiaircraft guns we were worried about."

Gutierrez shook his head. It didn't make a hell of a lot of sense. The rainy season was upon them. By all rights the NVA should have attacked already. Now even if they had heavy trucks and tanks they'd get bogged down on the muddy roads that were all this part of Thailand had to offer.

Sam Gutierrez shook his head in wonder. Senator Macallan had told him, during a second phone call, that not only was the United States getting ready to announce "joint exercises" with the Thais, but someone somewhere had a plan that would give them the amount of delay they needed.

It appeared to be working.

He just couldn't figure out how.

CHAPTER 24

"Why didn't we bomb this damn thing, back during the war?" Jim asked Dickerson, passing the binoculars back to the sergeant. The lake shimmered in the dawn, lights from the little bit of sun that made it through intermittent clouds dancing off the muddy water. Soon the clouds would join and thicken, as they did every day during this period of the year, and the rain would fall with such force it felt like you were breathing underwater without the benefit of scuba gear.

"I'm told the ambassador in Vientiane wouldn't let us," Dickerson replied, focusing the binoculars on the guard tower that dominated one side of the earthen dam. In the distance the other tower still stood in the shadow of the trees. Four guards in the tower, and they looked alert. DshK machine gun. Dick couldn't see them, but he would have bet a Yankee dollar that there were also a good stash of rocket-propelled grenades in the roomy tower. Tough nut to crack.

"Afraid it would wash out the rice farmers down-stream," he continued.

Jim grunted in derision. "Far as I know, there haven't

been any rice farmers downstream from this for the last fifteen years," he said. "Ever since the Viets came in and started using them for porters on the trail."

"Now, Cap'n, when is it you started thinking diplomats would be influenced by anything like the facts?" Jerry Hauck asked. He was lying on his back, enjoying the little bit of sun reaching them through the heavy canopy. They'd been wet for three days, ever since they'd started the march, in fact. Nighttimes they didn't dare light a fire for fear of discovery. Jerry was sure that various kinds of fungi were finding hospitable places in every crook and cranny of his body.

Jim, who had already caught a glimpse of some of the heavy antiaircraft cannon sited on the high ground around the dam, suspected that the ambassador's restrictions weren't the only thing that had held the bombers back. Low-level bombing down this valley would be a clear case of suicide and murder. Suicide on the part of the pilot, and the murder of the back-seater who had little choice but to go along for the ride.

Dickerson was watching the changing of the guard. Little sloppiness. Even as far away as they were he could see that their uniforms were clean and well maintained, they marched with purpose, and he would bet that their individual weapons had not a speck of rust on them.

Good commander around here somewhere, he thought. Damn it.

He put the binoculars away before the rising sun flashed off the lenses, alerting anyone within eyesight that there was something out there in the jungle that there should not have been.

"So what's the great plan, *Dai Uy*?" he asked.

"Plan? Hell, I thought you had one," Carmichael replied.

Both of them looked at Jerry, who roused himself from a near doze to claim he had no sort of plan, either.

Jim Carmichael took the binoculars from Dickerson, shading the lenses from the sunlight with a piece of cardboard taken from their last LRRP ration. Satisfied, he turned to the others, gave an exaggerated shrug. He thought he might have seen an opening, but wasn't going to tell the NCOs just yet.

"Guess we'll just go for the usual," he said. "Go in there, kill everything in sight."

"Ya gotta love it," Jerry said. "I guess brilliance like that is why they made an ossifer out of you."

"That and my pretty face," Jim replied. "Let's go."

In the end it proved almost disappointingly easy. Careful reconnaissance had confirmed Jim's initial assessment, that the enemy had placed his defenses expecting someone to come from downstream or to either side of the dam. Carmichael had chosen neither.

Instead the force spent the day scouring the jungle for dry branches, which they bundled together and then covered with ponchos, making field-expedient rafts. The ponchos held no air, were meant only to keep the branches as dry as possible. As it was, by the time they drifted to the dam the sodden packets were barely keeping the dynamite loads above water.

Jerry Hauck had primed the packets earlier—two blasting caps in each bundle, detonating cord crimped into the blasting caps, ends of the det cord left loose. When the teams converged at the center of the dam, the shadow of the great earthen berm shielding them from the watch towers, it was a simple matter to place the charges and tie the det cords together. Jim dove repeatedly as each charge was handed to him, embedding the explosive in the sodden earth six feet below the waterline. The weight of the water itself would serve as a tamping agent. Water is more dense than dirt, hence it would direct the force of the explosive where it would do the most good—against the dam. You placed an explosive charge without tamping and far too much of its force would be dissipated harmlessly into the surrounding air. This would produce a hell of a water spout, kill a bunch of fish, but most important, would drive the power of eight hundred pounds of dynamite against something that was never intended to withstand such force.

It took nearly two hours, and by the time the last charge was emplaced Jim was shaking with hypothermia so badly he could barely tape two more blasting caps to the exposed ends of the detonating cord. Into these caps were crimped lengths of time-delay fuse, and the fuse itself was inserted into military-issue fuse lighters. He finally finished, looked around to see that most of the Montagnards had already pushed their poncho rafts off and were headed back up the lake. He'd cut the fuse to burn for a half-hour before reaching the detonators. He hoped that would be enough time for everyone to get to the launch site where the rest of the group waited. If not, they were going to have a hell of a swim, trying to keep up with the contents of the lake as it poured into the valley. He allowed himself a bit of humor—while in Bad Tölz he'd gone kayaking in one of the Bavarian streams. Take a kayak here and you'd end up in Cambodia, he thought, letting his mind play on the sight of one of the thin boats skimming past half the North Vietnamese Army.

When he was sure the others had a good head start he removed the safeties from the fuse igniters, pulled the rings, and heard the satisfying pop as the incendiary inside was activated. Another couple of seconds to watch the time fuse bubble, showing that the powder inside was burning as it should. He then buried the igniters and fuse lighters in the mud. The fuse was waterproof. No way to stop the burning unless you cut it ahead of the flame. If some alert guard happened to pass by all he would see, if he saw that, would be a few bubbles popping to the surface. If he was smart enough to dive down below and pull the fuse and caps off the charges . . . well, sometimes you just had to hope things were going to go your way for a change.

He struck out, a side stroke for the first couple of hundred yards, less splash. Then an easy crawl, enjoying the feel of the water. The exercise warmed him back up. He felt like he could have done at least a couple of laps all the way around the lake, but thought that probably wouldn't be wise, given the circumstances.

He emerged from the water right where Jerry Hauck was signaling with a flashlight with a pinhole punched into the duct tape that covered the lens.

"Havin' a good time, Cap'n?" Jerry whispered.

"Not too bad," he replied, quickly shrugging into the dry camouflage fatigues he'd left on shore. "The others?"

"All accounted for. Gone to the rally point, just like they were supposed to." Jerry turned his wrist, checked his watch. "Should be happening pretty quick," he said.

As if in answer the ground shook, the tremors from the detonation reaching them even before the sound. Then a dull roar, and even in the dark they could see the column of dirty water reaching for the sky.

"Think it worked?" Jerry asked.

"We'll know in a minute," Jim said. He was intently staring at the waterline. The lapping of waves in the soft wind made it hard to tell, but was it receding?

"Look," he said, pointing to a rock that had been nearly awash, but was now almost out of the water. There would be no great rush, at least not at first. The very size of the lake made sure of that. An inch of water on a body this size would represent millions of gallons.

"B'lieve it might have worked," Jerry said, seeing that the rock was now completely out of the water, and that the recession of liquid seemed to be gathering speed.

"I think we might ought to go now," Jim said.

"Before we can't," Jerry replied, seeing headlights coming up on the dam. That would be the reaction force, he thought. And they're sure as hell gonna come looking for us.

They faded into the jungle.

Two days later Mark Petrillo was staring at the satellite photos, freshly delivered by courier. They'd sent before and after pictures for comparison. Where once there had been a town there was now a flat, mud-filled plain. Here and there the stronger structures—the province headquarters, a concrete rail house, a couple of houses that had the luck to be sited a little higher than the surrounding terrain—were still recognizable.

The Highway 9 bridge was completely gone. Worse, it had not only washed away the structure itself, but the revetments that anchored it on each side of the river. The rivers themselves, now neither of them being held back and the monsoon in full flood, rushed through the gap, eating away even more of the banks.

News reports being issued from Vientiane spoke of a great natural disaster and begged for aid.

They had a natural disaster, all right, Petrillo reflected. Jim Carmichael.

Time to bring the boys out. All Washington had asked for was a couple of months' delay. This would last at least through the rainy season and probably four to six months thereafter. More than enough.

He left for the commo room to compose the message.

"We're to head southwest," Dickerson said. "FOB says they've got a plan."

"Why does my asshole pucker when I hear that?" Jerry said.

Jim grinned. "O ye of little faith," he said.

"I've got faith in two things," the sergeant replied. "First one is that you've got a habit of getting me into deeper shit than anyone I've ever known. Second is that you always find a way to get us out of it. Them other dickheads, I don't know about."

They'd rejoined forces with Y Buon Sarpa and Willi Korhonen after a hard three-day march. Jim's feet felt like they were on fire, and when he pulled his socks off flesh came with them. The result, he thought ruefully, of spending several hours in the water softening them up, then jamming them back into jungle boots and walking at a pace that would have felled an Olympian.

He'd been doctoring them with tincture of benzoin, which of course burned like hell but was supposed to toughen up the skin, and was in the process of covering the worst of the abrasions with moleskin. Had hoped for a couple of days of rest. That, obviously, was not to be.

"They seem to think they have a route for us," Dickerson continued. "Due west at about thirty klicks is old Highway 23, not much more than a dirt path, I'm told. Goes from Highway 9 down to Saravane. Agency apparently still has some assets down that way. We're to link up with them, let them lead us toward the Thai border. FOB says the largest concentration of NVA troops will then be north of us. Nothing but some Pathet Lao and a couple of stiffener NVA battalions down that way."

Jim pulled the map from his rucksack, saw that the 1:250,000 map (that is, one foot of map distance equaled 250 thousand feet of ground distance) didn't even cover the section the FOB was talking about.

Dickerson handed him his own survival map, printed on silk so as to make as small a package as possible in case you had to drop everything else. Its detail left something to be desired, but at least it had the major roads and cities of Laos and the Thai border area.

"Nearly as I can figure, we're somewhere around here," Dick said, his big finger covering an area that was probably a hundred kilometers square.

"And we're supposed to go down here," Jim pointed. It was, he figured, at least a hundred miles to the border going in the direction indicated. Crossing four large and two smaller rivers, in the height of the monsoon. Avoiding contact at all costs, because the first time they got into a firefight it was going to bring down the entire goddamn North Vietnamese Army on them. All they would have to eat would be what they had in their rucksacks—three days' rations—and what they could hunt or scrounge. As a mini-mum, over terrain like this, it would be a ten-day march.

"I don't suppose they had an alternate plan?" he asked.

Dickerson shook his head.

"Guess we'd better get started, then. Willi, there's no chance I can get you to change your mind?"

Korhonen just grinned.

"Thought so." Jim had given up on the idea of drugging the former POW and sneaking him out. Wouldn't have worked anyway, he thought.

"Anything you want me to tell anyone?"

"My family already thinks I'm dead," Korhonen said. "Let's leave it that way."

Jim nodded, wondering about his own family. What about Alix? Does she think I'm dead too? He'd been gone much longer than the mission was supposed to take. Had anyone bothered to keep her in the loop? He doubted it. Frankly, he doubted that any word at all about the whole mission was going anywhere except some room in the basement of the Pentagon.

"So be it," he said.

Y Buon Sarpa came over as he was packing his ruck-sack. "I am sorry for having to fool you, Jim," he said. "But I did not know it would be you who they sent."

"Wouldn't have mattered," Carmichael replied. "Who-ever they sent, it would probably have worked out the same way."

"I think not," Sarpa replied. "It has been a very good thing, fighting alongside you again. Now it is time for you to go home. I hope that you will remember us, and our fight."

And your hopeless fight, Jim thought. You have

absolutely no chance. None at all. You and all your soldiers are going to be killed, and no one will know the difference.

For a moment he wished he was staying there with them.

"I wish you luck, and may the Buddha smile on you," he said.

Sarpa grinned. "I think we maybe need more than Buddha," he said. "Tell your people to keep the supplies coming, and we will keep up the fight."

Jim resisted the urge to tell the Montagnard commander that his people would, until it suited them not to. Then Sarpa and his men would be well and truly screwed, and nobody back in Washington would much care.

Sarpa surprised him by embracing him. The Montagnard had never been the most demonstrative of people, and the brief hug told him more than words ever could.

Fuck! Jim thought. I better get out of here before I start blubbering.

Nine days later they were in binocular distance of the Mekong. An escort of Sarpa's men had stayed with them until they made contact with the small group of Laotian smugglers still being funded out of CIA coffers, and had hung back out of sight but not out of reaction range until Jim finally called them on the Motorola radio he'd left with the lieutenant in charge and told him it was okay to leave. It had not passed Carmichael's attention that there was probably a fairly large reward waiting for anyone who turned the Americans over to the NVA, and if your only motivation was money . . .

The Laotians turned out at least to be honest thieves. When they were paid, they stayed paid. They also knew the area far better than anyone, either native or invader, possibly could. They'd been making their living off smuggling for generations, knew the back trails, the chokepoints, those places where the enemy might stay.

They were a happy bunch, laughing and joking in a mixture of Laotian and pidgin English, smoking cigarette after cigarette. This had at first bothered the Americans, before they realized that whenever the group came within range of either the Pathet Lao (who largely stayed to the villages) or the occasional North Vietnamese patrol (who didn't), they became deadly serious and stealthy enough to satisfy even Jerry Hauck.

They'd also established caches of food and ammunition at various spots along the trails they took, so the group ate as well as could be expected. Lots of sticky rice and dried fish, but it was a hell of a lot better than starving.

At one point they had, after first assuring the Americans that the enemy was well out of hearing, dropped a grenade into a pool of still water connected to the Xe Pong River, happily scooping up the fish that popped to the surface. They ate well for a couple of days after that.

And now, Jim thought as he observed farmers on the other side of the Mekong going about their business, it was almost over. It seemed almost anticlimactic. So much had gone on, so many battles and skirmishes, the loss of his friend, the deaths of so many of the others.

He didn't allow himself to think, For what? He'd done that after his final tour in Vietnam, crawling into the bottle to escape and very nearly killing himself. Now he had something to live for.

Alix, he thought. Soon.

CHAPTER 25

"Nature calls," Jerry announced.

Without a word Jim handed him his last packet of C-ration toilet paper. He needed to go too, but with any luck and a strong sphincter he could hold off until tomorrow, at which time he expected to be doing his business on a real flush toilet in Nakhon Phanom.

They'd stopped for the night, the smugglers maintaining their own small camp and the three Americans sitting back to back slightly off to the side. They'd come to trust the Laotians over the last few days, as much as you could trust anyone over here, in any case, but that didn't mean you shouldn't be careful.

The plan was to attempt the crossing of the Mekong sometime in the early morning hours, before it got true light. During the monsoon season the changes in temperature at that hour often produced a ground-hugging fog here close to the river. It would shield the boats that were to come from the other side to pick them up.

Jerry left the perimeter to do his business. The sergeant had little of Jim's distaste for shitting in the field, saying on more than one occasion he thought Jim's habitual bad mood was purely because he was always full of shit.

Jim settled down to try to grab a couple of hours of sleep, worming his buttocks into the soft ground, stopping for a moment to remove a branch that got entirely too friendly, then lying back on his rucksack. Dickerson was already asleep.

He heard a muffled explosion from somewhere in the direction Jerry had gone, followed by a low moan of pain. Dickerson, hearing it too, was already shrugging out of his rucksack, straining his eyes to see through the stygian darkness.

"Jerry?" Dick whispered.

Nothing.

Jim could sense the sergeant looking at him in question. He touched Dickerson's arm, pushing it in the direction Jerry had gone. Dickerson quickly moved out, Jim right behind. The only thing he could see was the glow of the fluorescent tape sewn to the back of Dick's boonie hat.

Dick followed the moans, louder now. In only a few seconds, though to Jim it seemed much longer, they reached Jerry Hauck.

Dick touched Hauck's shoulder, was rewarded with a soft-spoken stream of profanity, part of which was Jerry cursing himself for being so stupid as to step on a goddamn toe-popper.

At that point Carmichael decided the hell with operational security and switched on his flashlight. He sucked in a deep breath when he saw Jerry's mangled foot. The boot had been blown completely away, as had his heel and a major portion of the instep. Worse, the leg was turned around so far the remains pointed backward. He was bleeding profusely.

"Pressure," he instructed Dickerson, who quickly found the pressure point behind Jerry's knee and pressed down on it. That slowed the blood flow somewhat, but certainly didn't stop it. Jim hated to put a tourniquet on the leg, because given the fact that evacuation was obviously impossible in the short term, anything below the tourniquet was going to be lost.

But, he consoled himself, there would be no saving that foot anyway. He pulled a cravat bandage from Jerry's own pouch, tied it off as close to the wound as possible, and used a stick to tighten it. After a few turns the bleeding slowed, then stopped.

Only then did he cover the wound as well as possible with both Jerry's and his own field dressings.

He checked Jerry's vital signs—strong and steady.

"How about some drugs?" he asked.

Jerry, gray with pain from the injury itself and Jim's rough ministrations, indicated that he thought he might like just a touch of morphine. Jim injected him with a quarter grain, then stuck the needle of the syrette in Jerry's collar, bending it over to affix it there. While he didn't think there was any worry of another medic getting to Jerry anytime soon and giving him more morphine, old habits died hard. More than one man had died of an overdose when nobody knew exactly how much morphine had been given.

"Well, ain't this some shit!" Jerry said. Jim flashed the light in his eyes, saw his pupils pinpointing nicely. His face had relaxed from the grimace of pain, indicating the morphine was taking effect.

"Do anything for a little excitement, won't you?" Dickerson said.

"Fuck you, Dick," Jerry replied, his voice already taking on that dreamy tone that indicated that the drug was coursing its way not only to the pain centers, but to all the other parts of his brain as well.

"I think we'd best try to move," Jim said. "Whoever put that here is probably gonna be wondering what hit it. Go get our escorts, have them rig up a litter. We'll head for the river."

Dickerson moved off. Jim checked Jerry again, making sure the tourniquet hadn't worked loose. He was glad to see that the field dressings looked dry.

"Gonna lose my foot, ain't I?" Jerry asked.

"'Fraid so." Jim didn't see any reason to lie about it, give him false hope. Jerry Hauck had seen the results of too many of these to be fooled.

Jerry thought for a minute, then said, "Well, it ain't all bad."

"How's that?"

The sergeant grinned. "You won't be runnin' my ass up and down the mountains when we get back to Bad Tölz. At least not for a while."

Jim thought that to be true. Particularly given the condition of the leg above the wound. Its position spoke of the bones' being shattered. Jerry Hauck was in for some long, hard recovery time. He busied himself finding a stand of bamboo, cutting a length of it, and using it to splint the leg as well as possible. The bones inside would be sharp, and stood an excellent chance of cutting blood vessels and nerves if not immobilized.

He was just finishing up when he heard sounds of

someone moving through the brush; killed the flashlight and grabbed his gun.

"*Dai Uy?*" he heard Dickerson's familiar voice.

He relaxed. "Come on in," he said.

Dick moved close enough Jim could see the whites of his eyes. "Where's the others?" he asked.

"Ain't no others," Dick replied. "They've split."

Well ain't this just a fine how-do-you-do, Jim thought, unconsciously using a favorite phrase of his father's.

Without help they'd have to carry Jerry themselves, rendering them practically defenseless if suddenly hit.

Worse, if and when they got to the river there would be no boats.

They were in deep shit.

"Best make commo," he said. "See if the FOB's got any more bright ideas."

"I feel as bad about it as you do," Sloane said.

Yeah, Petrillo thought, I'll just bet your heart pumps purple piss about it.

They'd been arguing about courses of action ever since the message came in telling of the team's plight. The first thing Petrillo had done was contact the Agency office in Bangkok and tell him of the smugglers' betrayal, asking if there was any way he could get them back there to help Carmichael's crew. Not likely, the man had said. The smugglers had probably gone to ground, there was no regular contact schedule, and even if he could reach them the likelihood was that they'd refuse the mission anyway.

Too bad, so sad, sorry 'bout that.

Petrillo had then asked the military mission for a helicopter, and had been flatly refused. No way the ambassador was going to allow a U.S. aircraft to fly into Laos, possibly sparking the war that, at the moment, seemed less and less likely but could still erupt, given the right provocation.

No consideration was given to the fact that the team now in trouble was directly responsible for the decreased likelihood of war, with the front-line NVA troops pulling back to combat the insurgency in their rear.

"Contact your boss," he had then told Bentley Sloane. "Get someone in Washington onto this."

"Won't do any good," Sloane had said. "This whole operation was built on deniability. Carmichael and his people get caught, they're mercenaries. They knew the cover story before they went in there. They were willing to take the risk."

"They're fucking *Americans!*" Petrillo had shouted, so close to Sloane little flecks of spittle hit him in the face. "And I'm giving you a direct order."

So Bentley Sloane had sent a message back to General Miller, and had gotten the expected reply. The team was on its own.

"The general says we just can't risk it," he said. "They're on their own. God help them."

Petrillo, calmer now, thought that God wouldn't be doing much about it. But he would.

He turned on his heel, left Sloane standing there. Went back to the commo room.

"You still got the frequency and callsigns of those people we helped out over there?" he asked.

The commo man looked insulted that he would ask such a thing. Of course he had saved the information.

"Bring 'em up," Petrillo said. "Time for them to return the favor."

"The old man just called up," Bucky Epstein said. "He's about five minutes out. Wants to meet us on the chopper pad."

Finn McCulloden looked up from where he had been reading the intelligence reports. The sterilized NSA intercepts received directly from Gutierrez's office in Bangkok spoke of SIGINT indicators that the NVA was performing a massive pullback, something confirmed by the few recon teams he was still managing to send across the border. He didn't know what had caused it, but was sure as hell glad. Also on his desk was the official announcement from the Pentagon that a massive exercise was being planned between the governments of Thailand, the United States, and the few allies, mostly Australians, that they still had in the region.

It was a clear shot across the bows of the would-be invaders, signaling that the United States hadn't given up on Southeast Asia. Not at all.

Finn hadn't thought the administration had it in them, wondered what had made them change their minds.

Not that it mattered at the moment.

"He say why he's coming?" he asked Bucky.

"Negative."

Gutierrez had been there just yesterday, delivering the reports. Ordinarily he wouldn't have been due back for another week or so.

So something was out of the ordinary.

Best find out what it was.

*   *   *

"Think you can get a Bright Light together?" Gutierrez asked as soon as he got far enough from the whining turbine of the helicopter to be heard.

A sudden jolt of adrenaline hit Finn. Bright Light was the code name for recovery missions run out of SOG back when recon teams got into trouble across the border. Since he didn't have any recon teams out at the moment, that meant that someone else was in trouble over there.

"I expect so," he said. "Just happens we have a platoon of Thai Rangers on stand-down at the moment, but we can get them cranked up in no time. Air assets are pretty skimpy, though. Enough Hueys for the lift, couple of Cobras for support. How many people over there?"

"Three," Gutierrez replied. "And one of them is wounded. Nonambulatory."

That complicated things, but not so much that it couldn't be done.

"Can they get to an LZ?"

"They're about half a klick away from a clearing that'll take one ship at a time," Gutierrez replied.

Finn grimaced. That meant he'd have to land the Bright Light troops to secure the LZ piecemeal. Not the best of situations.

"Who are these guys?"

"Americans."

"Thought we weren't allowed to have any Americans over there," Finn said.

"I'm told these are freelancers."

And somebody up high enough to get to Sam Gutierrez is worried about some sorry-ass mercenaries in Laos?

What a bunch of bullshit! This smelled strongly of a black op that had gone to shit.

"These guys wouldn't happen to be former SF, now would they?" he asked.

"Could be," Gutierrez admitted. "I wasn't told, one way or the other. Does it matter?"

Of course it didn't.

"Gotta get back to Bangkok," Gutierrez said, turning back to the chopper, whose rotors had never stopped turning. "Some friggin' senator coming in on a boondoggle. Wants to see me personally."

Finn grinned. "You in trouble again?"

"Could be. Couple of things we've done here, didn't exactly ask for permission."

Just like I'm not going to, Finn thought as Gutierrez turned and headed for the open door of the chopper. You'd turn me down if I did.

"Get the Thai reaction force cranked up," he told Bucky. "And grab your own shit."

Carmichael and Dickerson had moved Jerry Hauck well away from where he had been injured, figuring at the very least that the sound of the explosion would bring curious villagers hoping to take advantage of any animal big enough to have set one of the toe-poppers off.

Worst-case scenario was that the local Pathet Lao troops had sown the mines themselves, and were even now on their way to see what they'd bagged.

They were leaving entirely too much sign. It wouldn't take a skilled tracker to follow them, but there was little they could do about it. No one to sweep the back trail. It

was hard enough to support Jerry, who insisted on hob-
bling along on one foot supported by one or the other of
them, maintain any semblance of tactical formation, and
blaze trail through the thick forest.

Not that they could do anything about it. Their only
hope was the cryptic message to move to the nearest LZ,
that someone was coming to get them.

Not someone from the FOB, who would have recognized them. Instead they were given a set of contact
instructions, including passwords and challenges. In Thai.

Right now Jim didn't much care who was coming, as
long as they were.

He jerked his head around at the sound of a rifle shot
somewhere behind them.

Shit! Some tracker had found their trail and was signaling others.

Things were about to get very interesting.

Finn McCulloden sat in the door of the chopper, surrounded by grinning Thai Rangers. Everyone, including
him, was loaded for bear. He carried a CAR-15 and six
hundred rounds of ammunition distributed in pouches and
in a small indigenous rucksack, eight frag grenades, two
willy-peters, and a tear gas. Two canteens nestled on his
belt, a claymore mine was packed in the rucksack, and a
Browning 9mm pistol hung to his right side. Taped to the
left side of his load-bearing suspenders was a K-Bar sheath
knife, haft down. Where there was the least little bit of
room he'd slipped field dressings, morphine ampoules, a
pen flare and bandolier of flares, and a strobe light. No
food.

They stayed across the border long enough to get hungry, likelihood was that they wouldn't be needing any food, anyway.

Across from him, the choppers flying so close together it looked as if their rotors barely missed one another, was Bucky Epstein, similarly equipped. Bucky had flatly stated that if his commander was going to disobey orders, he should be able to as well.

"D'you think Colonel Gutierrez didn't know you were going to do this?" he had asked after Finn had laid out a hasty plan. "That's why he didn't tell you specifically not to."

Finn reckoned that he was right. Gutierrez knew him entirely too well.

Besides, the thought of someone like Bucky Epstein beside him in a fight wasn't entirely unwelcome.

Behind them were two chase choppers, empty except for the pilots and door gunners. If one of the lift birds was forced down, the chase birds would swoop down, pick up the passengers and crew, and bring them back to the launch site. As loaded as they were it would take the two birds to pick up both passengers and crew, and the mission would have to be scrubbed.

If both lift birds went down . . .

Well, shit, Finn consoled himself. You can't plan for everything.

The plan was pure simplicity. The LZ would only take one ship at a time. He would go in first while the other bird orbited nearby, secure the clearing, the other bird would disgorge, and then all the choppers would head back to the launch site, sitting hot on the pad. Flying time was less than five minutes—better there than orbiting and using up fuel.

They were taking only two squads of the Thai Ranger platoon. More would have required more choppers, and they simply didn't have them. The other two squads would be on standby if things went to shit, and could come in and reinforce if necessary.

Once the force was on the ground they would leave one squad to secure the LZ while the other went to find the people they'd come to rescue. They'd rig a field-expedient litter for the injured man—a jungle hammock slung on a pole—two soldiers would carry it while the others guarded them. With any luck at all the entire force would be out of there in no more than thirty minutes.

A time period that could seem extremely short.

Or the longest thirty minutes you'd ever had in your life.

The choppers were dropping altitude in preparation for crossing the Mekong. It would be nap of the earth until reaching the LZ.

Finn felt the familiar tightening in his chest. He gave the thumbs-up sign to Bucky, who returned it.

Once more into the breach, dear friends!

"Y'hear that?" Dickerson asked.

Jim Carmichael nodded. The faint, far-off whopping of blades.

He just hoped it wasn't too late. The signal shots had been getting closer and closer. He estimated that the trackers, now probably accompanied by a sizable reaction force, were no more than a hundred or so meters behind them.

"Think you can keep going?" he asked Jerry.

The sergeant nodded grimly. The morphine had long since worn off, and he had refused more, feeling more of a need to keep his wits about him than for relief from pain.

"Keep moving then," he instructed them.

For a second Dickerson looked like he was going to object.

"All I'm gonna do is leave 'em a few little surprises," he said. "Then I'll be right behind you."

Both Dickerson and Hauck looked doubtful, but knew better than to object. It was obvious that one of them would have to stay back long enough to keep the bad guys off their asses, and Captain Carmichael had seized the initiative. All they could do now was waste time by arguing.

They shuffled off, Dickerson supporting Jerry Hauck as he hopped on one foot. Jim noted in passing that the bandage was getting very bloody—something had broken loose.

No time to worry about it. The pursuers were getting very close. He'd once been on his own Bright Light, had come so close to rescuing a downed F-4 pilot he could see the man's expression when the North Vietnamese took him away. The pilot hadn't returned during Homecoming. It had broken his heart.

That wasn't going to happen this time, he vowed. Dirty Dick and Jerry were going to get back. He'd promised that.

As for himself . . .

"You stay here and secure the LZ," Finn told Bucky. "Keep commo with the command ship. We get these guys, we're gonna need those choppers back in here fast."

Bucky Epstein recognized the tactical soundness of the command, though he would have liked to have been the one going with the recovery party. He cast a practiced eye around the clearing. The chopper had been forced to come straight down, testing the ability of the pilot as it had probably never been tested before. As it was the tail rotor of the second ship had chewed up some branches before the pilot corrected it.

The problem was a stand of young trees off to one side, like a green wall closing off the clearing from a slightly smaller one to the side. Get those out of the way and this would be a two-ship LZ.

He shrugged out of his rucksack, started pulling out the roll of detonating cord and the extra claymore he carried there. The Thai squad leader saw what he was doing, ordered his own men to divest themselves of whatever they were carrying that might make a big bang.

"We make a boom?" he asked, grinning.

"We make a goddamn big boom," Bucky replied.

Finn and his squad moved out in the direction they'd been told the evadees would be coming. Suddenly there was a burst of fire, and it didn't seem all that far away. His practiced ear told him that the sound was that of an M-16. Not more than a half-second later he heard the return fire from AK-47s. A lot of AK-47s.

All thought of stealth was abandoned as they moved to the sound of contact. He realized his palms were sweating profusely, wiped his gun hand on his pants leg, looked over at the Thai nearest him and was glad to see that the man's eyes were about as big as he suspected his own were.

It didn't really matter how many times you did this. The movement to contact was always tight-asshole. You had confidence in yourself, and in your troops, but you realized that all it would take would be one lucky shot. The odds simply were against you. You recognized early on that this wasn't the way to survive, that your chances grew smaller and smaller with each passing day, and you might console yourself with the thought that since you'd consigned yourself to death you didn't have to worry about the final act.

Which was, of course, bullshit. You still worried about it. Dreaded the thought of the bullet that would rip everything you had away from you. Woke up in the middle of the night drenched in sweat, having dreamed once again that awful dream wherein you were fighting against impossible odds, and the bullets you shot seemed to have no effect on them, and they just kept on coming.

Finn shook away the thought. Concentrate! A noise to the front. Someone moving, and very clumsily.

The point man gave the closed-fist signal, and the squad immediately stopped and took advantage of whatever cover and concealment the surrounding trees and rocks offered. Finn brought his rifle to his shoulder, sighted at the point of vegetation whence the noise came. Finger tightened slightly on the trigger. A couple more ounces of pressure and a bust of 5.56mm bullets would shred whatever it was that was coming.

"Don't shoot!" he commanded, seeing two Americans, one obviously wounded, come out of the jungle.

He showed himself, saw on the face of the unwounded one the immediate sense of relief. He sat down, clearly exhausted, forcing the wounded man with him, then immediately set himself to checking the bandage on the wounded man's foot.

The Thai squad immediately set up a hasty perimeter as Finn approached the Americans.

"Dickerson," the black man said. "And this here's Jerry Hauck. And we're sure as fuck glad to see you."

"Where's your other man?" Finn asked.

There was another burst of fire, and this time it was even closer.

"I expect that'd be Captain Carmichael," Dickerson said.

"Not Jim Carmichael?"

"One and the same," Jerry said. "Now, you gonna go help him, or do we need to go back there?"

Finn grinned. "Feisty little fucker, ain't you?"

In Thai he instructed the squad leader to detach two of his men to help get Dickerson and Hauck to the LZ.

"And we'll go help out Jimmy Boy," he said. "Before your little friend here gives me a good talking-to."

Jim saw two of the Pathet Lao soldiers trying to flank him on the right, shifted his firing position slightly, and waited until he had a clear shot. The first one folded like a cheap accordion when the burst of fire hit him. Jim shifted fire and was fairly certain he'd at least winged the second, who dropped out of sight.

Things were getting interesting. He'd tripwired a claymore but it had never gone off, suggesting either that it was defective or that these guys were savvy enough to avoid it. If the latter he was in even deeper shit than he had at first thought.

The PL, he had heard from veterans of the Laotian campaigns, weren't particularly good soldiers, sharing the common attitude in the country that it was better to shoot in the air and scare the hell out of the enemy and then walk in after he'd left. That way nobody got hurt, except by accident.

Maybe these guys had been taking lessons. They weren't running away and they sure as hell weren't shooting up in the air.

He shifted again, low-crawling to a position he'd picked out earlier. To stay in one spot too long was to give them a target. And he would just bet that one or more of them was carrying a B-40 rocket. The trees and brush that he was relying on for cover wouldn't stand up too well to a rocket originally designed to take out a tank.

Not that it was going to do him much good. They'd send out other flankers, and he wouldn't see them all, and sooner or later one would show up where he was least expecting it.

He had a sudden pang of regret. He'd never see Alix again, never see the baby that should be coming any day now. And the baby would never know its father, other than in fading pictures.

Goddamn it! It wasn't supposed to happen this way.

You've been rushing toward this day for most of your adult life, Jim Carmichael. Now that it's here, don't minge about it.

Three soldiers burst out of the brush in front of him, firing into the position he'd just left. He shot the first, moved to the second and pulled the trigger, only to feel the unresponsiveness that told him of a bolt locked back on an empty weapon.

Goddamn amateurish shit!

He punched the magazine release, the empty falling away even as he was clawing at another from his pouch. Not enough time. Not nearly enough. The other two Pathet Lao were no longer shooting at the empty position, were cranking off rounds that cracked by his head. They'd be on top of him in less than a second.

I'll take at least one of you motherfuckers with me, he thought as he hit the bolt release and felt it slam forward, chambering a round. No need to aim, just point and shoot!

He had to look at his own gun to confirm the fact that he hadn't shot a single round, but the two enemy soldiers were down, one writhing in agony, the other quite clearly dead.

A form slid down next to him, turned to grin.

"You about had enough of this fun, Jimmy?" he asked.

"Bishop? Where the fuck did you come from?"

"Why, heaven, of course. Now, would you like to go, or do you want to play some more games with these guys?"

While McCulloden, Carmichael, and the Thai Rangers were fighting an orderly delay against the Pathet Lao, Bucky Epstein was rigging the trees that unduly restricted the LZ with all the demolitions he could scrounge. To the biggest one he'd affixed two claymore mines wrapped with a dozen turns of detonating cord, with an M-26 grenade attached above the main charge, the fuse removed and replaced with another length of det cord. The idea was that the main blast would cut the tree, the M-26 going off milliseconds later would serve as a kicker charge, pushing the tree in the direction he wanted. The other trees he rigged with only one claymore, mainly because that was all he had, det cord and no kicker. Wouldn't really matter what direction they fell. He'd just finished double-priming the whole circuit, using a length of det cord to tie it all together and the detonating caps removed from the claymores to set it off. He strung out the firing wire, was just about to hit the claymore clacker when he saw the two Americans and their Thai escorts emerge from the jungle.

"Might want to take cover," he said, pointing to his handiwork.

"That's about some jury-rigged bullshit," Jerry Hauck said.

Epstein pretended insult. "And I suppose you could do better, you one-legged motherfucker," he said.

Jerry grinned, turned to Dickerson. "That's what I was looking for, some good old-fashioned sympathy. Blow the motherfucker! See if I care."

Bucky squeezed the clackers. The resulting detonation sheared all three trees neatly off at about two feet above the ground. The one with the kicker slowly, majestically, fell exactly where Bucky had intended.

Jerry spat out a great mouthful of dirt, ran his tongue over his teeth, spat again. Grunted.

"Not too bad for a cut-dick, weapons-man puke," he said. "How ya been, Bucky? Damned glad to see you."

"Gonna be hot," Finn said into the handset of the PRC-77 radio he carried. "Soon as we hit the LZ, 'bout five minutes nearly as I can figure, have the Cobras come in, try to suppress. Those Hueys will be sitting ducks, otherwise."

He got a Roger from Bucky back at the LZ, turned to Jim Carmichael and smiled. "Just like the good old days, huh, Jimmy?"

"Wasn't a goddamn thing good about them, and it wasn't all that long ago," Carmichael replied while changing magazines.

"Getting to be a cranky old fucker, ain't you?"

Jim fired a burst at a flitting target, was fairly certain he'd hit nothing, but what the hell. Hitting someone was a bonus. What you tried to do was keep them off you, make sure you weren't flanked, make them careful.

"And I suppose you're always sweetness and light," he said.

"That's what all my fans say," Finn replied. He shouted at the troops on his left, told them to move, laid down a base of fire with a full magazine of 5.56mm, then grabbed a white phosphorous grenade, pulled the pin, and heaved it as far as he could in the direction of the enemy. The choking cloud of white smoke would mask their movements and also serve as a marker for the helicopters orbiting above. Anything on the opposite side of the smoke was to be regarded as enemy, and fair game.

"C'mon," he said. "They're waiting for us."

CHAPTER 26

Deputy chief of staff for Intelligence General Miller met with the Army chief of staff Elmore Green in the latter's office. The meeting was at General Miller's request.

"Operation Playback is completed," he said.

"And the POWs?"

"One dead, the other chose to remain."

General Warren grunted. It was a less-than-satisfactory result. He'd had reservations about the operation from the beginning, feeling it far too risky for the results that were to be expected.

On the other hand, if the team hadn't been at just the right place at the right time Bangkok might right now have been occupied by the North Vietnamese army. The ancient monarchy would have been replaced by some Thai Communist stooge, and America would have lost one of the few allies it still had in the region.

"So we can claim Korhonen is simply an AWOL, if he ever shows up again," Warren said. "That's technically true, isn't it?"

"In that he refused repatriation when given the chance? Yes, that's true. The team itself took one casualty. Sergeant

Jerome Hauck stepped on a mine. They had to amputate the leg halfway up the calf. The others are okay. Exhausted, very much resenting the debriefings, but okay. Captain Carmichael is demanding to be reunited with his wife."

General Warren's head jerked up. "No one has told him yet?"

"We didn't think it would be appropriate before the debriefing was completed."

Warren shook his head. "Poor son of a bitch," he said.

Miller agreed. "Decorations?" he asked.

"You know we can't decorate someone for something that didn't happen," General Warren replied. "They've signed the debriefing sheets?"

"They have," General Miller replied. The debriefing sheet was a warning that, should you divulge any of the classified information on the operation or anything to do with it to anyone at all, you would be prosecuted under the provisions of the Uniform Code of Military Justice, and would serve a term of not less than ten years' confinement at the United States Military Disciplinary Barracks at Fort Leavenworth, Kansas.

"Keep a close eye on them," Warren said. "Make damned sure nobody gets a snootful and starts talking about this operation they were just on."

"They'll be watched," Miller assured him. "Now, as for the operation itself. As I had told you it was likely to be, it was compromised from the very beginning."

"And there's no possibility it was on the part of anyone assigned to it?"

"The people assigned to it were never privy to the operations of SOG, and the compromises appear to be generated from exactly the same source."

"You put the tell-tales in the messages?"

"We did. And got them back verbatim."

"Shit!" Warren swore.

Miller was silent. He knew the chief of staff was thinking exactly the same thing he was. That the compromise had to have come from somewhere in the classified message traffic from the FOB in Nakhon Phanom to CINCPAC in Hawaii. Just as the traffic from SOG headquarters in Saigon had been compromised, in the same route.

It meant that the chief of staff of the Army was going to have to confront the chief of Naval Operations and tell him that his precious codes had been compromised. It would not have been a pleasant task in the best of times, but since the new CNO and General Warren had a mutual personal distaste for one another that went all the way back to World War II, it was going to be particularly difficult.

But there was no alternative. Someone had been reading the mail, and had been using it to get a hell of a lot of good men killed. Those men were Army, and though they'd belonged to what the general often thought of as the Goddamn Undisciplined Special Forces, they were his.

Like it or not, the CNO was just going to have to suck it up. And find out where the compromise was, before it caused a lot more damage than just the loss of a few good men.

"So when are you going to tell the captain about his wife?" he asked, as much to change the subject as from any real concern about a very junior subordinate.

"I believe they're doing that right now."

CHAPTER 27

He came back to Bad Tölz in the dead of night, taking the last train out of Munich. He wanted no one to see him. He was, in technical terms, absent without leave.

After extensive debriefings, first at the FOB in Nakhon Phanom, then at CINCPAC in Hawaii, finally in a nondescript office building somewhere in Arlington, Virginia, he had been told that he was to be assigned to the Military District of Washington, specific assignment to be named later.

There was no reason for him to return to Germany. His household goods had already been shipped to Washington, were sitting in a warehouse somewhere outside Fort Myer.

Think of your daughter, the chaplain had said, the one they'd sent in after, when he'd demanded to be reunited with his wife, the colonel who was his final debriefer told him, with all appropriate expressions of regret, that he was sorry to inform the captain that his wife had died while he was in Laos. Complications arising from childbirth.

He'd sat, stunned, and the chaplain had come in. Terribly sorry, you have to be feeling horrible, etcetera, etcetera.

He'd been too numb even to rage at the man, knowing that he was merely an emissary, that it would do no good anyway.

You have a fine, beautiful daughter, the padre had continued. She's with your sister. Since your wife's parents are deceased, and there were no other close kin, and you were away, we thought that was best. Our deepest sympathies. Would you like to pray?

And that was when he came very close to losing it.

Pray? Ask a God who would do such a thing for something?

"Get out of here, Padre," he said, his voice low and venomous. "Before I hurt you."

Days later, as he worked his way from one bar to another, hoping to find someone who would still serve him, he saw a familiar face.

"Damn, Jimmy," Al Dougherty said. "You tryin' to drink up all the booze in Virginia?"

Jim took a swing at him, and when Al dodged his fist, fell flat on his face.

When he woke up he was somewhat sober, terribly hung over, and Al was still there, feeding him coffee.

"You were supposed to take care of her," he said, and with that broke down into racking sobs. *No, I was the one who was supposed to take care of her. And I failed. I left her, alone. She died.*

Why can't I?

Al told him later about the last days, how she had reported to the dispensary at Bad Tölz, bleeding badly, too sick to be shipped to the hospital in Munich. How Doctor

Beau Huckaby had made light of the problems, told her that it wasn't any big thing, that she could have the baby right there and he'd take care of her.

And how he'd panicked when the bleeding had become a flood. And had made the decision that had taken her life. The baby or the mother.

Now he was back. He knew where Huckaby slept.

In his rational moments, more and more rare these days, he knew that there was plenty of blame to go around. He knew that Beau Huckaby had made a mistake, but hadn't everyone?

Including himself, but his mind shied from the idea. To go that way was to invite madness.

Maybe he was already crazy. Did the insane know they were insane?

No matter.

He walked the streets up to the old Kaserne.

AUTHOR'S NOTES

Though the events described in this novel are, obviously, fictional, certain details are not.

For many years the survivors of Studies and Observations Group (SOG) were convinced that their own organization had been penetrated by hostile intelligence. There was no other way to explain why the teams crossing the borders of Laos and Cambodia in the highly classified recon missions they conducted were being shot out of every landing zone. Losses were so high among both the recon teams and the helicopter crews who flew them that in desperation SOG turned to infiltration by High-Altitude Low-Opening (HALO) parachute drops, but even these were, apparently, compromised.

At one point operations were shut down for an extended period of time while everyone with any knowledge at all of the operations underwent polygraph testing. Everyone came up clean.

Many years later the Walker spy ring was exposed. John Walker was a Navy communications expert who sold the codes to the naval communications system to the Soviets, who in turn passed on the information to their socialist brethren in North Vietnam. Soviet "trawlers," bristling with communications intercept equipment, plied the coasts of South Vietnam, snatching from the very air the messages sent from higher headquarters in Vietnam to the next command, CINCPAC, in Hawaii.

Most SOG veterans are now convinced that these traitors caused the deaths of dozens of recon men, helicopter crewmen, and others during the conflict.

THE MONTAGNARDS

The hill people collectively known as the Montagnards were the Special Forces soldiers' most fervent allies during the Vietnam War. They served in A Camp Strike Forces, as Mike Force soldiers, and as team members on the highly classified and incredibly dangerous missions conducted by SOG. Unflinching in their loyalty, they are the reason many SF men got to come home alive.

They were, as the novel indicates, abandoned after the war by the United States. Some, like the fictional Y Buon Sarpa, resisted by force of arms and were inevitably whittled down. The last of them straggled across the border into Thailand, where they were immediately put into refugee camps whose conditions were little better than those in the "re-education camps" the victorious North Vietnamese were running back in their home country. It took years of fighting the bureaucracy by a handful of dedicated former Special Forces soldiers before these allies were allowed to emigrate to the United States, where they have set up their own community in the mountains of North Carolina and are living in unaccustomed freedom.

The ones who remained in Vietnam are being oppressed to this day. For a full account of how the Vietnamese are essentially waging a campaign of extermination against these people, contact Amnesty International.